25th November 1993

To Katherine
    For all our memories and
for keeping the faith
through all these years.
I am grateful this
Thanksgiving for the
special blessing of our
friendship —

            With love,
            Cathy

OTHER AUTUMNS

OTHER AUTUMNS
Cathy Criss Adams

Atticus Press & Company

This is a work of fiction. The events described are imaginary, and the characters are fictitious and not intended to represent specific people.

Printed in the United States of America
L F S 9 8 7 6 5 4 3 2 1 0
First Edition

This book is dedicated
with love and gratitude
to Dr. Edwin Meek
of the University of Mississippi.

The harvest truly is plenteous . . .
Matthew 9:37

CHAPTER ONE

Kick Lambeth tossed his wire-rimmed glasses onto the kitchen table and squinted into the telephoto lens of his camera. The misty, filtered light of the early October morning was perfect.

He snapped the shutter three times in rapid succession, capturing his older sister as she stood in the stable yard behind their house. A chestnut horse nuzzled her neck as the Gordon setter at her side wagged his tail furiously, hoping to claim a share of her attention.

Candid shots intended to capture the essence of Lilly.

Home after years of vagabond life on the road, Kick found himself sharing with his sister the rambling Greek Revival house in which they, like generations of the family before them, had grown up.

He had come home to work on a book of photo essays tentatively titled *Seasons in a Small Town,* a pictorial chronicle of a year in the life of the small southern town he'd so long ago left behind.

On long drives and aimless ambles he found more than he'd expected, sometimes more than he would have liked, still the same, as if the physical byways of Brierley and the lives of its residents were held suspended in time.

His sister had had the house to herself for so many years that his return at times felt like more of an intrusion than a reunion. He accepted the fact that living in Lilly's house meant trying to conform to her haphazard ideas of housekeeping and schedules, but it was obvious that he was much too accustomed to his own lack of a regular lifestyle to stay on much longer. He liked to make his own rules. He was restless, already thinking of getting his work completed and moving on.

Kick Lambeth had carved his niche as a free-lance photographer, his work much in demand. It was a satisfying career, a career that had taken him around the world more than once, allowing him to yank up roots whenever they threatened to put down too deeply in one particular location.

He was home in part because of the book and in part because at age forty-two he found himself searching for the stability of someone to love him for more than one night. He was in a state of limbo, at loose ends in his personal life.

When the book offer came, he jumped at it, ending an emotionally empty love affair in New York and driving south, back to the house called home by four generations of his family. It was a house in which nothing had ever been thrown away, a house in which memories were as integral to the structure as the cracks in the plaster, the laugh lines webbing the faces of the rooms.

He had asked Lilly more than once why she stayed on in the house, if she didn't get lonely living in such an old barn. She always answered matter-of-factly that she shared the house with too many ghosts to feel lonely.

She believed in her ghosts, for the most part found them comforting, good company when the wind rattled old window frames on cold winter evenings.

Ghosts aside, she didn't mind the solitude. Lilly liked herself.

Still it was a big house, a house which often seemed to have a mind of its own, and Kick didn't think he'd like to stay there by himself. He wasn't so sure all the ghosts were settled spirits.

Out of film, he stood for a moment watching his sister through the filmy pane of thick, hand-blown glass in the kitchen window. The glass was original to the house, well over a hundred years old, granting only gossamer glimpses of the world outside.

The trees which formed a backdrop of woods were turning from the lush green of the summer he loved. In the six months since his return he had watched the trees bud and grow summer full, watched the seasons change.

It struck him how like the seasons the members of his family were. His younger sister, Laura, pale and blonde, was a Botticelli-like image of spring, windy, wispy, promise waiting for fulfillment. He had always considered himself a child of the summer, an actively alive man, with the sea and the sunshine his chosen milieus. And in Lilly there was much of the best of autumn.

Lilly was mellow, painted from the palette of that season with her long, uncontrollable tangle of bright gold hair falling down her back in waves like wheat fields ready for the harvest.

His older sister was heir to the family's characteristic strong jaw, her face freckled and punctuated with eyes that changed in the light from green to brown to grey. Eyes that, like Lilly, were mercurial and hard to describe. He wondered what she gave as eye color on her driver's license.

Lilly spent a lot of time out-of-doors. She had the slightly weather-beaten look of a woman unafraid of the sun or the wind.

She smelled of the autumn, too, a light, woodsy scent with the briefest hint of cinnamon and apples. He didn't know the name of the perfume or even if she wore perfume. Perhaps she exuded her own personal scent, spicy and pungent like the last fleeting days of Indian summer.

Lilly was a month away from her forty-fifth birthday, and if asked to sum up in a word his sister's life Kick would have chosen an autumn-appropriate adjective. Bittersweet maybe. Because her past held intensities of both the bitter and the sweet, she had grown philosophical enough to expect no less of the future. There was in Lilly a sense of balance.

Unaware of her brother's eyes on her, Lilly slipped a halter over the mare's nose and smiled at her dog Glamis as he took off at a mad run into the woods, barking as a fat brown squirrel scurried up a tree.

She took a deep breath of the early morning, her favorite time of day in her favorite time of year, this time of pumpkins and Indian corn, smooth brown acorns, and pale gold apple cider.

Autumn had blown in during the night after the hottest, driest September in living memory. No one, especially Lilly, mourned the passing of a summer that had burned on for far too long.

She thought of her grandfather, dead now some twenty summers but still in spirit very much by her side, telling her that in any life there are only so many golden autumn mornings allotted us and none of them given for the wasting. She intended to go for a very long ride in the woods.

In those woods surrounding the barn the trees flaunted their leaves like contestants preening for an evening gown competition. The native hickories wore a yellow gold, the sugar maples bright orange, the Bradford pear a dark wine red.

She kicked at a sweet gum ball. As much as she hated its spiny, impossible-to-rake fruit, Lilly had to judge the sweet gum, individual leaves bearing at once the colors green, orange red, purple, and yellow, the winner. The sweet gums wore their paisley well.

A fleeting memory brought a smile. She could still see so clearly the little girl with the long, golden braids and her grandfather, drying her tears after she stepped barefoot on a prickly piece of the sweet gum's thorny fruit. She could hear just as clearly their voices across the years. "It's a mean tree, Grandfather. Why did God give it those mean old gum balls?"

Her grandfather passed her a leaf from the same tree, a leaf bursting with the fullness of autumn color. "I expect He was seeking to level the richness," he said gently. "The name of this tree is *Liquidambar styraciflua*, liquid amber. Learn that name and remember it. When life bears bitter fruit, never forget that there are intense golden leaves but a short season away. Be grateful for the blessing of the balance. In windstorms to come many of these trees around us will fall, but when you're as old as I these native sweet gums will stand determinedly on, strong for having known both beauty and pain."

Liquidambar styrciflua she whispered. It was the only Latin she remembered, the only Latin she needed to know.

Divided by a narrow, gravel road from the banks of a sluggish, mud-brown river, the thirty acres on which Lilly lived was in her childhood a working cotton farm of many hundreds of acres. After the death of her grandfather, a judge by vocation and gentleman farmer by avocation, Lilly's father had, to her fury, sold most of the land.

Lilly hated her long dead father for many reasons, not the least of which was his decision to deny her chance to play the role of gentleman farmer herself.

On this morning she picked at the dirt under her broken fingernails and thought it was just as well. Every September she bought a hundred daffodil bulbs and every October wondered who in their right mind would set themselves up to dig all the little holes necessary to receive them. Heaven only knew what she'd have done with half-a-thousand acres of dirt.

She had a dog, and a couple of horses, and a never tallied number of cats. The pet pig was long dead and Kick had talked her out of getting a "just because I want one "cow.

Thirty acres was more than adequate for a good, hard ride and a few hours respite from her brother. She had welcomed him home with open arms, but she was well aware that too much togetherness had been the cause of more than one divorce, her own included. It was unclear how one went about divorcing a brother.

Five miles from the signposts announcing Brierley's police jurisdiction, Lilly's house was far enough from the civilization of town that in the absence of Kick and her crisis-prone younger sister, Laura, there was ample peace and quiet.

Kick's major problem, now that he was too old to be kicked out of military schools, was his habit of turning up in bedrooms where he didn't belong, and Lilly didn't see much that she could do about that. Laura couldn't seem to grow up at all. There wasn't a great deal that Lilly could do about that either.

A distance of five hundred miles would not have changed the fact that the slightest contact with either Kick or Laura seemed to immediately turn her ordered world into chaos. Yet, Lilly had to admit to herself that she would walk barefoot twice that distance to be with either her brother or her sister if they needed her.

Hawthorne Road, the widest street in the town of Brierley, derived its name from a founding family whose descendants had long since scattered to the wider world. Split by a median thick with grass and punctuated by rows of pansies in winter, daffodils in spring, and impatiens in summer, Hawthorne Road lay so canopied with huge sheltering oak and elm trees that even in high summer only dapples of sunlight filtered through the branches.

Around oversized houses built in the financial heyday of the 1920s, manicured yards and huge boxwood hedges spoke of the stability of time and tending.

To passersby on Hawthorne Road that October morning, Laura and Beck Kimble's white stucco house looked serene, solid and secure, at ease with itself.

A long structure with steep-pitched Tudor cross gables and red tiled roof broken on front and sides by potted chimneys, the house rested well back from the street on a lot large enough to have easily accommodated several smaller dwellings.

Tree branches bent gracefully in a light wind, saying good-bye to their leaves, shrubs bore the rounded edges of a recent clipping, and deep bronze and purple chrysanthemums replaced summer geraniums in the large stone urns flanking the arched front door. Beside tilled flower beds pansies were massed in flats, and the only disruptive noise was the hum of a leaf blower. Every sign was of things in order.

The second floor master bedroom facing Hawthorne Road was a large room ever-in-bloom with floral wallpaper and matching fabric on the bed-spread and canopy of the tester bed. It was a bedroom saved from utter fem-ininity only by the interjection of large, comfortable French armchairs and ottomans covered in muted plaids flanking the fireplace.

On the morning in question, serenity was far from the mood of the occu-pant of this room.

Laura Lambeth Kimble paced a path around and around the pale green carpet. All of her life she had been more than a little in awe of her older sis-ter. She brushed her long, blonde hair for the tenth time, rechecked her per-fect manicure, and told herself that she looked presentable enough to con-front Lilly.

There was nothing more that she could do to improve her hair, or her nails, or even the makeup applied so carefully that she appeared to be wear-ing none at all. Stewing about her appearance was not going to make the problem of talking to Lilly go away.

She made one post-final check before the mirror, brushing a bit of lint off the long, navy velvet robe. Her hand shook slightly as she picked up the telephone. Laura was a nervous wreck.

Lilly, having completed her morning ride, stood in the barn extracting briers from her horse's tail. She frowned in the direction of the ringing phone on the wall and added to her list of grievances functioning as an answering service for her brother. If he couldn't be bothered to answer the phone when he was busy in his darkroom, he needed to realize that she was equally busy in her barn, thank you very much.

"Lilly, I have the tiniest favor to ask, and I hope you won't say no." Laura's whispery voice carried an urgent "don't turn me down" undertone all too familiar to Lilly.

"Let me guess," Lilly responded, genuinely glad to hear her sister's voice. "You want me to keep the kids because you and Beck are going away for the weekend, and the maid can't sit. You're having a luncheon in two hours and need a massive arrangement of flowers from my yard. You're having a dinner party tonight, you forgot to call the caterer, and you need food for forty by four this afternoon. Or all of the above?" At one time or another Lilly had bailed Laura out of any number of similar situations.

"Oh, Lilly, you act like I'm totally incapable," Laura said in an exasper-ated voice. It didn't help that she did feel totally incapable most of the time. "It's nothing earthshaking. I just need your help with a little fund-raiser for the school."

"Are you asking me for help in fund-raising or for funds?"

"You'll be so proud of me, Lilly." Laura's words spilled out rapidly, words bumping into words, once she got going. "We had a meeting the other day about the auction we're going to have to raise money for the school's new library, and they made me chairman of the committee, and my committee has committees, and all I have to do is delegate, and we're going to raise tons of money, and everyone's going to be so proud of me for being so important." She stopped only because she was out of breath.

"And all you need from me is one tiny little favor to which I assume I'm already committed. Let me keep guessing. I'll bet I'm donating a night of frenzied sex with Kick."

Lilly ended her conjecture with the huge booming laugh which Laura had always found slightly embarrassing. Their voices and their laughter were as different as their physical appearances. Sometimes Laura thought of Lilly as an exaggeration of a person with her deep voice and her wild mane of curly hair.

Laura sighed and forced herself to continue. "Please stop making fun of me, Lilly. You ought to be proud that they've given me so much responsibility."

"I am proud of you, Laura," Lilly said in a gentler voice. "I'll mark my calendar right now and be there to help with whatever you need. Just tell me what my job is and consider it done. I've never done any auctioneering, but I've been to plenty of horse auctions, and I've been accused more than once of being a fast talker. I could probably bluff my way through it."

"It's not exactly a job," Laura whispered in a barely audible voice. "It's more like a donation." She took a deep breath. "I told them that you'd donate that horse painting that's hanging in your library."

"Grandfather's George Stubbs?" Lilly shrieked. "Laura, are you crazy? You know how much that painting means to me. That was Grandfather's favorite painting. How could you, in your wildest dreams, imagine that I'd give away something like that? No way, Laura. I would not part with that painting for a zillion million dollars."

"Lilly, what am I going to tell all those girls at the meeting this morning?" Laura begged, trying to resist the urge to chew one of her perfect, umber-painted nails. She looked at a small plastic bottle of tranquilizers on the bedside table, wishing she'd taken one before trying to talk Lilly.

"Lilly, I also told them that my mother-in-law would like to donate a piece of her celadon collection, and I haven't asked her either. What if she reacts just like you?"

"You're just going to have to be honest and tell them that you assumed wrong. You know how proud Eleanor is of that ugly old green porcelain. She's even less likely to help you than I am."

"To make a bad situation worse, Ginger Borland is in charge of publicity, and you know what a big mouth she has. She's probably on the phone right now asking Eleanor for a description of the piece she's donating, and Eleanor will come over here and kill me."

Lilly frowned. Ginger Borland had intimidated Laura since kindergarten, but Laura's relationship with her mother-in-law went far beyond mere intimidation. Laura was deathly afraid of the domineering Eleanor Kimble. In Eleanor's view Laura could do absolutely nothing right.

"Laura, I will donate the library if that will help you. I will write a check for whatever it takes to have it built, and I will get on a ladder and stock it with books, but I will not part with something that is as much a part of this house as the foundation," Lilly said firmly.

"Lilly, I will never understand why you are so obsessed with that stupid old house and all the junk that's in it. If all I needed was money, I could do it without you."

"The final answer is no, Laura. Have your meeting and tell them they'll have to come up with something else. Call me tonight and let me know how it goes." Lilly added a quick good-bye and hung up before her sister could argue further.

"Damn, damn, damn, damn," Lilly muttered to the big black dog as he pushed his nose under her hand. "Why does she insist on getting herself into impossible situations and dragging me along with her?"

She turned the horse out to pasture and started across the gravel stable yard to the house, kicking up pebbles in frustration.

Having left home for boarding school while Laura was still a toddler, Lilly had married, divorced, and continued to live abroad, roaming the world and only coming into Laura's life on a regular basis when the younger sister was already long married and out of the house.

Kick had been out and gone too, but Kick could take care of himself.

It occurred to Lilly that, despite almost daily contact with her sister, she didn't know Laura very well at all.

Lilly picked up a stick and broke it in pieces, threw the largest piece for the dog to fetch. She had to think of something to placate Laura. A simple no was never the last word with Laura.

Out of the corner of her eye she noticed that paint was peeling off the upper story cornice mold. She stuck out her tongue at the house as she calculated the astronomical cost of getting it painted. She had plenty of money, and she enjoyed spending it on things that she wanted to have or wanted to do. Spending it on things like painting and plumbing and plaster patching, things that had to be done, was no fun at all.

Maybe, as Kick too often said, what she needed was a little house in town. She couldn't picture herself in a little house in town. If this old house was a great white albatross, she loved having it around her neck.

Not by any stretch of the imagination one of the great southern mansions which existed more commonly in fiction and the movies than they ever did in real life, Lilly's house was actually more the typical type of the period. Green shuttered, white frame, and two stories like many that once dotted the southern countryside, it was just a big comfortable country house built in the prosperous days before a war disrupted the southern economy. Thanks to high ceilings and many windows it stayed relatively cool in the heat of southern summers and cold, despite its many fireplaces, in even the mild winters of that climate.

Wide porches supported by Doric columns wrapped both the upper and lower front and sides of the house and were hung with ceiling fans and ferns and furnished with rockers and swings for summer evenings.

On the back of the house a small porch, enclosed with insulated glass panels, was a slight concession to modernization while its upper story counterpart maintained its original identity as a screened sleeping porch.

The tall, paired front doors, encased within sidelights and rectangular transom, opened onto a large entrance hall with broad stairs and walls of dark stained mahogany paneling. Polished hardwood floors were softened by Kerman rugs deep-toned with age. The upstairs hall caught the breezes through a similar pair of tall, thin doors opening onto a balustraded balcony.

Most of the accoutrements of Lilly's house, from the 1810 American Empire sideboard to the massive bed in which she slept alongside the ghosts of Lambeths born and dying there a century ago, could have been among the prize displays in any fine antique shop. Her grandmother and great-grandmother had bought often and well to supplement inherited treasures.

Viewed from the distant vantage point of the road, Lilly's house might have appeared a showplace. Closer inspection would have reassuringly revealed to the envious onlooker that the place was more than a tad shabby. If she sold it and moved to a little house in town the new owners would repair the cracks, and sweep out the cobwebs in the attic, and paint the rooms decorator colors, or worse still, tear it down. Reason enough to stay where she was.

She let her eyes roam over the many tall, narrow windows of the house as if expecting to see remembered faces appear behind the glass, the faces of the ghosts who she knew were watching.

On some indiscernible plane of existence her grandmother still sat in the little boudoir chair in her bedroom and lifted a silver coffeepot over a delicate porcelain cup. Her grandfather continued to slam the back screen door after walking the woods with his dogs and to leave muddy prints from worn leather riding boots on the rugs.

There were ghosts to be sure, but she knew that both she and the house would be lonely without the reassurance of their presence, disturbed if some intruder had the nerve to hang new plasterboard.

They were the ghosts of those who had left to her a legacy that went far beyond a house, thirty acres of land, and a sizeable bank balance. Of far more value were their bequests of a sense of who she was, a security that she was someone without the need to be constantly reassured that she was somebody, and the common sense to identify and to go after those things that really mattered in life.

She had a responsibility to them and was confident that they would, as long as she stayed on, always be there for her. She knew that this was a comfort that the fates had denied her troubled younger sister.

For Laura, the only ghosts on the Old Post Road were those of her parents, after death still operating as they had in life, doing their best by word and deed to ruin the lives of each other and those around them.

CHAPTER TWO

*L*aura was falling apart.

"Beck, what am I going to do if Lilly won't help me?" Laura wailed in the direction of the cloud of steam floating over the glass doors of the shower. "They trusted me with this big job, and I have this meeting this morning, and how can I tell them that I've failed?" *Failed just like they expected I would* added a miserable little voice in the back of her head.

Brookland Beccles Kimble, III emerged from the shower ready to provide Laura a trail map for scaling whatever insignificant molehill she had made into a mountain while he enjoyed the play of three super-strength shower heads.

Having made up his mind to take the afternoon off and mulling over whether to play golf, or tennis, or some more stimulating indoor games with his attractive new secretary, he glanced out the window half hoping for clouds on the blue October horizon.

She passed him a towel and sat on the edge of the tub.

"What am I going to do, Beck? You've got to talk to Lilly for me. She's got to change her mind."

"I'm not getting the drift, Laura," he said as he walked into the bedroom, casually toweling his hair.

"She won't let me have that painting for my auction. She gave the museum all those great big pictures, and that's just a little bitty old painting. I told them she'd be happy to donate it, and all she can talk about is how much Grandfather loved it. Grandfather is dead, for goodness sake. He'll never miss it."

Having lived with Laura for a dozen years, Beck was accustomed to her perpetual state of dilemma and had his own classification system for solving her problems.

He cast himself in the role of the Secretary of State deciding what level diplomat was needed. Whenever possible he preferred to delegate the solving of her problems to someone else.

Evaluating her present level of consternation, Beck decided that today seemed to be a day for the top man himself. He turned and leaned against the carved-stone mantel of the bedroom fireplace and tried to give her his full attention.

Laura handed him a thick, gray terry cloth robe, monogrammed, like the towel he had just discarded, in deep burgundy. "I need help, Beck. Please, Beck, someone's just got to help me."

"First of all, Laura, why should your sister be expected to furnish you with some of her crap? Don't forget your grandfather left the house and all that land to her, not to you. She's too damn stingy to let go of anything in that grungy old barn, and Mother complains all the time that Lilly refuses to be on the board of directors of anything that might be construed as helping this town grow. The only thing Lilly cares about helping is Lilly."

A real estate developer who would have loved to get his hands on thirty subdividable acres, Beck often had trouble deciding whom he disliked most in Laura's family. Her sister, her brother, those objects-of-ancestor-worship dead grandparents, and even Desia, the venerable Lambeth housekeeper, all vied for the title. Beck took perverse pleasure in offending the aging family retainer by leaving her little notes with her name spelled just as it sounded, "Deeshuh."

By giving Lilly today's honor he found it convenient to forget that Lilly had not stopped with donating her grandmother's collection of early French Impressionists to start the fledgling local museum. She had also financed the new humane society animal shelter and given the use of a warehouse she owned rent-free for a recycling center. Lilly wouldn't have served on the board of a major multinational corporation if it meant having to sit in close proximity to Eleanor Kimble. He resented the fact that his wife thought her sister and brother so almighty perfect.

"They only put me in charge of the auction because I told them that Lilly and your mother had agreed to make big donations," Laura explained. "If Lilly won't help me your mother probably won't either. Beck, you've got to talk to your mother for me."

"Whoa, Laura, as usual you're about two paragraphs ahead of me in this story." He opened the door to his dressing room. The profusion of flowered fabric in the bedroom made his head spin so that he had trouble concentrating. The dressing room was his refuge.

"How did my mother get involved in all of this?" It was fine with him if Laura wanted to spend all day driving Lilly crazy, but his mother was a whole different ball game.

"Well, I told them that she'd donate a piece of her celadon. I guess I can understand that Lilly only has one painting like that, but your mother has gooboodles of that old green stuff. Surely she has one piece that she wouldn't miss."

"Laura, there are museum directors all over the world who would get down on their knees and grovel for one piece of my mother's collection. How can you, in even your wildest, most unrealistic, scatterbrained fantasies, dream of bothering my mother about some dumb little school fundraiser when you know how busy she stays with things that are really important? You're just going to have to come up with some other idea."

"I don't think it's all that dumb," Laura said quietly, feeling the last of the air go out of the bright balloon of self-esteem she'd happily carried only yesterday. "You're no more help than Lilly was."

Standing in front of the mirror, she brushed her hair furiously as if the act could put her brain in gear to produce an alternate plan.

Evidently it worked, because she suddenly smiled and turned to Beck. "I know what I'll do. I'll find Kick. My brother will help me. He'll talk Lilly into giving me that painting."

Beck wondered briefly if Kick would actually come up with a solution to Laura's problem and quickly dismissed that option. Her meeting was at ten o'clock, and she'd never roust that alley cat brother of hers from whatever bed he shared last night that early in the morning. Thinking about how women fell all over themselves when Kick Lambeth entered a room, Beck decided that it was possible that he hated Kick even more than Lilly.

Partly to remove the Kick option, but primarily because he didn't like the idea of her appearing a fool in front of their friends, he began to take a harder look at the whole situation. Maybe he should talk to his mother about donating something or other.

Moot point for now. He didn't have time to get tied up on the telephone with his mother. Tossing a pair of warm-ups into his tennis bag, he knotted his tie, slung his jacket over his shoulder, and gave his frowning wife a quick kiss on the back of her neck.

He left her looking perplexed and ran down the stairs whistling, without a care in the world.

Laura looked around the bedroom as if hoping to spot there a solution to her problem.

The bedcovers lay in disarray, and an almost empty glass of watered Scotch wept a white ring on an antique tea table alongside a slick-papered decorating magazine and yesterday's newspaper.

She didn't notice the mess. Laura's bedroom would be tidied, just as the lawn would be mowed, and the driveway swept, and the silver polished, without her giving much thought to any of it other than to write a weekly check to cover the wages of the people sent out by the efficient service she used. Her surroundings were handled for her as routinely as her nails were manicured.

Unfortunately, she didn't know of a service which specialized in finding the solution to her current dilemma.

Joining the coverlet and newspapers on the floor was a rapidly growing pile of discarded clothes as Laura tried and rejected one outfit after another in her general panic at the dwindling minutes before she had to face her friends.

Of medium height, almost too thin from nervous energy as much as diet and exercise, and with high cheekbones, a long patrician nose, and enormous blue-grey eyes in a face framed by luxurious, naturally ash blonde hair, Laura would have looked as beautiful draped in a garbage bag as she did in any of the expensive articles of clothing heaped on the bed and floor.

Growing up, Laura was a golden child, so beautiful that strangers stared, and she accepted the same treatment as an adult without being particularly aware of it. The constant checking and rechecking of hair, and nails, and clothing was more a nervous habit born of insecurity than a result of vanity.

Laura Lambeth Kimble had everything in the world money could buy and not one ounce of self-esteem. The ruling factor in her life was fear, and most days she felt that she was riding an out-of-control roller coaster. For Laura, fear was taking on a life of its own.

She was afraid of the panic which gripped her in the most unlikely places where she should have been enjoying herself, of being abandoned by her husband in the same way that her father had written off her mother, of her own body, which on a frighteningly frequent basis seemed to malfunction.

She was afraid of dying, and more afraid of living, and totally incapable of confiding the waking nightmare in which she found herself to even the people who loved her most.

There didn't seem to be an answer for the mysterious physical failings, the fact that her heart raced wildly when she stood in grocery store lines, or her vision blurred when she sat in church, or her fingers and toes tingled, and her mouth went numb, and she had difficulty getting her breath and swallowing whenever she had to go to her mother-in-law's for dinner.

The bewildering variety of symptoms had started after the birth of her third child. Her gynecologist, the same old and trusted family physician who had treated her mother and grandmother, had told her it was nerves and had given her a prescription for tranquilizers. Five years later she was still taking them like candy in hopes that one day they'd actually work, spiraling downhill so fast that she'd lost any hope of getting her foot on the brake in her life in time to avert disaster.

Some days just deciding what to wear seemed to represent a major decision. Finally, settling on a mauve cashmere sweater and mid-calf length camel wool skirt, she tied a paisley scarf around the sweater, slipped on a pair of boots, and went downstairs.

The three Kimble children, Brook, Marion, and Samantha, ages eleven, ten, and almost six, were remarkably independent children. They had been preparing their own breakfasts since leaving the high chair.

Entering the kitchen, Laura found her youngest child, Sam, sloppily spooning cereal into her mouth. The little girl's long tangled curls, which dipped in the milk every time she bent down for a bite, were a dubious legacy from her Aunt Lilly.

Laura frowned at the cereal, which was shaped like little brown fish. It vaguely reminded her of something inappropriate for a child's breakfast.

"Sam and Sunbeam like the same kind of cereal!" Brook shouted as he and a giggling Marion grabbed their book bags and flew out the back door.

"How could you give your little sister cat food?" Laura screamed at their hastily retreating backs.

"'Sgood!" pronounced Sam. "Me and Sunbeam both like Kitty Kibbles for breakfast!" She took another large spoonful and grinned at her mother.

Hearing her name called, the enormous yellow cat bounded onto the table and began to lap hungrily in Sam's bowl.

"Give me that!" Laura shrieked, sweeping the startled Sunbeam to the floor as she flung the contents of the cereal bowl into the sink. Sunbeam meowed a loud protest, and Sam giggled.

Sam gave her mother a defiant look and scooped up the offended cat. "Me and Sunbeam likes to share."

"Sunbeam and I like to share," Laura automatically corrected as she sighed in frustration at the child's overall appearance. Sam looked as if she'd taken a fashion cue from Lilly.

She wore pink overalls and a stained red tee shirt that smelled strongly of lemon oil, as if it might recently have been used to dust furniture.

Laura shook her head, wondering how she'd come to find herself the mother of three such different children. Marion was a smaller mirror-image of herself, Brook a carbon copy of Beck, and this pint-sized monster a miniature Lilly. Laura didn't have the energy to deal with two Lillys in one morning.

"Find your tennis shoes, brush that hair, and change that awful, smelly shirt just as fast as you can. It's my day to drive your carpool."

Finally relaxed enough from the pill she took after talking to Lilly to feel capable of driving, she took a deep breath before getting into the spotless, white Jaguar.

"Mommy!" An impish face popped up outside the car window.

"I'm late. Where's your ride to school?" Laura jabbed the button to roll down the window, doing nothing to hide her exasperation.

Sam, small fists on hips, said, "You just said it was your day to drive. My teacher's gonna be mad if we're late again."

Wanting very much to scream, Laura got out of the Jaguar and walked around to the station wagon. How was anyone supposed to keep riding groups straight with three children involved in a million different activities?

"Get in, Lilly," she snapped, ignoring the child's giggle at her mental lapse. Sam liked nothing so much as being compared to Lilly.

Preoccupied, Laura pulled out into the busy road without looking for traffic. Brakes screeched and horns honked.

In the wake of her leaving, serenity returned, the quiet autumn morning again disrupted only by the buzz of the leaf blower, dispersing the dead remnants of summer gone.

Kick was in the kitchen when Lilly entered the house. He opened his mouth to object to the fact that the jacket she wore was one for which he'd searched for weeks.

Lilly always seemed to be dressed in someone else's castoffs, usually appropriated without the owner's permission and more often than not returned with a stain or a tear.

"If it's not the lovely Lilly back from a morning canter and a survey of her well-appointed domain," Kick chattered, yawning as he spoke.

A glance at her hair told him something was up. Whenever she was bothered by something Lilly twisted her already unmanageable hair into knots.

"Horse throw you?" he continued. "Your hair's a positive rat's nest, sister dear."

"Falling off a horse I could handle on my own," Lilly snapped, suddenly conscious that she was giving way to the nervous habit of twisting her unruly hair. "Come with me. I need to talk to you."

"Lead on, O Medusa," Kick whispered as he followed obediently behind Lilly through the kitchen and down the hall to the morning room.

The room where they took their seats in matching wicker chairs was as cheerful as Lilly's expression was gloomy. By glassing in the old back screened porch, their grandmother had created a room at its best at this time of day, with French doors and floor-to-ceiling windows, comfortable wicker furniture with bright chintz cushions, ceiling fans overhead, and a white brick fireplace with a surround of painted blue and white Delft tiles.

Plants thrived in this atmosphere, ferns and palms and African violets, geraniums in summer and Christmas cactus in winter. The red tiled floor was softened with coconut sisal matting overlaid with Kelim area rugs in colors that picked up the brilliant red of the hedge of burning bush outside.

Lilly wore an absolutely murderous look, and Kick wondered which of her rules he'd broken now. He was too tired to be in trouble.

"Are you going to spank me for being out all night?" he asked in what he hoped was a suitably meek voice. He'd be lucky to get by with half the reprobate life Lilly assumed he led, but it would be a shame to take away the pleasure she got from imagining the worst.

"Never mind where you spent the night, Kick, although I worry about you." Lilly absently stirred her coffee. "I wish you'd settle down with somebody, but I'm not sure who could handle you."

"As much as I hate to shatter the image of my having spent a night of wild, abandoned lovemaking, the truth is that I spent all night working. I couldn't decide whether to shoot the picture at dawn or at twilight. I stayed up all night, very much alone, and did it both ways. Despite my image as a ne'er-do-well playboy I do work very hard you know."

"I know you do, and I'm proud of what you do," Lilly answered softly. Kick possessed a streak of modesty that he assuaged by putting forward an air of nonchalance about his work. His sister knew that his swaggering attitude and reputation with women were equally well-staged poses adopted to keep concealed an emptiness in his life.

Women dreamed about Kick Lambeth, chased him, and were often rewarded with the capture of his attention for an interlude, but deep down Kick was longing for a woman that he hadn't yet found.

No one wanted to see Kick settled more than Lilly. Having him around was like trying to keep a curfew-violating teenager from disturbing your sleep.

Their ancient housekeeper Desia had worked in the kitchen all the previous afternoon cooking vegetables for a man who hadn't even bothered to call and say that he wouldn't be home for dinner. Lilly herself had made his favorite cioppino, using a recipe she had learned years ago on a summer holiday in Italy.

She wouldn't admit to herself that they were more disappointed than angry as they sat down for dinner, two women companionable but alone as they had been in the long years he'd been away. They both enjoyed fussing over him.

"So what's up around here?" He interrupted her mental ramblings, sure from her scowl that he was somehow in hot water over something more than his absence at last night's dinner table.

"We've got a problem with Laura."

"What else is new?" He laughed, relieved to be off-the-hook personally. They'd figure out some way to solve whatever had their younger sister befuddled today. Laura's whole life was a series of problems.

"She's in charge of some fund-raiser for the school, and she's apparently told a bunch of her friends that I have agreed to donate Grandfather's George Stubbs."

"Is that all? Even dim-witted Laura ought to know you'd never give up that painting. You know very well that what she actually wants is to boost her image with all those empty-headed women she considers so important."

"What's bothering me so much is that she seems to see me as the solver of all of her problems, most of which are a lot more complex than this," Lilly answered.

"So what are you going to do?" he asked, knowing that both of them had a hard time saying no to Laura about anything.

"Maybe I humor her because I've always felt guilty that growing up in this house was as much a lonely nightmare for her as it was an adventure for us. We had Grandmother and Grandfather, and Laura got stuck with Mother and Daddy."

"Lilly, she's your sister, not your daughter, and she hardly lived the life of the little match girl," Kick replied, feeling angry with Laura for being the source of Lilly's blue mood. Lilly was usually a very upbeat person, but living with her when she was down could be pure hell.

Lilly stared up at the slowly revolving blades of the fan and sighed, knowing that much of the guilt she felt was irrational and that much of what Kick said was true. Growing up, Laura had everything she wanted and nothing she needed. Running off and marrying Beck when she was barely out of high school hadn't exactly forced her to grow up either.

Lilly would have found it convenient to place the lion's share of the blame for Laura's problems on Beck. She didn't like Beck any better than he liked her. She told herself that Beck enjoyed playing the father figure to Laura, and that his patronizing attitude, coupled with the constant interference of his overbearing mother, had resulted in the strange child-woman that was Laura.

Her conscience refused to let her off quite that easily. She and Kick were also guilty of patting Laura on the head and inviting her back to the nursery when Beck got tired of fixing things.

"I'm surprised that marriage has lasted as long as it has," she said. "Do you think he loves her?"

"I think probably as much as he's capable of loving anyone," Kick answered. "Talk about a terrible childhood. Can you imagine having the mighty, hard-boiled Eleanor Kimble for a mother? Bet she never even kissed him good night when he was little."

"Since I don't recall either one of us getting any advanced degrees in psychology I guess our analyzing Laura and Beck is pointless," Lilly said.

Kick studied his older sister. Although he would never have given her the satisfaction of admitting it to her, he felt that Lilly was very good at understanding people.

He reached over and ruffled her thick hair. "You still haven't told me what you're going to do."

"Beats me, but I'll come up with something." She frowned and twisted a

piece of her hair. "You know, Kick, sometimes I worry that Laura is mentally very close to the edge. She's so pale and so thin, and sometimes I have this
uncomfortable feeling that she's just going to evaporate or something.
Maybe if she could figure out on her own the solution to something simple it
would give her a pinch of self-confidence."

He yawned, ready to change the subject. "I'm getting too old to pull
these all-nighters."

"How's your book coming?"

"Pretty good I think. Spring and summer are wrapped up. Two seasons
down and two to go I guess you might say. So far the publisher's happy."

She resigned herself to the fact that he was trying to tell her that he'd be
underfoot for at least six more months.

"I still don't understand why anyone would be interested in pictures of
life in Brierley," she said.

"That should be obvious," he answered. "Brierley is everybody's idea of
the way things used to be, a place where the good old days aren't really
gone. Even people who didn't grow up with Ozzie and Harriet for parents
look back on the fifties like they did. In Brierley you still find things that go
back a lot farther than that. Look at the Feed and Seed for example.
Nothing's changed in there since Grandfather was a child."

"At least the smell hasn't," Lilly said, wrinkling her nose. To her the
Feed and Seed was a necessary animal grocery store stop. She saw nothing
romantic about the place. "It smells bad, Kick."

"Sure it smells bad. Eighty years of accumulated chicken droppings, and
tobacco spit, and dust would make any place smell bad, but people can look
at pictures of the Feed and Seed and remember going there, or some place
like it, as children and getting baby ducks and chickens at Easter. Remember
how they used to dye those chickens Easter egg colors when we were kids?"

"Inhumane practice that killed a lot of innocent chickens." She dismissed his comments with a wave of her hand even though she had very
clear recollections of one particular pale purple chicken that grew into a
ferocious mature rooster which chased both of them around the yard for
years.

"Look around you, Lilly, nothing's changed here. The Courthouse
Square and the Confederate Memorial and all those old men who sit on the
benches watching the traffic go by and reliving the past. Doesn't matter that
the traffic is cars instead of horses and buggies. Those green benches have
been rubbed to smooth, bare wood by generations of old men's bottoms.

Look at the train station. It's a Palladian gem of a building."

"The last time I looked at the train station the windows were all broken and boarded-up, and barn swallows were nesting in the gaps in the roof tiles."

"It's still a pretty building even if the trains have stopped coming through," he argued. It was his favorite building. He could look past the vacant windows and feel again the childhood excitement of boarding the train for a day trip to the city with his grandmother.

"You'd better be careful about staying around too long and getting all sentimental about this town," she warned. "Remember, not only have the trains stopped coming through here, there is no airport, and the interstate went through the next county. In a lot of ways it's hard to get into or out of this place. Lots of folks are stuck here, living in the past."

CHAPTER THREE

*B*eck Kimble leaned back in his leather chair and thought only briefly of putting his feet up on the massive antique partners desk, inherited, like the business, from his father. As a vision of his mother's disapproving face passed through his mind, he resisted the urge and buzzed for his secretary.

Beck Kimble believed in employing several secretaries. Doris Harris, also inherited from his late father, was the office mainstay. Nearing seventy and devoted to the company and the memory of the senior Mr. Kimble, she kept her opinion of the younger Mr. Kimble to herself.

Mrs. Harris currently shared the outer office with Bridget Dudley, the latest in a string of girls hired by Beck solely on the basis of face and body.

Mrs. Harris had not bothered to investigate or to utilize the girl's more-than-adequate capabilities, and Kimble could have cared less if the younger woman sat and filed nothing more than her fingernails all day.

He had plans to file her right between those flowered sheets the next time Laura left on an out-of-town shopping binge.

Bridget Dudley had taken the job as a stopgap between college and a hoped-for eventual move to an art career in New York. To earn enough money for the relocation, which her protective parents refused to finance, she had accepted the first local job available after her graduation.

Bridget was bored to death with her job and doing her best to avoid Beck. His leers and whispered comments left her little doubt that eventually he planned to propose something she had no intention of accepting.

It had never occurred to Beck that he was less than irresistible to any woman. He needed Mrs. Harris to keep the office running smoothly, but he needed a Bridget Dudley to keep his ego warmed.

Thoughts of that could wait he decided as Mrs. Harris marched through the door in her sensible, orthopedic shoes.

"Mrs. Harris, I need to review my mother's insurance file. I believe we also keep on file a list of acquisitions she's considering. Can you get me both?"

Mrs. Harris nodded and padded on the rubber soles back out to her office, wondering what he was plotting this morning. She had seen that something-up-his-sleeve expression too many times.

Beck swiveled in his chair, and the morning sun's reflection on a picture of Laura caught his eye.

Picking it up, he studied his wife. In the photograph she wore a blue ski jacket which made a bright contrast against the snowcapped mountain face in the background.

Beck couldn't remember where the picture had been taken. Aspen, or Utah, or Switzerland? Years of ski trips merged into one long, snowy trail in his mind.

If asked, Beck would have answered automatically that of course he loved his wife. If asked why he probably couldn't have formulated an answer.

He enjoyed Laura with her problems and insecurities because fixing up her little crises made him feel important.

He took pride in her appearance and her impeccable social standing.

He was very tired of her for the same reasons.

Beck Kimble was thirty-three years old, and some days he was so bored he felt a hundred and thirty-three.

Asking himself why he ever married her in the first place, Beck's mind traveled back to the night of the only truly impulsive act of his well-regulated life.

His marriage had begun as a prank. The guys lounging around the country club pool that summer placed bets on who could be the first to bed the unbeddable Laura Lambeth. A pool was formed, with a hundred dollars and a case of beer going to the winner.

Beck didn't need the money, and he didn't like beer, but he liked even less the idea that losing a contest might call into question his reputation as a stud.

He spent the summer wining and dining her, but all his powers of persuasion got him nowhere when it came to sex.

Laura was at the time just out of high school, a confused, frightened eighteen-year-old who had in the course of a year lost both of her parents.

All Laura wanted was someone to take care of her, and it didn't take much persuasion to convince her to elope with him. She was desperate for anyone willing to step into her life and tell her what to do next.

Marriage was no big deal to him. He could have a little fun with her and later get himself out of the situation when he got bored.

Marriage was, however, a big deal to his mother. All hell broke loose when they told his mother what they'd done.

He could see it as clearly as if it had happened late last night instead of a dozen years ago. Eleanor Kimble went to her desk, unlocked a drawer, and removed a small leather address book. Thumbing through it, presumably looking for a phone number, she turned her blackest stare on Laura and asked in a cold, firm voice how advanced they supposed the pregnancy to be.

Pregnancy? If Beck hadn't been so afraid of his mother, he would have roared with laughter. Who would have ever thought he'd find himself with a virgin bride? Did his mother have the name of that discreet doctor who had gotten him out of his last scrape filed away under "A" for abortion?

Laura's family did not pose the same sort of problem. Her sister was staying at the time with friends in the south of France, and Laura couldn't remember their names or the location. It was days later before Lilly chanced to call home and got the news.

Kick was on a photo assignment in Kenya, and it was a month after that before anyone got in touch with him.

With the exception of the vehemently disapproving housekeeper Desia, dismissed by Beck as the hired help, Laura had no family around to either complain or congratulate.

At the time he reassured Laura that his mother was no problem, that she would eventually come around. Who was he kidding? His mother had never in his life "come around" on anything. It was her way or no way, and she always got her way. Twelve years later she was still in a snit about his marrying without asking her permission.

His mother had planned to be the one to choose his wife, and an eighteen year old girl would not have been her choice. She was determined to get him divorced faster than he'd gotten himself married. That, of course, made him equally determined to stay married.

In the end they compromised.

Four months after a hasty marriage that remained a secret to everyone but the two principals and their families, Brookland Beccles Kimble, III and Laura Paulson Lambeth were married in a very correct, late evening, High

Church Episcopal service with the bride's brother giving away his sister but not her secret.

Planned to the last meticulous detail by Eleanor Kimble, the wedding and the many prenuptial parties leading up to it were the social focus of that Christmas season.

She's been running the show ever since Beck thought bitterly as his reverie was interrupted by a knock on the door.

"I have the information you need, Mr. Kimble," announced Mrs. Harris. "Your mother's favorite gallery in New York faxed us this list of available pieces in case you are considering selecting a gift for her. Will there be anything else?"

Flipping through the pages she placed on his desk, Beck gave her a smug smile and said, "I think I can handle it from here."

This was going to be easier than he had hoped. There were several suitable items for Laura's auction and a reminder that Eleanor's credit card numbers were kept on file by the gallery.

Beck laughed out loud. The office handled the mundane routine of bill paying for his mother. Whatever he chose could be bought and paid for without her ever knowing she'd made a contribution.

The sizeable amount he contemplated charging was not an issue that crossed his mind. Uppermost was the fact that it was a rare and a lucky day when he had a chance to put one over on his mother.

After dropping Sam and her three carpool compatriots off at kindergarten, Laura swung the station wagon through the massive, brick-pillared gates of Brierley Hall Preparatory School.

The school was housed in a brooding, dark red brick Gothic Revival mansion built in the early 1880s by a successful Reconstruction era carpetbagger.

The whole estate had been purchased, lock, stock, and barrel, from the old bachelor's distant heirs, and except for the addition of blackboards and desks very little had changed inside the house.

Even on this clear October morning the building looked forbidding to Laura. On some dark, stormy days of her childhood she had approached filled with absolute terror.

Trying to banish the frightened, insecure little girl who was never far from the adult's consciousness, Laura hesitantly pushed open the heavy front door and tiptoed into the cavernous hall.

The interior of the school, like so much of the town itself, clung tenaciously to the past. The hushed and heavy atmosphere was as much a part and parcel of the house as were the antique furnishings.

Brierley Hall was a school, but its setting was still very much that of a proper-Victorian private home.

Alone in the dining room where her meeting was to be held, Laura bit her lip and reflected on the dilemma she faced. To tell her friends, her friends who all seemed to handle everything so much more capably than she did, that she'd failed was out of the question.

She knew they laughed about her, that her latest snafu was often also the latest joke in the grocery store or on the tennis court.

Laura was surprised to find herself in such a position of authority. She remembered sitting in the beauty shop having a pedicure, flipping through a magazine, listening to several of her friends discuss having a fund-raiser to finance a much-needed new library.

As they tossed around ideas for an auction, Laura turned a page and saw an article on the increasing value of English equestrian art. That painting in Lilly's library had to be worth a fortune.

Without stopping to think, Laura blurted out that she could arrange for a real showstopper. The raised eyebrows that passed between the other women didn't escape her attention as she assured them that it would be no trouble at all for her to arrange for Lilly, and Eleanor, to make major donations.

Before another toenail was brushed blood-red, someone sarcastically suggested that she be made chairman of the benefit.

What have I gotten myself into this time she thought helplessly as she checked her watch again and confirmed that time was running out.

Laura felt the foul taste of fear start to rise from the pit of her stomach, making her heart beat too fast and cutting off her air supply. She felt like running out of the room, out of the school. She told herself that she couldn't do that, told herself to stop being ridiculous, told herself that she had to do something to keep from fainting.

She took a pill out of her purse, swallowed it without water, and hoped it would do its magic quickly.

There was only one other thing she could do for the moment. She'd tell them that it had all been arranged, and, Scarlett-like, she'd worry about the details tomorrow.

Laura sat down to wait for her committee. An event such as the auction for which Laura found herself responsible is, of course, never the result of the efforts of a single individual.

These otherwise unemployed women were pros at this sort of thing. They'd done similar fetes for the museum, for the church, for the local historical society.

It never occurred to any of them that if they pooled the amounts spent on appropriate dresses, shoes, and hairdressers, not to mention table settings, invitations, and lavish catered food and wrote one check they could more than fund whatever charity they supported without an hour's work being required.

To most of Laura's friends the real purpose of such an evening was as much to define their lives as it was to accomplish a goal. The chairman of the committee became for a time more than simply someone's wife or mother.

The fact that Cynthia Wilkins was the first to enter the room did nothing to shore up Laura's shaky resolve. Cynthia and her twin sister Ginger had always represented to Laura two halves of a coin of perpetually rising currency.

Growing up, the twins had dribbled, and cheered, and pitched their way to as many trophies for the school as they now garnered serving and putting for the country club. Always active participants in a world where Laura remained a spectator.

"Got it all under control, Laura?" Cynthia tossed a silver fox jacket over a chair back and popped the top on a diet soda.

Tall and muscular, with the trademark short-cropped blonde hair she and her sister had worn since childhood, Cynthia Wilkins towered over Laura.

"You look too clean to have exercised this morning," Ginger Borland said to her sister as she entered the room without acknowledging Laura's presence.

A mirror image of her sister except for the fact that her hair was worn swept off her forehead, Ginger wore electric blue silky shorts, a tight fitting red tank-top, and striped leg warmers. Having run the five miles from her home to the school, she went through a series of cooling-down exercises, purposely exhibiting her tautly toned muscles. She moved like a large predatory cat.

"Haven't seen you at aerobics class lately, Laura," Ginger said, extending a muscular leg. "Better watch out. Past thirty it's all downhill." She looked Laura up and down critically as if expecting to see fat where there was none.

"I've been working out in the pool at home," Laura said softly. "I just love teaching that arts and crafts class at the nursing home, and the only time they can fit it into their schedule is the same time that aerobics meets. I'm hoping we can start a regular bingo game after arts and crafts so I guess aerobics is out for a while."

"How can you stand to waste your time watching a bunch of drooling old people finger paint?" Ginger rolled her eyes, hard, glittery, contact-lens-green eyes. Her disgust was obvious. "Don't they have paid people to do mindless things like baby-sit?"

"The staff people have their hands full, and besides I love those people," Laura said defensively. "They don't just finger paint either. Some of them are quite talented."

The three mornings a week that she drove out to the nursing home were the best hours of her week, and the time she spent with the residents there the most satisfying. She thought of several of the ladies as the kind of grandmother she'd longed to have as a child, and it bewildered her that Ginger could make fun of them.

She felt safe, approved of, with the old ladies in a way that she never felt with her own friends. The nursing home was the one place in her life where she took care of others instead of seeking others to take care of her.

"I hope you're organized enough that this silly little meeting isn't going to last long. I've got a tennis match at twelve, and I'd like to hit off the backboard for a little while before that," Cynthia said, with a smirk in her sister's direction.

Ginger enjoyed seeing Laura squirm. Ginger Borland hated Laura Kimble with the intensity of one for whom jealousy is a gnawing, consuming cancer of the spirit. The fact that Laura, who had more money than she could ever spend anyway, had married someone with Beck's resources had irritated Ginger for years. She had had her eye on Beck in high school days when Laura had acted as though she didn't know he was alive.

Ginger's husband, Mark, made a decent living from his contracting business, but it wasn't close to enough to provide for things like the new fox jacket her sister flaunted.

Ginger hated her sister almost as much as she hated Laura. For Ginger there could never be enough, and she never tired of reminding Mark of what her sister and her friends had. Surely if he couldn't make the money necessary to satisfy her needs he could find a way to borrow it.

Before the now thoroughly intimidated Laura could answer that she couldn't begin until the rest of the group arrived, the chatter of voices told her that she wouldn't be able to delay much longer what was starting to look to her like the beginning of her own end.

It was just as well. The pill had calmed her down enough so that she felt like she could again breathe normally, but she was getting sleepy and having difficulty concentrating.

In they all finally came, singly and in twos and threes, women Laura had known all her life, women with whom she'd shared the common experiences of kindergarten and Brierley Hall, debutante parties and baby showers, cocktail parties and carpool lines.

They all seemed to Laura to have their lives completely under control. She watched miserably, feeling an outsider among these people she'd known for so long, as her friends laughed and poured coffee, exchanging the small talk of those to whom such talk comes easily, the experts at idle chatter.

Laura's lifelong best friend Christine Bradley laughed at another woman's comments about problems with her hair as she tore open a package of artificial sugar and spilled its contents into a cup of coffee.

"Let's get this show on the road, Laura," Ginger called out over the buzz of conversation. "I, at least, have a lot to do today."

As everyone took a seat in the shield-back chairs arranged around the table, Laura wished frantically that she could just sit unobserved and listen to someone else. Why had she ever agreed to do something like this? Her brain felt as fuzzy as one of her five-year-old's dinosaur slippers, and her eyes didn't seem to be focusing.

Knowing that all the other eyes in the room were clearly focused on her, Laura gave the group a bright forced smile and said, "I did it. The major donations are all arranged."

The room was silent as Laura held on to the edge of the table to keep her balance. They were obviously waiting for her to continue.

Laura forced herself to concentrate so that she'd know what to do next. She wanted to curl up under the table and go to sleep.

"That's really all I have to say," she blurted out as a feeble connection was made between brain and tongue. She gave in to her quaking knees and sat down.

The room was silent for a long moment before Christine Bradley jumped in to rescue her best friend.

"I've agreed to be Laura's co-chairman," she said to Laura's surprise and utter relief. "Now that Laura has done the lion's share of the work by arranging these fabulous donations it's time for all of us to pitch in and do the legwork on the nitty gritty of bringing the evening off. We'll each take an area of responsibility."

That's just great, we get the legwork while little Laura gets the limelight thought Ginger irritably. I'm expected to work my tail off arranging valet parking or something so that Laura can sit center stage in an expensive new dress and smile insipidly through the whole show.

Christine broke in on other thoughts half formed. "Come on, girls, you've all worked on things like this before. Speak up about where you want to work, or I'll have to assign jobs. It would be a shame to have some-one who has a real talent for handling the parking lot finding themselves in charge of supervising the caterer."

As they began to call out "flowers" or "invitations" or "staging" accord-ing to personal predilection for taking either responsibility or the easy way out, Laura closed her eyes and said a silent thank you for a friend like Christine.

She still hadn't allowed herself to think about the fact that she was no closer to what she'd rashly promised than she had been when Beck got out of the shower. Well, now that it was official Lilly had no choice but to help.

As if from underwater, or very far away, she heard Christine adjourn the meeting.

Laura was sitting silently, head nodding in a drug-clouded daze, as the others left the room. Christine had to ask her twice before Laura became aware that she was being invited to lunch at the club.

Lilly squeezed her muddy green truck into an empty parking space. She saw her brother's Porsche already parked in a slot across the crowded restaurant lot. She was late meeting him for lunch at Victoria's, a restaurant housed in a gingerbread Queen Anne house just off the town square.

It would not have been Lilly's first choice as a lunch location for the very reason Kick had suggested it. The courtyard dining area was the favorite spot of the Brierley ladies who lunched, and Kick wanted to get a picture of some of the now middle-aged women he'd known in high school for his book.

What he didn't want was a posed shot, and he reasoned that having Lilly in tow might make him somewhat unobtrusive. At six-foot-four it was hard for him to be unobtrusive anywhere.

Lilly got along much better with men than she did with women, and the crowd that frequented Victoria's was not her cup of tea at all. Her favorite restaurant was a truck stop on the other side of town.

A golden butterfly swooped past her head, and she smiled and waved to it before joining Kick at one of the white wrought iron tables.

Self-consciously he slipped his camera case under the flowered table cloth. Trying to take candid pictures was going to be an exercise in futility. He was the only man in the place, and every woman there seemed to be staring at him.

Maybe they were staring at Lilly who looked as out of place as he did. In a den of well dressed women she wore faded blue jeans and one of his old shirts which was much too big for her. Lilly hated to shop for clothes. The closest he'd ever seen her come to a shopping spree was the day that two big boxes were delivered from a mail-order hunting catalog, and one of those contained two pairs of hiking boots.

"Don't you just love this weather?" she asked as a brisk breeze blew a gentle dusting of leaves onto the tabletop. "October's my favorite month. Remember when I was a little girl, and my teachers complained because I always drew little jack-o'-lantern faces in the 'O's' when I dated my paper? I love the sting of the first frost when you open the back door in the morning, and the deer running in the woods, and the idea that it's going to get really cold soon, and I can snuggle down inside my house under a quilt."

"This is going to be a cold winter," she bubbled on. "All the signs are right. The horses have the thickest coats they've had in a couple of years. The spider webs are thick too, and there are a million acorns on the trees, and the geese look like they're getting out of Dodge with a sheriff chasing their tails."

Kick didn't respond to her enthusiasm. Kick hated cold weather. He was definitely not a winter person and, for all the pleasures of the sensual assault in the colors and smells of autumn, to him red leaves and the waft of wood smoke on the breeze were a wistful prelude to the dead dark chill of approaching winter.

"I just hate that Indian summer weather we've had the last few weeks, and I apologize that the heat has made me so mean lately," she continued. "I can't function when it's all humid and icky-hot. Now that the weather's changed, I promise to be a nice person again."

He thought to himself that her recent mood had more to do with the fact that she was in many ways as restless as he was than it did with the weather. Lilly's life had reached a sort of plateau.

She seemed to read his mind. "Kick, I'm thinking about doing something, and I want your opinion. I'm thinking seriously of buying that bookstore on the square." She sat back with a big smile, sure that he would back her up with the opinion that it was a wonderful idea.

The bookstore was a small, dusty enclave of first editions and old maps run by an elderly gentleman who hadn't taken inventory in decades. Kick couldn't visualize his outdoorsy sister spending her days in the dark recesses of a bookstore. Despite the fact that she loved books, had them spilling out of bookcases and stacked in corners all over the house, he thought the idea was crazy and told her so.

"Lilly, I think what you need is a change of scenery. Why don't you go to England and visit your daughter?"

Without giving up on the possibility of the bookstore she had to admit that his idea was a better one. It might be nice to make a spur of the moment visit to her ex-husband and her daughter. It had been several years since her last visit, much too long since she'd seen either one of them. The bookstore could wait for January when bad weather forced her indoors for extended periods.

"Great idea, Kick. Why don't you come with me? The grouse season will still be on in Scotland, and you know how good the trout fishing is in Edmund's streams. We'll have a great time."

"Wish I could, Lilly, but I need to stay here and get my pictures while the fall color's good," he said without bothering to remind her that she was the only one in the family who enjoyed the hunting and fishing their grandfather had loved. Kick was by nature more like their mother, dreamy and artistic.

"I'm going to call Cait and Edmund this afternoon and tell them I'll be there at the end of the week," she said enthusiastically. "Or should I just show up and surprise them?"

"People need to be warned when a storm is coming." He laughed. "Lilly, do you ever find it strange that you and Edmund have a relationship more like that of a very companionable old married couple than do most people who have remained together for years?"

"Not at all. The fact that we couldn't live together doesn't mean that we don't love each other. We'll always love each other. We were just very different people, classic case of opposites that attracted and then repelled like two magnets with the poles turned in the wrong directions."

"Maybe you ought to get back together. You're not quite the wild thing you were in those days. I'm not sure any man could have settled you down at twenty. Haven't you ever thought about getting married again?"

"I don't know, Kick. Sometimes I think I'm too set in my ways to make the accommodations necessary to live with someone else. I don't want someone else having the right to interfere with my plans for the afternoon."

"Don't you occasionally get lonely and want some companionship?"

"For companionship I have a dog who does nicely. If you're asking if I ever wish for a companion who's as starved for some heavy panting sex as I am the answer is yes." She spoke and laughed loudly enough that the women at the next table exchanged disapproving glances. Lilly winked at them.

"Anyway, you're a fine one to give advice on marriage, little brother. I don't recall buying you any wedding gifts lately."

Rather than coming back with his usual flip retort Kick looked troubled. "I think I'd like to be married, Lilly. I really do. I don't want to grow old all alone."

"Well there certainly hasn't been any shortage of women in your life," she answered. "What's holding you back?"

"Probably the same thing you'd find if you were honest with yourself. We both have a horror of ending up like Mother and Daddy."

Lilly chortled. "That's the most ridiculous thing I've ever heard, Dr. Freud. Daddy was a self-centered, philandering bastard, and Mother was nuts. I can't see either one of us playing those roles."

"I agree with you about Daddy, but I wish you wouldn't say things like that about Mother. Mother had emotional problems. Mother was afraid to leave the house, but she wasn't crazy. Mother was the sweetest, gentlest person I've ever known."

"I had this same discussion with Laura not long ago," Lilly said. "She was talking about how she felt like she spent most of her childhood in that bedroom keeping Mother company and how she hated it when Daddy took off with one of his women. I'm glad you and Laura have such fond memories of poor old Mother. I stick by my evaluation. I still say anyone who spent half her life afraid to leave the house was nutty as a fruitcake."

Finally, almost an hour after they ordered, a waiter served the crab bisque and artichoke quiche. Patrons of Victoria's were treated as if time were of no importance because for many of them it wasn't.

Kick and Lilly picked up their silverware and put away their respective memories of the troubled people who gave them life.

CHAPTER FOUR

*S*eated on the terrace of the Brierley Country Club, with a panoramic view of the autumn trees ablaze on the smooth green carpet of golf course, Christine gave Laura a big smile and reached over to squeeze her friend's hand.

"I'm so proud of you, Laura. The auction is going to be a huge success and all because of you. With the donations you arranged we can raise all the money we need in one night."

Laura seemed to be strangely fascinated by the eighteenth hole although there was not a golfer in sight. It took a few moments for Christine's words to register.

"Chris, there's something I have to tell you," she began, obviously fighting back tears. Despite the effects of the tranquilizer, she felt frantic again.

"Can I get you ladies something from the bar?" The young waiter interrupted before Laura could finish.

"Scotch on the rocks," Laura said in a shaky voice.

"Just coffee for me, thanks," Christine said, frowning at the obviously distressed Laura. "Listen, Laura, I'm all for celebrating, but wouldn't champagne be more in order? Since when do you drink Scotch with lunch?"

Christine looked closely at Laura.

"Laura, to tell you the truth what you need is a cup of black coffee," she said bluntly.

"I need help. There's nothing to celebrate." Tears began to roll out of the huge grey eyes. "Chris, I'm in the biggest screw-up of my life."

"Oh, I doubt it's as bad as that." Christine could think of more than one memorable catastrophe she'd helped Laura survive in the lifetime of years they'd been close friends. Sometimes she felt like Ethel to Laura's Lucy.

"Have you cheated on Beck, or wrecked your Jag, or gotten overdrawn at the bank? Just tell me the problem, and we'll figure out something to do to straighten it all out." She put her hand over Laura's.

"I haven't done any of those things," Laura said miserably. "I also haven't got those things for the auction. Lilly and Eleanor won't help me."

Christine tried unsuccessfully to hide her shock. Laura had pulled some stunts in her time, but she'd never live this one down. Big mouths like Ginger Borland's would roar for days.

"Oh, Chris, what am I going to do?" Laura reached for the drink, but Chris pushed her own cup of coffee over in substitution. She'd seen this spaced-out look on Laura's face before and didn't like the idea of mixing tranquilizers and alcohol.

"Ginger and Cynthia are telling everybody in town by now," Laura sobbed. "I'll never be able to show my face again."

"Well, you well know my opinion of those two," Christine reassured Laura as she tried to make eye contact with a waiter. She had to get some food in Laura quickly before she completely fell apart. "The day I start worrying about what the Boobsey Twins are saying I'm going to be in serious trouble."

Laura wiped her eyes and smiled a little, remembering the summer that she and Christine were twelve and flat as boards while the twins flaunted their newly overdeveloped figures in matching hot pink bikinis. It was a nickname so old Laura had forgotten it.

"Don't worry, Laura, we'll think of something," Chris said quickly before the sad little smile could evaporate. "We'll just tell them that the painting turned out to be a forgery, or that Eleanor's maid doesn't have time to dust a suitable piece of porcelain, or something."

Laura's tears subsided a bit. "I don't know what I'd do without you," she said in a tiny voice. Christine smiled gratefully at the waiter who finally arrived to take their orders.

Laura breathed a little easier and leaned back in her chair. She always took the chair closest to the exit because for her that represented a power seat. Sitting near an escape route gave her the power to run if she had to.

She concentrated on Christine's face and told herself that there was no need to run as long as Chris was there. As close as they had been since diaper days, Laura had never confided in Christine about the strange feelings which were running her life.

"Incapable" was a bad enough reputation. Laura certainly didn't need anyone thinking she was "crazy." She remembered her mother's often-repeated fears of being locked away somewhere. Laura understood that fear all too well.

It was almost two o'clock when Laura and Christine walked out of the club together.

"I'm going shopping to take my mind off of all this," Laura said. "Will you come with me?" Maybe with Christine along she could actually go in a store, even wait in a line, without feeling like she was trapped in a burning building.

She had stopped using credit cards because she knew in the time it took to get the charge verified her body could decide to go haywire. She paid cash for everything and only used the drive-in window at the bank so that she could avoid standing in line there. Sometimes, when she got that queasy feeling like she was going to faint, she didn't even wait for her change after a purchase.

"I'd love to, but I've got to pick Charlotte up at school and take her to ballet class," Christine replied.

"Oh, no! I forgot to pick up Sam's riding group again." Laura slapped her forehead. "I suppose the school has called someone else by now. I hope they didn't call Beck's mother again. I get enough of Eleanor telling me how not to do things without reinforcement from the kindergarten teacher."

Chris got into her car wondering for the millionth time how the Kimble marriage had managed to survive Eleanor's meddling. She waved a good-bye to Laura, who was too preoccupied on her car phone to notice.

There was no answer at the kindergarten. Laura tried to take a reasonable deep breath and tell herself that one of the other mothers had been reached. Obviously someone had taken Sam home, and there was no need to rush back.

Laura pulled out of the parking lot, making a left turn with total disregard for oncoming traffic. An angry truck driver blew his horn as he braked and swerved to avoid hitting her car.

She was oblivious to his reaction as she debated whether or not to go home or to try shopping without the safety net of Chris. If she actually fainted in a store, an occurrence which had thus far never happened, Christine would take care of her.

Laura decided to go it alone. Stopping in a half dozen stores, she made a few purchases in each one. So far so good. She was idly walking the aisles of the hardware store when the familiar feeling took hold of her. Dizzy, disoriented, and frightened, she felt her heart began to beat wildly and took great gasping mouthfuls of air.

Paramount in her mind was the uncontrollable urge to get out of the store as quickly as possible. She had to get out before she fainted. She imagined the scream of the fire engine, the buzz of paramedics as she lay in an unladylike position on the floor of the hardware store.

Round and round the room spun, a dizzy dance of light bulbs, and screwdrivers, and gardening equipment. A young clerk offered assistance as Laura tossed a can of furniture polish and a pair of pruning shears down on a shelf lined with paint cans and literally ran from the store.

Reaching the familiar safety of her car, she put her head on the steering wheel and tried to breathe normally. Sweat poured from her ice cold hands.

She was only steps from the shoe store, her planned next stop, but she knew that going in another store would only bring on another attack. It was time to go home, but she needed to go in that shoe store. When a new pair of shoes couldn't lift her spirits things really were bad.

Laura had over a hundred pairs of shoes, most of which had never been on her feet. The majority of them had been selected when she was in a similarly troubled mood.

She drove, concentrating on the center line, the air conditioning turned up full blast. Sometimes when she panicked she couldn't drive the car and had to pull off the road. She wasn't far from home, and she forced herself to keep driving.

Grateful to be home at last, she swung the station wagon into the garage. The car felt safe, but home felt even safer. The blinding headache that inevitably followed one of her out-of-control spells was building fast. She wanted to crawl in bed and pull the covers over her head.

Before she could get her key in the lock her brother's Porsche turned in the driveway. Laura smiled and felt a little relief. Lilly must have changed her mind and sent him into town with the painting.

"She's not going to budge about that painting," Kick said as he and a disappointed Laura walked into the house. "She's never even cleaned out Grandfather's clothes, and I suspect if she ever found the house on fire that painting would be the first thing she'd try to save."

"Kick, why is it that I can't ever seem to do anything right?"

"I think you do lots of things right, pretty girl." He put his arm around her. "Don't be so hard on yourself all the time."

He had stopped by her house for a reason, but he told himself that he needed to stop by more often just to visit. Laura rarely made the short trip out to their house.

"Laura, I wonder if I could borrow your youngest child for the afternoon? I want to get some pictures of the town square decorated for the high school homecoming parade, and I think Sam clutching a big orange balloon while the floats and cheerleaders go by would be perfect. Does the Homecoming Queen still ride through town perched on the back of a big Cadillac convertible?"

"You can have Sam for the rest of the day." Laura laughed, relieved at the removal of the biggest hindrance to a couple of hours of peaceful rest. "She's probably in the house playing with the cat. I'm at the end of my rope with that cat. She no sooner gets through nursing one litter of kittens than she has another."

Kick refrained from suggesting that she have the cat spayed. It was a logical suggestion he knew Lilly had made many times.

In the living room the housekeeper drew circles with a dust rag on an end table.

"Where is Sam?" Laura asked.

"I don't know, Mrs. Kimble. I haven't seen her. I assumed she was with you."

"Didn't someone bring her home from preschool?" Laura asked anxiously. Getting a negative response, she grabbed the telephone.

The first mother she reached had picked up the children. Laura hung up the phone and turned frightened eyes on Kick. "Sam was dropped off here a few minutes after noon. If she got home over three hours ago where is she now?"

"Probably hiding someplace," Kick suggested with a shrug. "I can remember doing that as a kid just to see how long it would be before Grandmother noticed I was gone."

"Not Sam," Laura wept. "Sam always runs in to show what she's made at school and to get something to eat. Sam is always starving after school." Laura felt and looked dangerously close to fainting as she gripped the edge of the table. Her heart was racing so wildly that she could feel it tap-dancing in her chest.

"Calm down, Laura," Kick soothed. "I'll make a thorough search of the house and yard. She's around here someplace."

Kick and the housekeeper made a swift but inclusive trip through the large house, calling to Sam and checking the many closets as well as the basement and attic.

The house had, as houses of its vintage do, numerous nooks and crannies from a wine cellar in the basement, to a tiny telephone closet under the staircase, to a trunk room in the attic. Doors behind doors. Kick opened doors that Laura didn't know she had.

When Kick reappeared without Sam Laura broke down completely.

He had a grim look on his face as he dialed first the police and then Beck's office.

Less than five minutes later a police officer stood in Beck's study holding a picture of a smiling Sam as he read out a description over a hand-held radio.

Sam's smile, her uncontrollable mane of hair, little chubby arms and legs all flashed through Kick's mind. He had taken that picture last summer at the beach. Sam had a new, bright pink bathing suit and sparkled as golden as the June day as she posed and giggled.

Sam was the closest thing Kick had to a child of his own. His stomach knotted with fear. Three hours was a long time for a five-year-old child to be missing.

He led Laura into the English-flower-garden bedroom. "What am I going to do?" she sobbed as he put his arms around her and stroked the thick, soft hair.

"I don't know, Laura. I wish I did." He could imagine a number of possible scenarios involving his favorite niece, and none of them included a happy resolution.

"What do you mean she's lying down? Typical of Laura to collapse with the vapors when she needs to take some action," boomed an unmistakable voice from the entrance hall.

Laura gave Kick a wide-eyed look of fear.

Eleanor marched into the bedroom without either a knock or greeting and glared at Kick before turning a cold look on her daughter-in-law. "Where is my son? How could you let something like this happen to my grandchild, Laura? Things like this do not happen in families like ours, young woman. I want you to know that if something has happened to that child I will hold you personally responsible."

Kick's impulse to slap the older woman was tempered by the slam of the front door and the sound of Beck's voice. Grateful to turn the two women over to his brother-in-law, he excused himself and left the room.

"No news I suppose," Kick said to the policeman posted by the front door.

"No, sir, but we've got everybody available out looking for her," the man replied. "We've got to proceed under the assumption that the child's been kidnapped. Cute little girl playing by herself out in the yard . . . people who obviously have lots of money . . . it happens, unfortunately."

"Obviously this is about all one can expect from the local police," Eleanor pronounced in a voice filled with disgust. "I am going to give you people one hour, and then I will personally call in the F.B.I. to find my granddaughter."

Kick studied Eleanor with his experienced photographer's eye as she continued to berate the young police officer.

Probably never considered classically beautiful as a younger woman, she belonged to that class of women who with years mature into the hard regality described as "handsome."

Her auburn hair was streaked with silver, a clear, bright-metallic color with none of the sallow yellow of old age hair, and her complexion was pulled relatively smooth.

The plastic surgeon was going to be needed again soon for the tiny crow's-feet around the cold dark eyes. It was from his mother that Beck had inherited those brown eyes so dark that they were almost black.

Today she wore a simply cut, navy blue wool suit and a pale pink silk blouse set off by a double strand of perfectly matched pearls. Her only other jewelry was a matching pair of pearl earrings and a three-carat diamond solitaire ring under which she wore no wedding band.

Kick had to admit to himself that she reminded him of his grandmother in many ways. She had the same kind of imperious sense of presence. She knew who she was and looked it in any situation.

His reverie was interrupted by the shouts of Marion and Brook.

"Hi, Grandmother, what are you doing here? Why are the police here?" Marion asked with a worried frown. "What's wrong?"

"There's a little problem with Sam. We can't find her," Kick said to the frightened child who had instinctively run to his side for the security of his arm around her shoulder.

"Oh, that's all." Brook sounded almost disappointed. "I thought we'd been robbed or something. Come on, Marion, let's get something to eat." Brook nudged his sister, and Marion, a pensive look on her face, followed him out of the study.

Kick watched the departing children and thought, as Laura had earlier that day, how much like their parents they were. Brook and Marion were unusually close, more often allies than adversaries. The younger Sam tried to keep up with them but was usually excluded.

Not only like their parents said a voice in the back of his mind. Like Lilly and Kick against the world while little Laura trailed behind.

Sam was unlike either her parents or her brother and sister. Sam from her hair, to her devil-may-care attitude, to the outlandish getups she wore was pure little Lilly.

Kick felt the cold sweat of fear. Where in the world could the child be?

Upstairs Beck Kimble was at a loss as to what he should do. As a rule he didn't think too much about his children, and it had never occurred to him that he might lose one of them. In Beck's well-ordered universe if you lost something you simply went out and bought another.

What did you do if you lost a child? He didn't like being unsure what to do in a situation.

"I complained about her shoes," Laura cried. "I fussed at her about her hair. What if I don't ever get the chance to tell her I'm sorry, to tell her how much I love her? Beck, if something's happened to Sam the world will never, ever be right again."

"Everybody bitches at kids, Laura. They don't even listen to you most of the time," Beck answered absently. He tried to remember the last time he'd paid enough attention to Sam to complain about something. There were at least a few days each week when he didn't even see Sam. He rarely had breakfast at home and often got in at night after she had been put to bed.

For an unsettling moment he couldn't even summon a mental image of his youngest child. Lilly, she looks just like Lilly, he thought as the little grinning face and long fan of hair flashed through his mind.

"I think I'd better go downstairs and call Mother off the police so that they can get their job done. Why don't you just take a nap or something," he mumbled in her direction.

From the uncapped bottle of pills on the bedside table and the expression, or lack thereof, in her eyes he assumed that Laura had probably already downed enough mind-deadener to kill a horse.

Downstairs Kick joined the older children in the kitchen.

Marion was crying. "Uncle Kick, we can't find Sunbeam either. Whoever took Sam probably got Sunbeam too, and Sunbeam is going to have kittens any minute."

The proverbial light bulb snapped on in Kick's head. If Sunbeam, who was Sam's constant companion, was about to give birth when Sam left for school then obviously Sunbeam would have been the first thing Sam checked on when she got home. Sam was very likely hiding out with the cat.

Cats made Kick nervous. They always seemed to be lurking in the most unlikely places and refused to come when called. Finding Sunbeam, with or without Sam, might not be easy.

"Well, Marion, my darling, there's only one thing we can do. While the police look for Sam we'll hunt for Sunbeam and see which is the smarter group of detectives. If you were looking for Sunbeam where would you go first?"

The children looked at each other, contemplating whether or not to share a secret. No grown-up they knew was more fun than Uncle Kick, but he was, after all, still a grown-up. It wasn't worth getting in trouble just to find Sam's dumb old cat.

On the other hand, Uncle Kick looked like he was real concerned about the cat. Brook weighed his options and decided that his uncle would be angrier if they didn't tell him their secret than if they did. At the age of eleven, Brook was almost as good as his father at evaluating lesser-amount-of-evil as far as he personally was concerned.

"Next door in Mrs. Trainer's old potting shed," he answered innocently. "Of course we're not supposed to go in her yard, and Marion and I never would, but Sunbeam likes to sneak over there. Desia says that house is haunted, and I'll bet she's right because Mrs. Trainer looks just like a witch. She dyes her hair black-as-tar and wears red lipstick that she puts on sort of crooked like she's not sure where her mouth stops. Mrs. Trainer hates Sunbeam more than she does us because Sunbeam likes to catch those birds that she feeds."

I'll just bet you'd never go over there Kick thought as he looked at Brook's smug expression. Deviling an old lady with small acts of malicious mischief was probably great fun for him.

"Let's go," he said to the children.

"Aren't you afraid of Mrs. Trainer?" Marion's eyes were wide, whether in fear of getting in trouble or of the reclusive old lady next door Kick couldn't tell. Probably a little of both.

"Of course not." He gave Marion a smile and took her hand. "Come on. We'll go together."

"Through here. There's an old gate in the wall," Brook said as he scrambled under a high hedge on the Kimbles' side of the brick wall separating the two properties.

Kick felt a childish thrill. Hidden access to forbidden territory. It was the kind of secret that he and Lilly would have loved at that age.

The back of the Trainer property, which had once been terraced rose gardens, was now completely overgrown. Kick fought his way through vines and thorny bushes in an attempt to keep up with the children who followed an invisible route through the undergrowth. This was obviously a routine trip for them.

Feeling blood start to flow from a scratch on his face, Kick could barely make out a rundown shed at the base of the terraced hill. The door stood open to what the children probably considered some sort of fort.

Marion reached the shed first. The mewing of newborn kittens was quickly drowned out by her screams.

In the little shed Sunbeam lay in the shadows licking a small grey kitten. Sam, still as death and covered with blood, lay on the ground beneath where the floor had given way.

Kick's hands bled as he ripped away enough of the rotten flooring to reach the child.

Adrenaline made progress through the jungle of vines and waist-high weeds quicker on the way out, and they were soon racing through the yard with no regard to the old woman who yelled threats from an upstairs window. Kick glanced over his shoulder and agreed with Brook. She did look like a witch.

"Call an ambulance, Sam's hurt, maybe she's dead!" Brook screamed as he ran through the back door.

Beck sprinted down the stairs and out the front door. Running across the yard, he was in the emergency vehicle right behind Kick and the child. The ambulance roared off.

Eleanor stood at the foot of the stairs with an expression of obvious disgust, glaring from the hysterical Marion at her feet to Laura, who held tightly to the banister as she swayed on the stairs.

"I have to go to the hospital." Laura's words slurred. She stumbled as she crossed the hall to pick up her purse from the hall table where she'd left it only a short time earlier. She felt as if the afternoon had gone on for years.

"You are certainly in no condition to drive," Eleanor pronounced. She turned from Laura to her granddaughter.

"Marion, straighten up right this minute! You must remember that you are a Kimble, and Kimbles do not display their emotions in front of servants." Her eyes went from the housekeeper to the policeman, who supposed that, as a public servant, he was included in the excluded group. He felt sorry for the little girl and her mother.

"Get that child calmed down," she barked at the maid who knelt on the floor next to Marion. "Then get Mrs. Kimble some coffee."

The telephone rang. Eleanor answered and watched through narrowed eyes as Laura tried, with shaking hands, to maneuver a coffee cup to her lips. Laura was making a supreme effort to get herself together enough to get to her child.

Never taking her eyes off Laura, Eleanor spoke into the telephone. "Of course there's a problem, Lilly. In this home there are always problems, chief of which is your vacuous sister. I can only marvel at the fact that one of my grandchildren hasn't already caught some disease from that filthy animal, and now this."

"I will criticize whenever criticism is due," Eleanor rebutted Lilly's defense of her sister. "But you're quite correct that Laura's deficiencies are not the primary issue at the moment. Samantha has been injured and is being taken to the hospital."

"You are responsible for what has happened," she continued. "If you had not given the children that creature, my granddaughter might have been spared a life threatening injury. The accident was your fault."

She saw Laura blanch but refused to let up. "You can speak to your sister at the hospital if she can arrange for someone to drive her there since she is obviously under the influence of drugs and certainly incapable of operating a motor vehicle. Good-bye."

The police officer helped Laura into her coat and led her to his car.

Eleanor collected her handbag and turned to the maid. "I'm sure you have better things to do than to stand there gaping, young woman. I couldn't help but notice that the books on the shelves in my son's study long since needed dusting. You are not being paid to eavesdrop on this family's private affairs."

Back straight and head held high, she made a perfect military turn and marched out of the house.

Once in the emergency room Beck was stalled by a nurse with a handful of forms while Kick followed the stretcher to a treatment room.

Confusion reigned as, in rapid succession, Eleanor, Laura, and Lilly appeared. Eleanor gave orders, Laura cried, and Lilly tried simultaneously to comfort Laura and to ascertain exactly what had happened.

Eleanor told everyone within earshot that her late father was the hospital's first board chairman. She demanded to have the chief-of-staff called in to examine her granddaughter. She ignored the security guard's repeated pleas to move her car which was blocking the emergency entrance.

Before Beck could interrupt his mother's harangue to request her keys Kick reappeared accompanied by a young doctor who asked to see the parents.

"Beck! Come here at once!" Eleanor demanded as, minutes later, her son and Laura emerged. "You must have that incompetent young doctor removed from the case at once."

"The young man seems extremely competent, Mother," he sighed. "It's only a slight concussion. Hopefully we can take Sam home in about an hour. I think you ought to go on home yourself."

Surprisingly, she acquiesced. "Very well. I am worn out from this whole unnecessary experience. I will await your call later this evening to update me on Samantha's condition."

It was hard to tell who was most relieved as Eleanor prepared to make her exit.

Ignoring all attempts to bid her good-bye, Eleanor fired her parting shot. With a hard look at Laura, she said to Beck, "Get that flea-bitten animal out of your home by morning. Tomorrow we will meet to discuss what is to be done about your wife. The situation as it stands is intolerable, and I am going to see that it ends."

At ten o'clock that evening it was difficult to gauge who could claim the most difficult day, but all involved were thankful it was at last over.

As the warm water in the whirlpool bubbled around him, Beck Kimble lay back and thought about what to do about his wife, and his mother, and his relationship with his children.

He had always taken for granted that he had a beautiful family, a spectacular home, no financial worries.

That night, for the first time, it occurred to him that their appearance of being perfect might be deceiving.

What troubled him most was the nagging feeling that righting the things that were wrong could be a hell of a lot of trouble for him.

Kick and Lilly stopped for dinner at the truck stop. Clouds skipped across the night sky, blanketing the sliver of crescent moon, and a sudden whip of wind made Lilly shiver in the thin cardigan sweater.

Kick, reluctant to offer his new jacket for fear he might lose it permanently, ordered for both of them. "Two large bowls of grease with cheese and a couple of beers right away."

"Very hot grease," Lilly added. The chili at Bo Tate's Truck Stop had been called "a bowl of grease" everywhere but on the menu for as long as anyone including Bo himself could remember.

The waitress returned with two tall bottles, and the pair sat sipping in companionable silence for a few minutes.

"I stopped by the travel agent's and made all the arrangements for my trip to London after I left you this afternoon, but I think I'd better cancel my plans and stay around to take care of Laura."

"Don't you dare. I'm telling you it's time we let Laura and Beck handle their own problems. In some ways we're as bad as Eleanor."

"Speaking of that, what do you think she meant by that last comment?" Lilly buttered a cracker and leaned back against the cracked, red plastic booth.

"I'm not sure." He frowned. "I'm a little concerned that she means to deprive the child of both her cat and her mother."

"Do you think Beck listens to her?"

"Probably not. He's made enough shady but brilliant business deals that I seriously doubt she has any monetary hold on him. Money is the only reason I can imagine Beck listening to anyone."

"I disagree. I think Beck goes along with his mother because deep down he's more afraid of her than Laura is. That evil-tempered old woman would like nothing in the world more than to break up the marriage and move him right back into her own house. She's pulled their strings like she was controlling two puppets for all these years, and it makes me nervous that her next move will be to cut Laura loose just to watch her fall."

Their food arrived, and Kick used the interruption as an excuse not to answer. He didn't like to admit, even to himself, that he was in total agreement with what Lilly said.

He took a big spoonful of chili, adding insult to an already deep sense of indigestion.

CHAPTER FIVE

At five o'clock the next morning Lilly woke to the steady drumming of cold rain and looked out the window on the flip side of autumn, a day as damp and gloomy as the one before had been blue-sky-bright and cloudless. The weather mirrored her mood.

Her bedroom, with its massive cherry bed, wardrobe, and dresser, was decorated in paisley patterns of deep greens and muted browns. The same colors which usually felt soothing and composed seemed on this grey, wet morning only dark and sad.

Having spent a mostly sleepless night under a heavy blanket of worry, she kicked off the covers and wrapped herself in the comfortable embrace of an old plaid flannel robe.

Frowning at her reflection in the mirror, she realized that doing anything to her hair was going to be an exercise in futility. She'd twisted it into knots while she slept.

As she reached the bottom of the stairs Lilly heard voices coming from the kitchen and was grateful to realize that she wasn't the only early riser.

Desia had for years hit the kitchen running long before either the sun or the family got up, but with age she now allowed herself a few extra hours sleep each night.

Kick, subject to nocturnal bursts of creativity, was a night owl, with his days and nights as confused as a new baby's. He was often working at one in the morning and still asleep at one in the afternoon.

It was a rare morning that Lilly didn't find herself in her quiet kitchen, having a cup of coffee and a piece of toast, alone but for the company of her dog.

"Well, if it isn't Sleeping Beauty," Kick teased. "We thought you were going to stay in bed all day."

"Very funny." Lilly took a mug from the cabinet and poured a cup of coffee. She smiled and sniffed the steam coming from the cup. It was her favorite blend from Harrod's in London. She had hidden the bag of coffee beans, the last in the supply which she replenished on visits to her daughter, from Kick. You couldn't hide anything from Desia. She winked her thanks in the old woman's direction.

Lilly looked at the pair at the table and thought to herself how lucky she was to have them. Kick, his light brown hair tousled from sleep and his wire-framed glasses magnifying the twinkle in his turquoise eyes, was saved from looking like a very huggable little boy only by the stubble of beard on his face.

Desia's crinkled grey hair was covered by the stocking cap in which she always slept. Looking at her lined face, Lilly realized with a pang that Desia was getting old.

Lilly took an empty chair at the worn, scrubbed-pine table around which she'd shared so many meals with the people she loved. The lashing of the rain, more muted in the kitchen than upstairs, combined with the crackling of logs in the fireplace to make the room feel as if it sheltered her in a protective hug of memories and security.

Years before, her parents and grandparents dead, Lilly had come home to the house she'd inherited on the Old Post Road as a brief stopping off place in her restless wanderings, a way station on the road to wherever her life was going.

She intended to pause for just a little while, a few weeks at most, but weeks and months slipped by into years. One day she realized that this old house was her destination. She was home.

Home for good at last, she told all but the friendly ghosts to be on their way. It was her house now and always would be.

Over the years Lilly had made few changes to the house. A house of its size and age required so much routine maintenance that she seemed to be constantly overhauling just to keep things running as usual, but she had extensively redone her grandmother's kitchen so that the efficiency of modern appliances now existed alongside mellow, aged cabinetwork.

Originally the kitchen was located in an outbuilding attached to the main house by a breezeway. Her grandparents had converted an informal parlor behind the drawing room to a kitchen and moved the cooking facilities inside.

The floor was of worn brick, salvaged from the foundation of the original kitchen. Countertops were dark green tile, the ceiling beamed and hung with copper pots, and baskets topped the glass-fronted china cabinets in the butler's pantry. It was a recently redone room that succeeded in having the old-fashioned feel of the rest of the house.

This was, like all good kitchens, a family gathering place as well as a room for cooking. Lilly had hung around Desia in here for so many of her growing-up hours, listening to her stories and sneaking bites of whatever happened to be in progress on the stove.

Kick gingerly touched the network of scratches on his face. It hurt to laugh, and he dreaded trying to shave.

Lilly looked at the scars of his rescue mission sympathetically. "How can that Trainer woman's family let her go on living there all by herself?"

"Bad blood in that family," Desia said darkly as she offered a basket of hot biscuits and a jar of homemade peach preserves. "That woman's mean as a snake. You know she poisoned her husband."

"Oh, Desia, where in the world did you hear something like that?" Lilly laughed.

"From your grandmother," Desia continued, ignoring Lilly's scoffing expression. "The Judge thought so too. Wouldn't be a bit surprised if that old Trainer place is haunted. The Judge'd be none too happy to know that little Laura is living next door to that place, and I told Beck so when they bought that house. Can't nobody tell that Beck nothing."

"I hope you're right about that, Desia," Lilly said with a frown. "Because I imagine he's due to get an earful as soon as the sun comes up."

Beck Kimble had not had a good night's sleep. Usually a long soak in the whirlpool accompanied by a double Scotch on the rocks could wash away the debris of even the most troubling day, but last night this time-tested combination hadn't worked at all.

After tossing and turning most of the night, he lay awake in the early morning, listening to the rain as Laura slept.

His mother's cryptic last comment at the hospital replayed itself over and over in his mind like a badly scratched recording.

He knew that his mother was always up by seven and that it would be no later than seven-fifteen when his phone rang.

When it came to his mother, Beck was outwardly a lion and at heart a coward, the classic product of a childhood spent in a home where a hand was never raised in anger but verbal abuse was a way of life.

His mother was thirty-five and his father forty when he was born. Neither had planned nor was particularly pleased by his birth, and most of his childhood was spent in the care of a succession of boarding schools, summer camps, and servants.

Because servants rarely stayed long in the employ of his tyrannical mother Beck grew up without even the security of a favorite household retainer as a friend or confidante.

The child who didn't have the option of terminating an unhappy situation by simply handing in a resignation envied the freedom with which employees could come and go.

When Beck's father died suddenly just before his fifteenth birthday he didn't particularly care. He supposed that his mother planned to prove mean enough to outlive her only child.

Beck closed his eyes to shut out the flowered fabric that made him feel so claustrophobic. Just being in the bedroom made him feel as if he needed to sneeze.

An ornate French clock on the mantel seemed to tick away the minutes with loud and alarming speed. He rolled over in a futile attempt to find a comfortable position on the rose-strewn sheets.

Maybe his mother had been right in her attempts to wipe the marriage out before it began. She could have solved it all with a few phone calls.

Once married, Beck stayed married in part to spite his mother. Initially he was fascinated by Laura. He could order her around just like his mother had always ordered him, and Laura did whatever he told her to do.

In those early days Laura had tried school for a while, dabbled in art classes at which she was actually very good. Aside from her art lessons she had led an aimless existence of shopping and cooking inedible meals from boxed mixes and the frozen food case.

Within a month of the wedding she was pregnant and too nauseated most of the time to try even prepackaged dinners. He couldn't recall Laura attempting anything more complicated than scrambled eggs in the years since.

By the time Marion was born, thirteen months after Brook, they had a house and a maid who did all the cooking. They had rolled on in a similar fashion for the past twelve years, losing themselves in their respective lives of work and too little to do.

All of her faults considered, he couldn't deny that in many ways Laura was a much better mother than his own. She loved the children so much that at times he felt something akin to jealousy. So she forgot a riding group every now and then or couldn't find her way around the kitchen. Laura was never too busy to listen to them or sit on the floor and play a game with them.

On the other hand, his mother was right that Laura was responsible for Sam's accident. As his mother pointed out, none of it would have happened if Laura had picked Sam up at school.

Beck looked at Laura as she slept, curled on her side in a soft, lacy, white nightgown. She looked like an innocent little girl.

His wife was one of the best looking women he had ever seen. He supposed she was a good wife because she never questioned anything he did. She knew better than to question what she was told.

He knew he was a good husband because she certainly didn't want for anything material. He paid the private school tuition, and camp fees, and showed up at least half of those damn soccer games. Obviously, he was also a very good father.

Beck enjoyed his little dalliances with his secretaries, but when it got right down to the doing-of-the-deed, it often represented more trouble than it was worth. There was the problem of getting rid of them once he was satisfied that they couldn't do without him.

At least that had been the case until Bridget. Bridget Dudley drove him crazy for the same reason he was initially attracted to Laura. She seemed to find it so easy to say no. He wondered if she were playing games with him.

Lying on his back, staring at the ceiling in the half light, it occurred to him that he wasn't particularly happy. None of his friends seemed especially happy either, and he supposed that this was just life. You rocked along, you tried to make more money this year than you did last, and one day you woke up and found yourself old. When you got right down to it, life could be a deadly boring proposition.

He rolled over on his other side, punched a nest for his head on the down-filled pillow, and sighed as he listened to the increased tempo of the rain. He hated winter, hated losing the escape of the golf course and tennis courts, the early dark and the holidays that winter brought. The whole season loomed over him like the clouds hanging over the balding trees outside.

Maybe what he needed was a vacation. They could go to Barbados for a couple of weeks and do nothing but lie in the sun and drink rum punches. When they got back, everything would look better.

Giving himself credit for a good idea, he called his problems solved and escaped back into sleep.

Travel plans also occupied Lilly's mind. She pulled strings, turning on the bare bulbs of the attic lights, and walked across the cluttered expanse of floor in the direction of the cedar closet where her winter clothes were stored.

As is the case with any family occupying the same home for generations, the Lambeths could have written the history of their family through the stories embodied in the dusty treasures and trash accumulated under the eaves.

There was something comforting about rummaging in the house's huge musty attic on a rainy day. Lilly loved to fantasize about the long forgotten garden party at which her great-grandmother wore the big straw hat, faded blue satin ribbons still trailing from its brim, or the summer trips to Europe on which the monogrammed steamer trunks were loaded on ships and trains.

More fascinating than the massive trunks, custom made in Paris and fitted with now tarnished brass, was a crude wooden box, obviously homemade and held shut with a simple leather hasp. Family legend said that it was sent home from Gettysburg with the few meager possessions of a young Confederate who did not return from his first and only journey north.

Her New England-bred grandmother's family war stories featured grand generals riding forth on spirited horses. The box belonged to one of her grandfather's great-uncles, and her grandfather didn't mind admitting that his forbear was a simple southern foot soldier plodding through the mud in search of a lost cause and a romantic ideal that had nothing to do with the life of a poor dirt farmer like himself.

Memories of those people familiar to her in stories told by her grandfather and in the yellowing photographs over which her grandmother loved to pore crowded alongside the memories of those people physically alongside her in the good and gone days of growing up.

Somewhere in the attic her mother's wedding dress slept silently in a sealed box, awaiting a similarly small-boned, small-statured bride to come. Marion perhaps would someday wear her grandmother's dress as well as her name. Lilly wondered what had become of her own wedding dress.

The tennis racquet with which a teenaged Kick won his first country club championship bore bravely its broken strings alongside a box of Laura's doll clothes. Their father's Navy uniforms hung in the cedar closet with Lilly's own winter garments.

Here was the tiny pony saddle, leather stiffened and cracked, on which she had proudly sat her first pony. She lifted it and read the engraved name-plate of a crown-warranted English saddler. Her grandfather must have bought it on one of his many trips to London. It bore the name of the shop in Piccadilly which furnished all of his riding gear.

Who in the world put a good saddle in the attic to rot? Who, for that matter, had made all the other countless trips up the narrow stairs in the deposition of all of these things?

Lilly sat on the dusty floor, hugging the little saddle in her lap and listening to the rain on the roof. She tried to imagine the house as it had stood new, redolent of freshly sawed wood shavings, rooms below an empty attic, waiting, waiting to be filled. Empty attic was almost an oxymoron.

For over a hundred years this attic had opened its arms to the no longer needed, the only slightly broken, the outgrown but still loved. This repository of memories must have been once just a huge, vacant cavern under the sheltering eaves.

Lilly forced herself to stop daydreaming. She had too much to do in the present to get lost in the past. She put the saddle down near the top of the stairs.

In years to come would one of Laura's children possess this house, this attic, and this legacy of the put-away-but-not-forgotten? She must spend more time with them, telling them the stories that she so loved as a child.

I'm closer to Laura's children than I've ever been to my own child she thought with a painful stab of regret. Caitlin has only known this house on summer visits, and she hardly knows me any better. So much lost time there is in any life. I had her, and I left her to others, and while I looked away for what seemed only a moment, she grew up without me.

Running away from her marriage when her daughter was barely two years old was the one regret of Lilly's otherwise satisfied life.

Despite her resolution not to let her mind drift back to the past, memories of her short-lived marriage crowded the surface of her thoughts.

Like many of her classmates Lilly had opted for a sabbatical term abroad and enrolled in summer classes in England. She considered herself a normal, carefree, typical college kid until she stubled into a class taught by a thirty-five year old history professor named Edmund McFarland.

She asked him an intriguing question one day after class, he invited her to discuss it further over tea, and to their mutual surprise Lilly and the quiet, intense Scotsman fell in love beyond the bounds of all reason.

Half again her age, Edmund McFarland was already widely respected as an historian who had thus far put the emphasis in his life solely on his work. Swept away by Lilly's exuberance, he let himself get caught up in the love she so freely offered.

Edmund had never met anyone quite like Lilly. He didn't plan to get involved with her, certainly never intended to go to bed with her, but once he did, he found himself as totally bewitched as one of the fairy-possessed characters in the Celtic folk tales read to him as a child. Lilly, with her wild hair and her ready laughter, seemed to Edmund as unreal as a magic being given human form.

Their affair grew in intensity as the summer progressed, and as August slipped toward September, Lilly became frantic at the prospect of leaving him and returning home.

On a weekend near the summer's end Edmund took Lilly to visit his parents' Grampian estate near Aberdeen. The ancestral family home was a tower house, a tall, slender structure described in later years by Lilly as an ugly stone pole.

The countryside was as richly colored as the house was grey and somber, and on a walk through lush green pastures where a thousand head of Cheviot sheep and black, hornless Aberdeen Angus cattle grazed against a spectacular backdrop of surrounding mountains, Edmund finally gave in to Lilly's pleas that they become engaged.

Her family was aghast when she telephoned them with the news that she planned to be married in early September and to stay on permanently in Britain.

Her father furiously threatened to disinherit her, her mother went immediately to bed, weeping and refusing food, and her grandparents caught the first available flight to London where they boarded a train to the north.

Lawrence Lambeth, in trying to assess the situation, was at the same time worried about his granddaughter's impetuous determination to marry a much older man whom she hardly knew and amused by a thoroughly Scottish family so economical with conversation that they could consume a four-course meal without feeling the need to utter more than an equal number of words.

His wife shared his concerns. Constance Lambeth had lived with him for a very long time, and she did not begrudge the fact that he loved Lilly more than he'd ever loved anyone else. He and Lilly had been inseparable for all the years of the child's growing up.

Lilly's grandmother's brisk approach to life did not allow for wasting tears or time on things she couldn't change, and it didn't take long for her to realize that her hardheaded granddaughter was not going to listen to any reasonable arguments.

With reservations, they gave Lilly and Edmund their blessing, and a few weeks later Lilly walked, on the arm of her grandfather, down the stone-floored aisle of the ancient parish kirk in a small Scottish village.

The long tumble of hair, which had blown so freely in the wind as she cantered through the woods on early morning rides, was swept on top of her head and tightly bound under the long, pearl-encrusted veil. Throughout the ceremony her grandfather silently prayed that Lilly's unique free spirit would not be similarly bound by the silent, brooding man who waited for her at the altar.

The troubled marriage of Lilly's parents, Paul and Marion, had been a constant source of worry and disappointment to Lawrence Lambeth who believed that marriage was forever. For his handsome, philandering son Paul he no longer felt any emotion beyond disgust. When he thought of his daughter-in-law, Marion, simple pity had long since replaced the impatience he once felt as he watched her retreat farther and farther from reality, turning the bedroom she refused to leave into her self-imposed prison cell.

What Lilly was doing was as reckless as her own parents' wartime marriage had been, and her grandfather could only hope it wouldn't come to a similarly disastrous outcome.

Looking back on the whole experience of being Mrs. Edmund McFarland, the word that came most often to Lilly's mind was cold.

There was physical cold in their house in London and in the big, grey house in Scotland where they spent most of their weekends, but mere physical cold was easy to bear when compared with the emotional frigidity that chilled the relationship when infatuation went its inevitable way.

Initially Edmund was fascinated by Lilly's zest for life. Before many months had passed, her high spirits threatened to drive him round-the-bend.

Given her background and temperament, Lilly's was not a malleable personality. Reserved and private by nature and by upbringing, Edmund cringed when Lilly seemed ready to bare her soul to the butcher, the postman, or anyone else who would listen.

Financially frugal, he dissected every expenditure and grew sullen when Lilly pointed out that she had her own annual income from family trusts. When his mother's sweaters began to look worn they were mended, and he felt that his wife should follow her thrifty example.

Perhaps Edmund McFarland's biggest mixed blessing came in following the advice of his father who suggested firmly that "all the lass needs is a wee bairn to settle her down."

Edmund casually mentioned one evening at dinner that he thought perhaps they should consider starting a family. Desperately lonely, and without giving a second thought to what she was doing, Lilly threw away her diaphragm with the remains of the meal.

Caitlin Lillesfield McFarland's was a difficult birth that kept Lilly in bed at her in-laws' house for almost a month. Edmund's old nurse saw to the baby's needs. The father returned to commitments in London within a few days of his daughter's birth.

As Lilly sank deeper and deeper into postpartum depression, Edmund's parents shook their heads, and, unsure what to do, left her alone and went about their business.

Cait was just over two months old when the family settled back into life in London. A capable nanny was installed, and, with the weekly exception of the woman's off day, Lilly had very little to do with the day-to-day concerns of her daughter.

Edmund's father, Ian, gave his daughter-in-law one of his fine Gordon setter puppies when they left Scotland, and she lavished her frustrated love on the little black and tan animal.

Lilly's puppy was true to the characteristics of his breed, steady, intelligent, and fanatically attached to his mistress. It was only a matter of days before she found his constant presence a stabilizing influence on her depression. She poured her considerable energy into his training while Edmund developed a belated but consuming interest in their daughter.

Edmund McFarland was a distant but not unkind husband to Lilly and an ideal father. He found his wife to be totally confusing, an enigma of a personality often doing the exact opposite of what he expected, but the amiable, even-tempered baby had a disposition very like his own, and he felt that they understood each other well.

Walking in the London park across from their house, they were often commented on by passersby, the tall, prematurely-greying Edmund pushing the pram and puffing on a pipe while the big, black dog ran alongside Lilly. At the least they made a lovely picture in their brief time together.

Caitlin was approaching her second birthday when Lilly got the call telling her that her grandfather was dead of a sudden, massive heart attack.

After putting her on board a plane for home, Edmund McFarland sat in his car at Heathrow Airport and, for the first time in his adult life, cried.

He loved Lilly deeply in his own quiet way and knew that to the end of his life he would continue to love her. Edmund was also realistic enough to admit that he would never be willing or able to provide the type of intense emotional interaction that a personality like hers demanded.

He did not expect her to return, but, to his credit, he put most of the blame for the failure of the marriage on himself.

A month later Lilly did come back, staying only long enough to work out the details of an amicable divorce.

It was agreed by all concerned that Caitlin's bonding to her father was far stronger than her attachment to her mother and that the child would be happier remaining in London in his care. Lilly's bitterness centered on herself and her awareness that it would have been far harder on the child if it had been Nanny who was leaving the household.

Leaving behind her hopes, her home, and her daughter, she took from her time with Edmund McFarland only her dog. She embarked on a journey covering many years and many miles, to a destination unknown.

Edmund McFarland's writing was recognized around the world. A shelf of books bore his name as author, and more than one prestigious award for a scholarly treatise came his way.

The fact that his books on bird-watching, a passionate hobby considered by Lilly disdainfully boring, were also recognized all over the world mattered to him almost as much as the fruits of his historical research.

He was a patient man content to sit quietly on a shooting stick for hours in hopes that a rare species would briefly beat its wings above his head, and he had asked one of the most impatient of women to sit by his side.

He also had interests which fascinated her. As an authority on the culture of the Celts who peopled early Britain and the fear of witchcraft that gripped later generations of their descendants, Edmund put great stock in the influence of the attitudes of ancestors on a person's state of mind. Lilly was a native of a little southern town. She knew all about that.

Edmund had a true scholar's patience, spending long lonely hours poring over old manuscripts and making detailed perceptive notes. Lilly knew how to type, and, bored by the cold, rainy days of a long English winter, she offered to transcribe his pages.

He found in Lilly an assistant who took a grisly delight in learning about the Celtic cult of the severed head. She loved to mentally picture a cozy family group admiring their enemies' heads displayed on posts around their home. It also didn't hurt that she had always longed to be a witch.

They took trips to the Highlands, to the Hebrides, to remote outposts where people still spoke Gaelic, the ancient language of the Celts.

Possessed of a romantic streak coupled with a vivid imagination, she soaked up information like a sponge for use in her daydreams.

Edmund grudgingly agreed to give his daughter the Welsh name Caitlin because Lilly's only other choice was that of Boudicca after the Celtic Queen of the Iceni who plundered and burned her way from Norfolk to London in the first century A.D.

Lilly loved the mysteries of prehistory, from the strange symbol stones of the Picts, the indigenous people of early Scotland whose lost language remains unknown, to the enigmatic brochs, stone towers of unexplained purpose that dot the northern countryside of that country.

Edmund's handwriting was so difficult to decipher that it might as well have been Pictish. Once Lilly mastered it he relied on her during their marriage and for all the years that followed.

Two decades after the divorce Edmund still forwarded his penciled manuscripts overseas for Lilly to type.

Like Lilly, Edmund never remarried. He devoted his life to Cait, and to his work, and was rewarded on both counts.

Nearing sixty, he enjoyed semi-retirement in the old stone home in the shadow of the Grampians, sometimes lonely but relatively content. His memories of the laughing girl who so long ago gave him the happiest summer of his life and the daughter who was the center of his world were sifted so that only the fond ones settled indelibly.

He thoroughly enjoyed Lilly's occasional visits, still envied her uncanny luck with the fish in his streams and the game fowl in his woods, and found with her in later years the easy companionship they lacked as husband and wife.

When she jokingly told him that if he had only earlier installed central heating she would never have left, he wished painfully that it could have been that simple. As he knew that day at Heathrow, his love for Lilly was too deeply a part of him to be destroyed by time or distance.

Her brother calling from the foot of the stairs that she had a visitor pulled Lilly back from the past. She had been thinking about a trip to Britain for weeks before Laura pushed her into the decision. Maybe she was running back to rather than away from something.

Her arms laden with the little saddle and a stack of winter clothes, Lilly trekked back down the attic stairs humming Vivaldi.

She grinned to herself. She was going to buy Edmund something crazily extravagant just as soon as she got to London. No need to let him know how very much she had grown up.

Edmund McFarland wasn't the only one who carried the torch long years after its flame had dimmed. For neither of them had it ever been totally extinguished.

CHAPTER SIX

*O*n Hawthorne Road Laura came groggily awake. Clouded with a sleeping pill hangover, her mind struggled to put into place the events of the previous day. Murky images swam through her consciousness before the angry face of Beck's mother broke to the surface.

She's going to make me pay for what happened to Sam thought Laura. She wants Beck to leave me, and what will I do without Beck? I mess up everything I touch.

Laura burrowed deeper into the flower bed of soft sheets, trying hard to hide from reality.

Also drifting between the shelter of sleep and the cold light of day, Beck automatically rolled over and put his arms around Laura.

"Your mother hates me. She wants you to leave me."

"Don't be silly," he mumbled into her neck. "Mother just enjoys keeping everyone upset."

"Are you going to leave me?" she asked in a trembling voice.

"Of course not. When have I ever let my mother tell me what to do?" he responded, knowing full well that the answer was most of the time. "What happened to Sam was an accident. Even my mother can't blame you for that. Everything turned out okay, and I think the best thing to do is just forget it."

"But that doesn't solve my problem with the school." She slid further down in her nest beneath the sheets.

"In all the commotion I forgot to tell you," he said sleepily. "I made a few phone calls, and it's all taken care of. Mother's favorite gallery in New York is sending you a painting which I'm sure is much more valuable than anything that's ever hung in Lilly's house as well as a very fine piece of porcelain. You're all set."

"Oh, Beck, you're wonderful!" She relaxed and snuggled closer to him.

"I knew you could fix everything. You always fix things for me. You're so good to me."

"That's what I'm here for," he answered, feeling more in control as his ego recharged itself. "I've decided that you and I need a few weeks away from kids and work and pressure. How does Barbados sound?"

"It sounds perfect," She smiled up at him. "We can just get away and forget everything that bothers us."

A quick look at the clock told him they had just enough time to make love before his mother called. He smiled a very self-satisfied smile. There really weren't any problems so big that he couldn't solve them with a minimum of effort, and he might as well enjoy the benefits of Laura's gratitude.

It usually irritated Beck that Laura always followed the physical act of sex by going immediately to take a shower. He wondered, but didn't care, if Laura on some level found the experience dirty.

On this particular morning he was just as glad she was in the bathroom with the water going full-blast when the telephone rang.

"Well, Beck, I assume you have formulated some course of action regarding your wife." He recognized the brisk voice on the other end of the line.

"Good morning, Mother. I'm sure you'll be pleased to hear that Laura and I are thinking of taking a vacation and getting away from the pressures of home for a while."

"Running away will hardly solve Laura's problems," she countered acidly. "I think it's time you either insist that she seek professional help or initiate divorce proceedings."

"Professional help because she occasionally forgets a carpool?" he asked incredulously. "Surely you're not suggesting that I get a divorce on the grounds that my wife is a little scatterbrained."

"I know from conversations with Samantha's school that the forgetfulness is more than occasional," Eleanor continued. "I have come to the conclusion that Laura is addicted to whatever medication she takes any time things do not go her way."

Startled by his mother's comments, Beck was momentarily at a loss for an answer. He couldn't deny that Laura did seem to go on vacation from reality with uncomfortable frequency.

Because the suggestion hinted at yet another crack developing in the smooth facade of his perfect life, he reacted by immediately dismissing it as one of his mother's dark fantasies.

"She tends to be high strung, Mother," he answered finally. "Maybe she does sometimes take something because she's nervous, but I hardly think that's sufficient grounds to classify her as a drug addict."

"Beck, either you will have a serious conversation with her or I shall be forced to do it myself." His mother's tone of voice left little doubt that she meant to do exactly what she said. "I cannot continue to sit idly by while the very health and safety of my grandchildren is jeopardized. I feel strongly that the only vacation Laura needs is at a good treatment facility, and I think you must insist that she go today."

"I can't insist that she do something absurd," he answered angrily. "Just how am I supposed to force her to enter some looney-bin if she doesn't want to go?"

"I will speak to our attorney about that this morning," Eleanor answered. "If she refuses to accept treatment on her own, then you will have her committed."

Wanting very much to tell his mother that she was the one who needed to be committed, he instead forced himself to speak calmly. "Please, Mother, let me handle this discreetly. We don't want to create a situation where the whole town will be talking about us."

"You have never been able to see the forest for the trees where that woman is concerned," she spat through the phone. "It was a dreadful mistake to allow you to marry her in the first place, and my worst fears have been borne out through the years. The whole town is already talking about you. I heard yesterday at my weekly bridge luncheon that Laura has been named chairman of a large fund-raiser at Brierley Hall. I have already called the headmaster and told him that under no circumstances do I want her placed in a position of authority where she will make fools of all of us. I don't mind telling you, Beck, that it is costing me a considerable sum of money to rectify the situation."

He wondered if she'd gotten wind of the pieces of art he'd charged to her credit card. "I'm not following you, Mother," he said in an innocent voice.

"Obviously, Beck, I had to put a stop to the auction or whatever it was they were planning. I told the headmaster that I had been thinking for some time of making a sizeable contribution to the school. I have agreed to personally fund the new library which will be built in memory of your late father. The auction will not take place."

"I'll think about what you've said," he acquiesced quietly as he heard

Laura turn off the water. "I'm sorry if I snapped at you, and I will consider your suggestions. I've really got to go now because I'm closing on that Brewer property at eight."

"Very well," she answered. She never argued with the idea that business came before all else. "But I am serious, if you do not take matters in hand, and do it soon, I shall be forced to handle the situation myself for the sake of the children. Act like a man, Beck."

Beck hung up and rubbed his eyes. Right behind them his brain was starting to throb painfully. She didn't give a damn about the children, but at least she hadn't asked whether or not he'd gotten rid of the cat. Maybe he could run over the cat with his car and solve that half of the problem.

His mother had planted a worrisome seed of doubt in his mind, and he knew he would have to think about what she'd said sooner or later. For now the expedient thing to do was to get Laura out of town as quickly as possible. Maybe by the time they got back his mother would be on someone else's case.

Laura emerged from the bathroom wearing a dark green silk robe and a towel wrapped around her wet hair. She noticed his preoccupied frown. "Was that your mother on the phone?" There was more than a hint of fear in her voice.

"No, just my secretary calling to confirm an eight o'clock appointment for a tricky closing," he lied quickly. He kicked back the covers and got out of bed.

"I'm sure it will all go just fine," she said. "After all, there's nothing you can't fix, is there?"

"Nothing I've run into yet," he said with a smug smile. "Maybe we can get away on our trip as soon as tomorrow."

"Oh, Beck, you really are just the most wonderful husband in the whole world!" She threw her arms around his neck.

She smelled of soap and a light, sweet bath powder, an innocent scent like that of a small child with freshly shampooed hair. He kissed her, pushing the troubling dark thoughts to the farthest back corners of his mind.

In a London flat on the top floor of a converted Kensington mansion, Caitlin McFarland rolled over in bed and planted a lazy kiss on the closed eyes of Viscount Lockingford, future eleventh Earl of Amberley.

"I think you'd better get up and start packing," she said softly. "This flat is too small to house both you and my mother."

"Afraid Mummy's going to find out you've a live-in lover?" he teased, making no move to go anywhere other than closer to her.

"You don't live here, Anthony. You just never seem to go back to your own home, and anyway you underestimate my mother's tolerance." She giggled as he tickled her.

Cait pushed him away and rolled out of bed in one smooth motion.

"Well, my love, I can't wait to meet her." He stretched lazily and smiled at her. "I'd hoped we could have a bit of a lie-in this morning, but if there are to be no fun-and-games in bed we might as well nip out for breakfast. I'm faint with hunger."

She knelt by the bed and put a freckled face, which very much resembled that of the mother just mentioned, close to the mop of blonde hair falling in his face. "Mother won't be here until day after tomorrow. I guess if you promise not to faint during the fun-and-games, we have time for those as well as breakfast."

"Breakfast can wait until lunchtime," he whispered as he reached out to her.

They made the easy, contented love of early morning, in no hurry for breakfast, or packing, or anything but their well-practiced pleasure in each other.

Lying afterward with her head on his shoulder, Cait again brought up the subject of her mother's unexpected visit.

"I want to do something terribly special while she's here. I know my mother worries about the fact that she left us when I was so little, and she really doesn't give herself credit for how much she's meant to me in the times I have spent with her. Knowing how different my parents are, I imagine it would have been much harder growing up if they'd stayed together because of me."

"What made them decide to get married in the first place?" he questioned, gently stroking her arm. He wanted to count every freckle on the pale skin, to know everything about her there was to know.

"Whirlwind romance I guess," she answered softly.

"I find it difficult to imagine the terribly no-nonsense Dr. McFarland engaging in anything even remotely whirlwind." He laughed, recalling her father's stern expression as they'd discussed Anthony's own career, or lack thereof. Anthony considered himself a gentleman rather than a member of the unemployed masses.

"That's because you haven't yet met Mummy." Cait rolled her eyes. "She's very spur of the moment, exuberant, a bit dotty, actually, and you find yourself getting caught up in her schemes despite yourself."

"Well, I know the perfect thing to make your mother's visit special."

"What's that?" She propped herself up on her elbow, tucking a wayward strand of the strawberry-colored hair behind her ear.

"A wedding?" he asked hopefully. "Marry me, Cait."

"Oh, Tony, you know how I feel about that," she sighed. "I need time to make sure it's right. I couldn't bear it if we married and found it wasn't. Just give me until Christmas."

"If you're sure you don't want to get married this morning the least you can do is get dressed and go with me in search of some breakfast."

"Whoever first said the way to a man's heart is through his stomach certainly had you in mind. I suppose if I do marry you, I shall have to learn to cook."

"On the contrary, my darling. Marry me and we'll take a suite at the Ritz and live on love and room service."

"Be careful about what you offer, Tony. I might just hold you to it." Cait pulled on her jeans and thought, not for the first time, about the responsibility of someday running the large country estate which marriage to him would inevitably bring.

She wasn't sure she wanted to give up her freedom, and her job, and her cozy, cramped flat for the life of a countess in a hundred room house. She knew she couldn't keep putting him off forever, but she wanted to wait at least until she got her mother's opinion of the whole situation before giving him a definite answer.

Lilly's upcoming visit to London had come as a surprise to Cait, but it was fortuitous timing. Her father couldn't see past the fact that Anthony seemed to care less about seeking any sort of employment. Lilly wouldn't be bothered in the least about a "minor detail" like that, and her mother was never reluctant to speak her mind about exactly how she felt.

What Cait most needed was an unbiased assessment of Richard David Anthony Amberley by someone whose vision wasn't hopelessly clouded by the blinding handicap of being in love with him.

Aerobics class met three mornings a week in the gym of the First Methodist church just off the square. It was an addiction in the lives of some of the women who attended. For others it was a casual, once in a while workout. The group consisted of a slightly different mix of people at almost every session.

On this particular morning most of the women who had attended the previous morning's meeting at Brierley Hall arrived at the church in sweat suits or leotards, attire chosen according to the degree of self-esteem in which they held their bodies. Those in sweat pants wanted very much to look like those in leotards.

"I tried to get Susan to join us," Laura's friend Christine said as she sat on a bench and pulled on purple and yellow striped leg warmers. "Poor Susan just can't seem to get her act together."

"Don't waste your time feeling sorry for Susan," Ginger Borland said sullenly. "She looks like a pig and lives in a pigsty, and how even that wimpy husband of hers puts up with her and those gross children is beyond me. Of course Daddy's money probably helps him overlook a lot."

"Jealous, jealous, jealous," her sister Cynthia teased. "Born with the wrong daddy, weren't we?"

"Well if I had her money I'd be heading to the best plastic surgeon I could find," Ginger continued. "It would take more than exercise to fix her. Speaking of things that need fixing, where's Laura this morning? At home having a crisis?"

"If she is, I'm sure Beck will handle it," Cynthia mimicked Laura's little girl voice. "Why does she put up with that jerk when she has money of her own?"

"Oh, Beck's just a lot of hot air," Christine said. "Maybe she sees something in him that we don't." She pulled her long blonde hair back into a ponytail and caught it with a rubber band.

"Yeah, and I know exactly what it is," Ginger said in a waspish voice. "He was drunk-as-a-skunk at the party Saturday night and offering to pull it out and show it to me in the pool house. I thought if he put his hand on my bottom one more time I was going to have to slug him."

"You should have taken him up on his offer. He might have paid you enough to buy something decent to wear to the next party." Her sister roared with laughter.

Ginger pretended to ignore her while the others snickered. What little there was of Ginger's dress had been the chief subject of conversation at the party.

"Well, I think we're all nuts to let Laura be in charge of anything," Ginger said to Christine as the others stood around fidgeting uncomfortably. "I just hope she'll be with us that night instead of in never-never land. Mark my words, if there is a way to screw it up, Laura will find it."

"I think we've done enough talking about this whole thing," Christine said. "Let's give Laura a chance for once."

The others nodded their assent as they heard the music start in the next room. Gossip time was over, and they all filed in to exercise.

While the women at aerobics pushed their muscles Laura pushed a trolley across the activity room at the Green Hills Retirement Home. It was the day of the month that birthdays were celebrated, and her two favorite residents were to be among those honored. Laura was so caught up in the festivities that she forgot all about Eleanor.

"Mrs. Hopper, you look just beautiful this morning!" Laura bent to kiss a wrinkled cheek and gently clasp an arthritic hand.

"Why, thank you, Laura. I don't often get compliments at my age." The old lady beamed.

"Oh, Mrs. Hopper, I'll bet you got enough compliments as a young girl to last you a lifetime. I've seen that wedding picture on your dresser, and I'm sure that good looking husband of yours had to fight some pretty stiff competition to win you."

"Laura, dear, the flowers you sent were just lovely," Miss Archer chimed in as an attendant wheeled her into the room. With her intense dark eyes and dyed-jet hair the tiny woman reminded Laura of a little bird. She and Mrs. Hopper fought like children for Laura's attention.

Laura motioned for the attendant to bring Miss Archer closer so that the three of them could be together for the cutting of the birthday cake. She had sent both of her special ladies flowers and also carried birthday gifts, antique gold lockets monogrammed with their initials, in the pocket of her volunteer's smock.

"I hoped we could enjoy our cake outside today. This is such a beautiful time of year, and the trees are already beginning to turn, but I'm afraid it's a little cool after the rain," Laura said. "I guess after that long hot spell it really is autumn at last."

"Do you know what I always associate with this season of the year?" Mrs. Hopper had a faraway look on her face, remembering other autumns when her life was still spring-fresh with promise. "Pomegranates. How I loved pomegranates! I haven't had one in years."

"What I associate with the autumn is spider lilies," Miss Archer responded. "We had lovely spider lilies every September. Did you have spider lilies in your yard, Daisy?"

"Oh, of course. Everyone did. I don't think you see them much anymore except in the older yards."

"One or two always come up in my next door neighbor's yard, and my sister has tons of them in her yard out on the Old Post Road," Laura said. "She says they remind her of our grandmother. I'll see if I can't beg a few the next time I'm out there. I'll try to bring pomegranates too."

The two elderly ladies exchanged smiles. Laura never came empty-handed.

"Your grandmother was such a lady," Mrs. Hopper reminisced. "She was older than I, of course, but I remember her well. My, how she did dress! In the days when most of us still had a local dressmaker or made our own clothes she bought most of hers in New York and Paris. We were quite impressed. I remember my mother clucking over Lawrence Lambeth marrying a 'damn Yankee' from Newport, Rhode Island!"

"They were an unlikely pair," Miss Archer agreed. "She was so stately and regal looking. Why, she had a bearing not unlike that of Queen Mary of England. I must admit that we did chuckle over the fact that she was a whole head taller than Judge Lambeth. I expect you have many fond memories of both of them, Laura."

"Of course," Laura agreed. Neither of her companions saw the shadow cross her face as she glanced at the cheap flowered china on the cake table and suffered the flash of a bitter memory of her grandmother.

She thought of another table, formally set for her birthday although she was only seven years old. She tiptoed into the dining room early, full of excitement, and picked up a plate to look at the pretty flowers painted on it. Surprised by her grandmother, she dropped the plate, antique Flora Danica, and looked down in horror at the shattered pieces of porcelain.

Her grandmother's quiet fury, and her mother's reaction to it, came back to her as clearly as if it all had happened yesterday. Her mother put a reassuring arm around Laura and reminded Constance Lambeth that the plates were Kicksworth family heirlooms inherited from her own grandmother.

Marion Lambeth told the older woman in no uncertain terms that the china belonged to Laura and that she had no right to berate a child who had every right to break the whole set if it made her happy.

It was one of the last times Laura could remember her mother leaving her bedroom during the light of day. She asked herself, not for the first time, the uncomfortable question of whether or not she could have somehow been responsible for her mother's retreat from society.

Shortly after Beck and Laura moved into their house, Lilly drove up one day with the china, carefully wrapped and boxed, along with a set of heavy sterling flatware, also a Kicksworth treasure. Lilly insisted that Laura should have both, and she accepted them without comment.

The silver she used when she entertained and needed to supplement her own service for twenty-four. The china had never been taken out of the box. Laura bought whole sets of china on a regular basis, her china, china that she could break without fear of consequence.

"Laura, they're lighting the candles." Mrs. Hopper pulled her arm. "It's almost time to sing."

Laura came gratefully back to the present as she joined the chorus of old and cracking voices.

As part of a midweek, midmorning ritual, Lilly carried her coffee and juice and Sam's pancakes and sausages to one of the picnic tables in the park outside their favorite fast food restaurant. They dried the remnants of the rain off a bench with paper napkins and Sam dug in hungrily.

"They cook better than Brook," said Sam, mouth full. "Sometimes he only cooks me cat food for breakfast. I wish I could come and live with you, and Uncle Kick, and Desia. Then I could have a dog, and wear my cowboy boots every day, and never have to brush my teeth." Sam gave Lilly a longing look.

"Oh, you wouldn't like living at my house at all." Lilly shook her head and put on a serious expression. "I make everybody at my house eat liver and spinach for breakfast and brush their teeth seventeen times a day. Besides that your mommy and daddy would miss you if you lived with me."

"Don't worry about them," Sam shrugged. "They'd never notice that I was gone."

Lilly didn't bother to waste her breath in disagreement.

"What are you going to be for Halloween, Aunt Lilly? I'm going to be a swamp monster."

"I haven't really thought about it, Sam, because I'll probably still be in England then." She knew it was a serious question and tried to look appropriately concerned.

"Do they have Halloween there?" Sam asked anxiously.

"Of course they do, that's where Halloween got started," Lilly answered. "But in Scotland they carve turnips instead of pumpkins, and in England they use big old hollowed-out mangel-wurzels that they call punky lights."

"What's a mangel-wurzel? Do they have witches there?" Sam was hoping for a story.

"A mangel-wurzel is an ugly orange beet that they feed to the cows, and oh, most certainly they do have witches!" Lilly took the bait. It was one of her favorite subjects, and Sam well knew it. "The Celtic people who lived in Britain long, long ago had a festival called Samhain honoring their lord of death. It was like their New Year's, only it was celebrated at the end of the harvest, about the same time of year that we have Halloween. They thought that on the night before Samhain a crack in time opened up, and all sorts of goblins and spooky dead things came back to scare the living people. The cemeteries were just chockablock with dead people running every which way!"

Sam was wide-eyed in glorious terror as she listened. It mattered not to her that Lilly's stories always involved a lot of words that she didn't understand. She liked to experiment with rolling funny words around on her tongue. They felt good coming out of your mouth even if they didn't make sense.

"They also thought that on this special scary night you could see into the future, because of the crack in time and all, and in Scotland they hid charms in bowls of champit tatties. If you found a coin, it meant you had great wealth coming, and a wishbone meant that you were going to get your heart's desire."

"What's a champit tattie?" Sam interrupted.

"Mashed potatoes of course," Lilly explained just a little impatiently. She wasn't through with the story. "Everybody put out the fires in their houses, and the Druids built huge bonfires out of oak branches because they thought oak branches were special. They wore these awesome costumes made out of hollowed out animal heads and animal skins, and they burned things on the bonfire and then relit their house fires."

She smiled at the rapt expression on Sam's face, thought about adding that some of the sacrifices burned were probably human, thought better of it.

"But you asked about witches. Oh boy, did they ever have witches in Scotland! Why, Scotland must be the witch capital of the world!"

"Tell me! Tell me!" Sam screamed. She knew that she'd have nightmares tonight, and that Daddy would get mad at Aunt Lilly and call her up and complain about her telling scary stories, but she didn't care. She also knew that Mommy would stay in her room until she got back to sleep. The stories were well worth the nightmares.

"In Edinburgh, that's a big city in Scotland, there's a big garden with a clock made out of flowers. It's called Princes Street Garden, but in the old days it wasn't a garden at all. It was a foul, foul swamp where people caught eels, and water rats, and dumped their rubbish. It was called Nor' Loch."

"Was that where the witches lived? Did they live in the swamp?"

"Don't interrupt so much. I'll forget my story. No, they used the swamp for the trial-by-water. That's how they knew for sure if someone was a witch or not. They rolled them down the hill and into the swamp. If they drowned that meant they were not witches and were really okay people, but if they floated it meant for sure they were bad news."

"And what did they do then?" Sam had goose bumps and was, as usual, totally ignoring Lilly's no-interruption directive.

"They took them up to Castle Hill and burned them at the stake!"

"Gross!" Sam shrieked with delight.

"Actually, it was," Lilly said, a little out of breath from her theatrics. It made a good story for Sam, but she knew that in truth the old Celtic love of superstition died hard, and fear of witches was once a decidedly ugly business in Scotland.

"Did you grow me a pumpkin this year?" Sam changed the subject slightly when she realized that the story was over. She licked the last traces of syrup from her plastic plate.

"A whole patch of them, and if I'm not back by Halloween you must make your mother bring you out to pick the biggest one," Lilly said. "You can get Uncle Kick to carve it."

"Last year he carved me two, but this year I'm a big girl, and I want five."

"Hmm, that may be a tall order, but I'm sure he'll try," Lilly answered. "If you'll throw away your trash I'll push you on the merry-go-round for a few minutes, and then we'll go to the bank and check out their lollipop supply."

Lilly was disappointed that Laura was not at home when she and Sam returned to Hawthorne Road. She felt badly about the unresolved donation situation and wanted to try to help Laura think of an alternate plan. Neither of them knew that Eleanor, using her favorite tools of telephone and checkbook, had arranged to have Laura fired from a volunteer position.

In the kitchen a delivery man from Nelson's, Brierley's gourmet grocery shop, was putting the Kimble family's dinner into the warming oven. He had already stocked the refrigerator. He knew his way around Laura Kimble's kitchen better than she did.

Lilly was amused when Laura and Beck remodeled the house and had a kitchen designer come for an interview. When questioned about the types of food she most enjoyed preparing, Laura smiled sweetly and said, "I'm very good at scrambled eggs."

He left the rest of the questionnaire blank and designed a state-of-the-art kitchen later featured in a popular decorating magazine as an example of every cook's dream kitchen.

Lilly thought to herself that the only dreams about cooking that Laura had were nightmares in which Nelson's went out of business.

Lilly assumed that her sister was incapable of following a simple recipe. She was unaware of the fact that what Laura loved most about Nelson's was that Nelson's would come to her. Laura could wait safely in her kitchen for her grocery bags instead of running the risk of passing out in the checkout line.

Laura wasn't simpleminded. She wasn't even, as her husband so often asserted, lazy. Laura was mortally afraid of being in a crowded supermarket.

Laura Kimble let them go on thinking what they liked. She would have traded a trip around the world or the services of a four star chef for the simple, normal peace of mind which would allow her the freedom to carry out the mundane routine of buying food for her table.

CHAPTER SEVEN

*H*alloween was Christine Bradley's favorite holiday, and she had done a thorough, if slightly premature, job of decorating. High in a front yard maple tree a dummy witch and black cat rode a broom. The porch was piled with pumpkins and corn stalks, and the stained-glass-paneled front door wore a grapevine wreath studded with Indian corn and tiny scarecrows.

Laura rang the bell wondering if she should greet Chris with "trick or treat."

Getting no answer, she walked around back. The Bradleys did most of the renovation work on the ninety year old Queen Anne Victorian house themselves, and Laura found Chris on a ladder reglazing a second story bedroom window.

"Chris, you're going to fall off a ladder and break your neck one day," Laura laughed. "Can't you hire somebody to do that kind of thing?"

"Can't hire somebody who'll do as good a job as I will." Christine grinned down at her. "This is original glass, and someone else might break it." She wiped a dirty hand across her already grimy forehead, pushing her long blonde hair out of her face, and climbed down the ladder.

"You and Lilly and that dumb old glass. It always looks smudged to me. I was hoping you could go shopping with me," Laura continued, "but you look much too busy, not to mention too dirty."

"At least come in and have a cup of coffee before you set out to single-handedly save the local economy," Chris said.

Chris took pottery cups and saucers from a pine hutch. "We missed you at aerobics this morning. Are you shopping for something special or just wasting time today?"

"Time is the one thing I can't waste today," Laura answered. "We had this awful experience with Sam yesterday, and Eleanor is on the warpath, and Beck is taking me to Barbados tomorrow, and I don't know where I'm going to find a new bathing suit this time of year."

"Slow down, Laura. One thing at a time." Typically, Laura was attempting to explain a whole series of incidents, related or unrelated, in such a manner that the whole story became incomprehensible.

As Laura told her about Sam's disappearance and accident, Chris could well imagine that Eleanor's reaction would be to blame Laura. Poor Laura stayed in hot water with her mother-in-law, but if Beck was taking her out of the country on short notice his mother must be more wound up than usual.

Chris shook her head in frustration. The more Laura was told everything she did was wrong the more disasters followed in her wake. It was a vicious cycle.

"She's not going to give up until he leaves me." Laura sighed and looked down at her lap. "I'm so scared he's going to leave me. What would I do if Beck left me?" Laura had a faraway look in her eyes as if she were trying to see a destination for her life.

"You and Beck aren't very happy, are you?" Chris asked, comfortable enough in their friendship to explore things deeply personal.

"Oh, Chris, I just don't know what's going to happen. Sometimes when he gets mad at me about something, and I'm so scared he's going to leave me, I try to picture myself not married to Beck, and I just can't do it. I've been with him my whole adult life. I don't know how to be anything but Beck's wife. Sometimes it's easier to stay where you are even if that's not a very happy place. Beck takes care of me."

Christine couldn't imagine herself anywhere other than where she was either, but in her case it was because she enjoyed an enviably happy marriage. At the same time she didn't doubt for a minute that if she found herself in something as empty as the life Laura led, she'd get out in a heartbeat. Maybe it was possible to get so firmly entrenched in a rut that you weren't aware that you were just spinning your wheels, foot on the gas and going absolutely nowhere.

"I'm glad we're going away for a while," Laura continued. "Maybe Eleanor will be on her high horse about something else by the time we get back."

"What about the fund-raiser?" Chris asked, hating herself for doing so but worried that in the commotion of the previous day it wouldn't have been totally out of character for Laura to have simply pushed the whole mess to the back of her mind. It had to be dealt with sooner or later.

"Oh, I forgot to tell you!" Laura shrieked. "Beck got the whole thing worked out! Isn't he just the best husband in the whole world?"

Chris didn't bother to answer.

As Beck flipped through his address book looking for the travel agent's number he had a bright idea. Bridget Dudley might as well make herself useful somewhere until he decided the time was right to see what tricks she could do with that marvelous body.

He had to justify her continued employment somehow because Mrs. Harris was already making noises about replacing her. It was just a matter of time until she made the same noises to his mother, after which Bridget would be on her way to the unemployment line before he'd gotten to first base. It had happened more than once before.

At his summons Bridget appeared wearing a bright green sweater that did nothing to hide her ample endowments. It was all Beck could do to keep from licking his lips.

"Mrs. Harris said you wanted to see me." She did not venture any farther into the office than the doorway.

"Actually my wife and I need a favor," he answered, enjoying the fact that she looked momentarily caught off-guard.

"We're going away for a couple of weeks and wondered if you'd be interested in staying with our children."

"Oh, Mr. Kimble, I'd love to." Starry-eyed about the kind of lifestyle she imagined Laura Kimble led, Bridget found the prospect of playing her role intriguing. The extra money wouldn't hurt either.

"You're sure this won't interfere with your social life?" he asked. "I wouldn't want to make your boyfriend mad."

"I don't have a boyfriend at the moment." She blushed.

Beck smiled to himself at this revelation. Two weeks with Laura might be more than he could stand with this one waiting, obviously eager for him, at home.

She turned to leave the office, and Beck, having trouble deciding whether her best aspect was front or rear as he watched her retreating side, forced himself back to the phone.

Fifteen minutes later he and Laura held first class seats on the next morning's flight to Miami with a later nonstop to Barbados and reservations at one of the island's most luxurious hotels.

Mrs. Harris gave him a disapproving look over the top of her glasses as he explained that he needed to show Miss Dudley around his house before she moved in to baby-sit.

"It would seem to me that should be more the province of Mrs. Kimble," she said curtly. Bridget fidgeted uncomfortably.

"Oh, I'm sure Laura's much too busy at the beauty shop, or the shoe store, or wherever she goes," came his unfazed reply. "I'm sure you can spare Bridget for a few minutes, can't you?"

"I'm sure I'll manage somehow," she answered dryly. Where did Beck find these big-breasted bubbleheads? It was time to call Eleanor Kimble.

Bridget slipped into the passenger seat of Beck's car and inhaled the rich scent of the leather upholstery.

As they turned up the long driveway, Bridget had trouble hiding her excitement at setting foot inside the house she admired so often as a passer-by.

"It must be hard to keep such a large house and yard looking so beautiful," she commented to Beck as they got out of the car.

"What? Oh, I guess so," he answered absently. He gave little thought to how things got done around the house. Beck could not have put a name or face to any of the staff who quietly came and went, dusted and spaded, polished and chlorinated in the tiny kingdom of the Kimbles.

Bridget smiled at the children who met them at the door. Three stony faces responded. Bridget imagined them to be sad at the prospect of their parents going away. The Kimble kids had been left in the care of baby-sitters since birth. They could have cared less.

"I'd love a tour of the house," Bridget said enthusiastically.

"Sure," Beck replied without looking up from the mail in his hand. "Brook, show Miss Dudley around."

Bridget obediently followed the sullen child. "This is the living room," he explained as they entered an enormous putty-colored room weighted with enough furnishings to have stocked a small antique shop. "We're not allowed to play in here so you probably aren't allowed to use it either."

A baby grand piano looked lost in one corner of the room. Twin love seats flanked a fireplace, over which hung an oil portrait of a solemn looking woman. The woman in the portrait, Beck's great grandmother, wore a satin gown and held in her lap a small terrier with a menacing expression which complimented her own sour smile."

Bridget looked from the crystal decanters on the Chippendale cocktail table to the leather bound books on the shelves of the tall mahogany secretary and sighed. She wondered if the Kimbles actually sat in such splendor every evening.

The tour continued on to an equally impressive dining room. A long, inlaid mahogany table with twelve Irish Chippendale chairs sat comfortably on a Heriz rug.

Another gilt-framed portrait hung over the sideboard, and Bridget studied the dark-haired woman, according to Brook his maternal grandmother. Her eyes were almost turquoise, and Bridget wondered how much the artist had exaggerated in capturing the unusual color.

Bridget drank in every detail, thrilled that she was going to live, even for a few weeks, in such surroundings.

In the breakfast room and kitchen white lacquered wooden cabinets with glass doors and brass knobs hung in high gloss contrast to brown granite countertops and large stainless steel commercial appliances. The butler's pantry contained a bar sink and glass-fronted cabinets. Bridget quickly counted five different patterns of china on display.

"Your mother must be quite a cook to have a kitchen like this." She whistled softly.

"My mom? No way," Brook answered. "My mom orders everything already cooked from Nelson's."

Bridget was a little offended by the idea of children eating prepared dinners from Nelson's, which specialized in things like green peppercorn pate and Peking duck. In Bridget's experience macaroni and cheese and meat loaf seemed more suitable entrees for little people.

Brook started up the back staircase. To Bridget's way of thinking there was something very grand about living in a house with more than one set of stairs.

Laura's upstairs sitting room, a small sunny enclave with green and white lattice wallpaper and a deep, overstuffed sofa and chairs upholstered in delicate flowered fabric, was the feminine counterpart of the downstairs study.

Bridget was the oldest of seven children. Her youngest brother was younger than Beck's youngest child. Having grown up in a house where privacy was virtually impossible to obtain, Bridget found it hard to comprehend living in a house where everyone seemed to have their own private space.

Bridget promised herself that someday she'd have something on the same scale. She was sure of her artistic talent. All she needed was opportunity, to be at the station on time, and to remain firm that Brierley was not her final destination.

The last stop on their house tour was Beck and Laura's bedroom. Bridget gasped when Brook, thoroughly enjoying her reactions, opened the closets, each the size of a small room. Bridget liked clothes as much as the next woman, but the sheer volume of Laura Kimble's wardrobe was mind-boggling. How could one person find the time to buy that many clothes, let alone enough occasions to wear them?

She had no way of knowing that most of them had been ordered from catalogs from the safety of home and never been worn on the occasions when Laura feigned illness to avoid large gatherings.

Brook giggled. "You haven't seen anything yet," he whispered conspiratorially. He lifted the dust ruffle and pointed out the shoe collection. Bridget was suitably amazed.

"I love this house," Bridget said in a dreamy voice. "My dad's an architect, and I was an interior design major my first two years in college. It took me that long to figure out that I enjoyed deciding what color to put on a canvas a lot more than deciding what color to paint a wall, but I'm still fascinated by houses. I've never been in anything that compared to this one."

"It's just a house." Brook shrugged.

They went back down the wide, curving main staircase, the kind of staircase designed for at-home weddings and the dramatic sweeping entrance of a bride in a billowy gown.

Beck was in the study. He motioned for Bridget to take a seat on the leather sofa.

"Mr. Kimble, this is the most beautiful house I've ever seen!" she exclaimed.

"Well I hope you'll be comfortable." He reached into a desk drawer and tossed her a spare key.

When Bridget stood up Beck rose from the desk and put his arm around her shoulders, suggesting that they stop off for a drink before returning to the office.

Uncomfortable with the physical contact, she was also unable to think fast enough to come up with an excuse for refusing his offer. She followed him to the Mercedes.

Bridget looked around nervously as she and Beck entered the dim interior of Lonnie's Tavern.

They took an empty booth and ordered, Scotch on the rocks for Beck and a glass of white wine for Bridget. When the drinks came, Beck raised his glass in a toast and inched closer to her.

Poor Bridget became more uncomfortable by the minute. She wondered how long she could prolong a visit to the ladies' room.

She told herself there was nothing wrong in having one glass of wine with him. She tried to push to the back of her mind that this man was very much married and that being here with him went against everything she had been taught about acceptable behavior.

Her mother would die if she saw her having a drink with Beck, but then her mother was highly unlikely to appear in Lonnie's at five o'clock on a weekday afternoon.

Kick Lambeth, however, often patronized the popular tavern in the late afternoon. When he entered, looking around the room for one of his beer drinking cronies, he saw instead his brother-in-law sitting much too close to a striking redhead.

Beck smiled and waved. Barely managing to keep his temper in check, Kick approached Beck's table and asked in the frostiest voice he could muster, "How are your wife and kids these days, Beck?"

Beck's composure was unshaken as he smiled smugly up at the tall man staring down at him. "Won't you join us, Kick?" He moved closer to Bridget. "There's more than enough room."

Kick hesitated before taking a seat on the banquette next to Bridget. He gave Beck a dirty look.

"I'm sorry. I seem to have forgotten my manners." Beck continued to smile insipidly. "This is Bridget Dudley from my office. Bridget, my brother-in-law, the famous photographer Kick Lambeth."

Bridget looked up into the face of the big man sitting next to her. Whoever had painted his mother hadn't exaggerated at all. His eyes were the most incredible turquoise, at the same time blue and green, the color of the sea off Bermuda in summer.

"Working late I guess," Kick muttered as he signaled to the waitress.

"Actually Bridget has been kind enough to agree to stay with the children while Laura and I take a little get away trip to Barbados," Beck explained. "We're discussing the arrangements now."

Thoroughly confused by this explanation, Kick was saved from the necessity of a response by the appearance of the waitress.

The tension around the table was as thick as the foam on Kick's beer. He couldn't help contrasting Bridget's fresh-faced appearance with his sister's cool elegance. Beck was really robbing the cradle with this one.

"I'm sure you can call on Kick for anything while we're away," Beck said smoothly. "He can handle any crisis."

"Oh, I doubt I'm as good at handling things as you are, Beck. I hate to run, but I think I'd better get back home and see if Lilly needs any help getting ready for her trip." He drained his glass and looked around for the waitress.

"It's on me," Beck said. "Tell Lilly to have a good trip." He didn't know where Lilly was going, didn't care, and didn't bother to ask.

Kick left without so much as a backward glance, much less a good-bye, in Bridget's direction. He knew his temper well enough to get out before he made a fool of himself.

Lilly was in the laundry room ironing a blouse when she heard the screech of brakes in the driveway. She turned off the iron and went into the kitchen to see what was wrong.

"I'd like to choke him," Kick stormed, slamming his fist down on the kitchen table.

"Take it easy," she said. "Who would you like to choke and why?"

"Beck. I just left him having a cozy tete-a-tete with a cute little redhead in Lonnie's," he said angrily. "You would think that if he can't be faithful he could at least be discreet."

"Discretion wouldn't provide enough fodder for his ego," Lilly said calmly. "I imagine he likes parading his conquests in front of his friends."

"I don't know, Lilly." Kick frowned. "I think he's mostly bluff when it comes to women, but I don't like him providing fuel for gossip that could get back to Laura."

"Did he see you?"

"I had a drink with Beck and the very attractive Miss Bridget Dudley. Apparently she's going to baby-sit while he and Laura are out of town."

"Bridget Dudley?" Lilly gave her brother a quizzical look. "Amanda Dudley's daughter?"

"We didn't discuss her mother. Who's Amanda Dudley anyway?"

"Max Dudley's wife. Real attractive redhead. She's Irish, and they live in a big old house near Laura's friend Christine and have six or seven kids.

They're very nice people."

"Well, I'm sure little Miss Dudley is equally nice," Kick said. "But I imagine Beck is far more interested in her forty inch chest than he is in her family background."

"Maybe you're jumping to conclusions, Kick. We spent so many years trying to cope with the damage that Daddy and all his women did to mother that I think it marked us in some horrible way. We've got a void in the trust department."

"Why does Laura put up with him?"

"I was thinking about that the other day. Did you ever think about the fact that there's one major difference between you and me and Laura?"

"What's that?"

"You and I chose to wash our hands of Mother and Daddy. With Grandfather's help, we wrote our own marching orders and got the hell out of a bad situation. Laura didn't have that option. We left, but she, poor child, was abandoned."

"Speaking of leaving, when did all this trip business come up?"

"I gather this morning. Of course for all I know they could have had this trip planned for months without Laura bothering to mention it. You know how Laura is. She could tell you in great detail about the various shades of red in the roses on her dining room table and forget to add that the house burned down around them an hour after they were delivered. For whatever reason they're going I'm relieved that he's getting her out of town and away from his mother for a few days."

"Some days I feel like I should have stayed in New York, where it was nice, and quiet, and uncomplicated," Kick grumbled. "I'm too old to keep up with life in Peyton Place."

"Well, I'm glad you didn't. It's nice having you back here. It's hell growing old and senile all by yourself."

"You never know, Lilly. By the time you get back from England I'll probably be married, moved out, and have two kids on the way, and you'll be sorry to have the house all to yourself again."

"It will never happen, little brother," she said, playfully punching him on the arm as she went back to the ironing board.

She'd begun to want the house to herself again about fifteen minutes after he first reappeared.

Bridget got into her little car and waved good-bye as the big Mercedes pulled away. She needed to stop by her mother's house as she'd been promising to do for a week.

She told herself again that she'd done nothing wrong. Her conscience wasn't listening, and it continued to nag as she put the car in gear and drove out of the lot. After the unpleasant encounter with Beck's rude brother-in-law she felt guiltier than ever.

If guilt or anything else was readable in Bridget's face it escaped Amanda Dudley's notice as she mopped up a spilled glass of milk and tried to referee an argument between two of her younger children.

Total chaos as usual, Bridget sighed as she surveyed the mess in the kitchen and said hello to her family.

"Join us for dinner," Max Dudley called from the crowded table. "I'm sure your mother has plenty."

"Always." On her hands and knees on the floor, her mother smiled up at her. "We don't see enough of our Bridget these days."

"I'm busy, Mom," Bridget answered as she looked in vain for a vacant chair. "I don't need any dinner. I just thought I'd stop by and say hello."

"Is something wrong, honey?" her father asked after sending the younger children off to do their homework. "Are you having problems with your job?"

Bridget wished that she had not come. Her feelings were all too evident from her expression.

"No, the job is fine," she answered just a little too quickly. "I'd rather be doing what I'm trained to do instead of a lot of busy work filing and fetching coffee, but the old battle-ax who runs the office won't give me any responsibility. At least it pays the rent until something better comes along."

"I have a hot apple pie just out of the oven, and I know that's your favorite." Amanda smiled at her morose daughter. "Ice cream and cheese as well?"

"Nothing, thanks. I'm on a diet as usual," Bridget mumbled. She frowned at her mother's ample waist as Amanda cut a large piece of pie. Bridget wondered what her mother's figure was like before seven pregnancies took their toll.

Bridget was barely five feet tall and, despite the big breasts, didn't weigh a hundred pounds soaking wet. She intended to stay that way.

"I'd better be going. I've got to pack so that I can move to the Kimbles' tomorrow. I'm going to be baby-sitting for a couple of weeks while they're out of town."

"You're staying in that great, huge house?"

"Of course, Mom. I could hardly fit three children into my little apartment," Bridget said more sharply than she meant to. "They're used to quite a bit of space and their own rooms."

Amanda frowned, concerned that her oldest child seemed to be talking all around some problem.

Bridget gave her father a quick kiss before fleeing the kitchen. She was going to cry, she wasn't sure why, and she didn't want to find herself in the position of trying to explain why she seemed so unhappy.

Driving back to her apartment she did cry. Bridget felt terribly confused about where she was, sure only of where she wanted to go. She began to wonder if accepting the baby-sitting job had been a mistake.

Two weeks of living out the fantasy of Laura Kimble's life was only going to make her more dissatisfied with her own circumstances. Maybe her best move would be to borrow enough money to pack up and get out of Brierley as soon as the Kimbles returned.

Beck also came home to chaos. Sam was in tears because Sunbeam had hidden the kittens. Brook and Marion were fighting over the rights to a video game. Laura, seemingly oblivious to the children's distress, swam in a sea of clothing as she packed for the upcoming trip.

Beck retreated to his study and poured himself another drink. He began to wish that he'd planned a solitary business trip instead of including Laura and her damned wardrobe. He wondered if the parcel delivery service had needed one whole truck to deliver the boxes that were stacked by the front door.

Also wondering how the woman could possibly cram another garment into the closet gave him an idea, and he dialed Mark Borland's home number.

"Hello, Mark, Beck Kimble here. I was wondering if you still have the plans for the proposed addition to our house."

"Sure do, Beck," the contractor answered. "If you're thinking about doing it soon, your timing is perfect. I've got a large crew hired because we were scheduled to begin building a new house that's suddenly going to be delayed indefinitely. The lady of the family can't make up her mind what she wants."

"I don't give my wife the option of making up her mind," Beck responded. "The best way to handle a woman is to tell her what she's going to do and refuse to take any back talk."

While silently wondering how poor Laura put up with such a buffalo, Mark Borland reminded himself that he had a crew to pay and a desperate cash flow problem. "That's the way to handle them all right," he agreed.

"How soon could you start?" Beck asked.

"Would tomorrow morning be soon enough?" Mark laughed nervously, relieved at the promise of an unexpected turn around in his dismal financial situation. Ginger's spending was getting totally out-of-hand.

"I knew I could count on you," Beck replied.

"If the weather will stay on our side we should be able to get the whole thing done in about four weeks."

"Great. Go for it. I'm going to be out of town for a couple of weeks, but I'll call the bank and set up a line of credit. Just draw on that for whatever materials you need."

Beck hung up the phone and leaned back in his chair. It would be great having his own bedroom. He'd have a buzzer installed so that he could summon Laura when the need arose.

He studied the painting of his father hanging over the fireplace and was sure the old man's heavy jowls quivered as he nodded his approval. After all, the older man had spent his own married life sleeping a long hall away from Eleanor.

Mark Borland undressed in anticipation of his first good night's sleep in weeks.

He didn't like Beck Kimble, had never liked him, and had sworn that the renovation of the Hawthorne Road house was the last work he'd ever do for the man.

That had been years ago, and in the intervening time he had learned an important lesson. Personal likes and dislikes had nothing to do with meeting a payroll or covering the overdrafts on Ginger's account that the postman seemed to bring with the regularity of junk mail.

Ginger complained constantly about the alimony and child support Mark had to pay his ex-wife each month. She hated it when his two children spent one weekend a month with them.

Mark had a vasectomy before his first marriage ended. Ginger knew that when she married him, and it suited her just fine. Ginger didn't want any children of her own.

She said she didn't like children, but Mark suspected that what she really didn't like was the idea of doing anything to knock out of whack the shape of the body which was such an obsession for her. Ginger exercised compulsively and went completely to pieces if she gained half a pound.

"My sister Cynthia has a new fur coat." She finally came out with the reason behind her sour mood at dinner.

"Good for Cynthia. You know we can't afford fur coats, Ginger. I'm too tired to discuss it right now, but you're overdrawn by several hundred dollars that I don't have as it is. If you're going to keep spending like there's no tomorrow, you're going to have to think about swapping the tennis court for a job."

"Every other husband I know seems more than capable of supporting his wife. Weren't you on the phone with somebody about a new job?" she questioned as she peered closely at her reflection in the mirror. She was pinching her thighs and flat stomach, finding both reassuringly devoid of excess flesh.

"Yeah, Beck Kimble." He frowned at his own reflection. His hair was going grey, and he knew it was more a result of worry than age.

"Don't tell me Laura Kimble has bought a house even bigger than the one she has now." Ginger pinched so hard that she left a red mark on her leg.

"They're not moving. He's adding a bedroom for himself onto the house they're in now. It was part of the original renovation plan, but he got tired of construction before we got through."

"Well, now isn't that interesting." She smirked. "Separate bedrooms for Beck and Laura. Wonder who he's seeing on the side?"

"Ginger, Beck and Laura's sex life is none of my business — or yours. I need this job, and I'd very much appreciate it if you didn't go running that big mouth of yours about it to all your little buddies at aerobics. If he wants to sleep down the hall from his wife, it's no concern of yours. Maybe they get up at different hours. Who cares what his reasons are as long as it helps me keep the wolves at bay."

"He's not the only one who wants to sleep down the hall. Don't wake me up if you leave here at some unholy hour of the morning." She grabbed her nightgown from a hook on the bathroom door and slammed the bedroom door behind her. He made no move to argue. It didn't matter to him if she slept in the street.

Ginger Borland was thirty years old. Mark was her third husband. He was beginning to doubt that he'd be her last.

CHAPTER EIGHT

*I*n London Caitlin was furiously cleaning her cluttered flat. Anthony watched with amusement from behind the pages of a satirical tabloid.

"I never knew you had such prodigious housekeeping skills, my love." He grinned, dodging the dust cloth swatted in his direction. "Someday when you're mistress of a hundred-room home in the country, you'll be able to engage in a veritable orgy of dusting."

Cait moved the dust cloth in furious circles wishing that he would stop referring to her future as a *fait accompli*. His family's monstrosity of a house in the country was one of the main stumbling blocks which had kept her thus far from agreeing to marry him.

Like his parents, Anthony was passionate about Summerfield House and determined to someday take up the constant battles with dry rot, roof leaks, and deciding what painting to sell this year in order to heat half the place through another winter.

"My, what a black look for such a pretty face," he continued to tease. "Why don't we just ring up a maid service and abandon the place to a Mrs. Mop? It will only be dusty again by morning, and it's much too nice a day to lay about here."

"Unfortunately I, at least, must pay a visit to the office." She picked up his discarded magazines and popular press tabloid newspapers with an expression of distaste. The more lurid the words and pictures the better he liked it. Cait's taste in newspapers ran more to the Sunday literary supplement which she read each week from cover to cover. "I have what's called a job. It keeps me occupied and brings in the odd farthing. You ought to have a go at it yourself some day."

"I've been saving some dreadfully sad news. On the first January I'll begin moldering away at the bank," he said with such a sad expression that

Cait began to laugh. "I shall slave away there in order to provide for your upkeep and only see the sunshine on occasional forays to Savile Row and Jermyn Street where I will outfit myself in appropriately somber dull grey banker suits, black wing tip shoes, and dark felt hats. Eventually I will end my days in the same sad state that my grandfather did."

"What happened to your grandfather?" Cait asked, still laughing.

"An agonizing demise. Mildew of the brain," Anthony said solemnly. He shook his head, his hair fell in his face, and he looked like a little boy just in from a day in the sunshine.

"Well pack up the rest of your rubbish and go and sit in the fresh air-while you can." She gave him a peck on the cheek. "Maybe if we keep you regularly scrubbed with disinfectant we can save you from the same fate."

"Doubtful, doubtful," he mumbled as he considered for the first time that he hadn't made arrangements for lodging during Lilly's visit. His least favorite sister was camping out in the family's London town house, and he hadn't yet had the funds handy to join his father's club. Maybe he'd just ignore the cost and put himself up at Claridges.

He had to go somewhere, and it was important to enjoy life to the fullest in the two months of leisure left him.

Morning brought the coldest temperature of the late blooming autumn. Lilly paused at her bedroom window to watch the horses play an equine version of tag in the pasture. Canada geese circled over the pond, contemplating a brief stop on their migratory journey.

"Get a move on, Lilly," Kick called from the foot of the stairs. "After I've gotten up this early, it would be a shame for you to miss your plane."

She took one last look out the window, her glance sweeping the yard and the woods, the purple leaf plums and coppery beeches, a bright, bright splash of ginkgo. She gave them a silent command to hold onto their color until she returned.

She walked slowly in the direction of the barn where Kick loaded bags into her car.

"Are you staying on permanently?" He scowled at the pile of luggage. "You know you're going to have to pay extra for this many suitcases."

"You know perfectly well that I'd rather pay extra than try to jam everything into two little bags."

They had had this exchange more than once before. It was useless to argue over her assorted baggage, which ranged from expensive luggage to overflowing grocery sacks. Lilly didn't like to leave home without taking a little of it with her.

"I hate driving this thing," Kick continued to complain as he slid the driver's seat back to accommodate his long legs. "It's worse than that old truck of yours."

"If I had known what a pleasant companion you were going to be I'd have called a cab."

"Don't be ridiculous. It's seventy-five miles to the airport. It would cost more to take a cab there than it does to fly to London."

"Kick, what in the world is your problem?" She had lost a little of her enthusiasm for the trip, and his bad mood wasn't helping things.

They were hardly out of the driveway, and she was already homesick. She'd found a maple leaf, half-gold half-green, and tucked it in her purse. It was still fairly supple, but she knew that before she returned home it would be crumbs of brown in the recesses of the lining of the bag.

"Sorry, I guess I didn't sleep very well," he mumbled. "I kept thinking about Beck and his little friend."

"I still say you're jumping to conclusions there, Kick. I haven't met the girl except once or twice in passing, but I can't imagine Amanda and Max Dudley having anything but lovely children."

"Oh, she's lovely all right," Kick said. "Maybe lusty is a better description."

"Are we maybe just a tad jealous?" Lilly laughed.

"Me? Jealous of Beck's flirtation with an oversexed teenager? I can just visualize a fiasco in which the only one who doesn't get badly hurt is Beck. He'll have his fun and go on to something else while Bridget and Laura end up the losers."

"Well, there isn't much we can do about it." Lilly rummaged in her purse hoping she hadn't forgotten her passport or airline tickets.

"Maybe and maybe not," he answered. "Perhaps in the next two weeks I can get to know Miss Dudley well enough to convince her that the last thing she wants to do is fool around with my sister's husband."

"Be careful," Lilly warned. "I think you're playing with fire."

"So is Bridget." He gave his sister an unhappy look.

They drove the rest of the way in brooding silence, Lilly looking out on the fields of bare brown stalks stripped clean of their little puffballs of cotton. Like huge wire playpens, the mesh-enclosed flatbed trucks lined up on the roadside. They were as fluffy-full as cotton candy machines at a fair, overflowing with the gin-ready harvest.

She looked at the snowy loads of cotton and thought of Desia telling stories of the days when the cotton was picked by hand and the pickers paid by the pound weight of their burlap gunny sacks.

She tried picking cotton once as a child. It was slow and tedious and hard on the back. Her grandfather obligingly took Lilly and her little sack to the gin. Two hours work weighed only ounces.

When the first cool breezes of autumn blew, Desia got a faraway look in her eyes, remembering, singing softly the songs of her youth. Apparently in her selective memory bank Desia chose to save singing friends over an aching back.

Lilly studied history and found the parallels of the ages amazing. The harvest customs of her childhood resembled those buried in the mists of European history.

In Edmund's Scottish village there was a modern re-enactment of the ancient festival of harvest home. She thought of the strong young Scot standing proud as King of the Mowers, compared him with the enormous young man who carried in triumph the first bale of cotton through the streets of Brierley in a seasonal celebration.

She must ask Edmund if the parallels were mere coincidence, traditions borne across the Atlantic by the sons of serfs on immigrant ships, or just a common thread in the cloth of the human experience.

Lilly thought again of the harvest time in Scotland, the kern baby made from the last sheaf of corn, the ceremonial "crying the neck" when the ploughmen threw their sickles in the time-lost tradition of the harvest home, and the harvest of the sea thanksgiving service in the port towns on the cold North Sea.

Wind-reddened Scottish crofters, superstitious old herring fishermen, back-weary southern sharecroppers, singing the same songs of gratitude that the season of sowing had reached culmination.

"Wake up, Lilly, here's the airport." Kick gave her shoulder a gentle shake.

"Take care of Desia." Lilly gave her brother a quick kiss and signaled for a skycap.

"I will. Give my love to Cait and have fun. While you're in London stop by Fortnum and Mason and bring back the fixings for Christmas dinner."

"Better hurry, Ma'am," the porter interrupted. "I think they're already boarding your plane."

After dropping Lilly at the airport, Kick walked around the town square snapping pictures at random. He found that his best work happened when he abandoned planning and relied on the serendipity of chance.

The pictures of small town life were there for the taking, a small boy bouncing on the time-scarred "wonder horse" outside the hardware store, two work-weary women in smocks sharing a cigarette in the doorway of the Korner Kut and Kurl next door. "Beauty parlor," he said to himself with a smile. Salons were for New Yorkers.

He made a detour into the stained-glass-softened sunshine of the red brick Episcopal church, pausing wistfully at the third row pew where he spent so many Sunday mornings fidgeting next to his grandmother. He hadn't attended an organized religious service in years, and he wondered if his grandmother knew and rebuked him for it. In penance he dropped a twenty-dollar bill in the offering box by the door.

The A. & P. grocery store was still on the corner of Main and Laurel, the corner gas station opposite now a bright green instead of faded blue. Ace Butler waved to him from the used car lot where every five years or so Lilly bought the latest in the family's traditional series of second-hand trucks. There had been a rusty truck, usually a green one, in the driveway at home for as long as he could remember.

Memories. So many years ago that Lilly, too young for a driver's license, ran away from home in Desia's husband's truck. Frantic with worry, their grandfather had the sheriff mount a county wide manhunt for her. Worry replaced with anger once she was apprehended, he had them go through the motions of booking, and fingerprinting, and telling her that if she was lucky the sentence for vehicular theft wouldn't be more than about thirty years.

Kick smiled to himself. If there were real justice in the world, she'd still be doing time instead of nagging him about wet towels and underwear left on the bathroom floor.

He drove home slowly, scanning his surroundings, reassuring himself that Brierley was still the same unbroken capsule of little town America that it was in his childhood.

Sure there was a new subdivision between "uptown," as Desia referred to the environs of the square, and the Old Post Road. There was a new strip shopping center with a two-screen theater out on the road commonly known as "the four lane." A few fast food chains now competed with the cafe next to the Feed and Seed and Bo Tate's Truck Stop for the town's appetites.

There was progress, but as long as Deb's Dress Shop, and Fraser's Footfair, and Leon's Rexall were not only in place but still staffed by people who thirty years ago took his grandmother's checks with a smile instead of a request for two forms of identification things were pretty much the same.

Maybe Lilly was right that half the people in Brierley were stuck in the past, but if the past was still a place where you didn't worry about locking your door at night and you not only knew your neighbor but also knew how his grandmother was getting along in the old folks home, was the past really such a bad place to be? Maybe, like Lilly, he had also come back full circle to the destination he had sought for so long.

Back at home, he worked in his basement darkroom until after two o'clock. He was more than satisfied with the final set of prints. Let them show R-rated movies at the twin cinema. He could still smell the popcorn and taste the pickled eggs, plucked from a huge jar of brine, sold at the old "picture show" standing vacant across from the United Daughters of the Confederacy Hall.

He frowned down at the black and white print swimming in its final chemical bath. Only a few letters clung stubbornly to the rusted marquee, its outline of colored, flashing lights long broken and dark. In his teenage years in Brierley the one screen theater, where the feature changed approximately every two months, had been the only Friday night diversion. He'd had his first real kiss in that dark theater, wondered at the magic of the feeling it produced and if all girls tasted faintly of popcorn and pickles.

The last set of prints in the dryer, he came upstairs in search of lunch.

"Got anything to make a sandwich?" Kick asked Desia, who was sitting at the kitchen table stringing the last of the summer beans from her garden. He was hoping for a vegetable dinner, and it looked as if he might get his wish.

Kick watched as she removed ham, thick white bread, and a bowl of cherry gelatin salad from the refrigerator. The comfort foods of childhood which she kept on hand for him. He wished he had the nerve to ask Desia how old she was but knew she didn't consider him too old to feel the back of her hand.

Desia's age had been a matter of speculation around the house for years, and Lilly had lately been making a federal case out of the amount of work generated by his presence.

She winced as she began to slice the meat, and he felt guilty. To Kick, Desia was still the warm capable woman of his childhood, and he didn't want to admit to himself that she could be classified as an old woman. Desia was ageless, and he didn't like to consider the possibility that she might also be mortal.

He gently removed the carving knife from her hand.

They shared lunch with laughing reminiscences of childhood misadventures for dessert. It was a comfortable, familiar-as-an-old-pair-of-jeans scenario that could have been lifted from the days when Kick was an eight-year-old.

For all his nagging about a little house in town, he knew that Lilly couldn't consider selling the house in Desia's lifetime. It was her home too, and she'd be even harder to displace than the ghosts.

He rinsed the dishes and grabbed an apple from the basket, placed as it had always been, just to the left of the refrigerator. Desia settled down with a cup of her private recipe herbal tea, ready for her afternoon nap in the kitchen rocking chair.

"I'm going to run into town and see if everything's okay with Laura's children. I'm not sure I trust that kid they've got baby-sitting. Maybe I ought to bring them out here."

"Suit yourself." Desia shook her head. "I just don't want to make any trouble for Laura. I worry about my little girl. She just don't seem real happy anymore."

"Well maybe this trip will do her good." Kick sounded unconvinced of his own words.

"Laura doesn't need a vacation," Desia said. "What Laura needs is something to do. She's got too much time on her hands."

She didn't need to voice to Kick the thoughts that went through both their minds. Desia remembered all too well the sad haunted eyes of Marion Lambeth, a woman they both had loved, the most powerfully unhappy woman she had ever known.

CHAPTER NINE

*T*he Kimbles' driveway was lined with trucks as workmen began the preliminary foundation excavation work for the addition of Beck's private quarters.

Sam Kimble, a sweatshirt over her nightgown, sat on the patio with Bridget, stroking a kitten that she had smuggled out of the house.

"When I grow up, I'm going to live at Aunt Lilly's house and have twenty-five dogs and forty-seven cats," she announced to Bridget. She wiggled her toes in the dinosaur slippers. Her feet were cold.

Bridget laughed as she spooned a marshmallow into her hot chocolate. She reached across the table for the ringing phone, hoping it would be Laura so that she could report on how well things were going. It was probably Mrs. Harris making sure she wasn't going to be late for work.

"I am warning you to stop them. Stop them now." The voice on the telephone was muffled, quavery.

"Who is this?" Bridget demanded, trying not to sound as shaken as she felt. The disembodied voice had a strange quality, and it was difficult to understand the stream of words coming through the line.

"If you don't stop them, I will have to do it myself. The children will get hurt."

"Stop who?" Bridget questioned. She knew she should hang up, but the crank call caught her off guard and momentarily held her spellbound by its unreality.

"You were warned!" shrieked the caller.

Bridget shivered and looked at the dead receiver as if it held the answer to what she should do.

"You run on up as fast as you can and put that baby kitty back before Sunbeam gets upset," she said to Sam in the calmest voice she could muster.

The child reluctantly did as she was told, and Bridget followed her into the house to telephone Mrs. Harris and explain that in light of the bizarre call she planned to remain at home with the child. She needed the older woman's advice.

"I haven't time for chitchat, Bridget. Someone has to do your work you know," Mrs. Harris said curtly.

Bridget wondered to herself why Mrs. Harris seemed to dislike her as much as Kick Lambeth did. She'd never done anything to either of them.

She told herself that as soon as Beck returned she would resign and rid herself of the whole situation and the characters in its cast. She had seen enough of these people.

Bridget and Sam spent a largely uneventful day filled with cartoons, coloring books, and no more frightening calls. She read two storybooks to the yawning child and tucked her in for the nap Sam insisted she didn't need.

The morning's phone call now seemed no more than an aggravating wrong number, and Bridget felt a twinge of guilt about missing work as she settled down with a magazine on the flowered chaise lounge in Laura's sitting room.

She often looked longingly at Laura and her friends on the days when Beck sent her to Nelson's to pick up lunch. Unlike her mother, who always seemed to be in a rush to get everything done, the Laura-set seemed to shop aimlessly as if their rationale for being in the store were more chatting than buying food.

She daydreamed about living their lives, and now that she had the chance to be a lady of leisure she wasn't sure how one went about it.

By the time she flipped through all of Laura's art, antique, and fashion magazines, gave herself a manicure and pedicure, and tried unsuccessfully to follow the complicated plot of a soap opera, Bridget began to suspect that Laura's life might not be as exciting as she'd imagined.

After Sam's nap they walked outside to play on the swing set. The construction crew was packing up for the day, and Mark Borland waved from his truck.

"If we keep going at the rate we did today, we'll have this thing almost done by the time they get back," he called out. "Cross your fingers that the weather will hold because there's a nice bonus included if we get through ahead of schedule."

The older children got off the school bus and joined them in the driveway.

"Can we see your hole digging machine?" Sam asked.

"Sure you can if you promise me that you won't go around any of the equipment without a grown-up," Mark answered. "A construction site is a dangerous place to play."

The three children were happily perched high in the driver's seat of the huge machine, and Mark and Bridget had their heads together over the blueprints when the first shot was fired.

The contractor screamed in pain and the children in terror as Mark Borland fell to the ground, blood mingling with the mud.

Bridget said later that her gymnastics teacher deserved the credit for the speed with which she scrambled to the top of the big machine and pushed the children to the ground and behind one of the tires in what she hoped was a sheltered position.

Lying in the mud on top of the terrified children, Bridget's mind raced frantically as two more bullets shattered windows in the house. The gunman was either a poor shot or firing at random.

She also had no idea whether or not Mark was still breathing, but it looked like suicide to make a run for either the wounded man or the house.

If she had ever doubted the power of prayer, she developed a renewed belief when she heard a car turn into the driveway.

"Someone's shooting at us! Get in the house! Call the police!" she screamed as she heard the car door slam.

In what seemed hours, but was in reality only a few minutes, the Brierley police pulled into the driveway.

It took them less than a minute to subdue ninety-three year old Lucille Trainer, who sat calmly in a rocking chair at her bedroom window, her late husband's rifle pointed at the house next door.

Her explanation to the police officer was that she had to do something about her noisy neighbors and their trespassing children.

Kick knelt in the mud with his arms around his sobbing nieces as a disheveled but surprisingly calm Bridget comforted a violently shaking Brook.

Paramedics loaded Mark Borland into a waiting ambulance. To Bridget's enormous relief, it was quickly determined that his wound was serious but not life threatening.

The muddy little band finally collapsed into the safety of the house, and Kick sent the older children off to hot showers while Sam snuggled in his lap with her thumb planted firmly in her mouth for added security.

"You know your quick thinking saved those children's lives," the police officer said as he handed Bridget a towel for her muddy face. "Crazy old woman should have been locked up years ago. Up until now she's been satisfied with driving the neighborhood crazy with telephone calls."

Kick squeezed Sam tightly to stop his own trembling.

After all three children were bathed and bundled in robes, Kick prepared soup and sandwiches and got them settled in bed while Bridget took her own well deserved time under the hot water.

Toweling her long red curls and wearing a silk robe borrowed from Laura's well stocked closet, she came downstairs to find him in the living room. He had a stiff drink in hand and a warm fire going in the fireplace.

"I imagine you could use one of these too," he said rising from the sofa as she entered the room. "You were really brave this afternoon."

She sat shivering on one of the matching sofas. "I think I drained the hot water tank, and I still can't seem to get warm."

He poured a healthy measure of brandy from a crystal decanter and passed it to her without comment.

"Just a little of this," she said in a barely audible voice. "I need to be alert tonight in case one of them wakes up with a nightmare. What a horrible thing for children to experience."

"I'll get up with the children. I wouldn't think of leaving you here alone tonight," Kick said quickly. "I can sleep in Brook's room."

"That's awfully kind of you, but it isn't necessary." She smiled at him, wondering if her first impression of Kick Lambeth had been off the mark. He really could be quite nice when he wanted to be.

Kick was thinking the same and more about Bridget. It took a lot of nerve to handle a situation like the one she'd faced, and he was coming to the conclusion that there was more than empty space inside that red head. This was not one of Beck's usual bimbos.

After a few sips of the brandy-laced tea, Bridget suddenly began to cry as the events of the afternoon finally took their toll.

With an apology for her loss of composure, she wiped away the tears and said very softly, "I was so frightened. I thought she was going to kill them and that it was all my fault for not taking the phone call more seriously."

"Why didn't you call me this morning?"

Bridget laughed a little through the tears. "I was under the impression that you didn't like me very much, and I didn't want to bother you."

"Can I ask you a very personal question?" he asked.

"I guess so." She gave him a quizzical look.

"Are you involved with my brother-in-law?"

"I am not and don't intend to be!" she shot back angrily. "What kind of person do you think I am?" She jumped to her feet and looked down at him with the green eyes blazing.

He pulled her back down on the sofa beside him. The red hair was the exactly the color of the firelight as she shook her head.

"I'm sorry," he apologized. "My sister has always said that jumping to conclusions is one of my biggest faults."

She stared into the fire without answering or accepting his apology.

He thought how nice it would be to kiss her, even nicer if that led inevitably on to other things. He wondered how soundly asleep those kids were because right here in front of the fire would be even better than upstairs.

Before he could act on his fantasies, the front door was slammed, startling them both.

"I am shocked, simply shocked," Eleanor said as she glared at them. "I suppose with the example Paul Lambeth set as a father it's understandable that you are totally lacking in morals, Kick, but the very idea of your using my son's beautiful home as a staging ground for your tawdry assignations is beyond my comprehension. Who is this little half dressed tramp?" She pointed a bony finger at Bridget. "You! Out of my son's home immediately!"

Bridget shrank back as if the woman were going to strike her. Horrified, she tried to pull the robe tighter. She had been too preoccupied with the events of the afternoon to give much thought to modesty, and in an embarrassing flash she realized that the robe, too small and too thin, revealed more than she would have allowed under normal circumstances. She wondered if she should try to explain that her own ample quilted robe had been left behind in her hasty packing.

"The moral fiber of this country is collapsing due to the total lack of values on the part of young people," Eleanor ranted on before either of the pair on the sofa could answer. "I don't know whether the blame rests more with young harlots willing to sell themselves or unstable, middle-aged men anxious to buy their favors, but the two of you will be held among those accountable when this society falls just as surely as did that of Rome."

As Bridget burst into tears Kick felt a dampness in his own eyes. He was laughing so hard that he feared he might go from tears to a fit of choking.

"Where is my son?" Eleanor demanded.

"If you're through blaming me for the collapse of the Roman Empire, I'll try to explain," Kick sputtered, still unable to control his amusement.

"Beck and Laura are out of town. This is Miss Dudley, Beck's secretary, and she's baby-sitting for the children. I can assure you that the farthest thing from her mind is any hanky-panky with me."

It suddenly struck Bridget as bewildering that everyone assumed that she, with no more than a whisper of sexual experience, was sleeping with every man with whom she came in contact.

"Well, I suppose that it is too late in the day to make other arrangements for tonight, but you can be assured that first thing tomorrow morning I will see that my grandchildren are adequately chaperoned." Eleanor pursed her lips and glared. "Perhaps Doris Harris can be persuaded to move in here until I can summon Beck and Laura back home. I would take them myself, but Laura has taught them wretchedly little in the way of manners, and it would be a dreadful strain on my maid to have them underfoot."

"I'm sure I could take over some of her work at the office," Bridget said in what she hoped was a placating voice.

"Your only future function at my son's office is to pick up your severance pay, young woman. Oh, never mind that. I will arrange to have your check mailed to you. Good night."

"Drive carefully, Eleanor," Kick called out as the front door slammed behind her.

He stood up and yawned, disappointed that the potential mood had been broken before it got started and amused to think that if Eleanor had timed her arrival just a little later, she might really have gotten an eyeful. "I'll bunk in with Brook and see you in the morning, Bridget. Don't let Eleanor scare you."

Bridget shrugged. "Unemployment is what scares me." She felt at the same time too tired to worry about it and greatly relieved that someone else had made the inevitable decision for her.

Lilly put her initial bout of homesickness behind her and allowed herself a surge of excitement as the plane touched down in London.

Searching the throngs of multinational travelers she spotted Caitlin, to her surprise in the company of a very tall, very thin, very blonde young man wearing horn-rimmed glasses and a tweed jacket.

"Mummy, you look wonderful!" Caitlin exclaimed as she threw her arms around Lilly. "I can't believe you're here!"

Lilly returned the embrace and held her daughter at arm's length. She smiled over Cait's shoulder at the young man, who seemed to be regarding the reunion with amusement.

"I'd have known you anywhere," he said in a rich, deep voice. Lilly knew well the accent of the British upper class. The voice belied the jacket, which had obviously seen better days.

"There is a resemblance," she answered, receiving the strong handshake he offered. He wore a heavy signet ring of dull gold.

"This is Anthony Amberley, Mummy. He's a great friend of mine." Cait blushed as she spoke.

"Rather more than that I would hope." He looked reprovingly at Caitlin.

"Yes, well, more than a friend." Her blush deepened.

"Unless your mother wants to spend her vacation in the airport we'd better be off." Anthony took Cait's arm in a proprietary way.

Outside he loaded Lilly's luggage into a double parked maroon Bentley and pulled out smoothly into the traffic and toward the motorway for the thirty-mile trip into London.

"It's certainly nice to be picked up in style." Lilly smiled at Anthony. "I had expected to wrestle all this luggage onto the train myself."

"Well, luckily my mother was in town for the day and loaned me her car. It would have taken both my little sports car and Cait's Ford to have transported you otherwise. Extraordinary amount of luggage you've got for a brief stay."

"The name Amberley certainly rings a long silent bell in my mind," Lilly said, wondering why men always bothered so about the extensity of women's equipage. "Could I perhaps have known your parents?"

"Caitlin has told me that you were at Oxford at about the same time my Uncle Frederick was in school."

"Of course. I knew him slightly." Lilly struggled to bring up forgotten associations. "I tagged along with some friends to a house party in the country. Great huge castle of a house. Can't remember what it was called."

"Summerfield House, perhaps?" he asked, stealing a glance at Caitlin.

"That's it! A big old pile of stone in Dorset. I couldn't believe that anyone actually lived in something that size. Not a very warm and homey sort of place. Must be ghastly to heat," Lilly rambled on, oblivious to the looks that passed between the other two. "Do you come from that area?"

"Anthony grew up at Summerfield House," Caitlin chimed in. "It's his parents' home. His father is the Earl of Amberley."

Lilly mumbled something about removing her foot from her mouth, and she and Anthony continued a friendly banter for the remainder of the drive. When they pulled up in Caitlin's street, he announced that he had to be off to meet his mother.

"Call me tonight," Cait whispered to him as he put the final piece of luggage down and gave her a kiss. She had no choice but to temporarily evict him, but she suddenly realized how much she was going to miss his presence.

"I'll do better than call. I'd love to take you both for dinner. Shall I come round about seven?"

"With bells on!" Lilly answered for Cait.

Giving Cait another good-bye kiss, he was off at a long-legged run down the three flights of stairs, the void when he left obvious. Lilly liked this "more than friend" very, very much.

"When you said you had a surprise, I didn't expect it to be quite so tall, blonde, and handsome," Lilly said as she settled into a flowered chintz chair and kicked off her shoes. "He seems to be smitten, darling."

"He wants to marry me."

"Well, well, well. Now that is interesting. And do you want to marry him?"

"I don't know what I want to do." Caitlin gave her mother a troubled look. She placed a tray with stoneware teapot and cups and saucers on the coffee table and poured for her mother. "Tony's truly the most interesting, most exciting man I've ever known, but I'm not terribly sure I'm ready for marriage to him or anyone else. I'm enjoying my independence. I've been dying to talk to you about it, but I decided you needed to get to know him first."

"Well, I certainly have a favorable first impression," Lilly said slowly, weighing her words. "You mentioned that you were seeing someone, but I had no idea things had gone this far. How long have you known him?"

"Not so very long when you consider that he's asking me for forever." Cait smiled over her teacup. "His mother's writing a book about Summerfield House, and I was assigned to edit it. I went down there for a weekend in late July, and things just snowballed from there. We've been pretty much inseparable since."

"Oh dear, I'll bet I've dislodged your roommate." Lilly grinned maliciously at the red-faced Caitlin. "You should have booked a hotel for me."

"Am I that transparent?" Cait laughed. "He doesn't really live here. He just sort of made camp one night and never went away."

"And what does the future Lord Amberley do for a living?" Lilly questioned.

An unhappy expression crossed Caitlin's face. "That's part of my problem. He barely made it out of Eton and left Cambridge with only a general pass degree. For the past year or so he's played at betting on the horses and helping his mother with the book. He spends most of his time going through mounds of musty old documents that he hauls down from the attics. I told him that I couldn't consider a future with him until he proves to me that he has some kind of employment outlook."

Lilly knew that at Cait's age she herself would never have worried about a silly little detail like whether or not a man with the charm and good looks of Anthony Amberley planned to work.

She silently complimented Edmund for raising a daughter who was sensible as well as hardworking. Cait had taken a first class honors degree and had a good job with a publishing house.

"He's going to join his family's bank after the new year," Caitlin continued. "That makes me feel as if I've forced him into something he'll find dreadfully boring."

"Well, I don't think it's unreasonable to expect a person to have a job," Lilly answered. "On the other hand, if the Amberleys have money enough to support that sort of lifestyle, it's probably hard to get excited about being stuck in a bank."

"I don't think they have the financial resources one might suppose," Caitlin mused. "That dreadful old house just sucks up money, and all Anthony's father has ever done is play the role of lord of the manor. His mother is determined to preserve Summerfield House as a private home if it takes their last tuppence to do it."

"Might I assume from the expression on your face that you don't relish stepping into her shoes someday?" Lilly frowned.

"You know titles are meaningless to me. I wish old King Canute had never introduced earls to England."

"Does the Amberley title go back that far?" Lilly thought of her grandmother's self-important pride in being a member of the Daughters of the American Revolution.

"Not quite. The first recorded Amberley is a Roger de Amberle who came over with William the Conqueror. He was a feudal lord of the manor, granted the land on which they still live. The earldom dates from the Restoration and was granted in appreciation for their loyalty to the Crown during the Civil War. Lady Amberley is a peeress in her own right, and I think her family's titles are at least as old as her husband's."

"Oh, Mummy, I just can't imagine leaving London for the country," Cait continued. "I love my job, and my flat, and my two little pots of geraniums. Summerfield House has about twenty acres of gardens to worry about. I'd rather continue editing new books than constantly be worrying about mice and mold eating away at a library full of old ones. I just find it all too over-whelming to think about."

"Darling, I wish I had an easy answer for you, but I don't know what to say." Lilly bit her lip, feeling hopelessly inadequate as a mother. "What does your father say?"

"Ah, lass, you can do better than to marry an idle son of an idle father." She imitated perfectly Edmund's deep brogue.

"Marriage is just such a huge step to take," Cait continued with a sigh. "I can't help wishing I'd met him five years from now."

Lilly wondered what would have happened if she had been five years older when she met Edmund. With a little more experience under her belt she might never have been attracted to him in the first place and wouldn't now be having this conversation with the daughter she adored.

"Life doesn't happen according to a schedule, darling," she said. "Sometimes things happen when they do because they're meant to be."

Lilly studied Cait's worried face for a long moment as she groped for reassuring words. Her daughter had the strong Lambeth jaw and a light dusting of freckles. She was painted from a palette of summery colors, peaches and pinks, soft hair the color of sand, and intense blue eyes the color of the ocean where it is very deep, Edmund's eyes.

"Give me a day or two to think about all this," she said softly. "Let me get to know your Tony a little better."

"Oh, Mummy, I'm sorry to have sprung all this on you," Cait apolo-gized. "You must be exhausted from traveling, and I'm asking you to tell me whether or not to commit the rest of my life to someone you've only known for an hour and a half. Let's change the subject. You can fill me in on all the news from Brierley."

"That should take all of about five minutes," Lilly replied with a laugh. "You know nothing ever happens in Brierley. That little town can be as dull as dirt."

CHAPTER TEN

*B*eck and Laura arrived on the green and peaceful island of Barbados late in the evening. Laura pleaded exhaustion from the long day of traveling and went alone to bed.

After taking a solitary walk on the beach, Beck morosely nursed a drink in the hotel's poolside bar. He felt no happier here than he had at home, and he wondered why they had made the trip.

He had second thoughts about everything in his life as he listened to a Bajan band play steel drums and sing the trite songs he supposed tourists considered romantic island music.

There sure as hell wasn't any romance in his life, and this hotel, with its well-behaved clientele of wealthy British and American travelers, was not the type of place where he was likely to stumble onto a willing, lonely lady in the bar.

He pondered what to do to amuse himself for the next ten days and thought briefly of inventing some business crisis that would necessitate an early return home. Of course that would only put him right back in his mother's line of fire.

By telling his mother, his office, and Bridget that they would be at a different hotel from the one where they were actually staying, he figured to buy himself ten days away from Eleanor's constant carping. Maybe it was enough to be satisfied at that respite.

He congratulated himself on his cleverness. A vacation wasn't a vacation when someone constantly called from home with some minor irritation. Whatever they couldn't handle on their own could just wait until he got back.

He downed the last of his drink, signed the check, and went upstairs to rummage through Laura's makeup bag. There was something to be said for traveling with Laura and her personal pharmacy on a night when it would be impossible to sleep without some kind of chemical assistance.

He tossed aside aspirin, muscle relaxants, something labeled "take as needed for symptoms of P.M.S.," and a plastic bottle with enough pills to tranquilize the entire population of Barbados. At the bottom of the bag he finally located the sleeping pills.

The damp drizzle falling outside penetrated the walls and gave the flat the musty but not unpleasant smell that Lilly associated with London in the same way that the fragrance of hyacinths brought her grandmother immediately to mind.

It was good to be back in the city she loved, listening to the sounds of traffic from the street below and in the distance the pealing of evensong bells from a neighborhood church.

London was Lilly's city as Paris was Kick's. She thought back to their first trip to Europe with their grandparents the summer that she was fourteen and Kick twelve. Kick fell hopelessly in love with the lights of Paris and announced with a conviction later carried out that someday he would live there.

But it was London, with its grime, and its green parks, and its roots deep in the past, that claimed Lilly's heart. She found happiness just walking the streets and looking at the doorways, for no city in the world boasts such a variety of enticing entrances as does London.

Late one evening, walking down Park Lane on their way back to the Dorchester Hotel, Lilly and her grandfather almost collided with a man who appeared from the shadows between two buildings. He was a large, round man dressed in antiquated clothes and carrying the lighted torch of a lamplighter.

"Is he going to a costume party, Grandfather? Why has he got that torch? Maybe he's going to be in a parade." Lilly danced on the sidewalk with excitement.

When Lawrence suggested that they inquire they turned to find that the man had simply disappeared into thin air. One minute he was there, torch blazing, and the next he was gone.

"London is like that, Lilly love," her grandfather said without a trace of teasing in his voice. "The city is like a vast time warp, and perhaps, just as that gentleman fell through from the past and into the present, in this city you too can travel between today and yesterday."

Later, as an adult living in London, she explored to her heart's content the neighborhoods from Hampstead Heath to Chelsea, tried to picture herself riding in the magnificent state coaches in the Royal Mews, spent hours wandering among the vast treasures of the British Museum and the National Gallery. She bought cashmeres in the Burlington Arcade and fish and chips in Apple Tree Yard, went boating on the Thames and horseback riding in Hyde Park.

Kick could have the flash and dash that was Paris. For Lilly, the solid, eyes-on-the-past attitude of London was as comforting as a hot cup of tea on a cold rainy day.

"Join me in a glass of wine," Caitlin called from the tiny kitchen as Lilly emerged from the bedroom. "Tony is always late."

As the two sat before the gas fire flickering in the small fireplace, enjoying their wine and idle conversation, Anthony surprised them by being five minutes early. He opened the door with his own key and bounded in with a huge smile and a dozen yellow roses under each arm.

"Oh, my goodness, how beautiful!" Cait exclaimed. "I hope I have a vase large enough to hold a whole garden!"

"Just in case you don't I stopped off at Thomas Goode." He grinned as he pulled two beautifully wrapped packages out of a shopping bag.

Unwrapping an exquisite cut glass vase, Lilly thought with amusement that whatever was left of the Amberley estate might soon be depleted in the pursuit of her daughter.

Anthony held a large black umbrella over the three of them as they walked a half block to his customized sports car. Streetlamps glowed through the misty rain.

"My brother Kick would adore this car," Lilly said as they drove in the direction of Drury Lane. "He's been car mad since he was a little boy."

"From what Caitlin has told me your brother sounds like an interesting sort of fellow."

"He keeps things jumping to say the least," Lilly said. "I'm afraid his two main interests, outside of his work, are fast cars and faster women."

"No prospective aunts on the horizon then?" Cait asked.

"He'll never find anyone willing to put up with him." Lilly shrugged her shoulders.

They found the Indian restaurant and its Punjabi cuisine delightful. The Tandoori beef marinated in yogurt and spices was lightly seasoned and the service excellent.

Lilly enjoyed thoroughly Anthony's wit as he regaled them with amusing stories about the myriad problems inherent in the day-to-day operation of a home the size of Summerfield House.

She knew Caitlin found the anecdotes about mice shredding priceless papers or the removal of mildewed wallpaper revealing strange erotic frescoes on the drawing room walls unsettling. Such stories would only be amusing to people who knew they would never have to try to cope with similar situations.

Also knowing that her level headed Scots-bred daughter could cope better than most people convinced her that this was one young man too special to lose.

"We must pop out to Summerfield House for a visit while you're here," Anthony said as he signed the dinner bill and included a larger-than-usual tip for the young Indian who was his favorite waiter. "Perhaps we can arrange something for the weekend."

"That sounds wonderful," Lilly answered. "I don't know what Cait has planned, and I hope to make a quick visit to Scotland while I'm here."

"For now the night is young, and I know a wonderful little wine bar with music in Camden High Street," Tony said as they waited for the car to be brought around. "Are you too tired, Lilly?"

"Just getting my second wind," she answered with a wink in his direction.

Anthony Amberley couldn't believe his luck. He might soon be the only man in England thoroughly in love with his mother-in-law.

Beck's plan to avoid telephone calls resulted in no end of frustration for Kick. The airline confirmed that they had arrived from Miami, but where on the island they were was anybody's guess.

Not too very long after dawn he paced around Laura's pool trying to decide if he should consider the situation under control and assume that they'd call home eventually.

Every muscle in his body hurt from the contortions necessary to arrange his length in one of Brook's narrow bunk beds. Thoughts of Bridget crowded his dreams in the little sleep he got.

"It was good of you to stay the night." The soft voice startled him.

In a sunny yellow warm-up suit, with the long red hair tied back with a bright green ribbon, she looked to Kick not so much young as morning fresh. Fresh and clean and innocent. Far too long since he'd been involved with anyone who hadn't seen far too much of the world.

He found himself glad that Eleanor's interruption had prevented any spur-of-the-moment seduction the previous evening. Bridget intrigued him, and he didn't want to ask her to embark on one of his usual quick flings.

He asked himself repeatedly during the night whether or not he was ready to commit himself to something from which there might be no turning back.

Looking at her in the morning sunshine he wondered how he could have questioned. This girl was like a videotape of springtime that could be played over and over in any kind of weather.

"Everything looks better in the morning, doesn't it?" She smiled at him. "I'm so sorry for that poor old woman. What do you think will become of her?"

"I imagine they'll send her to some retirement home which is where she should have gone years ago," he answered. "I can't get in touch with Beck and Laura, and I wonder if we should get the children out of here for a couple of days, give them a chance to settle down."

"They have a school holiday on Monday," Bridget answered. "Some sort of teacher workday I think, and I suppose after last night I'm unemployed. Where did you have in mind?"

"I know exactly the place." Kick grinned, hoping she would agree to his idea. "Are you up for a weekend at the beach?"

"The beach? You must be kidding." She laughed, a soft musical sound that made his heart catch. "I've never been to the beach in October."

"That's the best month of the year there," he went on quickly. "It's not that far really."

"Where would we stay?" Bridget asked, warming to his enthusiasm.

"In my house of course." He put a hand on her arm and led her back into the house. "Just throw some jeans and jackets in Laura's station wagon."

"Are you always this spontaneous?" She made no move to escape his arm around her shoulders.

Only when I'm falling in love he thought happily to himself.

Though not nearly so tall as her brother, Lilly had also spent a fairly cramped night on her daughter's living room love seat. She was formulating a tactful suggestion that she spend her nights in a suite at the Dorchester instead of in the small flat when Caitlin emerged yawning from the bedroom.

"We really must make some plans, Mummy," she said sleepily as she filled the tea kettle. "There's a good exhibit at the Tate, and Christie's is having a sale of silver which might interest you, or perhaps we should make an appointment with that wonderful new designer who works only with cashmere."

"Slow down," Lilly laughed. "You don't have to entertain me, you know. I'm sure you have work to do. By the way, what's going on in the world of book publishing?"

"Actually, I'm caught up at the office except for a long-term project, editing the book on Summerfield House."

Cait frowned into the small refrigerator. It held nothing remotely suitable for breakfast. "I hope you don't mind nipping down to the bakery for a bit of breakfast."

"I'd love a walk," Lilly responded. "Let's pick up some fruit and cheese and have a picnic."

Caitlin put on corduroy slacks and an oversized cable knit sweater which smelled comfortably of Tony's after-shave, and the two set off down the wide, tree-lined street.

Lilly savored the simple pleasures of the Kensington neighborhood. In the early days of her marriage she had longed to live in Kensington, but Edmund was unwilling to pay the rents there. Many mornings she took "the tube" or a red double-decker bus and walked the streets of the former Victorian village within the city, pretending that it was her neighborhood.

Blessed with an overactive imagination, she told herself that she was the Duchess of Holland Park Avenue returning home to one of the creamy stuc-

co houses. She had only to walk through the gate of the black wrought iron
fence and up the short sidewalk to the porticoed entrance. Just the other side
of the heavy mahogany door would wait a liveried butler only too happy to
fetch a mink-lined raincoat as protection against the ever present chill.

Lilly knew Kensington better than Cait did. Holland Park, with its Inigo
Jones gates and peacocks, the High Street which was once the old Roman
road to the West, and the statue of Peter Pan in Kensington Gardens were all
old friends.

Kensington Church Street, the ancient heart of what was once a country
village, ends at Notting Hill Gate. On this street she had paused at the parish
church of St. Mary Abbots and looked longingly in the windows of antique
shops where Victorian jewelry, Meissen figurines, and Oriental carpets all
vied for her attention and her checkbook.

The shopping center Lilly loved best was north from Notting Hill Gate
along the Pembridge Road. Many a Saturday morning found Lilly slipping
out of the house early for Portobello Road, site of London's biggest outdoor
flea market, and returning hours later with bags full of junk.

She still kept an Edwardian blouse despite the fact that it was painfully
rotted and a teapot, assumed to be fake silver and bought for a song. It
turned out to be the genuine article and a rather fine piece at that. Souvenirs
of misty Portobello mornings.

"Penny for your thoughts. You seem to be a million miles away," Cait
said softly.

"Oh, I was just thinking about a duchess I used to know who lived in
this neighborhood. I think her house was pale pink instead of yellow then."
Lilly smiled at the memories, wondering who would have the audacity to
repaint "her house" without asking permission. She did approve of the
recently installed bright striped awnings over the windows.

They passed art dealers' shops, tiny nooks filled with antiques, and
flower sellers behind pushcarts before stopping at a canopied cafe with
wrought iron tables and colorful umbrellas.

"So tell me about this book," Lilly said between bites of a banana nut
muffin that looked much better than it tasted. She eyed Cait's Eccles cake
and decided that it would have been the better choice.

"Lady Amberley has always wanted to compile a definitive history of
her house. She's made notes for years, and I'm trying to help her assemble
all of the information. Tony has spent months in the attics with the bats and
spiders searching for old records."

"Sounds marvelously interesting to me," Lilly said as she abandoned the gooey muffin to a rubbish bin and began peeling an orange. "How old is the house?"

"The oldest parts date back to medieval times. There is mention of a dwelling on the land in the Domesday Book of 1086, but most of it is seventeenth century and Victorian. It's had its ups and downs depending on the proficiency or profligacy of the previous earls. I'm just not sure the future earl is industrious enough to keep it all going."

"What about this banking job?" Lilly questioned.

"It's a position with a private bank owned by his mother's family. They manage portfolios, give tax and general financial advice, specialize in one-on-one relationships. Considering Tony's dismal scholastic record, it's a wonder even family would take him on in any sort of responsible business position," Cait continued. "Can you imagine turning for trustee services to someone who is convinced that the future will take care of itself because he's destined to someday win the betting pools?"

"I gather Tony prefers the life of a country gentleman to that of a banker slaving away in the City." Lilly sympathized with Tony despite Cait's dismal estimation of his future employment potential. "I can understand that."

"Please don't do anything to discourage him at least trying it," Cait said, suddenly dismayed at the idea that her whimsical mother might back him up in backing out. "You don't make payments on the type of car he likes or dine at four-star restaurants on a minor book editor's salary."

"Let's accept the invitation to tea with his mother and let me take a look at the situation in its larger context."

Much larger context Lilly added to herself as a misty-memory vision of Summerfield House passed through her mind.

The suggestion of a trip to the beach brought no arguments from Brook, Marion, and Sam, and before Bridget had time to think about it, she and the children were in Laura's station wagon following Kick's Porsche out of town.

They turned up the Lambeths' long driveway on the Old Post Road and drove through a shower of falling oak and hickory leaves up to the big white house.

While Bridget was still awed by the elegance of the Kimble home, she felt at home here without even walking through the door. It was on a larger scale than the house where she'd grown up, but the traces of peeling paint, a few missing window screens, and the scattering of unswept leaves on the porch steps all told her that the interior would be decorated in her mother's favorite style of day-to-day disarray. This was a house where screen doors were slammed, where no one cared that dogs shed on rugs and cats sharpened claws on upholstery, a house in which it would be unthinkable to declare any room off-limits to children.

Desia met the assemblage at the back door and took it in stride when Kick announced that he was leaving for the beach with three children and a cute little stranger in tow.

She crossed her arthritic fingers that his childlike excitement had more to do with the auburn haired girl than it did with a trip with his nephew and nieces. The "sophisticated" ladies he had brought around in the past were not to her liking at all, but this little girl would make him a fine looking wife. She was even tiny enough to wear his mother's wedding dress, and Desia knew exactly where to find it in the cluttered attic.

By the time they crossed the state line Kick was hopelessly in love. From his first romance at age thirteen through his more recent bitter breakup with an icily beautiful New York model, he had had more than the average man's share of experience with women. Never had someone affected him so profoundly in such a short time. Despite a veneer of sophistication he was at heart romantic enough to believe in love at first sight.

There was little off-season traffic as they neared the Gulf. Driving past a few strip shopping centers, with the ubiquitous quick marts and beer joints, they came to an almost deserted stretch of beachfront road.

Around a slight bend in the road, the house, grey-shingled and wrapped with screened porches, came into view. It looked an incongruous antique neighbor to the high-rises standing shoulder-to-shoulder just a half-mile down the beach.

Bridget rolled down the window, sniffing the air and savoring the vague hints of saltwater and fish carried inland by the October breeze.

"Great, isn't it?" he asked, wanting to reach over and take her hand. "And as long as I'm alive this will stay just as natural and undeveloped as it is now."

"Driftwood patrol," he announced to the excited children as they piled out of the car. "Got to have enough wood to keep us warm this weekend, and anyone caught getting in the water without a lifeguard will have to sleep in the cellar tonight."

As the three children dashed off in the direction of the water, he smiled down at Bridget. "They'll come up with enough washed up pieces of some kind of junk to feel like they've made a contribution. I have an old guy down at the fishing camp who brings a supply of wood every year."

"So you come here all year round?" Bridget asked as they unpacked the station wagon.

"I actually prefer it off-season." He took the bags from her. "When my grandparents built this place, this was pretty much a deserted beach. There wasn't even a grocery store for miles. I feel like all the people who have condominiums in those high-rises are interlopers. This little strip of coastline is sort of Kick's private beach," he said with a grin.

"The children certainly seem to love it here," she said as they walked up the short flight of steps.

"Beck and Laura have a condominium in that second building down the beach." He struggled with the screen door lock, stiff from the salt air. "As the main investor in the development Beck received a very slick, modern penthouse that doesn't look at all like a beach place. I think the kids prefer this house."

The furniture, a motley collection of pieces that had all seen better days, begged for a book and a rainy afternoon. Dusty magazines dozed on tables, and traces of sand from summers past filled the grooves between the pine floorboards.

Upstairs the bedrooms were simply furnished with quilts on the beds and rag rugs underfoot. Kick insisted that Bridget take the large master bedroom where eyelet curtains framed windows with dramatic views of the crashing surf across the dunes.

Bridget opened a window and stood for a moment letting the sea air fan her hair as she watched gulls swoop over the waves.

"It's absolutely the most perfect place I have ever been," she said to him as they stood together and watched the children struggling to pull part of a palm tree's trunk across the sand.

The autumn sunshine was warm on their backs as they walked from the house to the sandy beach on a boardwalk across the dunes. The sea oats and seaside goldenrod danced in a gentle breeze, and Bridget kicked off her shoes and rolled up her jeans before taking off at a run down to the water.

"I want to sail, Uncle Kick, I want to hang off the boat," Sam begged as the three children danced around him, each eager to have his attention.

"We've got all weekend," he assured them. "Plenty of time to sail, and fish, and catch crabs, and have a bonfire on the beach." He caught Bridget's eye and winked at her. This was his world, and he wanted to be generous in sharing its pleasures with her.

Kick rigged the sails on his catamaran, and the gentle breeze that took the boat out seemed to conspire with him to win her heart. Bottle-nosed dolphins danced and jumped with their singularly natural grace in the water around the boat.

Later they bought shrimp and oily black squid from a little market down the road and fished in the bay from their private pier, catching nothing but the memories of an autumn afternoon, golden before the sky turned the pinks and blues of a coastal twilight.

The three children sat at the end of the dock, feet dangling. An occasional fish jumped in the water, tantalizing them with its proximity. The resident great blue heron kept his vigil on a piling in the water.

"I'd love to paint this scene," Bridget said softly. "It's magic how the colors of the sky reflect back in the water."

"I know. I've taken many a photograph from just this spot. The colors are best very early in the morning or late in the afternoon, about the time of day the French call l'heure bleu. I guess right here is the most peaceful place I've found in the world."

With the twilight sky heralding the coming of October's evening chill, Kick and Bridget and the children put on sweatshirts and built a fire on the beach. They sat on a faded quilt eating hot dogs and rolling on their tongues the incomparable taste of blackened, gooey marshmallows.

The setting sun seemed to know that it had spectators eager to share in its concert, and it didn't disappoint in its closing song.

Unlike the summer sun, seeing the days as lazy idylls and taking its time in descending below the horizon, the autumn sun slid down quickly. The sky became a rainbow of purple and turquoise streaks on a background of pink and the sun a giant, pumpkin-colored fireball. It exploded and sank from view in a moment, and if they had not been looking, they would have missed entirely its passing.

They lay on their backs as Kick pointed out the stars most visible at this time of year, the "wet region" stars. He had been no older than the children, now growing sleepy on the blanket, when his grandmother had sat with him on the porch of this same house to tell him fanciful stories about the Water Carrier, the Southern Fish, the Whale, and the River Eridanus.

A giant yellow harvest moon had taken center stage after the sun's performance. On its face a jack-o'-lantern's grinning countenance replaced the normal man in the moon.

Bridget and Kick took turns with the guitar. He played with more enthusiasm than talent, and not a member of the group other than Bridget could come close to carrying a tune. They happily improvised, a little band of balladeers singing late into the evening, inharmonious voices floating harmlessly out to sea.

They doused the fire, and Bridget, Brook, and Marion gathered up the remains of the picnic as Kick shouldered a yawning Sam.

As the children snuggled sleepily in the big beds upstairs, Kick and Bridget built a fire in the large fieldstone fireplace in the living room. They settled down with snifters of apple brandy and the sound of the sea providing the background music no mortal composer could ever match.

"Thank you for a wonderful day." She stretched out contentedly on the rug in front of the fire, bright lights reflected in her green eyes.

Kick studied her smooth golden skin, still bronzed from the summer past, and the coppery hair, and thought it would be difficult to do her justice with a camera. It would take a paintbrush to capture the soft, dreamy quality of her expression. While he had been described as an artist with a camera, he knew he could never capture on film the essence of the way she looked lying in front of the firelight.

She was so tiny, not much bigger than Brook, and he had a momentary sensation that she was really a small, magical Irish fairy who might disappear as quickly as she'd entered his life. A fey fleeting glimpse of the promise of happiness.

"You're so quiet." She spoke softly to his pensive gaze. "This is a special place for you, isn't it?"

"The most special in all the world," he answered. "I often came here with my grandmother when I was a child. I don't guess I ever saw her touch bare feet to sand, she wasn't a barefoot kind of person, but she got up early every morning to have her coffee on the porch and watch me play on the beach. My grandmother grew up in New England, and she had a sort of mystical bond with the sea."

"I was the only other person in the family who shared that bond," he continued in a dreamy voice that made Bridget wonder whether he was telling her a story or reminiscing to himself. "Lilly was always more at home in the woods than she was by the water."

"A woman from the fishing camp came and did the cooking, mostly fresh fish from her husband's boat. When I got old enough to go out with him, it was a great adventure."

"I guess part of the reason I love it so much is that my grandmother, who ran such a tight ship at home, never threw anything away here. There must be forty years of old *Life* magazines and *National Geographics* here. I could never change anything here. Grandmother was a very private person, but she left me a lot of herself and a lot of good memories in this house."

"She was terribly disappointed in my father, and I think she felt a special responsibility to see that his shortcomings didn't carry over into my generation."

Kick seemed to be unburdening some part of himself to her under the spell of the firelit evening. "Was your father her only child?" Bridget asked comfortably, without fear of intruding on his private thoughts. She had never felt more comfortable with a man in her life.

"I don't think anyone could have handled more than one Paul Lambeth," Kick said, bitterness evident in his deep voice. "My father was the center of their universe. Absolutely everything, from school, to sports, to very blonde good looks, came easily to him. He followed my grandmother's family tradition and went to Yale, where he was a football star and number one in his class. He was commissioned a Naval officer when the war started."

"How could anyone be disappointed in a son like that?" Bridget questioned.

"Oh, I think the problem was that they were so proud of him that they convinced him that he could do no wrong," Kick continued. "I think my grandmother always felt guilty about that."

"He was stationed in Newport briefly before being sent overseas, and he met my mother through some of my grandmother's relatives. She was a tiny little thing about your size with beautiful expressive eyes and very dark hair, quiet and sheltered and hoping for a career as a concert pianist which her family violently opposed. It was one of those wartime things where the wrong people came together. They did something irrational that they'd never have considered doing under normal circumstances. I think she saw in my father a romantic figure who promised to take her away from a constricted life. Before she knew what hit her, they were married, and he was sent to the Pacific for two years. They had as little in common as any two people could have."

"Lilly makes a bitter joke that she was conceived the day he got back home before they had a chance to realize what a mistake they'd made, and that's probably not far from the truth," Kick said. "After the war housing was difficult to find. They moved in with my grandparents on what was supposed to be a temporary basis and wound up spending the rest of their lives there. I think my mother had some sort of nervous breakdown after I was born, and she was never exactly right again. At first she refused to leave the house, and, after a time, even her room."

"Oh, Kick, how sad for all of you!"

"It was certainly a sad life for Mother," he said over his shoulder as he refilled their glasses. "Lilly and I were sort of taken over by our grandparents, and we had Desia to love us. After Laura was born my mother retreated farther and farther from reality. I remember her as a pathetic little figure sitting late at night in the dark at that huge grand piano playing moody nocturnes. The only time she ever came out of her room was after dark when no one was around. Listening to her music float up from downstairs was like attending a concert performed by a ghost."

He stretched out on the floor close to Bridget and stared into the fire. "I looked at her life as a complete waste of a gentle person with enormous talent. I hated my father for his part in it. I acted like a terribly rebellious teenager, hoping, I suppose, to snap them out of their self-destructive private worlds. In desperation my grandfather finally shipped me off to military school when I was sixteen. I went in the Navy right after college, spent a year in Vietnam, and then just roamed the world until six months ago when I decided it was time to come home again."

"I tend, as I guess all men do, to measure other men by my father, and Beck is a little too much like him to suit me. That's why I jumped to the conclusion that the two of you were involved. I apologize again for that."

"Can I give you my personal opinion of your brother-in-law? I feel sorry for Beck Kimble."

"Sorry?"

"Sure," she answered. "I feel sorry for anyone who has an ego like a leaking balloon, constantly in need of refilling with hot air. I've spent the last two months trying to avoid him and wondering what in the world I was going to do when and if he did make a move."

Kick laughed out loud. "You can't imagine the steamy relationship I'd invented between the two of you. Why in the world are you wasting your time and talent working there anyway?"

Bridget sighed and stared into the fire. "My parents absolutely refuse to loan me enough money to be on my own in New York. Jobs in commercial art are non-existent in a town the size of Brierley, and I just took the first thing that came along."

"Forgive me for saying this, but I agree with your parents," he said. "I love New York, loved most of the years I spent living there, but it's a tough city, and you find yourself getting hard, defensive, just to survive. I'd hate to see that happen to someone like you."

"Somehow I've just always wanted more than the life my mother leads. I don't want to wake up one day and find myself forty, saddled with a husband, and kids, and the knowledge that I missed my chance."

"Maybe some of us wake up at forty and realize that not having a family and a home means that we missed a lot," he interrupted. "The world is still out there to grab even if you are married, and sometimes when I've been in a beautiful place at a certain time of day or a special season of the year, I've thought how sad it was that I had no one beside me to share it. I was lucky to find my calling, but I can assure you when you wake up in the middle of the night after a bad dream, a successful career isn't a very reassuring partner. A career can't put its arms around you when you're cold."

"Haven't you ever considered getting married?"

"Of course, I suppose anyone who gets to be my age has considered getting married once or twice. It's just that I've never been involved with anyone about whom I felt strongly enough to be sure that I wouldn't make the same mistake my father did. Most of the women I've known have been very dependent, fragile people like my mother or so New York independent that they didn't need me enough. I want an equal partner."

"I wish you luck in finding her," she said softly, staring into the dying fire. "Do you think you'll know her when she does come along?"

"I have no doubt," he smiled down at her as he banked the fire and prepared to go upstairs.

For the first time in years he felt not only at home but at peace with himself. He was going to force himself to give Bridget all the time she needed before asking her to make any commitments.

For the second night in a row Bridget was disappointed when he said an almost formal goodnight before they climbed the stairs together.

CHAPTER ELEVEN

*T*he only wake-up alarm came from the cries of the gulls. Shivering, Bridget snuggled under the quilt. The sea sounds and smells were worth the chill the early morning breeze brought through the open window.

Coming out of the bedroom, she heard laughter from below and realized that instead of being the earliest riser she was obviously the last stirring.

In the kitchen Bridget found Kick juggling pancakes as Sam shrieked and giggled. Sausages sizzled in an ancient cast iron skillet, and the warm, morning smell of coffee filled the room.

"Guess I got a little carried away." He pretended shame as she eyed the mess. "I did a photo spread on buskers once and got a guy in the London tube to teach me juggling. It works better with tennis balls than it does with pancakes."

"What's a busker, Uncle Kick?" Sam asked as she licked honey from her fingers.

"Someone who juggles, or sings, or plays the flute, or draws chalk pictures on the street in Europe," Kick explained. "They have a hat or a can, and you toss them a few coins as a form of applause."

"Bridget could do that!" Sam exclaimed. "She can draw anything!"

"The answer to your dilemma," Kick teased. "You could support yourself in the big city by drawing Cubist masterpieces on the sidewalk outside the Museum of Modern Art like the street artists outside the Louvre sketch the Mona Lisa!"

"I can't imagine why such an obvious solution didn't occur to me before." She playfully elbowed him aside and put a kettle of water on an empty burner.

"What time is it?" she asked. "I couldn't find a clock."

"Clocks are not allowed in this house," he said, losing another pancake to the floor. "In this house we sleep when we feel tired, and eat when we feel hungry, and read when we feel lazy without regard to normal routine. Time is meant to be forgotten in a place where you're happy."

Kick dug in the pocket of his jeans and produced a coin which he held high above his head. "You kids know that pirates once sailed right here in these waters," he said solemnly. "I happen to have here a leftover gold doubloon which I will award to the person who can bring me back the biggest shell to be found on this beach this morning. Everybody outside."

"You'd better get a head start because as soon as I've cleaned up after the juggler I'm going out to look. I am descended from black Irish pirates with eagle eyes for spotting shells," Bridget chimed in.

Bridget found the largest shell. She put the "gold doubloon" in her pocket, a souvenir of a perfect weekend, a reminder of the good times when she found herself back in the Tuesday-morning world of looking for a job.

The children found lots of shells, and Kick knew the names of every one from the dark brown blood ark clam to the broken piece of Scotch bonnet which he proclaimed the morning's greatest treasure.

Bridget smiled at the picture perfect scene of the big man kneeling in the sand next to the giggling little girl with her long soft hair. She thought it a shame that Kick didn't have any children of his own.

They sailed again with the morning breeze, lost an elaborate sand castle to the incoming tide, and finished the contents of Desia's well stocked picnic hamper before sending Sam upstairs for a nap.

Brook and Marion set up a board game on the porch, and Bridget browsed through the bookshelves stocked with best sellers from past decades of summer reading. She fell asleep in a hammock on the porch and stole a surreptitious look at the forbidden watch in her pocket when she woke up. She was surprised to find that it was already four o'clock.

"Kite flying time," Kick announced as he looked up from his book to see her yawning awake. "The wind is picking up, and the radio says it's going to storm tonight. Perfect kite flying weather."

"I feel a little like I'm back at summer camp," Bridget laughed as he pulled her out of the hammock. "When do we get to do arts and crafts?"

"Wait until you see his kite!" Brook said. "It's called a trilby, and it's five kites tied together, and you have to hold it with both hands. He can make it do tricks!"

"A talent to fall back on if you don't make your name as a juggler," she teased.

The trilby was a splendid series of colored kites which dipped, and danced, and chased the sea birds in the gathering clouds. When Bridget attempted to control the double handles, she found that the wind was exerting more force on the strings than she could handle, and her inexperience at controlling the lines quickly resulted in a crash landing.

"Just like Aunt Lilly," Marion sighed. "She can't fly it either. Daddy won't even try. Daddy hates the sand. He likes to stay inside and talk business on the phone at the beach."

"Daddy says Uncle Kick lives in a grubby old place that's as nasty as that fishing camp," Sam chimed in.

"Sam!" Marion shot her little sister a warning look as Brook smirked. "That's a terrible thing to say."

Sam looked as if she were going to cry.

"It's okay, honey." Kick scooped her up. "Your uncle Kick is a grubby kind of guy."

Bridget felt a sudden stab of pain, aware that time was passing so quickly. She wished that the absence of clocks meant that time was truly standing still, that the weekend didn't have to end.

A streak of lightning suddenly split the clouds. They hurriedly gathered up the kite as fat drops of rain began to fall.

The rain continued, hammering on the tin roof of the dingy restaurant where they had dinner. In the dim light a nearly nude woman flashed a smile from an ancient beer sign. For years she had surveyed the scene of scratched pine bar, faded football pennants, and yellowing framed photographs of fishermen and boats long sunk or relegated to the graveyards of wrecks in the backyards of the marshy surrounding neighborhoods.

A huge man in a greasy apron and his equally rotund wife greeted Kick with the bear hugs of old friends. They served them fried mullet, the abundant Gulf fish which is the poor gourmet's caviar, onion rings, and the best hush puppies Bridget had ever eaten.

When Bridget protested that she was too stuffed to even consider one of the large slices of lime pie offered as dessert they insisted she take one home.

"Bad storm coming in, Kick," the gargantuan Riley commented as he passed out candy to the children. "Better have your boat tied up good tonight."

"Thanks, Riley, I've already done that," Kick answered. "They can blow up fast this time of year, can't they? I guess if that boat has made it through twenty-five years of storms, it'll last through one more."

"I reckon so," Riley mused. "I remember the summer your grandmother bought you that boat. We thought a sailboat was mighty highfalutin for 'round here. Now all those new folks down at the condominiums got themselves sailboats."

"New boats and new people, Riley." Kick shook his head. "I'll take my old boat and my old buddies any day."

"Take care," he cautioned again as he counted out Kick's change. "I don't like the sound of that wind at all."

As they ran from the restaurant to the car, Bridget realized with a flicker of fear that the wind had greatly intensified from the gusty singing breeze which earlier propelled their kite. It now screamed loudly with the furious violence of what promised to be a major gale-force storm by morning.

Drenched by sheets of rain windblown so hard that they appeared to be falling horizontally, they reached the safety of the station wagon. Bridget and Kick exchanged worried looks as he attempted to find a weather bulletin on the radio.

"Although no major evacuations are being planned by Civil Defense, beach residents are advised to take normal precautions during the night. The storm we reported on earlier has dramatically changed course, and the tail end of Hurricane Elisa could pass near this area," the mechanical voice droned into the black, rainy night. "Small craft advisories are in effect, and flash flooding is possible. Those in low-lying areas should seek higher ground immediately. Tides are expected to be several feet higher than normal."

"What should we do about the children?" Bridget whispered.

"My first choice would be to start driving for home," Kick whispered back. "But I don't like being on the road with them in this kind of weather any more than I like the idea of them being in that old house. These roads can flood in a matter of minutes. I think I'll call Sally and Tom Craig who live in the condominium on the floor below Laura and Beck's and see if they can spend the night with them. I'd feel a lot better if they were in a sturdier place than the house. Would you like to go with them?"

"I'll stay with you," she answered. "You may need help in weather like this."

He reached over and squeezed her hand in gratitude. It was going to be a long night, maybe even a dangerous one, and he didn't relish spending it alone.

Sally Craig, a friendly woman in her late fifties, welcomed the wet little refugee band with hugs and mugs of hot chocolate.

"Are you sure you and Bridget won't stay here too, Kick?" she asked as Bridget got the children settled and toweled dry. "I've lived here all my life, long enough to know that a storm like this is unpredictable enough to do just about anything."

"Thanks for the offer, Sally, but I feel responsible for Grandmother's house. Bridget and I had better get back and make sure everything's secure."

Tom winked at Kick and whispered, "I like the girl. Why don't you try to keep this one?"

Battling the wind to keep the car on the road, Kick and Bridget drove the half mile back down the beach in silence and made a mad, wet dash toward the yellow porch light that beaconed like a tiny lighthouse in the intensifying storm.

"Where do we start?" she asked anxiously as the wind slammed the door closed behind them.

"With some dry clothes." He smiled down at her, hoping to dispel the worried look she wore. "Then we'll tape the windows. There's a box of candles in the kitchen and fresh batteries for the radio. The power won't last much longer in this kind of wind."

As he predicted, an hour later the house lights went down with a violent surge of lightening and thunder. Bridget stretched out on the floor in front of the fire and listened to the wind. There was an exhilaration in the sounds of the storm, and she wondered if that were the cause of the sense of anticipation she felt.

Kick joined her, bringing a quilt and Sam's cassette player.

"What a perfect evening," he said softly. "A roaring fire, a raging storm, and, thanks to battery power, even a little Bach to accompany the wind."

"I love storms," she said. "When I was a child, I always wanted to go outside during storms and let the wind carry me away, but my father invariably spoiled my fun by bringing me back in and telling me that it was much better to be in a safe place."

"Want to come upstairs and take shelter with me?" he whispered.

"I think right here in front of the fire is perfect." She held out her arms, and Kick's resolve to take his time flew away on the violent breeze.

As he pulled her close, she wrapped her arms around the strong back well aware that she was setting her course for waters yet uncharted.

As experienced as she was innocent, he'd long ago found that he got the greatest pleasure from giving pleasure. It was well into the early morning before he finally carried her up the stairs and to bed, where she curled her small body tightly against his large one, two pieces of the jigsaw puzzle that is love, mismatched in size but perfectly interlocking.

He woke early to find the sun rising behind scudding clouds and slipped reluctantly from the warmth of Bridget snuggled beneath the quilt.

Standing on the porch with a mug of coffee in hand, he watched the screaming gulls glide down to pluck fish blown in from the sea with the storm tossed tide. They'd flown all night against the angry winds and now claimed their reward from the turbulent sea.

Dunes had shifted, shells littered the beach, and the waves crested and rolled in as if seeking shelter from the wider waters stretching to the horizon.

The sea laid on the shore a foam like a wreath of baby's breath and Queen Anne's lace that yellowed quickly to the color of old, dried flowers and crumbled away. Calm was returning after a restless night.

Bridget joined him and encircled his waist with her arms. He put his large hands over her tiny ones, silently thanking the wind and the cloud-filled skies for the most remarkable night of his life.

"Marry me, Bridget," he said softly.

"It's all happened very quickly, hasn't it?" she responded as she felt the pressure of his hands tighten. "Just a few days ago I didn't even know you, and now I can't imagine spending the rest of my life any way but with you."

"Does that mean yes?" He couldn't keep the excitement from his voice as he turned and held her at arm's length.

"Are you sure we're not rushing into this?" She laughed, imagining the reaction of her mother who wanted nothing more than to see her oldest daughter securely tied down. Amanda would be horrified that she was thinking of taking such a big step so impulsively.

"I've been waiting about forty years for you," he answered quickly. "That's hardly rushing into something."

"Won't people make the inevitable remarks about your being old enough to be my father?" she teased.

"Doesn't matter." He stared down at her so intensely that she had to suppress a giggle at his determined expression. "We'll just have a baby of our own. I'm more than ready to be a great daddy."

"What would our families say if we went away for the weekend and came back married?" she asked, shocked to find herself actually considering the idea.

"They'd say congratulations, of course."

"Gosh, we came down here on such short notice that I completely forgot to pack my wedding dress," Bridget teased him as she collapsed laughing on the porch swing.

"That doesn't matter," he grinned back at her. "If you insist on wearing the white to which you are no longer entitled you can always wear my bathrobe."

"My mother will die if I get married in blue jeans, but then my mother is probably going to die over this whole thing anyway so I guess what I wear doesn't really matter."

"Great, then it's all settled." He pulled her out of the swing and gave her a lingering kiss. "We'll go into town and get the license. There's a justice of the peace out near the fishing camp. We can get Riley and Maureen to be witnesses, and the kids can be our attendants."

"I can just see this written up in the newspaper," Bridget said. "Guests at the lovely reception feasted on all the fried mullet they could eat. Is the rest of my life going to be like this?"

"I promise not only to love, honor, and cherish, but most of all to make every day an adventure."

"What a fun day this was," Lilly said to Cait. "There's no city in the world like London for shopping, and now I can cross off half the people on my Christmas list. I'm just sorry we didn't have time to go to Trafalgar Square to feed the pigeons. I loved to do that when I lived here. I fed the pigeons some days, and other days I went to the Battersea Dogs' Home and visited the homeless animals."

"It was fun, and I expect the pigeons will still be there waiting for you next week. Let's spread out your treasures." Cait rummaged through the pile of shopping bags overflowing with Lilly's purchases.

In the course of the day they'd ridden the tube, the bus, and in a couple of cabs as they made stops in the expensive boutiques of Bond Street, the trendy shops of Knightsbridge, and the department stores of Oxford Street. Shopping with Lilly was a whirling dip and dive into the best that London had to offer.

Struggling under a load of packages, Cait could have cried with relief when they were told that the small pony saddle could be shipped to the United States by the same shop which had counted both the Queen Mother and Lilly's grandfather as customers.

Out of time, if not energy, Lilly had agreed to save for another day trips to her favorite bookstores, J. A. Allen, a literate horseman's paradise near Buckingham Palace, and Foyles in Charing Cross Road.

"The rosewood decanter box you chose for Uncle Kick is lovely."

"It's hard to shop for him," Lilly answered. "Anything he needs he buys for himself. I think most men are like that. I can never come up with anything for your father either."

Cait sat down across from her mother and spread a bit of Brie on a thin slice of apple before speaking. "What a strange relationship the two of you have! In some ways you've remained so close. As a child, I used to dream you'd remarry."

"We're friends, darling, very good friends I'm glad to say, but we could never have kept that friendship going if we'd remained together under the same roof. We were just dreadfully incompatible as husband and wife, and I'd have long ago frozen to death in that drafty old house in Scotland."

"Papa told me once that he hoped by marrying you to absorb some of your zest for life," Cait said.

"I must admit there were two sides to that coin." Lilly grinned. "I loved the fact that he was so steady, and stable, and mature. However, when I'd been married to him a couple of months, I realized that I also found those traits boring as hell. I remember the first trip we made to the Hebrides. I knew we were going to find all sorts of Celtic grave sites and meet up with a witch or two. Instead all he wanted to do was to sit in some bird stand and speak Gaelic with an old crone who knew more about migratory patterns than magic spells."

"I know what you mean," Cait chuckled. "I've made a few jaunts to the islands with him myself." Cait now expanded the conversation to include the unspoken territory that lay behind their words. "You know Tony can be lots of laughs. I don't think I'd ever be bored with him, and we do enjoy doing ever so many of the same things."

"That was an important element missing in my marriage," Lilly said. "I was happiest standing on the corner watching the crowds in Piccadilly Circus while Edmund's idea of an exciting day was sitting in the woods with his binoculars. We really had so little in common."

The jingle of the phone intruded, and Cait picked up quickly, anticipating a call from Tony.

"Uncle Kick, how smashing to hear from you!" she said with pleasant surprise. "It's so wonderful having Mummy here. I wish you could have come with her."

"Any problems at home?" Lilly asked anxiously. Her brother hated talking on the telephone and had, when he lived in New York, gone for months without communicating. It was totally out of character for Kick to call just to chat.

"You did what?" she shrieked so loudly that the startled Cait could only wonder what might be the latest escapade of her renegade uncle. From Lilly's wide-eyed expression she couldn't tell if it was something wonderful or tragic.

"I know I've suggested more than once that you ought to get married, but this comes as a bit of a shock," Lilly sputtered into the phone. "Of course I'm happy for you. I'm just astonished."

Cait thought briefly of picking up the bedroom extension so that she could hear both sides of the conversation, but before she could collect herself to leave the room Lilly hung up. She looked dazed.

"What in the world was all that about?" Cait asked.

"Several days ago I jokingly suggested that by the time I got home your unpredictable uncle would probably be married and have a baby on the way. He eloped this afternoon with Laura and Beck's baby-sitter and says they started working on the baby part last night."

"Is this someone he's been dating for a long while then?" Cait asked her bemused mother.

"He's known her less than a week, but then when he makes up his mind about something, he goes after it full steam ahead and damn the consequences."

When the phone rang again they both jumped.

"Mummy, Anthony's mother wants us to come out to Summerfield House tomorrow and stay the night," Cait said, hand cupped over the mouthpiece and eyebrows raised in question.

"Tell her we'd be delighted," Lilly responded quickly. She sensed that Caitlin was getting close to a decision regarding Anthony's proposal.

After assuring him that she preferred to drive out in her own car rather than having the Amberley chauffeur call for them, Cait reciprocated his assurances of love and placed the receiver back in its black cradle.

"You're not going to keep him waiting until Christmas, are you?" Lilly asked gently.

"No, I suppose not." Cait bit her lip and looked around her flat as if she might be seeing it for the first, or the last, time.

Lilly followed her gaze and thought how attractive the room was, with its heavily molded, cream-colored mantel wrapped with shelves filled with books and the Toby jugs Cait loved.

A window seated bay, hung with simple blue shades on rollers, looked out on a green park, and the bright geraniums in the window boxes bloomed stubbornly on against the coming winter. Anthony's roses filled the room with their scent and, now in full-blown bloom, dropped a few of their velvety petals on the glass-topped cocktail table.

In the tiny bedroom an etching of St. Paul's in a gilt frame hung over a heavily carved sixteenth century headboard. The green and white of the ticking-striped duvet was repeated in the toile de Jouy on the table skirt and windows.

This flat, very much the home of one individual, bore the stamp of her daughter's personality in every corner.

She's reluctant to give up her own little private space for a museum stamped through the past centuries by others, thought Lilly, and I don't blame her one little bit.

CHAPTER TWELVE

"*I* can't wait to develop the wedding pictures." Kick squeezed Bridget's hand as he turned the station wagon north toward home on the interstate highway.

"Mom would never have gotten married with a ring from the quick mart," Marion whispered to her brother.

Overhearing his niece, Kick responded. "We're going to do something about getting Bridget a proper ring just as soon as we get back to Brierley."

"There's nothing improper about this one, thank you very much," Bridget protested, holding her left hand before her face and admiring the cheap metal ring. "I'm proud of it. I don't intend to take it off for as long as I live."

We'll get you a ring and anything else your heart desires Kick thought happily to himself. "There's probably not a very good selection of stones in Brierley, but Eileen has a brother in the jewelry business who can arrange for anything you want," he said to Bridget.

She became aware suddenly of all the facets of his life, his friends and acquaintances, likes and dislikes, about which she knew nothing at all. "Who is Eileen?"

"Eileen was my landlady in New York. She and her husband are the best friends I've ever had outside of Riley and Maureen."

"Well, I hope I'll get to meet them someday."

"I've still got a lease on my old apartment. Would you like to spend the winter in New York?"

"Are you serious?" she asked, her green eyes wide. "Are you saying we could really live in New York?"

"We can live on a mountaintop in Nepal if it would make you happy," he said softly. "You may find my place above a delicatessen a little rough, but Eileen has been awfully good to me, and if we're going to be in New York I owe it to her to stay there at least a month."

"But first things first. Before we decide where to live we have to choose a honeymoon destination. Any ideas about where you'd like to go, Bridget?"

"Suggest something," she said dreamily.

"Well we could go to Europe, or Rio's nice in winter," he answered, mentally trying to conjure up the most romantic place he'd ever been.

"I've never even been to New York." She laughed and hugged herself. "Be careful or you'll spoil me. Rio indeed!"

"Why not?" he asked innocently. He had been around the world more than once, and he found it exciting to imagine showing her all the places that he thought he'd grown too jaded to appreciate.

"Could we really go anywhere?" Her eyes sparkled at the possibility.

"Absolutely. You'd love Venice, or I know a little chateau in the Loire Valley where you can take hot air balloon rides. I can just imagine how perfectly at home you'd look in the Irish hill country. Lilly loves Kenya, but Africa's not my cup of tea."

"Oh, Kick, we are going to have fun, aren't we?"

"Of course we are, and I fully intend to spoil you just as rottenly as I can." Unlimited hopes, and plans, and dreams were running pell-mell through his mind. He felt like a child given the keys to the toy store.

Lights in the house shone a welcoming glow as they turned in the long driveway on the Old Post Road. Desia was at the kitchen table soaking her feet and watching a game show on television when they burst in the back door.

Sam shouted the news. "Guess what, Desia! Uncle Kick and Bridget got married, and I got to be a real bridesmaid!"

The old woman froze midway between chair and full stance. Bridget shrank behind Kick unable to evaluate the obvious emotion playing on the lined face. She could well imagine a less than enthusiastic reaction later in store at her parents' home.

Desia was delighted and anxious to hear all the details which Sam and Marion eagerly provided. Bridget seemed the answer to years of her prayers for Kick.

Brook escaped out the back door. He ambled along kicking aimlessly at the pebbles in the driveway. He had an uneasy feeling about the events of the past few days. Something deep down told him that his father was going to be angry, very angry, about Uncle Kick marrying Bridget. For some reason he didn't fully understand, a nagging voice in his head told him that because she worked for Daddy she shouldn't have done this without Daddy saying it was okay. And what if Daddy somehow blamed him for being a part of it?

He watched, frowning, as Kick and Bridget got in the Porsche for the drive into town.

As the dark car shot out into the darker night, Bridget begged Kick to slow down.

Kick laughed. "I may have made a commitment to give up fast women, but you're going to have to accept the fact that fast cars are a part of my life."

"I have no objection to fast cars." She laughed nervously. "I'm just not looking forward to the reception we're going to get."

"Stop worrying. They'll be happy for us."

They weren't. "How in the devil could you do something like this to your mother?" Max Dudley roared. The redness of her father's face frightened Bridget. Her mother sat sobbing at the kitchen table, too shaken to speak.

"Relax, Mr. Dudley." Kick made a conscious effort to modulate his own voice, hoping to calm the other man down. He felt ludicrous addressing someone so close in age as "Mr." Dudley and realized that the proximity of their ages was probably at least part of the source of Dudley's fury. "I realize you don't know me, but I can assure you that I love your daughter very much."

"Oh, I know you by reputation, Lambeth," Max growled. He refrained from mentioning that Kick's father had broken up his best friend's parents' marriage. "I suppose that my daughter just happens to be the first young, inexperienced girl who insisted that you actually marry her first. I'm sure you consider this quite a lark. Let me assure you that, while your family doesn't take marriage vows very seriously, this family does."

The words stung, and Kick groped for an answer. He took a deep breath before answering. "I have been around. I don't deny that. Maybe that's all the more reason that I knew right away when I found the right person. I like to think that I'm not so cynical that I can't still believe very much in love at first sight."

They finally left Bridget's sullen father, weeping mother, and gaggle of gaping brothers and sisters with nothing resolved and the parting spate of words unfriendly.

The drive home was silent except for Bridget's tearful self-recrimina-
tions. He cursed his inability to think of anything to say that would comfort
her.

While Kick was at a loss for the right words, he was well experienced in
the giving of physical comfort. As she relaxed into sleep with her head on
his shoulder, she closed her eyes and breathed deeply. She liked the way he
smelled, faintly of sweat and toothpaste. As Kick snuggled next to her, big
and warm and full of life, Bridget smiled to herself. Her future outside of
Brierley was finally realized, just the other side of the town line.

The autumn sun began to dissipate a misty rain as Cait and Lilly set out on
their early morning drive to Dorset.

"Shall I put down the hood?" Cait asked.

"I've been away so long that I forget little British things like the hood
being the top, and what I'd call the hood being the bonnet, and the trunk
being the boot," Lilly laughed. "By all means let's enjoy the fresh air."

The roof of the bright blue car opened to a matching sky, Lilly leaned
back in her seat to enjoy the brilliant foliage as they sped west away from
London.

"I'd also forgotten how October here can be warmer than July," Lilly
said. "I imagine the gardens at Summerfield House will still be beautiful."

"Actually, they're spectacular all the year round, and Lady Amberley
takes great pride in them." Cait dug around in her bag for a pair of oversized sunglasses. "Around the turn of the century they employed a gardening staff of over twenty-five. There are some charming old photos from
Anthony's great-grandparents' day showing the household and gardening
staffs all got-up for a grand party for the visiting Prince of Wales."

"How in the world do they manage to keep it up today?" Lilly asked.

"They've sold off much of the parkland, but the gardens still require a
tremendous amount of planning and upkeep."

"I'm looking forward to meeting them. If Anthony's parents have his
same delightful outlook on life we'll get along splendidly."

"You'll love his father. His mother is a bit of the bluestocking, hard to
get to know."

They stopped for lunch, enjoying spiced pork with Stilton cheese and apple turnovers in the cozy dining room of a small restaurant in Salisbury.

The elegant spire of Salisbury Cathedral, the tallest in England, outlined behind them against the clear blue sky, they took the main road out of Salisbury and drove through the village of Netherhampton toward Wilton, once the capital of King Egbert's Wessex and Kent.

Reaching the rolling pastures of Blackmoor Vale and the chalk uplands, Cait and Lilly were at last deep in Thomas Hardy country. It was a part of England which Lilly had visited only a few times, having spent most of her married life in Scotland. As much as she loved the busy bustle of London, she had to admit that this picture postcard area was England at its best.

She tried to imagine living in a stone cottage in a town like Evershot, a village only one street long by one street wide, and decided that she could be very content in such a setting.

Wonderful names the neighboring villages had, Piddletrenthide and Puddletown, Grimstone and Godmanstone.

They came at last to the closest village to Summerfield House, a hilltop town with old stone cottages painted purple with lilac and wisteria, elegant town houses, medieval walls, and the ruins of a Benedictine Abbey. In the quiet churchyard cattle and sheep grazed among the tombstones beneath thousand year old yew trees.

Cait turned the car into an unnumbered road and shortly turned again through massive stone gates into an avenue of chestnut trees.

They proceeded for almost half a mile before Summerfield House loomed before them, its two foot thick walls of locally quarried grey Purbeck stone broken by dozens of windows, some of which had once reflected the sun of twelfth century harvest seasons.

"It's bigger than I remembered," Lilly gasped as the little blue car came to a stop in the circular driveway.

"Thirty-three bedrooms excluding the servants' quarters," Cait whispered to her mother as a butler in full livery opened the enormous oak door and ushered them into the great hall with its intricately carved seventeenth century staircase.

"Welcome to Summerfield House," he intoned with the slightest trace of a smile on his lined face. "Lady Amberley is waiting for you in the music room."

Anthony bounded down the stairs, his booted feet on the Wilton runner breaking the museum-like quiet of the house.

"You're here!" he shouted as the staid old butler winced. It was not a setting where one shouted. "Come and meet Mother and have your tea, and then I'll take you on a tour."

Caroline Amberley, looking in every aspect Countess of Amberley and the several other positions that her titles proclaimed her, rose gracefully to meet her visitors.

Her face unlined and framed by upswept blonde hair going grey, she extended a cool, pale hand to Lilly.

Stifling the impulse to curtsy, Lilly instead sat down gingerly on a delicate Louis XVI chair beside a small table set for tea.

A maid in traditional black uniform appeared as if by magic to pour tea and offer out-of-season strawberries, clotted cream, and delicate iced cakes.

After dismissing the servant, Lady Amberley expressed the hope that Lilly would be comfortable during her stay and explained that her clothes would be put away by a lady's maid.

Lilly resisted the urge to giggle at this very nineteenth century scenario. She had been sure that this way of life long ago died either with Victoria or during the servant shortages of that followed the First World War. It was obvious that Lady Amberley's desire to preserve her home as a private residence also included preserving the lifesyle that had once defined it.

And what a home it was. The cavernous music room, with its twin gilt grand pianos and elaborate plasterwork ceiling, was, Lilly rightly suspected, not the largest room in this massive house.

Tea and small talk having taken up the better part of an hour, Anthony suggested a tour of the house, an offer that was readily accepted.

Lilly itched for a behind-the-scenes look at the places where the family actually lived on a day-to-day basis. She wanted reassurance that such a house contained things mundane.

"We know from old records that there has been a large home on these foundations since the twelfth century," Tony explained as he took Lilly's arm and led her back into the high-ceilinged hall.

"The earliest deed to the property in our possession is written in Norman French, and there is mention of a house on the site in the Domesday Book, William the Conqueror's census of 1086. I'm hoping to beat the mice to even earlier documents which will give us some of the missing pieces of the puzzle. Our muniments room is in disarray because most of the documents were stored in the attic and stables during the war."

"There have been at least three major periods of construction leading to the present house," he continued. "The first house that we can describe with any certainty was a Tudor one of about 1550. It was enlarged in the 1740s and again around 1810. Many of the furnishings are from the Victorian period, a time in which one of my ancestors married a lady with the face of a horse and the dowry of a princess."

Anthony proved himself an enthusiastic and knowledgeable tour guide as he led them through the eighty-foot long yellow drawing room, its walls hung with Spitalsfield silk. Twenty-two feet above them on the ornate ceiling painted cherubs frolicked around massive Irish crystal chandeliers.

The oak-paneled dining room contained a table large enough to comfortably seat twenty-four. A George III mahogany sideboard was dwarfed beneath a huge Gobelin tapestry.

"The entrance hall was originally a great assembly hall," he explained. "This staircase was carved in London about 1683 and brought here in pieces to replace the original stone one underneath. In the 1740 renovation the kitchen was removed to another wing and accessed by a subterranean passage. I imagine the food was dreadfully cold by the time it reached the dining room. It still is most days!"

Lilly studied the staircase, cantilevered and turning in straight flights around an open, square well. The banisters were inches thick wood carved with heraldic devices. It was a busy piece of work, but then the whole hall was a compilation of architectural exaggeration. Doorways were crested with pediments resting on pilasters, the huge stone fireplace was heavily carved with armorial representations, and high above the ceiling was an overflowing centerpiece of carved garlands of fruit and flowers.

The whole arrangement would have been attractive enough if about four hundred years before someone had had the innate good taste to say enough is enough.

On the main floor they entered a magnificent state bedchamber with an elaborate fireplace with an Elizabethan chimney piece and the largest bed Lilly had ever seen.

"This was decorated for an upcoming visit by Charles I, but unfortunately he and his head were separated before he could make the journey. As far as I know the sheets haven't been changed since," Anthony said with mock solemnity.

They viewed the sixteenth century long gallery with its linenfold paneling, Flemish Renaissance chimney piece, stone-mullioned casement windows, and ancestral portraits of family members who centuries ago took their winter exercise there.

The minstrel gallery was hung with antique musical instruments which, Anthony explained, were found in the attics.

"In houses such as Summerfield that have remained in the same family for hundreds of years very few things are actually thrown away. Things tend to get banished to attics and storerooms rather than tossed in rubbish bins," he commented.

"Cataloguing everything in the house is a project that Mother has had occupying my time, and I must say it's more dusty and time consuming than I would have dreamt when I agreed to do it."

Lilly mentally contemplated the pros and cons of cleaning out her own attic when she got home. For all her family's pack-rat clutter tackling it would be child's play compared to sorting what must lie under the rafters of a place this size.

"We must show her the tower room," Cait interrupted. "Although I have to warn you first, Mummy, that we may encounter the ghost."

"Well, I would certainly hope that any self-respecting house of this age would have at least one ghost." Lilly laughed. "It would be a shame not to meet her."

"I notice you said meet 'her,'" Anthony said without a trace of teasing in his voice. "Has Cait told you about our 'Blue Lady' then? We haven't decided yet who she is, but I hope, as I pore deeper into old records, to hazard a guess to her identity in case I need to converse with her. The monk is easier to explain."

"The monk? I haven't heard about him," Cait interrupted.

"I naturally assumed you'd seen him. He's frequently prowling around, but fortunately he's a good-natured, Friar Tuck sort of chap. A good deal of the stone in the house came from the ruins of a local monastery. When Henry VIII dissolved the monasteries in the 1530s about a third of the total acreage of England suddenly came available at fire sale prices. One of the conditions of sale was that the monastic buildings involved be demolished. I suppose some ancestor of mine couldn't resist the combination of cheap land and ready-dressed, near-to-site stone. We've always just assumed that the monk came as part of the masonry."

"You don't seriously believe in this I hope." Lilly looked at him quizzically.

"Oh, but of course," he answered seriously. "Quite without permission my brother and I stole the key to the tower and snuck up there one night, and I can assure you the woman's very much there. We took candles instead of torches, wanted to create the proper atmosphere, you see. The candles suddenly burnt blue, and as you must know that's a definite sign that there's a ghost about."

Lilly felt her skin prickle as he used what was obviously one of the oldest keys on a large ring to unlock the door to the worn stone steps spiraling up the tower.

Conversation with his mother had been difficult enough, but she had absolutely no idea what she'd say if confronted by a blue-faced apparition.

"No doubt some poor maiden locked up here by her father so that she couldn't marry her true love," Cait mocked as she winked at her mother and followed up the narrow stone steps.

The tower room was cold, dark, and damp. The only visible inhabitants were scuttling mice and spinning spiders, and to Lilly it seemed an ideally gloomy venue for a ghost seeking a permanent abode. She was only too happy to retreat back down the claustrophobic stone stairway.

"What's down that hall?" Lilly asked.

"Oh, just the kitchen wing." Anthony shrugged his shoulders as if dismissing the whole area as unimportant.

"I love kitchens," Lilly announced, pushing open a closed door without invitation. "I'm much more at home in kitchens than I am in drawing rooms. Let's take a tour of the kitchen."

Anthony hesitated. "To be perfectly honest I don't know much about the whole area. It's always been off-limits to us, but I suppose, if Mrs. Keddington is about, she can explain it to me as well."

Mrs. Keddington, a capable looking woman with short grey hair, proved to be the housekeeper. She was at first taken aback, then obviously pleased, when asked to give a brief tour of her domain. Mrs. Keddington was much more accustomed to making her way to the Amberleys' side of the door than she was to finding an Amberley in her quarters.

In general, the area consisted of a large two-story kitchen along with enough smaller ancillary rooms to comprise in square feet a fair-sized residence. To Anthony, who had grown up in the house, it was a territory as foreign as the jungles of Africa.

A room for brushing clothes adjoined a boot cleaning room and a drying room for the wet clothes that invariably find their way into English houses. The butler's domain was as extensive as his duties. Adjoining his comfortably furnished bedroom was the fire and burglar-proofed plate room. Lilly whistled at the amount of silver stored in cupboards and baize-lined drawers. A separate room held linens, china, and vases of every size and description.

The path back to the main quarters was a winding one.

"It's almost as if they wanted to keep the staff hidden," Cait said thoughtfully.

"Oh, decidedly so," Anthony agreed. "The children were hidden as well. The day nursery, night nursery, and school room are at the complete opposite end of the house from the master suite. My father has often said that in his father's day the children were kept so removed that visitors might spend a month in residence without being aware of their existence."

He startled them by laughing. "I was just thinking of my own years in the nursery and how the staff didn't fit the stereotypes. Nanny was young and pretty and sang delightful little songs while we had our pease porridge and chocolate. The French governess, on the other hand, was an old toad of a woman with no sense of humor. She came over the Channel during the war, and I wouldn't be surprised to learn that she was a Nazi collaborator. She was certainly mean enough to have been."

Lilly had an uncomfortable mental image of a world in which the vast majority of the citizens, including the small heirs, were considered second class. Surely when Cait took over this house she could find some superfluous little room in which to install a practical, convenient kitchen with a microwave oven and a dishwasher.

"You know this stone makes a lot more sense than wood," Lilly said, thinking that this house at least had a lot of surfaces that would never require the repainting she faced at home. "Hard as the devil and meant to last forever."

"Dorset is stone country," Anthony said. "Most of London is built of Portland stone from this area. Must have been a hell of a job to transport it by water and packhorse before the railways were built."

"As I'm sure you have no desire to visit thirty or so more or less similar bedchambers I will show you to your own and leave you to rest before cocktails at seven-thirty," Anthony said as they climbed the broad main staircase.

The large pleasant bedroom which Lilly was assigned was furnished with a four-poster bed hung with heavy green velvet draperies, comfortable chairs covered in striped silk, and a small Queen Anne writing table on which lay cream-colored stationery embossed with the Amberley crest. The windows looked out on wildflower dotted parkland.

"What do you think?" Cait asked anxiously after Anthony had closed the door behind him. "Overwhelming, isn't it?"

Lilly took a deep breath before choosing her words. "I would hate to think of having to vacuum the place or going to bed only to remember that you didn't turn off the lights a half mile down the hall."

"When Lady Amberley started on her book, there were rooms that hadn't been entered since before 1914," Cait said. "Who knows what's here."

"And in the process of finding out they hope to locate hidden treasure or turn up some long forgotten old master, the sale of which will provide enough funds to keep the National Trust, the tour groups, and the need for public toilets at bay for a few more years," Lilly mused.

"You're very perceptive," Cait replied. "In a house like this who knows what's hidden where, or wasn't even valuable when it was first purchased, or was, as Anthony said, relegated to a back attic because it went out of style."

"There is a room in the attic stacked floor-to-ceiling with paintings. No one has ever done a complete inventory of the art in this house. There's everything from Lily portraits, to Italian chiaroscuro, to Dutch genre pieces, to very bad pastoral water color scenes executed by maiden aunts with no talent. Every member of the family who ever took the Grand Tour of the Continent apparently brought back large souvenir pictures like you would buy postcards, and I'm sure there wasn't one of them who didn't have a portrait done. I look at some of them and wonder at the wisdom of marrying someone who carries the genes for such truly awful hook noses."

"Tony's mother took a dreadfully dreary nineteenth century landscape down to have it cleaned. When the frame was removed they found a Canaletto hanging behind it. While no one has come right out and said so, I think its subsequent discreet sale is the only reason this ceiling isn't still leaking. There are even family legends that treasures were sealed in the walls during Cromwell's time when the family remained loyal to the crown."

"Ghosts and hidden treasure behind secret panels." Lilly gave a low whistle. "I guess my question is how anyone could not die to live in a place like this?"

"You seem to forget that along with your impossible romanticism I also inherited a hardheaded Scotswoman's practicality." Cait smiled. "Up until now my only interest in chairs has been an eye to the relative comfort of sitting in one versus another. In one room alone here there is a hideous thing which is 'Etruscan' and shows up in the 1806 inventory, a carved gilt Adam chair made about 1777, a 1610 Jacobean armchair, and a buttoned, horsehair-stuffed, carved walnut Victorian piece that arrived in 1885. Every one of them is ugly, valuable, and uncomfortable. How am I ever supposed to learn about all of this?" She flashed Lilly a frantic look.

"You're not. You decide what you truly love and hate, what's important because of some historical significance to the house itself, call in some expert from Sotheby's who's paid to know for an appraisal, and spend the next winter warm, dry, and minus one Etruscan chair." She was relieved to see Cait's smile return. "You mentioned an inventory. I imagine some of the cataloguing has been done in the past, hasn't it?"

"Of course. There is a muniments room downstairs up a little staircase behind the estate office. It's chockablock with big black deed boxes and little string-tied bundles. No one has yet had the courage to tackle that room. During the Second World War this house, like many large country houses, was requisitioned by the government, and the contents of the muniments room were dispersed to the cellars and even the stables. The house was vacant for some years after the war."

"Tony says that everything in that room is a victim of 'Triple M Syndrome,' suffering from mice, mold, and moisture. If it was ever in any sort of order, which I seriously doubt, all semblance of system has been lost."

"It's all stuffed in there in the most appallingly haphazard fashion. Detailed architectural drawings are underneath Victorian valentines, and the early Norman French deed was tucked in with horse breeding records from the eighteenth century. He probably wants to marry me only because I can translate from the Latin. It's frightful how many important papers are in fragments, torn, or stained, or even partially burnt. Clues to the puzzle of this house written on faded foolscap."

"House aside, I wanted you to be the first to know that I have made my decision, and I shall tell Anthony tonight that we can set a date and start making preparations for a wedding. It means a great deal to me that you seem to like him so much."

"Oh, Cait, darling, I am pleased!" Lilly hugged her daughter, feeling the prickle of tears start. "As long as you love him, and he loves you as much as he seems to, it's silly to let a little thing like a house get in the way."

"In this case a little thing like a big house." Cait rolled her eyes. "Now let me have a bath and change so that I'll be presentable enough that he'll not change his mind. Cocktails will be in the library I'm sure. I'll see you there at seven-thirty."

With Cait and Kick married maybe I'd better start thinking along the same lines myself Lilly thought as she stretched out on the bed. She wondered if Edmund, in his old age, could be persuaded to learn to dance.

CHAPTER THIRTEEN

On a flagstone terrace, with the sun setting beyond the distant yew hedges bordering the formal gardens of Summerfield House, Caitlin McFarland agreed to assume the title of Viscountess Lockingford.

"Cait, I'll make you happy. I promise I will," Anthony said, taking her face in his hands. "You'll grow to love this house as much as I do."

"I'm marrying you, Anthony, not the house."

"I understand that, darling, it's just that the house sort of comes along with the package." He smiled. "It will be ages before we have to worry about that anyway. For now we'll find something closer to London, and you can continue at Birnley's while I try to handle the daily stimulation of counting someone else's money at the bank."

"Are you sure you're not taking the position with the bank just because of me?" she asked with a worried expression.

"Of course I'm taking it because of you," he said. "I love you enough to do whatever it takes to have you."

"Well, I guess all that's left is to set the date," she answered, not entirely comfortable with his response. "Do you think your mother will insist on a large spectacle?"

"Of course," he answered. "Shall we go in and share our news with the others? I know Father will be frightfully pleased that you've agreed to be the future Countess Amberley."

Cait rose and took his hand, as uncomfortable with the prospect of the title as she was with the onus of the house.

Lilly tried in vain to do something with her hair before frowning one last time at her dressed-up reflection in the mirror. She felt a great deal of pity, if no respect, for anyone who had to suffer in panty hose and high heels every day.

In the library, a fussy rococo room, the worn bindings of priceless books melted into the shadows of gilded bookcases and two-foot-deep carved moldings. Amberleys, attired in the ruffs and laces of long ago, surveyed the scene from portraits hung around the room.

Francis Amberley was busy at a drinks trolley while his wife sat straight-backed on a damask-covered French fauteuil.

Skirted tables, tasseled chairs and footstools, and heavy drapes with swagged pelmets all argued for attention in the room. All the Georgian kings were represented. George II giltwood mirrors hung over George III satinwood commodes flanked by japanned Regency chairs from the time of George IV.

The room was fussy, fussy, fussy.

Lilly eyed the drinks trolley and wondered if Cait knew anything about china and silver. She herself knew enough to recognize the small bowl which held the limes as Meissen, and she'd be willing to bet the silver pitcher was the very Paul Storr she'd seen described in a magazine as part of a private collection.

The earl smiled warmly as he handed her a gin and tonic. "I hope you've found your accommodations comfortable."

"Very much so," Lilly quickly assured her host. "You have an admirable amount of hot water for a house of this age."

"I can assure you that wasn't always the case," he responded with a chuckle. "This house was serviced by a single well, and all water brought inside by pail for the first several centuries. When Caroline and I took over the house after the war, only two of the bedrooms had *en suite* baths."

"Up until the sixteenth century the servants slept on little truckle beds in the master bedrooms. When privacy became more of an issue adjoining cubbyholes were carved out for them, and these attached servants' quarters redo nicely into bathrooms or at least space for a sink and loo."

"Early attempts at plumbing were quite primitive of course. My ancestors had to make do with garderobes which drained into the cesspool built into the exterior walls. 'Soil men' came at night and did the dirty job of transferring contents from cesspool to moat. The W.C. wasn't even patented until 1775."

"Really, Francis, I'm sure our guest finds the subject of antique plumbing distasteful." Caroline shuddered. The little liver and white spaniel at her feet thumped his tail, at the same time directing a menacing low growl in Lilly's direction. He looked as if only good breeding kept him from nipping at her ankles.

"Not at all. I'm fascinated with the evolution of a house like this," Lilly responded. "My house is only a century old, and I should be ashamed for the complaints I make about the difficulties of keeping it in working order. Tell me about your library. You must have some fine old volumes here."

"To be perfectly honest we don't know what we have here." Caroline took up the discussion, relieved to be off the subject of plumbing fixtures. "The shelves are very deep because of the thickness of the walls, and many of the books you see are actually positioned in front of others. For generations a story has passed down that secret caches are built into the walls, but without removing over a thousand books, one by one, we have no idea where to look. As the walls are almost two feet thick it is certainly possible."

Before Lilly could ask any further questions a glowing Anthony appeared with Cait in tow.

"Caitlin, my dear, you look even lovelier than usual," Francis said as he took her hands.

Lilly agreed with him. Her daughter, too freckle-faced to be classified as beautiful, tonight looked elegant in a raspberry chemise with a ruffled hem which showed off her long legs to their best advantage.

She noticed an unfamiliar ring set with a large cabochon ruby on Caitlin's left hand.

"Have we any chilled champagne, Father?" Anthony asked as he bent to brush the air near his mother's cheek with a perfunctory kiss. The little dog growled again.

"I can have Harold fetch some from the cellar," his father answered. "Quite right that we should celebrate Lilly's visit with something more festive than gin. Let me ring for him."

Lilly thought to herself how easy life must be with a Harold around the house as moments later the somber butler arrived with a silver bucket of French champagne and a tray of crystal champagne flutes.

"May I propose a toast." Anthony raised his glass. "Before we acknowledge our charming guest, I feel it's entirely proper to first drink to the future lady of the house." Cait blushed beneath her freckles as he put his arm around her and proudly continued, "Caitlin has agreed to become my wife." He bent to kiss her.

"Well done, my boy!" Lord Amberley exclaimed and rushed over to embrace Cait. "We've so looked forward to this day, and you couldn't have chosen anyone we'd rather have join this family."

"I share your father's feelings, Anthony," his mother beamed, her normal reserve melting into obvious pleasure. "I know Caitlin will be more than capable of someday running and preserving this home for our descendants."

Can't leave the damned house out thought Lilly as she saw Cait flinch.

"The gardens will be at their best in early June," Caroline Amberley continued. "We can set up a tent in the rose garden for the reception."

"Really, Mother, don't you think that's putting the wedding off a bit too long?" Anthony asked.

"Well, my darling, I feel strongly that it would be inappropriate for you, as the future heir to this house, to be married anywhere else, and everything is so dreadfully dull looking in winter. You have your whole lives ahead of you. Surely you can be persuaded to wait for a few months."

Lilly's frown was as deep as Caroline's smile as Anthony responded, "Of course you're right, Mother. We'll leave all the arrangements up to you."

Cait sat silently, unconsulted about the timing of the most important day in her life.

Beck stood on the balcony of the luxurious hotel suite and watched the waves crashing below on the rocky beach. He knew that on the other side of the island stable boys were forcing the race horses out into the waves for an early morning workout in the sea. He had suggested a trip to the races to Laura, but she was adamant in her refusal. Despite having grown up on a farm, Laura was terrified of horses.

Now that he thought about it, she was terrified of a number of oddball things from escalators, to crowds in football stadiums, to Italian restaurants. He felt cheated of all the things they no longer enjoyed because of her peculiar fears.

"Good morning." Laura spoke softly from behind him.

He turned and marveled that she could wake up looking so unaffected-by all the junk she took to make herself sleep. His head felt like it was full of cement, and the morning didn't feel good at all. He was restless, edgy and dissatisfied.

As he looked at Laura, it suddenly seemed to him that she must be in some way to blame for his unhappiness.

"I wonder what time the shops in Bridgetown open?" She stretched, and yawned, and fluffed out her hair like a lazy cat considering the day's hunt. With Beck along she could shop all day. Beck would take care of her if anything happened. She felt happier and calmer than she had in ages.

"Who cares?" he mumbled. "Surely we didn't come all this way to shop."

"I want some of that Hungarian porcelain, and it's much cheaper here."

"Laura, we must have ten sets of china. What difference does cost make? If you want another set of china surely some store in Brierley can send it out."

"I suppose you're right." She yawned again in lazy acquiescence. "Should I order breakfast? We could eat it out here on the balcony."

"Whatever you want to do," he snapped. "I'm not hungry, but I do need some coffee."

He continued to glare at the waves beating on the jagged rocks and wished he could beat out his anger and depression on something as easily and relentlessly as the sea did.

Laura puttered around in the bedroom, humming to herself and as oblivious to her unhappy husband as she was to the European antiques scattered around the suite.

The full English breakfast, enough to sate the hunger of a table full of people, arrived and was served on the balcony. In silence Beck drank the dark, rich, tropical coffee while Laura nibbled on half a piece of dry toast. Eggs, bacon, sausage, fruits and oatmeal grew cold, ignored under silver lids.

"What are we going to do all day?" He finally broke the silence. "Would you like to go snorkeling or play golf?"

"I don't know. If you don't want to shop, maybe I'll just sit by the pool and read a book," she answered, reaching for the coffeepot.

"Great." His voice was heavy with sarcasm. "We come thousands of miles to sit by a swimming pool and read a book. I can do that at home." He slapped his napkin down and got up from the table.

"Good grief, Beck, what in the world is wrong with you?" Laura asked, bewildered at his reaction. "You're so jumpy this morning."

"I don't know what I want," he said, under his breath but audibly enough for her to hear.

Laura was idly trying to remember whether or not the hotel had any shops where she could buy another bathing suit, and the empty note in his voice totally escaped her attention.

"Well, Beck, there's all kind of food left here. You ought to be able to find something that appeals to you."

He shook his head at her retreating back as she put down her coffee cup and went into the bathroom to brush her teeth.

Faced with a lack of anything concrete to do, rather than from any sense of duty to the people left unable to reach him, he decided to telephone his secretary.

Laura, still singing little off-key snatches of song, was carefully applying her makeup when she heard Beck raise his voice. Something must be wrong at home.

She ran out of the bathroom terrified that something had happened to her children. The look on his face as he held up a hand and motioned for her to be quiet did nothing to reassure her.

"What hospital is Borland in?" he asked as he furiously scribbled notes on the little pad by the phone. "And what have they done with Mrs. Trainer?"

Laura frowned as she listened. The only Borland she knew was Ginger's husband. What in the world could Lucille Trainer have to do with his being in the hospital?

"They did what?" Beck screamed into the phone, and Laura watched his face get redder and redder as his fury mounted. Beck hung up and shook his head in disbelief.

"Apparently Lucille Trainer didn't like the idea of our adding on to the house and decided to go on a shooting spree," he explained.

"Beck, you're making no sense at all. I don't know anything about adding onto the house, and who in the world has she shot? Are the children all right?" Laura felt the jitters overtake her like an out of control train. She sat down on the bed to relieve her wobbly legs.

"The kids are fine," he said. "I decided to add that extra bedroom we planned when we bought the house. I was going to surprise you when we got home. From what Doris Harris tells me crazy Lucille got her husband's gun and decided to stop the construction by playing sniper from her bedroom window."

"Well, thank goodness the children weren't at home." Laura sat down on the bed next to him. "Was Mark hurt?"

"Mark has a shoulder wound that's apparently not very serious, and the children were at home at the time. They were all out in the yard when it happened, and it seems that only some very quick thinking by Bridget kept them from being injured. She pulled them under a bulldozer or something until Kick came along and called the police."

"Oh, Beck, how awful for them! Thank goodness for Kick. We have to call him right now." She reached for the phone, but Beck put out a hand to stop her.

"You haven't heard the end of the story. Kick then took Bridget and the children to that awful old house of your grandmother's for the weekend."

"The beach house?" She was having trouble following the story.

"Yes, and with a hurricane coming, but that's not the worst of it. Your crazy, irresponsible brother and Bridget also managed to get married over the weekend."

"Kick and Bridget got married? Don't be silly. He doesn't even know her. You must have misunderstood. Why would Kick want to marry Bridget?"

"Don't ask me to explain anything the damn fool does," he answered sharply. "All I can say is I hope she knows what she's gotten herself into."

"I want to go home right now, Beck." Laura put a hand to her throat as she felt the familiar tightening sensation. The room started to spin.

Beck threw up his hands in frustration. "We just got here, Laura. We can't just pack up and go home. I'm sure everything is under control at home."

She ignored his comment, rose from the bed, and crossed the room. He followed her to the bathroom where, instead of throwing things into her makeup bag as he'd expected, he found her tossing everything out in a frantic rummaging.

"What in the hell are you looking for?" Leaning against the door jamb, his whole body felt strung tight and topped by a brain that threatened to explode at any minute.

"My panic pills. I need something," she mumbled as an incredible number of bottles, jars, and tubes spilled out of the monogrammed bag.

The frustration and irrational anger, simmering inside for days, had in the few minutes since he'd learned that Kick had taken something he considered his property intensified to a rolling boil. He grabbed Laura's shoulders and spun her around to face him.

"No, Laura, you're not going to turn into a zombie on me," he spat at her as she turned large, frightened eyes on him.

"But I need something," she mumbled weakly. The expression on his face frightened her.

He said in a deadly cold tone of voice, "Need? You need something? My mother was right, Laura. You're nothing but a stinking junkie." All control now gone, he shook her, then slapped her so hard that her head snapped backward and forward, long hair swinging.

When he at last let her go, Laura collapsed sobbing on the floor. She finally got the childproof cap off the bottle and threw three of the pills in her mouth as the door slammed behind him.

CHAPTER FOURTEEN

As hours passed, Laura remained on the cold tile bathroom floor, unwilling or unable to make it back to the bedroom. Beck found her there, hair disheveled and eyes red, when he returned to the room from the bar.

He jerked her up from the floor.

"You're hurting me," she whimpered as he dragged her into the bedroom and pushed her onto the bed.

"You're the one hurting yourself, Laura. You've got to pull yourself together. We've got a flight out of here in a couple of hours." He managed to spit out the words although his brain felt fogged from the effects of two hours of steady drinking and the confusion produced by the sight of his usually immaculately groomed wife sprawled on the bed like a cheap truck stop pickup.

"Beck, everything will be fine if we can just go home," she whispered, struggling to sit up, head nodding like a child fighting sleep.

"Things are far from fine, Laura. I've had it with you. I'm bored, and right now all I want is to be out of the whole situation."

"Beck, please don't leave me," she sobbed. "I can't make it by myself."

"If it hadn't been so much trouble to rearrange my life, I would have left you two weeks after we got married. I'm worn out with your inability to decide what to order from the grocery store for dinner, with all the maids who stay one day and leave, with all those damned shoe boxes under the bed and pills in the bathroom."

Laura made a staggering lurch for the bathroom, and it hit Beck's subconscious like a sledgehammer that if she could get to the medication she would be yet again, however negatively, the one controlling the situation. A violent wave of nausea rolled through him, and the taste of sour Scotch, mingled with a straight, neat shot of the distillation of years of frustration, rose in his mouth

He lunged for her, grabbed the long tangled hair with one hand and the thin silk robe with the other.

He tightened his grip on her hair as the robe fell away, and the sight of her, slender, pale, and vulnerable, loosened his usual firm grip on self control

She put up a feeble resistance which he somehow perversely found exciting.

Men have been sentenced to long years in prison for acts far less violent than what Beck Kimble forced on his wife during the rest of that long afternoon.

Lilly took a deep breath and smiled with the joy of remembrance. She inhaled the smells of sausages frying, damp-wool clad people, and ancient smoky trains as she walked through King's Cross Station in the direction of the departure platform.

She much preferred trains to planes. During her short marriage she had managed to see a great many British towns and cities as she made temporary excursions from the unhappy reality of her home life.

Settled in a first class compartment, she found it ironic that she was, at this stage in her life, on a train running, perhaps back, to the man she had once sought so often to escape.

Lilly was considering suggesting a reconciliation to Edmund. The slow rail journey gave her time to think. She asked herself if she were jealous that everyone close to her seemed to have someone to make winter nights seem not so long, but that seemed too simple an explanation. No, the simple truth was that she still loved Edmund as much as she did the day they married.

She had talked with Cait far into the previous night, trying to explain her firm belief that falling in love is succumbing to the most primitive form of magic spell. Love didn't need or want a simplistic basis in rational reason. Reducing the feeling to lists of "whys" and "because ofs" would lead only to a marriage of practicality.

Love was just as often a matter of "in spite of," a chemical confusion which didn't require a logical sequence to reach its conclusion. Anyone who could, deep in the safety of the right person's arms, give you a "why" for the feeling, hadn't yet really emerged into the glade in the spellbound forest of the spirit.

She drifted off to sleep, thinking of how much she had changed in the past twenty-five years, long ago outgrowing the need to dance the night away. If birdwatching still didn't hold much allure, the idea of having Edmund to hold every night held a promise she was prepared to keep for the rest of her life.

Sleeping longer and more soundly than she would have thought possible, Lilly barely had time to wash her face in the tiny lavatory compartment before the train pulled into Edinburgh's Waverley Station.

With over an hour to kill before her connecting train to Aberdeen, she made her way through the glass and steel modernity of the Waverley Market Complex and out onto the comforting old world atmosphere of Princes Street.

Wishing she had time to trek up the High Street to the Royal Mile, she instead dashed across the busy street to Jenners, Scotland's largest department store. On a whim, she bought a picnic basket full of fancy goodies that she knew Edmund would enjoy but consider much too extravagant to purchase for himself.

Lilly took a brief detour through Princes Street Gardens where once the unfortunates alleged to be witches had been rolled into the swampy water. She climbed the 287 steps of Walter Scott's monument, and looked out through the rain at the grey and beautiful city.

Back in the station she bought a newspaper, and a Scotch egg, the traditional Scottish fast food snack of a hard-boiled egg wrapped in sausage, and a paper mug of tea.

Her train was called, and she discarded the unread paper and boarded. The spectacular scenery between Edinburgh and Aberdeen was blurred by a cold, gloomy rain.

Despite a second warming cup of tea bought from the dining car, she shivered, remembering how the chinks in the McFarland's old stone castle let in the most brutal elements of the Grampian climate.

She closed her eyes, reviewing pictures from the past. When, in the early days of their courtship, Edmund referred to his parents' home as "the castle," Lilly envisioned with awe something on the scale of the great royal homes of England. On her first visit to Scotland, she found Edmund's castle actually closer in feeling to a small French chateau.

Disappointed, she accused him of exaggeration, and Edmund patiently gave her a lecture on Scottish baronial architecture. When the house was built in the early 1600s, Scotland was much more closely allied with France than with England. The large homes built in Scotland during that period bore a much greater resemblance to their counterparts in France than to those in England.

A traditional L-plan tower house, Edmund's castle was a prime example of the local architectural transformation of a defensive rough stone tower built as a military stronghold into a domestic residence.

Forbidding from the exterior, the tall structure was covered in grey harl, or roughcast, and was topped by a steep slate roof. The few tiny windows were buried deep in the thick walls. The castle's only embellishments were at the roof line, where corbelled turrets and chimneys with pepperpot domes ran riot alongside Renaissance balustrades and crow-stepped gables.

That the balustrade was a replacement for an earlier roof parapet, from which Edmund's ancestors might have poured boiling oil on their enemies, gave Lilly the same thrill of goosebumps she felt when Edmund took her down to see the dungeon under the house.

The house rose from the main floor, with its great hall, up through five additional stories. The upper regions of the house, where the McFarlands had their everyday living and sleeping quarters, were accessible only by a tortuous climb up a narrow winding turnpike stair. In this skinny shaft of a house each floor contained only one or two rooms. The library occupied one whole floor and was, during Lilly's residence, the only room in the house where she ever felt warm.

The tiny bedrooms were icy even in full summer. The Victorian mahogany encased bathtub was deep enough for a hot soak, but hot water was as scarce as a day without rain. On the cold slate floors anything that chanced to be dropped broke into a million pieces. It was not a house where one ran barefoot.

In the vaulted cellar kitchen, with its ancient black range, copper boilers, and pudding basins, she tried her hardest to learn to cook the dishes on which Edmund had been raised.

She developed a violent distaste for Scotch broth, a thin, peppery mutton soup. At the same time she had to admit that never after leaving Scotland had she had a soup as good as the crab-filled partan bree. Chicken casserole somehow tasted better when it came to the table as "stoved how-

towdie" followed by the apple and raisin boiled pudding known as cloutie
dumpling.

She could still close her eyes and smell the cloves, and ginger, and bub-
bling apples when cook made black bun and taste the sweet Scottish honey
served with scones and cakes at tea.

Lilly left Scotland swearing that her lips would never again touch herring, kippered or otherwise, or eels, or "bashed neeps," the mashed turnips
Edmund's mother seemed to serve at every dinner.

But how she had missed through the years the fresh salmon and the rich
cranachan, a dessert of oatmeal and raspberries kissed with Drambuie and
cream!

Cold she'd been in that house and hungry as well on the nights when
the local fare had been more than a pregnant digestion could handle.

As the train rolled over the rails on its journey from Edinburgh to
Aberdeen, Lilly decided that no other place on earth could touch the beauty
of the Grampian mountains. The mountains, bronzed with heather and
sparkled with mica, blazed in the clear autumn air. If the castle was not an
abode for any fairy-tale princess worth her salt, the grounds and surrounding countryside were so breathtaking that being outside made Lilly's heart
ache.

The younger Lilly had longed to climb the forbidding heights of
Lochnagar. She had picnicked on the banks of the river Dee, splashing its
way from its source at the Linn of Dee in the Forest of Mar to the granite
cliffs and headlands of the cold North Sea. In the forests of fir where the red
deer run she had walked for hours at a time, trying to assuage her loneliness
for home with the beauty around her.

She had fished for the salmon that taste nowhere in the world as they do
fresh from the depths of the Spey. She had even convinced Edmund to take
her sea angling. They had set off early one morning on a boat from
Stonehaven with a fisherman who had entertained her with his serious
admonitions about refraining from using the words pig and salt, supersti-
tions as old as the neolithic long cairns of Macduff.

In a region strewn with Pictish stones and Iron Age forts her imagination took her back to a time when fierce men with tattooed faces roamed the
very woods where Edmund would sit for long silent hours hoping to see
overhead some straggling, endangered avian survivor.

Strange how much it felt like coming home as the train drew closer to
what was once the ancient Celtic province of Mar, the magnificent valley

nestled between the twin rivers of Dee and Don. Home to a cold stone house she'd left two decades before and a man on whom she hadn't laid eyes in several years.

Impulsively, and in mischievous anticipation of Edmund's disapproval, she rented a bright red Jaguar outside the Aberdeen station.

She drove west from the rockbound coast toward the mountains. Along the roadside the yellows and purples of the heather and bracken called out their swan songs of October.

To her delight the aged gentleman who sold her a bottle of Edmund's favorite port in the off-license shop in the tiny village recognized her, and, in a rare burst of effusiveness, welcomed her back.

"It's been years!" she cried. "How in the world did you remember me?"

"The hair, lass," he smiled. "Still na hae it unner control, do ye?"

"I gave up on that long ago." Lilly laughed with him, and the bell over the door tinkled in agreement as she went out to begin the last leg of a journey that had taken years rather than days.

The house stood, as it had for centuries, commanding the top of a hill in a glen. Lilly stopped for a moment at the gate and thought that somehow with the change in perspective brought by the passage of years in her own life it looked more solid and stable than forbidding.

Proud symbolic seat of generations of McFarlands, this little castle surely bore the weight of its history as heavily as did the larger and more imposing Summerfield House. Lilly could imagine this vantage point as it might have looked two thousand years before, topped by one of the vertically-oriented stone brochs which provided refuge from wild beasts and even wilder humans.

She wished desperately that Edmund could claim kinship with one of the romantic kings of Scottish history, Macbeth, or perhaps Malcolm, who lived with his saintly queen Margaret in the castle still standing on the highest point in Edinburgh. When he assured her that his roots were with more humble souls she assigned him imaginary heroic forbears who peopled the farther distant mists of history, leaving their legacy in remnants of stone.

The shopkeeper had no trouble recognizing Lilly, but she was not sure that she would have known the Edmund who answered her knock if she had met him on the street. His long face was gaunt, and the hair which had, in going grey, looked distinguished was now almost white. To her shock Edmund looked old.

But the gentle smile hadn't changed, and his arms still felt strong and safe as he embraced her with a pleasure at her arrival that she knew was genuine.

He looked down at her intently as he'd done after any separation in their early days together.

"She stood, a sight to make an old man young."

"Help me out." She blushed despite herself. "You know I was never any good at Shakespeare."

"Obviously you weren't any better at Tennyson." He smiled at her. "You haven't changed a bit, Lilly."

"I'm glad you think so. Kick has promised to give me a gift certificate for an eye tuck for my birthday." She laughed, as if displaying with pride the crinkles around her eyes. "These are just laugh lines, and I've earned every one of them."

"How are Kick and Laura?" He led her into the hall and closed the heavy oak door behind them.

"Well, Laura is as mixed up as ever, and no sooner than I turned my back and left Kick unsupervised he eloped with Laura's baby-sitter who's young enough to be his daughter."

"Love can make the wisest of men do foolish things, and that's a quotation from me," he answered with a gentle smile.

"Oh, Edmund, it wasn't entirely foolish." Lilly sighed. "Look at the wonderful daughter we have."

"Speaking of our wonderful daughter, what do you think of her plans?" He frowned, an expression that brought deep creases to his forehead.

"Well, I think Anthony is wonderful," Lilly replied. "I think Caitlin has given this a lot of thought, and I hope they'll be very happy."

"Will you be wanting your tea before I go, sir?" The housekeeper interrupted after a discreet tap on the door. She was relatively new on the job and consumed with curiosity about Edmund's former wife.

"I'll make something for us later," Lilly answered for him. "What I'd like is a walk in the garden before it gets dark, and if I remember correctly it gets dark here this time of year about an hour after the sun comes up."

"Let me whistle up the dogs, and I'll show you the changes I've made in the garden."

Around the house came three of the magnificent Gordon setters, tails waving a welcome to Lilly. She bent to rub a silky ear.

"They have much more energy than I can handle in my old age," Edmund commented. "Twice in the last week they've gotten in with the cattle and caused all sorts of annoyance to Peters, who's a grumbly sort on the best of days."

"Peters is still here?" Lilly cried. "He must be a hundred and ten years old."

"Still an old crofter on a peppercorn rent. Peters is the sort who will keep working until his last breath is drawn," Edmund said. "I've been after him to take a bit of ease now and then, but he's convinced that no one else can do his job."

"Sounds like Desia," Lilly said. "Ever since Kick's been back she's been waiting on him hand and foot, and every time I complain about it to either one of them I get a dirty look in return. With me gone she's probably trudging up the stairs every morning to bring him breakfast in bed."

"Lilly, Lilly, Lilly," he laughed. "You still want to control everyone else's behavior. I'm sure that the formidable Desia doesn't do anything that she doesn't want to do. Did you ever stop to consider that she gets great pleasure from doing little things for Kick because she loves him? She's like a mother with a prodigal son returned. Surely, now that he's married, he'll be moving out soon anyway."

"You're right," she said with a frown. "As much as I've complained about his camping out with me I'm going to miss him terribly. I just wish I knew this child bride. I can't imagine what possessed even someone as impetuous as Kick to pull a stunt like that."

He laughed until tears came. "You sound exactly like your grandfather when he came over here to try to talk you out of marrying me. No one should have to tell you of all people that falling in love makes people do things that make no common sense at all. I'm the first to admit that I was old, and contemplative, and boring even as a young man, and it certainly didn't take me weeks or even days to throw all good sense to the wind and fall hopelessly in love with you. Your brother has always been the sort who's in love with love, and I imagine at his age he's getting a bit tired of chasing skirts."

Edmund unfastened the little wooden gate that separated the rose garden from the rear court of the house.

"Your mother's Reve d'Ors are still blooming!" She bent to sniff a yellow bud. "These were always my favorites."

He followed her gaze around the garden, taking in the herbaceous border of dahlias, zinnias, and purple Michaelmas daisies, the dark red leaves of the Canadian maples in the distance, and the apple trees dropping their autumn bounty of tart fruit. Beyond them were centuries old yew hedges and further still in the background a striped banner of color in the green Douglas firs, the yellow larch, and purple and brown heather and bracken on the hillsides.

It was hard to decide if the earth were yielding one last burst of enthusiasm or screaming with fury at the dying of the summer.

"We've had an unusually warm October," Edmund said. "A frost is predicted for tonight, and tomorrow the garden will be on its path toward death."

"Edmund! What a depressing way to put things." Lilly shuddered. "Don't be so gloomy."

"I've enjoyed the garden so much this past summer," he sighed deeply as he looked around him. "There is so much of my parents in this garden, and I wonder if anyone will care to keep it up after I'm gone."

"Is it just the coming of winter that puts you in this kind of mood, or are you sad that Cait is marrying a man with that ridiculous house looming in his future? You know she loves this house as much as you do."

"Oh, I'm practical enough to know that she'll sell this place after I'm gone. Someone will open one of those horrid bed and breakfast establishments for tourists and invent all sorts of stories about ghosts, and rattling chains, and Macbeth having slept here."

"Edmund, stop it! You're being positively morbid." Lilly felt a shiver of fear when she saw the expression of terrible sadness on his face. "Is there something wrong? Something you're not telling me?"

"Actually, Lilly, there is, and I might as well go ahead and get it out in the open," he said bluntly. "I have an inoperable form of cancer. The only good thing the doctors have told me is that I will be relatively free of pain until the end."

"No, no, no, no!" she screamed, taking a step back from him, childishly putting her hands over her ears as if trying to block out his voice before he could say more. "We'll just get you to another doctor. We'll take you somewhere where they can fix this. I won't let you die."

"Lilly, you never could handle the inevitable when it was unpleasant. I assure you we have some of the best doctors in the world right here in Scotland, and I have seen most of them in the past few months. I intend to enjoy the days I have left and wailing over something I can't change is not the way to do that."

"Stop being stoic. I hate you when you're stoic," she sobbed. "I came here hoping we could start over. I started remembering all the things I loved about you. I wanted to grow old with you. And now you have the bloody, unmitigated nerve to tell me that you're going to die?"

For the first time since he'd been given a sentence of death from which there could be no commutation Edmund McFarland let his emotions come roaring to the surface. He began to laugh and then to cry until the tears came, as they needed to, hard and fast.

With his mother's roses blooming bravely against their own sure end, he and Lilly held each other, caught in a frozen moment which held neither the past nor the future.

"Stay with me," he whispered. She nodded wordlessly as they clung to each other in the gloaming, the fading light of an early Scottish dusk.

CHAPTER FIFTEEN

Silent tears streaming down her cheeks, Lilly lay next to Edmund in the dark room. On the other side of the heavy velvet drapes dawn had broken pink and purple over the surrounding mountains, but she was reluctant to get up for fear of waking the man who slept so peacefully beside her.

Lilly couldn't believe how easy, how natural it had been. She and Edmund hadn't made love to each other in over twenty years, and yet they had been able to slip back into the familiar touches as if they had been only a night apart.

She was committed now for the duration, no matter how long, or short, or difficult the time they had together might be. How did a person make up for twenty lost years in a few months or, don't even think it, a few weeks?

He stirred, and she wrapped strong arms around him. "Marry me, Edmund," she whispered to the back of his neck where a younger man's long auburn hair once curled.

"I tried that once, Lilly." He turned to face her and smoothed the confusion of her hair.

"But I'm a grown-up now," she argued.

"I doubt that very much," he said, "and I don't know what kind of burden we'd be facing."

"I'm here for the better or worse, sickness or health part, whatever we do, so you might as well make an honest woman of me," she answered firmly. "How would it look to Cait to have her parents living together in sin?"

"Oh, I imagine Caitlin would be delighted, but that's beside the point. Be reasonable, Lilly. You can't just pick up and leave your life to move in with me. You know how you hate the winter here. It's cold, and isolated, and I doubt very much that I'll see another spring."

"Yes, you will! We'll see it together. What have you got to lose by taking me on again?"

"Probably my sanity along with my health." His voice was firm in its conviction despite the teasing quality of his words.

"Do you love me?" she asked quietly, searching his face for the answer.

"Of course I do, Lilly. I've loved you from the day I met you, and I long ago stopped trying not to love you. I just can't cope with living with you any more than you could adjust to being here with me. What you're doing is feeling sorry for yourself because your brother has found someone to love at a point when your own life doesn't seem to be going anywhere in particular. You're looking back through the forgiving fog of memory and trying to rewrite the past. We did have some happy times, but we also had some pretty hellish ones. If you'll remember, you spent more time on BritRail than most of their conductors."

"Damn it, Edmund, you're an expert on history, not psychology."

"You're right, but it doesn't take a trained expert to see right through you. You wear your emotions on your shirt sleeve for all the world to see."

"I suppose you're right as usual. Would you suspect an ulterior motive if I asked you to make love to me again?"

"Even if I did, I don't think I could refuse such an offer. It's not one I get very often anymore."

Lilly moved closer to him, willing herself not to cry.

Later, the drapes still drawn against the world outside, they talked, as they had been unable to the night before, about their lives and their futures. Lilly let her tears flow freely, aware that he knew her well enough to know that the tears were there whether shed or held inside.

"Does it hurt, Edmund?" She finally asked quietly the question she had been most afraid to voice.

"No, except for feeling tired occasionally, which I imagine is as much a function of aging as anything else, I don't feel badly at all," he answered. "It's such an insidious disease, Lilly. It can sneak up on you with few if any symptoms until it's too late to do anything."

"How did you find out then?"

"Routine physical examination with my physician in Aberdeen. He ran a few tests and sent me to Edinburgh and Glasgow to specialists. I'm satisfied that there is nothing more that they can do."

"You're going stoic on me again." She sniffled, and he took a handkerchief from the bedside drawer and handed it to her. It smelled of the past, of his mother's rose petal potpourri. "Surely there is someone, somewhere, doing research or something. We'll just have to keep looking until we find the top person."

"Lilly, this is something your money can't fix, and, as difficult as it may be for you, you're going to have to face that fact. All you're doing by refusing to face facts is making things harder for me."

"Turn your mind off, Lilly," Edmund said firmly. "Let's get dressed and go to the market fair in the village. I haven't had any pointless fun in years, and now that you're here perhaps it's time I tried to do just that."

"Oh, Edmund, do you remember when we went to the Nottingham Goose Fair? It was just this time of year because it was right before Cait was born."

"Well this is just a small fair, originally held to celebrate the Old Michaelmas, which was in October rather than September, but I expect there will be a fair number of geese for sale."

"Can we buy one, a great fat one?" She bounced like a child on the overstuffed feather mattress. "Think what fun the dogs will have chasing it!"

"I suppose if you must have a goose it can be arranged." He laughed for the sheer joy of having Lilly back even if for a moment. "Just don't eat any blackberries after the fair."

"Why not?"

"Very unlucky. Didn't anyone ever tell you that the devil spits, or worse, on blackberries on Michaelmas Day as a way of spiting his rival the Archangel?"

A shadow passed over Lilly's heart. She couldn't dispel the feeling that the devil had already spit on both of them.

Kick and Bridget took Laura's station wagon to the farmer's market on the outskirts of Brierley.

"Isn't this the absolutely best time of the year!" Bridget cried as she ran toward an enormous mound of pumpkins. "Oh, Kick, look! Sugar cane!"

"What are we buying anyway?" she asked as she examined a basket of apples that a vendor pushed her way.

"Photographic props. I've got to get the 'autumn' section of my book nailed down fairly quickly before all the color is gone. While we've got three cute models as houseguests, I figured I'd get all sorts of fall produce and set up some shots."

Bridget threw herself into her assistantship, bargaining lightheartedly with the local farmers for pumpkins of varying sizes and shapes, apples fat and shiny red, pomegranates and persimmons, tall stalks of sugar cane, and bunches of higgledy-piggledy colored Indian corn.

They bought jars of honey and locally produced molasses for the Thanksgiving pecan pies Desia planned to make early and freeze.

The back of the station wagon was soon overflowing with the fruits and colors of the season.

"Have to get one more thing," Kick called over his shoulder as she opened the car door. He soon returned with a small paper bag of grapes.

"What's your sister like, Kick?" she asked as they pulled away from the market. It's weird to think that I have a sister-in-law who I don't even know. How long do you think we'll be staying with her?"

"That's a tough assignment, asking someone to describe Lilly." He shook his head and laughed. "When they made Lilly they threw away the mold. I think she was ready to kick me out months before you came on the scene, and I have an idea about where we might want to live. There just might be a house that would suit us coming up for sale."

"Really? Which one?"

"It's a secret I cannot reveal. You'll just have to wait and be surprised. In the meantime pass a couple of those grapes this way."

Bridget reached into the bag and felt something hard. When she looked inside she saw among the pale green grapes the darker green of the largest emerald she had ever seen. She gasped as she drew it out of the bag and slipped it on her left hand.

"Must be all the pesticides they're using these days," Kick said with a wink in her direction. "Never know what you're going to find at these local produce places."

The first class cabin was almost empty, and Beck and Laura made the flight sitting in silence, nursing their separate wounds, on separate sides of the aisle. They returned to a cold, dark and silent house.

"Aren't you going to bring in the luggage?" she asked timidly as he unlocked the door and went in without holding it open for her.

"Surely in the vast resources of your closets and your medicine cabinet you can somehow make it through tonight."

"Are you coming up to bed?" She was still bleeding and sore, and one eye had swollen shut from the afternoon's encounter. As frightened as she was by his behavior, she told herself that she was willing to submit to anything rather than lose him.

"Go ahead. I'll sleep in here." He stalked into his study. Laura stood for a few minutes, bracing herself against the door frame, and watched him pour a large tumbler of Scotch which he drank without his usual addition of soda and ice.

When he poured the second drink, Laura, exhausted and afraid, closed the door and slowly and painfully dragged herself up the stairs to bed.

Lilly didn't get her wish to purchase a goose at the fair, but she did come away with a hand-loomed tartan blanket for Desia, kilts for Marion and Sam, and a worn leather-bound set of the novels of Sir Walter Scott for herself.

"I can't believe you're not aghast at my extravagance," she teased Edmund as he loaded the car with her purchases.

"You know, Lilly, in retrospect many of the things I chided you for were inconsequential," he said as he got behind the wheel. "I disapproved of your buying things when I felt you were shopping out of boredom, but generally I think you spend money for the intrinsic pleasure that the things you buy bring to you or to someone else. There's nothing wrong with that."

"I wish I could say the same for Laura." Lilly sighed. "She goes on these crazy binges and comes home with ten pairs of shoes at a time."

"Lots of women are compulsive about shoes," he mused with a smile. It was years since he had lived with Lilly, but it would take a lifetime to forget the horror of sharing a closet with her.

"No, Edmund, I really think she's an emotional mess." Lilly frowned as she sought the words to describe her sister. "She takes tranquilizers like they're candy and goes around in a trance half the time. I don't know how she functions as well as she does."

"Have you tried talking to her about it? How does her husband feel? How long ago was it that they spent that weekend with me?"

"The time they came over on the golfing holiday?" Lilly tried to put her sister's Scottish holiday in some sort of time frame. "I know it was before Sam was born because Brook and Marion stayed with me. Must have been about seven or eight years ago."

"I must admit I wasn't terribly taken with her husband." He lit his pipe and drew deeply on it. "Seemed rather self-absorbed as I recall."

"That's a nice way of putting it," Lilly responded. "He can be a real S.O.B."

"Well, I'm sorry to hear that," he continued. "I like Laura very much, and if she does have a problem, he's going to have to be a part of the solution. You know, Lilly, I've often thought about the things you've told me about your mother. Who knows how treatable your mother's condition might have been?"

Lilly stared out the window and didn't answer. The rain which had threatened all day now obscured the view.

"She obviously had agoraphobia," he continued. "I realize that those of us in the general public didn't know much about that sort of problem back then, but if someone had tried to help your mother instead of encouraging her to hide upstairs like a character in a mystery novel, who knows what kind of productive life she might have led?"

"Well, obviously Laura has a different problem entirely from what ailed Mother. I worry about her infatuation with pharmaceuticals." Lilly frowned at the view out the window as an unbidden and unwelcome vision of her mother lodged stubbornly in her mind. Her father had refused to allow an autopsy. No one would ever know the true cause of Marion Lambeth's death.

"I know how much you love your sister, Lilly," Edmund said. "Perhaps she'd welcome your bringing the problem to the fore. Promise me you'll do something as soon as you get home."

Lilly bit her lip and nodded.

They had turned off the heat in the house before leaving town. Laura, tossing and turning chased by nightmares, woke cold and aching with the sheets soaked and the covers in disarray.

The house was as quiet as it was cold, and she passed through its many rooms as might a lonely ghost seeking the solace of any available human companion.

Beck's car was not in the driveway. The children were still at the farm. It was the maid's day off. A long, lonely, empty question mark of a day stretched ahead of her. In desperation she picked up the telephone.

"Good morning!" The warmth of Christine's voice did nothing to lift the gloom that hung over Laura. "I didn't expect you back so soon."

"Well, the weather . . . ." Laura struggled for any excuse for being back at home, for an excuse for calling her friend at all.

"Laura, what's wrong? You sound terrible," Christine asked anxiously.

"Nothing, everything, I don't know. Chris, can you come over? I have to talk to somebody." Laura began to cry.

"Sure, Laura, I was on my way out anyway," Chris lied in what she hoped was a reassuring tone of voice. "I'll be there in a few minutes."

Laura stood in the shower under the hottest water her body could bear scrubbing at the dried blood. It had run for hours and stained her clothes, and she felt like the broken parts of her life had streamed with it from somewhere deep inside her spirit.

Beck, in his mindless fury, had done more than physical damage. In washing away the physical evidence, she wished desperately that she could at the same time wash the whole ugly ordeal from her mind.

The hot water ran out, and she shivered as she opened the shower door. Christine, who had followed the sounds of the running water when Laura did not respond to her calls, stood in the bathroom. Her face was an open mask of her horror as she stared at the bruised and dripping wreck standing on the threshold of the shower.

"Laura, what in the hell has happened to you?" she screamed at the sight of her shivering, shaking friend. Gathering Laura up in Beck's robe, she led her into the bedroom. "Who did this to you?"

"Beck," Laura whispered as she collapsed into a chair, unconcerned that she was soaking the delicate fabric with bathwater and blood.

"Chris, he's going to leave me, and I don't think I can take it," she mumbled through chattering teeth.

Christine was nauseated with disgust and angrier than she ever remembered feeling. She took Laura's shoulders in her hands and looked deeply into the big, grey eyes.

"Laura, you've got to tell me exactly what happened if I'm going to be able to help," she said firmly. "What went on in Barbados?"

"He was in one of those black, depressed moods. You know how he can get. He called home and found out about Mrs. Trainer and about Kick and Bridget getting married. It was like he went crazy, Christine. He accused me of being a drug addict just because I needed something to calm me down, and then he stormed out of the room."

Christine was, as usual, having trouble following Laura's narrative. She wasn't sure what Laura was trying to tell her about Mrs. Trainer and Kick, but there would be time enough later to get the details of that. The immediate problem was what to do about Laura.

"Laura, you look like you've been run over by a train. Tell me what he did to you."

"Isn't it obvious?" Laura let out a little hysterical laugh. My own husband raped me, and when he ran out of sexual steam he beat me up."

"Son of a bitch." Christine held Laura close and tried to control her fury enough to make a rational decision about what to do next.

"Let's get you dressed. I'm going to call Jack Connor. You need to see a doctor."

"Chris, it's bad enough that you know. I can't go running to Jack Connor looking like this." Laura shrank back in the chair, pulling the robe tight around her as if it could hide what Christine had already seen.

"This is no time to worry about how you look, Laura. You need a doctor." Chris pulled Laura up from the stained chair and began to dress her as if she were a child. Too weak to fight, Laura meekly accepted the garments and let herself be led to the car. Her teeth were still chattering.

"You need a coat, Laura. I'll be right back," Christine turned on the car heater and dashed back into the house.

After pulling Laura's coat from the closet, she picked up the phone and dialed the number of her gynecologist and close friend Jack Connor.

"This is Christine Bradley," she told the receptionist in a voice that she hoped carried some sense of urgency. "I've got an emergency, and I need to speak to Dr. Connor." She said a silent prayer that he wouldn't be tied up at the hospital delivering a baby.

In seconds she heard Jack's familiar reassuring voice on the line. "Christine, what's wrong?" he asked with concern at the obvious emotion playing in her voice. He was her close friend as well as her doctor.

"I'm fine, Jack, it's Laura Kimble who needs help. She's been raped, and I need to get her into your office without half the town sitting in the waiting room gaping at the shape she's in."

"Have you called the police?" He felt a knot form and twist in the pit of his stomach as it always did when he saw this sort of case. He hated the one weekend a month that it was his turn to be on call in the emergency room.

"I don't think there's much the police can do," she sighed.

"Well, you know she's not my patient, but bring her to the back entrance. I'll be waiting for you there."

Jack Connor buzzed his receptionist to stall his next patient and waited by his private entrance. He tried to remember who Laura's doctor was, had a vague feeling that it was old Sam Tarver, who should have retired years ago. As much as he dreaded facing Laura's problem, he knew he was better able to cope than the geriatric Tarver.

Rushing out to help Chris get Laura out of the car Jack wondered now why Beck wasn't with them.

It didn't take a lengthy examination for him to determine the extent of Laura's injuries. Most of the physical damage would heal quickly. He wasn't so sure about the prognosis for emotional recovery when he looked at the hurt in those big, grey eyes.

Laura begged him not to make her talk about what had happened, and he agreed to respect her request for at least the immediate time being. Completing the examination, he entrusted her to the ministrations of a sympathetic nurse and left the room to talk with Christine Bradley.

Jack ushered her into his office and closed the door behind them. He motioned for Chris to take a chair, sat down behind his desk, and ran his hands over his eyes. "She needs to be in the hospital," he said. He wished he could shut out what he'd just seen. "Whoever did this to her needs to be locked up. Why is she refusing to get the police involved, and where in the hell is Beck?"

"In hell is exactly where I'd like to see Beck Kimble," Christine said angrily. "Getting the police involved wouldn't do any good. Eleanor would just find some way to get him off the hook."

"Wait a minute, Christine," he said with alarm. "Surely you aren't trying say that Beck did this to her?"

"That's exactly what I'm saying. You mean she didn't tell you?" Christine watched Jack Connor's face contort with rage, as the truth of what had happened angered him as much as it had her.

He closed his eyes tightly for a few minutes trying to assess the situation dispassionately as if he were dealing with strangers rather than with two people he'd known all his life. He had legal, moral, and ethical obligations in a case like this, but uppermost in his mind was dealing with it in a way that would cause Laura the least amount of future pain. He'd known since high school fraternity initiation week that Beck had a cruel streak, but what he'd seen today frightened him.

"She has to be admitted to the hospital, Chris. At the very least she's got a couple of broken ribs. I can't treat all that in my office. Can you stay with her after she's settled in a room?"

"Of course, Jack. I appreciate this. I realize that you have a waiting room full of patients." Christine rose from the leather chair.

"I'm going to cancel the rest of my appointments," he said. "I don't guess I've ever known a kinder, sweeter, more loving person than Laura Kimble, and I can't tell you how sick this makes me."

"Jack, I'm sorry I got you involved, but I didn't know what else to do. Please don't feel like you've got to stay with her. I'll be there."

"I know you will. Just as soon as we have Laura taken care of I'm going to find Beck."

CHAPTER SIXTEEN

"Do you want me to call Kick?" Christine adjusted the blinds and darkened the room as Laura requested.

"No, please don't. I don't want anyone else to know about this," Laura pleaded. "Kick doesn't even know we're back in the country. I just want to sleep. I don't want to think about things."

"You're going to have to think about things," Chris said softly. "Maybe not right now, but you can't just hide out indefinitely."

"Do you think Jack will tell Betsy?" Laura asked.

"Of course not. Jack's a doctor, Laura. He's a good friend, but right now you are his patient. You don't think he goes home at night and says to his wife 'I told Chris and Wade to have sex standing on their heads in hopes of making a baby' do you?"

Laura laughed, wincing as her bruised and swollen face reproached her. "You can always find a way to make things funny even when they're miserable. Did he really suggest that?"

"No, but it's the about only thing we haven't tried," Christine rolled her eyes and laughed with Laura. "Believe me he's seen me shed many tears, and he is a very compassionate guy. I'm in his office bawling on a monthly basis."

"Funny how life treats people differently," Laura grimaced as she tried unsuccessfully to shift to a comfortable position. "Beck was so furious when I told him I was pregnant with Sam. Why is it that the people who don't want children seem to make them so easily, and the people like you and Wade who want them so badly can't seem to have the same luck?"

"I guess, if I could answer that Jack wouldn't have that waiting room filled with desperate people," Christine answered softly.

Jack drove the short distance to Beck's office determined to get his emotions under control before the unpleasant confrontation ahead.

He ignored Mrs. Harris's protests that he had no appointment and left her staring open-mouthed as he pushed open the door to the plush enclave that was Beck's private office.

"Hi, Jack, what brings you here?" Beck put down a sheaf of papers and smiled at the other man as if he hadn't a care in the world.

"I just got through patching up your wife, Kimble." Jack leaned over Beck's desk and gripped its edge.

It took a lot of restraint not to grab the nonchalant Beck and beat him to a state resembling Laura's. "You made a real mess of one of the nicest ladies I know, and I want to hear some explanations."

"Sit down, Jack," Beck said calmly. He was caught off guard and unsure whether to deny the accusations or to try to defend himself. Leave it to Laura to go babbling to anyone who would listen about something that was private.

"I don't know what you're talking about, Jack," he answered, tapping a monogrammed fountain pen on the palm of his hand. "Where did you see Laura?"

"You know exactly what I'm talking about. I saw her in my office before I admitted her to the hospital."

"I didn't know you were my wife's doctor, Jack." Beck continued speaking calmly.

"I'm not. Christine Bradley brought her in, and I repeat that I am waiting for some kind of explanation for what could have prompted the fit of insanity that made you do what you did to Laura."

"Oh, Jack, you know how it is." Beck gave him a leering grin and winked. "We were out of town, a romantic place, Laura wanted to try something a little kinky. She gets all kinds of crazy ideas from those afternoon talk shows she watches. Things just got a little out of hand. Laura can be so prudish sometimes that she's probably just embarrassed that she enjoyed herself so much."

"You're lying, Beck, and not doing a very good job of it." Jack's voice rose, and Beck wondered how much of this Mrs. Harris was hearing. "No one could have 'enjoyed' what you did to her. You raped her, and then you beat her up. Why, Beck?"

"All right, Jack, I'll be honest with you, although I don't think what goes on between my wife and I in the privacy of a bedroom is any of your damn business," Beck said. He leaned over his desk, deciding it was time to go on the offensive. "I did it because I lost my temper."

"You lost your temper," Jack mocked. "What on earth could make you lose control like that?"

"Lots and lots of little pills, Jack. Laura spends the hours she isn't zonked on sleeping pills in some private, drug-induced never-never land. It's about time somebody jerked her out of the stupor."

"I don't know anything about that. If she needs help for some kind of substance abuse problem, then get her some help, but if you're at the point where you could let yourself do what you did, you need help as badly as she does," Jack shot back.

"It's not my problem, Jack. She's going to have to fix her own little red wagon. If she does, fine. If she doesn't, it's her life she's throwing away. She's not going to waste my life in the process any longer."

Jack stared at him in silence, and Beck returned the stare, seemingly unmoved.

It was Beck who finally broke the stalemate. "You said she was in the hospital. Mental or regular?"

"Regular of course." Jack sighed. "I'd like to keep her there for a couple of days. Where are your children?"

"I suppose they're out at the Lambeths' being supervised by good old Uncle Kick who has run off and married the cutest little piece of ass you've ever seen," Beck said bitterly.

Jack looked at Beck in disbelief and wondered how someone could be at the same time an old friend and a monstrous total stranger. He didn't know how much of what Beck had alluded to was truly a problem and how much a fabricated justification for what he had done. All he knew for certain was that someone had better get a handle on the situation before Laura was released from the hospital and sent right back to the private nightmare she was apparently living.

"I think it might be well to leave the kids right where they are for now," Jack said. "Laura's face is not a pretty sight, and I think it would be very unsettling for them to see her in this condition."

"Great. Keep her as long as you like. As far as I'm concerned you can have her," Beck said, still maddeningly tapping the fountain pen. "We'll tell everyone she had some female crisis that needed immediate attention and that she doesn't feel like having company."

"I'll go along with your 'story' for her sake, Beck, but on one condition. You will get some professional help, immediately, for both of you. I can recommend several good people, and I will be happy to set up the appointment myself."

"I don't think you understand, Jack," Beck said patiently. "It's Laura who has a problem, not me. Find her a good shrink and I'll be happy to pay for it."

"You're the one who doesn't understand," Jack stood up and leaned over the big desk, holding tight to his own thin grip on self control. "Either you will get some help or I will encourage her to make things very ugly for you, and I'll be more than willing to help her do it. Think about what I've said and call me this afternoon."

He turned and left the room, almost knocking Mrs. Harris down as he pushed the door to the outer office open. Beck sat frowning, the staccato beat of the pen against his hand picking up in tempo.

Edmund was outside conferring with Peters and the veterinarian on the condition of a sick cow. The housekeeper was in the village doing the marketing. Lilly felt that she could make a necessary phone call without being interrupted or overheard.

Lady Amberley herself answered the phone.

Lilly explained the state of Edmund's health and his adamant refusal to inform his daughter until his condition deteriorated.

"Oh, Lilly, I am so very sorry to hear such dismaying news," Caroline said with sincere sympathy. "I totally agree with you. We must forego the idea of a large wedding and encourage them to proceed with their plans with all speed. How can I be of help?"

"Thank you for being so understanding, Caroline. I know it's a tremendous disappointment for you, but Cait and her father have been unusually close because of our family situation, and I feel very strongly that it's important for him to be a part of her wedding. Perhaps you'd talk to Tony. She's going to need a great deal of support from him as her father's illness progresses, and I think he should be made aware of the situation. Of course we must, at the same time, respect Edmund's wishes that Cait not be told."

"Yes, I'm sure that we can trust his discretion, and I shall do whatever is necessary to convince them that a spring wedding here is totally out of the question," Caroline replied. "Do you think perhaps I should tell them I'm having the house painted?"

Lilly laughed, relieved to know that a sense of humor lurked behind the formal, aristocratic facade. "What a wonderful idea. That should take several years at least!"

Hearing Edmund call to her from the hall below, Lilly quickly terminated the conversation and went downstairs to enjoy, for a few days at least, the sense of being a part of his life.

The absence of both Christine and Laura was not particularly noticed at aerobics class. The other participants were too preoccupied with the ups and downs of their own lives to worry about anyone else as they went through the perspiration producing gyrations.

Ginger Borland was substituting for the regular instructor, and she was obviously more interested in demonstrating her own stamina than in meeting the capabilities of the class as a whole as she led them through a grueling workout. When two of the women sat down in frustration, Ginger simply picked up the pace.

Physically in perfect shape, Ginger was mentally exhausted from dealing with her injured husband. The shoulder wound had rendered him unable to use his right arm and therefore pretty much helpless. The vocation for which Ginger had the least natural aptitude was nursing, and she was not enjoying her new role at all.

"Push! Push! Push! Push!" she screamed over the music blaring from the tape player. "I see lots of ugly bodies. I know my percentage of body fat. Do you know yours? Let's get busy or be ready to compare some numbers."

Cynthia Wilkins could physically keep up with whatever her sister dished out to the class, and she found the whole thing amusing. She didn't particularly like her brother-in-law, who was much better looking than her own husband, and she felt only a twinge of sympathy for his pain. Ginger's daily verbal sniping had to hurt a lot more than any gunshot wound.

Cynthia didn't hold out much hope that this marriage was going to last any longer than Ginger's previous two had.

Cynthia didn't particularly like her own husband either, but she'd wheedled him into agreeing to buy her a new car, and she knew how much pleasure she was going to get when she asked Ginger to help her select it after class.

Ginger looked around the room, satisfied that her assessment of the class was right. Most of them were getting flabbier with each baby and each passing year. Even Cynthia looked as if she might be developing a little pouch. Maybe Cynthia was pregnant again.

A shiver of revulsion went through Ginger as she thought of that prospect. If there was anything good to be said about Mark it was that he had rendered himself incapable of making her pregnant.

She also had the tennis pro in bed every Wednesday afternoon, and he didn't charge for lessons off the court. She was having to be careful, very careful, about that. He was young, insatiable, potent, and probably, as a tennis pro, made even less than a building contractor.

As Laura slept, Christine sat nearby, flipping without concentration through a magazine.

Hearing a tap on the door, she rose to whisper to the nurse that Laura was finally sleeping, albeit it a disturbed rest in which she frequently cried out.

To her amazement on the other side of the door was Beck, barely visible behind an enormous bouquet of several dozen long-stemmed red roses.

"What in the hell are you doing here?" she hissed under her breath as she shoved him back into the hall. "How can even a lowlife like you have the nerve to show up here?"

"Butt out, Chris," he spat back at her. "This is between Laura and me, and I don't think the hall is the place to have this conversation. Why don't you just go home where you belong? Leave us alone."

"Beck Kimble, I have stood by for years and watched you and your mother abuse her verbally," Christine said, voice rising, too angry to be concerned about who might overhear. "If you think I am going to stand by and let you get by with what you have done this time, you're more full of it than I thought."

He pushed her aside and entered the room. Laura's black eye and swollen lip did look worse today, and he found it interesting that in some ways the sight of her bruises aroused him. She stirred in her sleep and called his name.

"Right here, sweetheart, everything's going to be just fine," he said soothingly, smirking at Christine who stood, arms akimbo, glaring at him as he sat down on the edge of the bed.

Laura's good eye fluttered open at the sound of his voice. "I've explained to Jack that we were just trying some fun that got out of hand," he said in an oily voice that made Chris's stomach turn. "I told him that you just wanted to experiment with something you saw on one of those television talk shows."

Laura took a deep breath. Her hands were shaking. "You know that wasn't what happened, Beck," she whispered.

"Well, we don't want this getting out among all your gossipy buddies, now do we?" He stroked her arm as he talked, and Christine wondered how Laura could let him touch her without her skin crawling at the contact.

"Beck, I look so awful," she whimpered.

"No, darling, you could never look awful. We're going to let you stay here and get some rest for a few days, and you'll be as good as new in no time. If anyone asks, I'm going to tell them that you had a small problem that Jack fixed and that you're just not up for company. No one has to know."

"Sure, Beck, if you say so," she acquiesced in a tired voice. "Can I go back to sleep now?"

"Of course you can." He bent over and kissed her gently on the forehead. "Just rest, and I'll take care of everything."

"Thank you, Beck." Laura, eyes closed, gave him a little crooked smile.

"Come on, Chris, I'll buy you a cup of coffee," he said firmly, leaving her very little choice but to follow him from the room.

They took a table in the farthest corner of the cafeteria. Beck unloaded a full lunch from the tray and began to eat as Christine stared at him. "Sure you don't want some lunch, Chris?" he asked between bites.

"No thanks, Beck, just being with you makes me nauseous. Say whatever you have to say so that I can leave."

"Now wait a minute. If anyone has a right to be nasty, Christine, it's me and not you." He made a face at the slightly congealed piece of chicken before pushing it aside and taking a forkful of rice. "You and Jack Connor both showed a lot of nerve today getting involved in something that really doesn't concern either one of you."

"When my best friend is lying up there in the shape she's in, it very much concerns me," she answered. "It's a good thing I got her to Jack when I did. She should have had medical attention last night."

"Oh, come on, Chris. She was in such a stupor yesterday that I doubt she felt a thing." He buttered a roll with deliberate motions.

Jack Connor crossed the room and pulled up a chair, "Have you thought about what I said, Beck? I meant every word I said."

"Sure I have," Beck answered, slowly, infuriatingly, playing with the rice. "You're absolutely right about getting Laura some help for her problems, and I'll be glad to talk to whomever you suggest. I'm free all week. Make me an appointment with someone, and I'll fill them in on all her neuroses."

He put his napkin down and rose from the table. "If the two of you will excuse me, I need to check on my kids."

They sat in silence as he strode out of the cafeteria, looking very much a man in control of his fate.

"What was that all about?" she questioned.

"I told him earlier that they've got to get some professional help and that if he won't agree to participate that I'll do everything I can to see that she prosecutes him."

"He knows she'd never do it," Chris said. "She's scared to death of him." She took the tray of half-eaten food and carried it to a trolley as if trying to remove all vestiges of Beck from the table.

Christine rejoined Jack at the table, wearing a mask of worry, and Jack took her hand. "You're a good friend, Christine. Tell me what's really going on here."

"Oh, Jack, I don't know. I think she does have some sort of drug problem, and I haven't been much of a friend sitting by and watching things progress. Maybe on that score Beck is right, although I hate to admit that he could be right about anything. I think she's just trying to escape from her life half the time."

"Are you sure it's tranquilizers that she's taking, Chris? Almost no one indiscriminately prescribes those anymore." He thought again of Laura's regular doctor and realized that Sam Tarver would be exactly the type to respond to a complaint with a panacea.

"I know what they look like. The doctor gave me some when my mother died. I've seen her take them lots of times, any time she has what she perceives to be a crisis, which can be several times a day. I just wonder how Beck is going to explain this whole situation to Kick."

"That, my dear, is his problem." Jack rose and gave her a smile. "When Kick Lambeth finds out what happened to his little sister I imagine Mr. Kimble will be admitted here in far worse shape than his wife."

Beck tried to remember on what floor of the adjacent parking deck he had earlier left his car and cursed any institution that didn't offer valet parking. Small wonder his mother always double parked outside the emergency room.

His mind raced as he considered the possibility of his mother finding out about this fiasco. He unlocked the chocolate brown Mercedes and slipped behind the wheel.

He drove out of the deck and put on his dark glasses against the late afternoon sun. There were few things that Beck hated as much as the end of daylight saving time, and October was fast drawing to a close.

Damn. He'd forgotten to ask that miserable Jack for the name of a condition to assign to Laura. He had to figure out a plausible excuse for keeping Kick and the children away from her until her face got back to normal. Maybe he should invent a traffic accident.

The native sweet gum and sassafras trees along the Old Post Road rained down a frenzy of yellow, red, and orange leaves on the car, but Beck was too absorbed in his own machinations to notice the brilliance around him.

He was very sorry about what had happened, not so much about what he had done as about the difficulty of handling the situation without the truth getting out.

He took some small comfort in the knowledge that Jack and Christine would be discreet for Laura's sake.

He had to have a believable story for Kick. Kick and Bridget. He had put that situation as far back in his mind as it would go, but he supposed he'd have to face that now too. Possibly Kick would be so preoccupied with Bridget that he wouldn't have time to be worried about Laura.

Maybe he could just grab the children and leave without having any contact with Kick. Kick was probably spending every waking minute in bed with Bridget. Beck ground his teeth in frustration.

Luck was not with him. Kick met him at the door. "Hello, Beck, what are you doing back so soon?"

"Oh, Laura had a little flare up of an old problem she's had several times before, and we decided to come home and let Jack Connor do some minor surgery. She's fine and should be home in a couple of days." He'd repeated the story to himself so many times that he almost found himself believing it.

"What exactly is wrong with my sister?" Kick questioned as he poured Scotch for Beck and took a beer for himself out of the small refrigerator in the library.

"Oh, I don't understand all the medical terms. I haven't asked Jack too many questions because I find all this talk about the female reproductive tract embarrassing at best."

"Bridget and I will be over to see her later this evening." Kick took a sip of beer and stared as Beck downed his Scotch straight, neat, and rapidly.

Without waiting for an offer, Beck went to the bar and fixed his own refill. "Please don't do that, Kick. She's been very nauseated from the anesthesia and was very specific about not wanting any company. Wait until she gets home."

"I'm sure she didn't mean her brother and new sister-in-law when she said no company," Kick countered. "By the way, you haven't congratulated me yet."

"Sort of robbed the cradle didn't you, old man?" Beck tried to sip the second drink at a more normal pace. What he really wanted was to turn up the liquor bottle and guzzle until his mind went blank.

Before Kick could think of a reply to the comment, which was beginning to sound to him like a refrain on a broken record, Bridget burst into the room.

At the sight of the large emerald on Bridget's left hand, Beck decided that he had to have a third drink fast. To hell with what Kick thought about his drinking habits.

"Mommy's car is full of pumpkins!" Sam screamed as the children ran in the back door.

"Hello Dad," Brook said. He hestitated in the doorway, knowing that the moment he dreaded had arrived. Here were Daddy and Bridget and Kick all together, and as he'd expected his daddy did not look happy.

"Get your things together, and let's go home," Beck said to the three children who stood close together like little soldiers awaiting their marching orders.

"Where's Mommy?" asked Sam. "Did you bring me a present?"

"Mommy isn't feeling well, and she's going to be in the hospital for a few days. On the way home we'll stop at the toy store and let you choose your own present, anything you want."

Sam seemed pleased with that offer. She had never been shopping with her daddy. Maybe, after the toy store, they could buy a real pony. She smiled in anticipation.

CHAPTER SEVENTEEN

*I*n the great stone-floored dining room of the castle, Lilly and Edmund and Caitlin and Anthony sat down to a dinner of tender filet of Scottish beef.

Lilly closed her eyes as Edmund offered grace. She could imagine the same room torch-lit in past years, other earlier McFarlands drawn close as a family. She added her own silent prayer of thanks that they were, for even a brief time, all together.

"We'll make a good Anglican of her," Anthony said as he tried with a straight face to take a serving of the mashed turnips Lilly had warned him would surely appear, "but something tells me that the soul will always be true to her Calvinist heritage."

"Aye, I should hope so. It was the way she was raised," Edmund answered. "If she doesn't have too much of her mother about her, she should run a thrifty household."

"Have you set a date yet?" Lilly turned her gaze on Caitlin.

"We were talking about it just last night, and Anthony's mother said the most surprising thing." Cait, who had been raised on turnips, took a large portion of the vegetable. "She seems to be backing away from the idea of some sort of extravaganza. In fact, she made the startling comment that in some ways she'd prefer a simple ceremony as soon as arrangements can be made. I found her turn of mind quite amazing."

"Mother's not as young as she used to be," Anthony chimed in. His eyes met Lilly's across the table. "I think she finds the idea of a large wedding exhausting, and it would no doubt be a relief to her if we insisted on being married right away. I know I'd like to call you my wife as soon as possible."

"This is such a lovely time of year," Lilly mused. "Why not right here, in the church where your father and I were married, two weeks from now?"

"Two weeks," Cait gasped. "Could we put it together that quickly?"

"Don't forget we've done this spur-of-the-moment marriage routine once before," Edmund said, shooting Lilly a warning look lest she push things too hard and arouse Cait's suspicion.

"By the way, Caitlin, I found something in the linen chest that I thought you might like to have," he continued. "I'll get it for you after dinner."

"How mysterious," Cait giggled. "Quite unlike you, Papa."

"He's mellowing in his old age." Lilly smiled lovingly at Edmund.

Later, assembled in the library over Gaelic coffee, rich with cream, sugar, and whisky, Cait drew in her breath as she lifted Lilly's wedding gown from protective layers of tissue paper. Edmund's eyes brimmed with tears. Lilly silently thanked him for the uncharacteristically sentimental gesture.

"Edmund, I had no idea where that dress was," she said in a breaking voice. "I assumed that my grandmother had it packed away somewhere. I had no idea it was here."

"One of the last things my mother and I discussed before she died was how lovely you looked that day, Lilly," he said softly. "She told me where she'd stored the dress and asked that it be given to Caitlin at the appropriate time. I hope it will fit."

"Oh, it's the most beautiful gown I could imagine." Cait's blue eyes, her father's eyes, were sparkling as she unfolded the white satin against the simple dark wool dress she wore.

"It's settled then," Lilly interjected. "Call your parents, Tony, and tell them we'll expect them up here in two weeks."

No one made a move to contradict her, and Edmund gave her a look of such profound thanks that she felt her heart would break.

Lilly grinned. One thing nobody found unusual was a suggestion on her part to do something impulsive.

"Never heard of him," was Beck's initial reaction when Jack Connor called and suggested that he make an appointment with Duncan Eagan.

"I'm not surprised that his name is unfamiliar," Jack responded to Beck's gruff attempt to brush off the suggestion. "He's only been in town a couple of months. I guess you could say I'm responsible for his coming to

Brierley. I've known him since medical school."

"Duncan had a very successful psychiatric practice in Chicago and decided last year that he wanted to relocate to a smaller town. I invited him down here for a weekend of fishing, and he decided to stay," Jack continued. He wasn't telling Beck the whole truth, but his conscience was satisfied with the version he put forward.

"Nobody just leaves a successful career in a big city to move to a town the size of this one unless there's some sort of problem," Beck said irritably. "Sounds to me like the guy was running away from something."

"Some people just don't like the pressure of living in a big city, Beck, but Duncan's motives for being here are irrelevant. He's good at what he does, and, as I told you this morning, you're going to talk to someone for Laura's sake. I meant every word I said."

"All right, Jack, you win. I'll see this Eagan guy if it will help you with your little 'save Laura' crusade," Beck sniffed. "I suppose this guy also brought his Chicago fee scale with him."

"I have no idea what he charges, Beck, but I'm sure you'll never miss the money."

Jack hung up the phone and lay on the bed staring moodily at the ceiling. He hated the idea of the gossip that was going to fly all over town when the news of this trouble got out. Inevitably, in a town the size of Brierley, where everyone knew just a little too much of their neighbors' business, it would.

He thought about Beck's speculations about Duncan Eagan. Duncan had his own problems with the past and was trying to make a new start. It was no one else's business, least of all Beck Kimble's, why he had come to town.

Raised in a poor Indiana family, Duncan Eagan had struggled for years to put himself through school and advanced training, years when he and his wife were unable to stretch the budget far enough to afford children.

After a child did arrive, Duncan was so busy hard-charging up the big city professional ladder that he rationalized that there would be plenty of time for applying himself to family life after he'd made a big name reputation and the big money that went with it. He had to provide for Linda and his son before he could relax and enjoy them.

Duncan and Linda's only child was four when he rode his new training-wheel bicycle into the path of an oncoming car. A bitter Linda Eagan walked out on her husband six months after the child's death.

Jack Connor knew that divorce was not an uncommon occurrence after such an experience. Duncan Eagan knew it too, but it only compounded his pain.

Linda was remarried and pregnant again. Duncan wished her happiness and whatever measure of peace he supposed time might bring.

Jack didn't consider Duncan's move to Brierley running away. He knew that Duncan was smart enough to know that he could never run far enough or fast enough to escape his memories.

The following morning Laura lay propped up in bed, mindlessly flipping through the television channels.

A home shopping service wanted to sell her a genuine zirconium pendant. A ranting, wild-haired evangelist promised to save her soul for a contribution of five dollars or more. An earnest young Indian woman exhorted her to do something to save the rain forest.

Numbed by fatigue and boredom, she didn't hear the knock on the door and was startled when an unfamiliar face appeared in the room.

"Who are you?" she asked, shrinking back under the sheets.

"Duncan Eagan." He smiled down at her from the foot of the bed.

She burrowed deeper under the covers, reminding him of a pale soft little rabbit desperately seeking shelter. "I just don't think I can stand to be touched anymore." The apparently unintended double meaning behind her words was not lost on him as he gave her the warmest smile he could and pulled up a chair.

"I'm not that kind of doctor," he explained in a gentle voice. "I'm a psychiatrist."

"You don't look like a psychiatrist." She rose slightly from her position under the blanket and studied him. He had an amiable face topped by soft hair that looked a little flyaway, as if he'd just washed it, brown hair that had probably in childhood been sandy blonde.

He was stocky, maybe ten pounds heavier than what would be considered ideal, with a very fuzzy chest partially showing through the open neck of the red golf shirt. His hands were short-fingered and covered with the same thick hair. Laura was reminded of a large teddy bear and relaxed visibly.

At her comment he threw back his head and laughed. It was a good, rich sound. "And what is a psychiatrist supposed to look like, might I ask?"

"Well, your hands, and your hair, and your face are all wrong." She stammered a little, embarrassed by her words and his laughter until she realized that he was laughing with rather than at her.

"For another thing you have too much of a suntan for a psychiatrist. They spend all their time in dark little rooms."

"Well this one spends as much time as he can out of doors," he contradicted. "You have a remarkable eye for physical detail. Most people never look at another person's hands."

"I took art classes for a while," she said softly. "I was always the best in the class at drawing hands."

"And do you still enjoy drawing hands?"

"No, I haven't touched a canvas in years," she said wistfully. "I thought at one point that I had some talent, but I was probably wrong."

She looked down at her own hands and wondered what she ever did with them anymore except to rub in lotions and put on nail polish. In high school she was perfectly happy with burnt umber caked under her nails and the scent of turpentine stinging her nose when she brushed her hair out of her face. Her teacher encouraged her to pursue art in college. Beck came along, and college never happened.

"What are you thinking," he asked gently.

"Oh, I was just thinking about someone I used to know," she answered. "Why are you here?"

"Jack sent me. He thought you might need to talk to someone."

"My husband thinks I've done far too much talking already," she said with a bitter, brittle laugh.

"I know. I talked with your husband earlier today on the phone." He watched her face for a reaction.

The expected response was immediate. She winced visibly as if she'd been struck again, and he saw the fear in her eyes. Laura Kimble was obviously afraid of her husband's anger, and Duncan had the feeling that the fear was of a more deep-seated sort than that produced by physical abuse alone.

"You talked to Beck?" she asked in disbelief.

"I did, and he's agreed to meet with me this afternoon at four o'clock."

"Can he make you lock me up?" The rabbit again dove for cover.

"Laura, he can't make me do anything," he said firmly, taking her tiny cold hand in his own large warm one. "All I want to do is help, and I don't think you can deny that you, and your husband, need some help at this point. If you don't think I'm the right person that's fine, but if you don't turn to somebody, and do it soon, I think there's the potential for some real disaster ahead in your life."

"You don't think I'm beyond help?" she asked miserably.

"Of course not. The only people beyond help are the people who refuse to try to get help. Sometimes we just get so mired in our own problems that it takes a third party to help us pull out of the muck and get back on our way."

"Okay. I'll do whatever you say," she answered.

"Not whatever I say. Whatever you decide, on your own with a little help from me, is the best course for living your life on your own terms. You need to be on a different road than the one you've been traveling, and all I'm here to do is show you a map with a choice of destinations."

"You make it sound almost fun."

"At times it can be," he agreed, not adding that the process of finding oneself also could involve taking some very slow and painful steps. "Exciting, too, finding out who the lady is that Laura's yet to be. Will you call my office and schedule an appointment?" He removed a card from his wallet and handed it to her.

"Sure." She turned the little card over and over in her hand as he moved to leave the room.

"Dr. Eagan," she said as he opened the door. "Thank you."

"If you need me before I see you again, just call." He gave her the reassuring smile again. "And call me Duncan."

Laura lay back against the pillows and felt relief flood through her. Duncan Eagan had just thrown her a lifeline. He was offering her something she hadn't felt in years.

The security of hope had been absent from her life for such a very long time that she almost didn't recognize the feeling when it came.

Duncan agreed to meet Beck at the Kimbles' house. Beck suggested this with an insistence that bordered on demand.

Duncan knew that Beck assumed that meeting on his home field offered him an advantage. He also knew that he could concentrate so entirely on what another person was saying that they could just as easily meet in the middle of Grand Central Station at rush hour without the surroundings affecting him.

He didn't care where they met, and so he honored Beck's request, parking his ancient little convertible behind the long brown Mercedes in the driveway on Hawthorne Road.

He walked around to the front of the house, taking in the immaculate yard, impressed with its size only to the extent of being grateful that he didn't have to mow it.

The heavy brass knocker on the front door thudded solidly against its plate as a tall grandfather clock inside chimed the hour. He could see through the little window in the door that the hall was dark and wondered as he waited if Kimble were standing him up or simply keeping him waiting on the doorstep. Either was possible.

Beck was keeping him waiting, another transparent attempt to show Duncan Eagan that he was firmly in control.

When at last Beck opened the door he ignored Duncan's outstretched hand. Duncan followed his silent host down the length of the dark hall and into the study.

Beck motioned for Duncan to take a seat in one of the large leather chairs flanking the desk behind which he himself took a seat as if the heavy piece of furniture were a trusted shield in the elemental armor with which he intended to enter this battle.

"I saw your wife this morning," Duncan began, totally at ease and even slightly amused at the other man's posturing. "She's very beautiful."

"The classic dumb blonde?" Beck asked rhetorically. He leaned back in his chair and gave Duncan a sneering smile.

"No, quite the contrary," Duncan answered. "She doesn't strike me as dumb at all. Frightened, insecure, unhappy in the extreme maybe, but definitely not dumb."

"Well, since you seem to have formed a great many deep insights after a very brief encounter, have you also decided what we should do about her?" Beck countered.

"I don't think it's up to anyone else to 'do' anything about her. She's got to decide for herself what she's going to do about making some changes in her life. No one has the right, or even the capability, to do that for another person. My role, with what I hope will be your help, will be to help her find the direction she wants her life to take."

"You're aware, are you not, that Laura is a drug addict?" Beck asked in a cold voice. "What do you propose to do about that?"

"I am aware from talking to Jack that there may be some problem in that area," Duncan said slowly. "I don't know enough yet to characterize her as addicted to anything. She and I did not discuss that aspect of the problem. I'm sure you're aware that there are various methods of tackling that sort of thing."

"Don't you think we'd be smart to have her committed to some good treatment center?" Beck leaned forward and stared hard at Duncan as if willing him to agree to what he and his mother had decided was the easiest route to take.

"Certainly not." Duncan remembered Laura's frightened comments along those lines and quickly and correctly assessed that simply getting physically rid of Laura would take tremendous pressure off her husband.

"From what little I know of the situation, I'd say it's pretty safe to guess that what your wife is doing is running as fast as she can from something that she finds either terrifying or extremely unpleasant. When we find out what she's trying to escape we can deal with her method of escape. The drug taking may be a symptom rather than the disease itself."

"Well, don't you think it's unfair to expect me to share whatever hell she's creating for herself?" Beck asked. "It's hardly my fault that she does what she does. I mean, for goodness sake, Eagan, look around you. She has everything money can buy. What in the hell does she have to be unhappy about?"

"I'm not saying that anything is your fault, Mr. Kimble." Duncan returned the steady, unsmiling gaze. "But your wife does not live her life, however privileged that life may be, in a vacuum. Like it or not, you are involved. How much you're part of the problem I don't know at this point. What I do need to know is to what extent you're interested in being part of the solution to her problems."

"Dr. Eagan, for the last twelve years I have been a perfect husband to Laura." Beck leaned forward over the desk. "I'm not proud of what happened in that hotel room, but surely you can understand that someone can be driven beyond their limit. I don't know what kind of future we have, or even if it's worth the effort to keep trying. Laura was very young when I married her, and frankly I don't see that she's done much growing up in the intervening years."

"Tired of being a father figure, are you?"

"Yes, as a matter of fact, I am. I have three children as it is, and I'm not sure that they wouldn't be better off with the fourth child out of the picture."

"And who would fill her role as their mother?" Duncan asked.

"Oh, that's easy enough," Beck answered, dismissing the problem with a wave of his hand. "We have servants, my mother, anyone could do what Laura does."

"That's where you're wrong, Mr. Kimble." Duncan's voice was firm. "You can hire someone to drive them, or cook for them, or buy their clothes, but you can't replace a child's mother, and I think you'd better think about that. Would you have wanted someone to replace your mother when you were ten years old?"

"Now that you mention it, yes, I would have loved it." Beck laughed bitterly. "I used to have a recurring, pleasant dream that a lady appeared at the door with a little boy my age and told my mother that there had been a terrible mix-up and that I really belonged to her."

"And what was the other lady like?" Duncan asked gently.

Beck closed his eyes, remembering the dream that he hadn't thought about in years. His defenses slipping ever so slightly, he answered quietly, "As I recall she was someone who liked to bake chocolate chip cookies."

Before Duncan could pursue this further, the armor clanked back in place, and Beck's face again became a mask.

"So you're proposing to do what?" he asked. "I'm a businessman, Eagan, and I'm used to solving problems with concrete remedies rather than a lot of psychoanalytical mumbo jumbo. How long do you think this process will take?"

"If I could tell you that I'd be in the fortune telling business," Duncan answered. "I can't give you an absolute time frame, but I'd like to start out seeing your wife at least three times a week."

"Fine," Beck replied, rising from his chair, calling an end to the meeting. "Just bill me at my office, and give me an update from time to time."

"I don't think you understand," Duncan said. He remained firmly planted in the leather chair. "If we're going to get anywhere I have to see you at least a couple of times a week too."

Beck started to protest, weighed his options, and decided that it would probably be easier to humor this witch doctor than to continue to hassle with Jack.

"Fine, whatever you think we need to do to get Laura back on her feet. I'll be glad to meet with you and fill you in on how she's doing on whatever basis you think best."

"Thanks for your time," Duncan said as the chimes of the clock signaled the end of his allotted hour. "Just call my office in the morning and set something up for tomorrow or the next day."

Not sure why he didn't feel more pleased with himself, Beck saw Duncan to the door, returned to the library, and poured a drink. He watched through the French doors as the little car went down the driveway.

It was late afternoon, the time of fading light called in Scotland the gloaming. Cait had departed for London, happy that even for a brief weekend the three of them had been a family.

Edmund was engaged in a telephone conversation with a colleague.

Lilly walked alone in the garden, letting her mind ramble.

The prevailing southwest wind was building, a gathering storm visible in the distance, coming toward her across the loch. She liked the feel of the wind in her hair, the thrill of menace in the black clouds that hung just beyond the summits of the mountains. The sky was purple, and mauve, and gold, as if drawn by a child eager to try each color in a new box of crayons.

They had driven Cait and Tony to Aberdeen, had lunch there in a tiny pub reached by a circuitous walk through the pends and wynds off a side street. On the return trip Edmund and Lilly had stopped in Banchory and bought some of the local lavender.

Lavender, with its misty scent and color, made Lilly think of Laura. She felt inexplicably sad.

One of Edmund's dogs nudged her, begging for attention. For want of a proper ball Lilly bent and picked up a fallen apple and tossed it for him.

She looked at the ancient gnarled alders, the windbreak of rhododendrons, the sad, pale color of the late hydrangeas.

One of the flock of small, wild birds tamed by Edmund swooped and landed at her feet, hoping for a bread crumb treat. Lilly took a packet of crackers, pilfered from the pub and already crumbled, and obliged it. Poor little birds. Who would be there to feed them when the wild Scottish winter came racing down from the north and all was cold and dead and gone?

"What do you want to do, Lilly?" She hadn't heard his approaching footsteps. She didn't turn but continued to stare moodily out at the gathering storm.

"I want to be out stalking the grouse. I want to take a boat from Stonehaven and go sea angling. I want to go back to Old Deer and have a picnic in the ruins of the abbey and daydream about St. Columba and the Celtic monks compiling the 'Book of Deer.' I want to go back to Oxford and walk the High and the Cornmarket and watch the Cherwell punts at Magdalen Bridge and hear the choristers sing a hymn in Latin. I want to be young again."

"Dear me. I only meant do you want to stay in the garden for a bit or go in and have your tea. We could go hunting, or fishing, or certainly make a brief visit to Oxford or Old Deer if it would make you happy, but neither of us is ever going to be young again."

"Why do you always have to be so realistic?"

"You're in one of your moods, Lilly, and you and I both know that it will pass as unpredictably as it came on. It doesn't take being realistic to notice that it is beginning to rain. Let's go inside, enjoy the nice tea that Mrs. McLean has left for us, and let me tell you about an idea I have for spending the upcoming week."

The gentle Scotch mist suddenly became a downpour, and they ran for the safety of the old stone house.

Over tea Edmund broached the subject of his plans. "Lilly, I've been thinking for some time about making a short trip before the foul weather of winter sets in. I can't think why I've delayed as long as I have, but now that you're here perhaps we could go together."

"Where?" She gave him a puzzled frown.

"I want to make one more trip to the Hebrides, a sort of pilgrimage. Will you go with me?"

"Oh, Edmund, I'll even take binoculars and help you bird hunt! What a grand idea! How soon can we leave?" As he'd predicted the bad mood had flown. Her dark sky was clearing.

"I don't know of a thing in the world to stop us leaving early tomorrow unless you're anxious to get busy with wedding plans."

"I'm only anxious to be with you." She threw her arms around him in childlike excitement. "Is that witch still there?"

"Lilly, just because a lady is elderly, wrinkled, and speaks Gaelic, there is no reason to accuse her of being a witch. And no, sadly, she died some ten winters ago."

"Sorry she's dead, but the old hag gave me the creeps. If I'm going on a second honeymoon, I don't want to spend it with some old crone who I can't even understand."

"I didn't realize that this was to be a second honeymoon."

"Sure. We can be just like Flora Macdonald and Bonnie Prince Charlie going over the sea to Skye."

"She was trying to keep him alive after Culloden, Lilly, not taking him on a honeymoon."

Lilly gave him a solemn look for a long moment. "I'm floating in tea, Edmund. Do you think it's late enough in the day to break out the single malt whisky? I feel badly in need of a lift from the revitalizing waters of Corriemulzie."

CHAPTER EIGHTEEN

*L*aura neatly folded the camel hair blazer over the back of the chair and smoothed imaginary wrinkles from her plaid wool skirt before taking a seat with her legs crossed at the ankles in a perfect finishing school pose. Her appearance was carefully constructed, and makeup camouflaged the yellowed, fading bruises on her face, but Duncan knew she was nervous.

A psychiatrist's office is, after all, an unnatural place to find yourself. Duncan had a recurring fantasy daydream in which someone came in, sat down, and proceeded to tell him how very happy they were.

"How are things going at home?"

"Things are okay, I guess," came the whispered reply. She looked down at her hands. "Beck's sleeping downstairs."

"And how does that make you feel?"

"Safe, lonely, I don't know." She avoided eye contact with Duncan. "He's adding a bedroom for himself. He says his mother and father always slept in separate rooms."

"I gather from our one meeting that he doesn't have a very harmonious relationship with his mother, but I don't recall his even mentioning his father," Duncan said.

"His father's been dead for years, and no one could have a harmonious relationship with Eleanor."

The vehemence with which she said this intrigued Duncan. "Tell me about your husband's mother."

"While I was in the hospital she brought her maid over and cleaned out all of my closets. I know the closets were overflowing, but, Duncan, it made me absolutely sick to come home and find out that she'd thrown out things that meant a lot to me. I had a big box full of the childrens' drawings, every picture they'd done for me since they were old enough to hold a crayon. Gone, all the small special things that I treasured are just gone. Of course she didn't touch Beck's closets."

"Eleanor would love to see Beck put me away somewhere. She has hated me from the day I married him, and she has so much power that it frightens me."

"Power over whom?"

"Over us, over everyone she touches from her maid to her bridge group. No one, and I mean no one, dares to cross Eleanor Kimble."

Duncan began to suspect that he was dealing with a marital relationship that had three very unequal partners.

He suddenly shifted gears in his questioning. "Who are you, Laura?"

"What do you mean?" she asked. The personal question perplexed her because she was still thinking about Eleanor.

"Tell me who Laura Kimble is. Describe her for me as if you were someone else telling me about Laura Kimble."

She took a deep breath. "She's married to a man who is terribly successful at everything. She has three perfect children. She lives in a beautiful home. She has an older sister and brother who are very sure of themselves. She and her mother-in-law do not get along very well. That's about all I can say."

"That doesn't tell me a lot about her except that she sees herself as an extension of other people," he said. "What do those other people think about her?"

"Her husband wishes that he were married to someone else. Her children don't think much about her at all unless she forgets to pick them up at school. Her maid takes care of her house. Her brother and sister wish that she would stop dumping her problems on them, and her mother-in-law thinks she's totally incompetent."

"And you see yourself as pretty much all of the above?"

"I guess so."

"Not a very good self-image, is it?"

"Not very." She looked down at her hands again.

"Have you been taking a lot of pills to get away from someone you don't like very much?" He shifted gears again.

"You've been talking to Beck," she said defensively.

"It's become a problem, hasn't it?"

"I guess," she whispered.

"You know you're going to have to do something to solve this problem, Laura."

"Will you help me?" She turned the big, blue-grey eyes on his face, and he tried to keep them locked there by the force of his own gaze. If she looked at her lap he would lose her.

"In every way that I can," he promised, leaning closer and gripping her hands. "Don't throw away what could be a good, happy, productive life, Laura. I don't know whether or not you and Beck have any future together, but I'd like to think that you as an individual have a good future, with or without him. The decisions about where things go from here are all yours. Do you believe me?"

"I wish I were as confident as you that people can simply take control of their lives and turn things around," she said. "I think a lot about my mother's life, about her death. Toward the end of her life she never even left her room. She was buried on a beautiful April morning when it sounded like every bird in the world was singing, and the air smelled so good, and Kick slapped Lilly for saying that Mother had finally gotten what she wanted. I don't want to be my mother."

"Then don't be. It's your choice, Laura, and you do have a choice you know."

"I guess I do, don't I?" The briefest hint of a smile flickered across the tear streaked face, and she felt again the little tugging of hope.

"Thank you, Duncan." She slipped back into the jacket and walked to the door, unaware that she had bitten off not only her lipstick but a good portion of her left thumbnail as well.

She hesitated as though there was something else she wanted to tell him. A brief shadow crossed her face before she turned and literally ran from his office.

Duncan stared at the closed door long after she had gone.

Laura's escape mechanism was a symptom of some larger problem. He was sure of that. Life was a complex puzzle, and in Laura's case some of the pieces were still missing.

On his first visit to Duncan Eagan's office, Beck Kimble was as uncomfortable as Laura had been.

Unlike his wife, however, Beck was adept at hiding any nervousness he felt even from himself. The field of combat had changed. This time it was Duncan behind the desk and Beck the visiting challenger.

"How about coffee?" Duncan asked in an effort to put Beck at ease. He came around the desk and took a seat in the chair that matched the one in which Beck held a stiff-postured seat.

"I'm not here for coffee and chitchat, Eagan." Beck declined with a sour expression. "If I'm going to pay you to waste my valuable time, we might as well get down to discussing Laura."

"Let's discuss you instead." Duncan gave Beck a relaxed smile.

"Me?" Beck snorted. "There's nothing wrong with me."

"I didn't say there was," Duncan responded in the same affable tone of voice. There had to be a way to penetrate the defenses of what he suspected was a man very nearly as unhappy as the woman with whom he shared his life. He didn't think it would happen today, but given the luxury of time, it would happen eventually.

"Tell me about yourself and Laura, about your family," Duncan continued, leveling a gaze at Beck that the other man met with equanimity. Beck had years of practice in staring people down, but he had met his match in Duncan Eagan.

"As I told you, she has a perfect life." Beck wanted to shift the focus of the conversation away from himself. "All of her needs are met. She doesn't have to lift a finger and most days doesn't."

"What does she do all day?" Duncan asked, mentally noting that sheer boredom probably loomed large enough in Laura's life to make it a major source of problems. He had been popular with rich women in Chicago, and he had seen the deadening results of too much time and too little to do more than once.

"All sorts of useful things." Beck gave the other man a sarcastic smile. "Shops compulsively, gets her hair done, talks on the telephone, reads magazines, just sits staring into space."

"I expect the children take up a great deal of her time," Duncan interjected.

"Oh, right." Beck laughed unpleasantly. "She complains about all the car pools she has to drive and then forgets to pick them up about ninety percent of the time."

"What happens when she forgets? How do the children get home?"

"The school calls my mother, or my office, or one of the other mothers."

Duncan could well imagine the scenario. Someone else fetched the children and then followed up by reminding Laura that she was incompetent.

"Take what happened last week for example. My mother was, naturally, enormously irritated when her bridge game was interrupted by a call from the kindergarten teacher. Mother sent her maid, Grace, to get the children, and when Grace drove up at our house with them Laura was getting out of the car with ten boxes of new shoes. In that sort of situation Laura deserves to be reprimanded." Beck's choice of words made his wife sound like a disobedient child.

"Sometimes the children call my office, and I have to send one of my secretaries, but now that that stupid Bridget has ruined her life by getting hooked up with Laura's oversexed brother we're going to be shorthanded. Damned guy had the nerve to offer to buy my children a puppy. Can you believe it? It would probably dig up every azalea in the yard."

"You don't like dogs very much I gather?" Duncan asked as he tried to compartmentalize Beck's dissembling.

"No, I don't. My mother would never allow animals in the house. She reminds me regularly that the filthy cat that Lilly gave the children probably harbors all sorts of diseases. Sunburn, Sunshine, I can't remember what the hell they call the animal. I've tried to catch her in the driveway so that I can run over her."

"Sounds like your mother exerts a great deal of influence at your house." Duncan hoped that Beck was too busy holding his position on the soapbox to recognize a leading question.

"Someone has to see to it that things are run properly," Beck sniffed. "Laura cannot keep a maid for more than a few days because she can't seem to convey to them what is expected. If Mother didn't come in to give directions and then follow up and fire them when her instructions aren't followed properly, nothing would ever get done around our house."

Duncan felt a stirring of disgust and wasn't sure whether it was because Laura "couldn't keep a maid" or because her mother-in-law ran off what help she did have.

"You certainly have a beautiful home. I imagine you and Laura entertain frequently."

"Sure, doesn't everyone?" Beck asked. Duncan pictured his own one bedroom apartment. He wouldn't have room to entertain if he knew anyone in town to invite to dinner.

"Most women seem to have that one special recipe that they won't share, don't they?"

"Laura? Recipes? You've got to be kidding." Beck erupted with sardonic laughter. "Laura has never cooked anything more complicated than scrambled eggs, and she can even screw up something as simple as that. The longest time Laura ever spent in the kitchen was the hour she spent trying to figure out how to program into the telephone the number of that grocery store that delivers so that she can order dinner by punching one number instead of seven."

"She mentioned that she used to enjoy art classes. It's too bad she doesn't do much with that any more." Duncan continued to probe for Beck's opinions.

"Actually she was pretty damn good," Beck mused. "She's no Michelangelo, but she's got a good sense of color."

"Yes, I can tell that from your house," Duncan agreed.

"She had nothing to do with that. She brought in some hot shot Atlanta decorator who stayed about a month and sent me an outrageous bill for the thousands of dollars it cost to swaddle our bedroom in flowered English chintz. I get a headache every time I go in the room. Laura would have gone along if he'd told her to paint the whole house black. She's totally incapable of deciding anything for herself. I'm sure he got some kind of kickback on that fabric."

Duncan added the decorator to his mental list of Beck's perceived enemies.

"I believe Laura mentioned something about your adding on a bedroom for yourself," Duncan said as casually as he could. He didn't want to get Beck's guard up by implying that he and Laura had spent their time discussing her husband.

"Should have done it when we bought the house." Beck smiled. "My father and mother never shared the same room, and it was a very satisfactory arrangement. Why bother having some woman and all her clothes and makeup around when you can have peace and privacy?"

"Might I suggest that sex is usually one of the main reasons people share a bedroom?" Duncan asked.

"I imagine my father found more of that away from home anyway. I'm sure Laura will be willing enough to make a trip down the hall when I call her. I'm having a buzzer installed."

His smile was not returned as Duncan glanced at the chiming clock and wondered why an hour was never enough.

In the red Jaguar Edmund and Lilly sped north, then west. Driving was one of the few things Edmund did with abandon, and they made excellent time in the finely tuned car.

They had traveled these roads on past pilgrimages. Lilly wondered wistfully if she ever would again.

Through the Great Glen they came to the ferry port of Kyle of Lochalsh where they took the short boat trip over the Sound of Sleate to Kyleakin and the Isle of Skye.

Checking into a seventeenth century inn, Lilly was eager to drop her baggage and see what changes time had wrought in her favorite group of islands.

Little had changed since Lilly's last visit decades before or, for that matter, since the days of a lost-cause prince and a girl called Flora Macdonald whose memory is honored by a Celtic cross in Kilmuir churchyard.

They played tourist for a short, sunny span of days on the islands where the fairies are said to have built their bridges and castles and bequeathed their magical battle flag to the Clan MacLeod of Dunvegan Castle.

There is magic everywhere in the Hebrides, in the misty black gabbro mountains and the fanciful names of Iona, Eigg, Rhum, Tyree, and Colonsay.

Visiting one of the last outposts of the Gaelic way of life, Lilly and Edmund island-hopped to familiar destinations where the links to the past still held firm and strong.

On Harris, Lilly bought yards of handwoven tweed while Edmund conversed in the ancient language that is the Scottish form of Celtic with the women who spin the virgin wool on hand looms. He seemed at home in the "black houses," low, thatched, windowless one-room buildings in which humans and animals have sheltered together for centuries. Lilly listened as Edmund joined in singing the Gaelic folk songs on the island of Barra and knew that he was in the land of his roots.

On these islands, "the Kingdom of the Western Isles," Scottish kings had their ancient burial ground, Reilig Oran, final resting place of Macbeth and Duncan. The fog swirled in a mystical, spiritual atmosphere that Lilly drank deeply to replenish a searching soul.

A magic land in many ways, it was for them a place to drift back through the mists of time, through the music, the ceol beag played on the bagpipes, and the classical strains of the Piobairochd. Unpronounceable names for beautiful, haunting music. In a local artisan's shop Edmund bought Lilly a necklace wrought with the mysterious Pictish symbols of Z-rod and disc.

Happily caught up in past and present, sad future for a while forgotten, they took the ferries and chartered boats when necessary, going from island to island, visiting the monoliths and chambered cairns of North Uist, walking on the sandy beaches of Barra. On the island of Staffa they visited Fingal's Cave, called in Gaelic "An Uamh Ehinn," the musical cave, and stood between its six-sided pillars of standing rocks, listening to the songs sung by the pounding sea.

The nature of idylls is that they are sweet in their brevity, and too soon Lilly and Edmund ferried back to the mainland and turned the car toward home.

In the short days following, they managed to visit Deer Abbey and enjoyed a memorable meal of venison and game pie. It was a restaurant dinner rather than a picnic, but it sufficed.

They didn't find the day necessary for sea angling but did arrange a morning's fishing from the breakwaters at Lossiemouth and an afternoon of golf.

The grouse were saved Lilly's expertise with a gun, but she promised them, not really believing it, that she'd be back next year.

CHAPTER NINETEEN

*D*uncan buttered a blueberry muffin and removed the top from a paper container of coffee. A regular at the little French bakery on the town square, he knew that he was going to miss this morning routine after the new year when, he promised himself, he was going to do something about his extra weight.

Eating at home by himself was lonely, but eating every meal out provided too much temptation to live on bakery goods and French fries.

The muffin was delicious. Maybe, if he took Jack's challenge to renew their old rivalry at handball, he could continue to patronize the bakery. Duncan had put Jack off, afraid of the old memories that came along with old friends, and buried himself in work.

He had not allowed himself to make any new friends, a feat not particularly difficult given the closed society of a small town. The chains of friendships in a place like Brierley were forged of links from a common past which he did not share.

Losing himself in work wasn't difficult. Duncan had found more demand for his specialty than he would have dreamed possible in a town the size of Brierley. He listened to problems real and imagined all day, everyday, and three nights a week as well.

He was smart, well trained, and very good at what he did. His chief problem was that as a Midwesterner he was often baffled by the southern minds with which he now came in contact. The sanest members of the population were hard to figure out at times. The people of Brierley were like members of some long lost tribe, sharing their language, and customs, and hierarchies with outsiders only when they chose to do so.

Some of it he found amusing. There was a great emphasis on family and a maddeningly confusing custom of repeating the same name over and over in succeeding generations.

In Duncan's family both his mother and grandmother shared the same first name. Confusion was avoided by calling one Margaret and the other Peggy. In Brierley they would have been "Big" Margaret and "Little" Margaret. There were dozens of "bigs" and "littles" in Brierley, and in no case was the reference to size. Duncan's barber was a three hundred pound behemoth who answered to "Little" Jim Bob.

There were also a great many women with names double or diminutive. In one morning he met Elizabeth Sue, Martha Jean, and Betty Ann, followed by two large women with the curious nicknames of Bitsy and Tee Weeney.

Some days he longed for the simple normality of his hometown in Indiana. Other days he found Brierley a hell of a lot more interesting.

He looked over the growing file marked "Kimble" as he waited for Laura, his first appointment of the morning. He considered subdividing the file according to the emotions represented. Resentment, fear, manipulation, emptiness ran amok in the big house that presented such a perfect front to the world passing by outside.

"I hope I'm not late." Laura entered and smiled at him with the expressive, blue-grey eyes lowered. She had a way of averting her eyes so that they revealed very little of what she felt. "I've been tearing my hair out trying to finish the children's Halloween costumes. No sooner do I get one get-up put together than they decide to be something else entirely. I spent two hours at the sewing machine this morning trying to transform a swamp monster into a Druid. Can't think where a five year old child ever even heard of Druids. Some of Lilly's nonsense I expect." She looked up and rolled her eyes.

"Finish your breakfast," she added, eyeing the half-eaten muffin and cooling coffee on his desk. He took the chair beside her.

"Guess what!" She was almost childlike in her enthusiasm and her desire to share something she was obviously bursting to tell him. It was a Laura he hadn't seen before today. He liked this glimpse of a Laura he didn't know.

"You know we're adding on to our house, and they've moved much faster than they expected." She rushed on breathlessly. When Laura had a lot to say, she talked in a manner that would translate on paper to sentences without any periods.

"I called the decorator we used before, and he's going to be all tied up for two months and can't come."

"And?" Duncan asked as she paused for breath, a look of triumph on her face.

"And so I decided to pick everything out myself!" Her self-satisfaction was obvious. "Remember how you told me to find something in my life and just take charge of it? That's what I'm doing."

"And how does it make you feel?" he asked, pleased at her news and her bubbly enthusiasm.

"Scared to death!"

"What does Beck say about this? Isn't it his bedroom?"

"He doesn't think I can do it, but, you know, I think he's proud of me for trying."

"Laura, do you know that you look happy?" he asked softly.

"I know. I've been so busy with this project and the bingo games I've started at the nursing home. You wouldn't believe how those sweet little old ladies like to gamble for dime store prizes! Being busy makes the bad times come further apart. It really does."

"How about your mother-in-law? What does she think about your projects?"

"Maybe that's one reason I'm happy. She's away getting her eyes retucked or something. We haven't seen her in a week." Laura laughed again.

"What about the holidays coming up? Holidays are hard for people sometimes."

"Well, we always go to Lilly's house for Thanksgiving dinner so I don't have to do anything," she said, slowly, as if thinking about how one handled holidays. "Beck and I usually go to New York to go Christmas shopping, but I don't know if I want to do that this year. I don't want to go away with him." The rabbit was back.

"You've got an easy out, you know." He tried to will her to raise the downcast eyes and look at him. "Tell him you're terribly busy with the plans for the renovation."

"But that would be lying," she said hesitantly. "I've done my part of that, choosing the colors and fabrics and telling the store what to send out. It's all being handled by someone else now."

Her words struck a chord in Duncan. Having most of the responsibilities in her life "handled" by someone else was one of her biggest problems.

"Laura, you have a beautiful yard. Who keeps your yard in such perfect shape?" he asked in his carefully structured but disconcerting way of seeming to entirely change the subject in the middle of a sentence.

"The yard service does," she answered automatically as if he'd asked the dumbest question in the world. "Do you need someone to work in your yard?"

"I don't have a yard. I live in a small apartment."

"I'm not following you," she said, frowning at him.

"I want you to do something. When you leave here go by the nursery and buy a big bag of bulbs. Go home and plant them."

"I'd mess up my manicure." The response came as automatically as the comment about the yard.

"So get your fingernails redone tomorrow. Plant those bulbs, and think about how they'll look next spring. Think about how good you'll feel when it's February, and it's cold, and spring feels far away, and one morning you look outside and see those little green tulip shoots coming up. When that happens, I want you to think about today and realize how very far you've come."

"You know, it would be nice to have some tulips. Maybe some hyacinths." There was a dreamy, faraway look on her face. "My grandmother always forced hyacinths in the winter. She had pots and pots of them in her morning room, and they smelled wonderful. They smelled like spring was coming."

"It must have been wonderful growing up with your grandparents around." He wanted to hear about her childhood without having to ask her about it directly.

"Actually they died when I was pretty small." She looked down at her hands again. "Lilly and Kick thought they were absolutely fabulous." She closed her eyes, caught up in memories to which he had no access.

"I was scared to death of my grandmother. I don't think she liked my mother or me very much. She didn't think much of Daddy either, but then he wasn't around all the time like we were."

"You loved your mother?"

"I adored my mother. She didn't come out of her room much, but every night, before Desia put me to bed, I'd go in Mother's room, and she'd brush my hair. She told me I had fairy-princess hair that was spun from gold. I imagined that my mother didn't come out of her room because she was a beautiful queen locked away in a tower. Of course, when my father went away, I just pretended that he was the handsome knight off on a quest."

"And what was it like when your father was at home?" Duncan asked.

"My father was so big, and so handsome, and he had a moustache that tickled when he kissed me goodnight. He made me feel safe from dragons and monsters and the dark outside my window."

She closed her eyes. "When my father was around he made me feel like I was a special princess. My father read stories to me sometimes, but my mother's stories were better because she made them up."

"It's time to put the fairy princess back in the story book," Duncan said gently. "Your hair is beautiful, but it's not spun gold, is it?"

"I don't care about being a princess with golden hair." She looked at him longingly. "I guess the part of the story that I want to believe is the ending, the part about happily ever after."

"Trick or treat, lady. I am here to drink your blood, but if you have none, I will settle for beer instead."

"Come in, Dracula, and let's see if we can quench your thirst with something." Laura laughed at the sight of her huge brother in full Halloween regalia. He wore a long black cape over a formal, tucked dress shirt and tuxedo pants and had obviously been playing in Bridget's makeup.

"I'm not sure the children are safe on the street with me," he said. "Somehow the glasses just spoiled the look, and you know I'm blind as a bat without them."

"Some people just can't seem to grow up," Beck said as he passed them in the hall. "I hope you know how ridiculous you look."

Kick was saved from making a nasty reply by the shouted greetings of Sam and Marion, dressed respectively as a Druid and a ballerina. Brook felt that he was too old to participate in the trick-or-treating ritual. He and Beck were going to a movie instead.

"Have a popcorn ball before you go," Laura said, offering her brother a basket of cellophane and orange ribbon tied treats.

"Delicious," he said as he took a big bite. "Where'd you buy these? They're as good as the ones Desia used to make."

"That's because I used Desia's recipe," she said with a big grin. "I made them myself."

"Good for you!" Taking a child by each hand, Kick left to make the rounds of the neighborhood.

"Waste of time," Beck muttered. "You know children aren't allowed to take homemade treats anymore. I hope you didn't forget to put in the razor blades."

Laura's face fell. "What am I supposed to give the kids who ring our doorbell?"

"Go raid Sam's piggy bank and give them change. Kids today would rather have money than candy anyway. Probably half of them are on drugs. Maybe you could find some extra pills in your medicine cabinet. Better yet, just turn off the light and ignore the door. You know how I hate these stupid holidays."

Jack-o'-lantern light illuminated their way as Kick and the children stopped at house after house. He snapped pictures of other groups of goblins as they made their way to the center of town.

"There aren't any houses around here," Sam complained. "Where are we going?"

"To the graveyard, my dear," he whispered in what he hoped sounded like a Transylvanian accent. He had had a photographic assignment in Transylvania once and found that the people there didn't sound at all like the movie concept. "Lilly and I used to visit the graveyard every Halloween. She liked to share her candy with the ghosts there."

Kick led the children through the wrought iron gates of the century old consecrated grounds across from the Episcopal and Presbyterian churches. It was a perfect night with a full moon occasionally obscured by scudding clouds and gusts of wind whipping the trees.

Kick had spent a whole afternoon in the cemetery the week before, photographing the old headstones, final milestone markers of the prominent lives in the town's history. He knew his way around pretty well even without his glasses on.

"Look at this one. Isn't this great? 'Died from drowning while taking his weekly bath.' Don't you just love it? Some of these old inscriptions are just hilarious!"

Marion stuck to his side like glue. She wanted to go home. Sam, however, skipped through the tombstones, looking in her long white "Druid" robes like a lively little ghost, dropping candy on selected graves.

"Uncle Kick, Uncle Kick!" she suddenly screamed. "Look in this little play yard. There's our name. I can read our name."

"That little 'play yard' is our family plot," he said as he and Marion joined her outside the ornate iron fence separating the Lambeths from the rest of the town folks.

"What a pretty angel," Marion said softly. "She looks so sad though."

Kick felt a shadow cross his heart and wished he hadn't brought them on this lark. He looked at the carved-marble headstone on top of his mother's grave, the headstone he had commissioned by a New York sculptor friend and installed himself.

Marion's comment made him realize why the figure had always looked so appropriate to him.

It was, like the mother he remembered, an angel with a pretty face, missing only a smile.

All Saints Day was a reflective day in a poignant season of the year. There were purple asters and white lilies on the altar when Duncan stopped in church to light a candle.

Prayers for the souls of the dead would have to wait for another day when he had more time. Just too many to pray for. Except for a sister his whole family was gone.

He sat in his office waiting for Laura, thinking that some people couldn't seem to take advantage of the things real living offered. He felt not a trace of condemnation for her situation. Material goods were worthless when the spirit was caught in a terrible cycle of poverty.

Somehow he had to get at the root of what was devouring Laura's sense of well being. It was more than a self-centered husband and more than an escape in drugs. It was something private, something deep inside of her.

Laura came in mumbling apologies for being late. This struck Duncan as odd because she was usually late and usually seemed unaware of the fact.

"I was caught in a long line at the grocery store," she said with a visible shudder. "It was awful. I had to just abandon my cart right in the middle of the aisle."

"You're not that late. You should have finished your shopping. Now you'll have to go back later."

"I can't. I can't go back in that store. I thought I could. I thought the lines would be short this time of day." She shuddered.

"You don't impress me as the impatient type," he said.

"I get so sick. I get so scared. I can't get my breath, and my eyes won't focus, and my hands start to shake." She blurted it out as much to herself as to Duncan.

"This happens to you in stores?" He held his breath waiting for her answer.

"It happens to me everywhere except at home. It's getting so bad that I'm scared to go out. Everyone thinks I'm lazy, but I would love to be able to do the things normal people do. They don't understand. I can't cook because I'm afraid I'll have one of these attacks and pass out and burn the house down. I can't go in a restaurant because I'm so afraid of choking to death and embarrassing Beck. I'm just like my mother, and Beck's going to leave me just like my father left her. I have all these weird symptoms. I don't know whether I'm physically sick or just going completely nuts. Help me, Duncan." She started to cry.

Suddenly all the pieces fell into place. The family history, the fairy-tale fantasies of being taken care of, the constant self-criticism and lack of self-esteem, the sublimation to a dominant husband were all textbook symptoms of a panic-prone personality.

Laura's demons could be categorized by a variety of clinical names from generalized anxiety disorder to agoraphobia, but the common element in a condition like hers was the terrible fear of loss of control. Fear that took on a life of its own and took her life out of her hands.

Laura had just handed him the key that would open the door to the hay-wire house of her mind.

She was fueled by fear, and apparently what she was most afraid of was herself.

There were no tents in the spring sunshine or massive arrangements of flowers from the gardens of Summerfield House when Cait and Anthony exchanged their vows, but, if anyone regretted the fact, they kept tactfully silent.

Instead the ceremony was a simple one with only family and a few of Edmund's village friends invited. Lilly included among the guests her old friend from the off-license shop and one or two others still around from the days when she was a young bride.

Lilly kept her sentimental tears to a respectable mother-of-the-bride minimum as Cait made the traditional walk down the aisle of the ancient kirk on her father's arm. The only extravagant display of emotion came from Peters, the aged crofter, who sobbed noisily throughout the vows. Edmund found this departure from the old man's usual sulky silence so amusing that he was more than able to suppress any outward show of inner feelings himself.

Cait gained a title but signed the parish register with a simple "Mrs."

In the days leading up to the wedding Lilly drove everyone around her to distraction recalling every superstition she had ever heard. No one seemed to notice the chimney sweep standing outside the church, or if they did notice, they little realized that Lilly had hired him to be there, bowing to the old adage that a bride who passes a sweep on her wedding day will carry happiness with her always.

The white horses that pulled the carriage taking the newlyweds off toward their new life had garlands of daisies and roses from Edmund's garden woven through their bridles. White horses for luck, roses for remembrance.

The day after the bride and groom departed on a short honeymoon to Paris, Lilly was in the kitchen climbing down the ladder-like stair from the china room when Edmund called out that he had a surprise for her.

There, among the huge copper fish kettles where years before she had tried to learn to cook the foods he loved, he presented her with his gift, a ring made especially for her, set with a stone of the translucent, yellow quartz crystal found in the granite of the Cairngorms.

He slipped it on her finger, not a wedding band, but a little bit of Scotland, and of himself, to take with her always.

CHAPTER TWENTY

*T*hanksgiving morning dawned cold, and grey, and damp. Storms spawned the previous day by a cold front colliding violently with the last warm temperatures of Indian summer had brought down whole tree limbs along with most of the last of the leaves.

Lilly stood looking out her bedroom window. She felt as woebegone as yesterday's brilliant trees now appeared.

She tried to summon her usual early morning energy, knowing that she ought to be downstairs in the kitchen helping Desia who daily showed increasing signs of age.

Lilly uncharacteristically dreaded the holiday season to come. Christmas seemed to represent a punctuation mark on the calendar instead of a day to celebrate.

Even thinking of the simple ritual of addressing Christmas cards depressed her. The names on the list seemed a reminder of people gone in the year past and people to go in the year to come.

She continued to stare moodily out the window. The big sweet gum in the south pasture was dead, but it had withstood the storm's high winds. It stood still, outlined against the stark November landscape, as it had when her grandfather was a child and for a hundred years before that.

Last as long as you can, Edmund, she sent a silent plea as tears as cold as winter rain dripped slowly down her cheeks. She cursed herself for leaving him, for agreeing to run away when the sun still shone on the hills they loved and the heather held the purple and gold. She twisted the ring with its golden stone around and around on her finger.

After giving her the ring, Edmund told her that he'd booked passage for her on an early morning flight to London.

"Go home, Lilly," he urged despite her protests. "It's been an interlude, and that's all it can be. The past few weeks have been the happiest I will ever know, and I want us to leave it at that. Do that for me."

And so, far sooner than she intended, she left him for the last time.

"Lilly, are you talking to yourself again or have you got a man hidden under your bed?" Kick called out as he banged on the door.

Quickly wiping away the traces of tears, she crossed the room and opened the door to face her brother. His constant good mood was becoming a major source of irritation in her life.

"I think you're lucky your fence is still standing this morning. We have got to find someone to take that big tree down," he said, striding into the room and flopping down on her bed.

"Leave it until it falls. I don't want it cut down," she snapped at him.

"Lilly, be reasonable. I know how much you love that tree, but if you let it fall you'll have a major fence repair on your hands. Trees die, that one has, and it needs to go."

"Well, maybe I don't want it to be dead!" she screamed, startling him into a sitting position. "You have trees of your own now. Go cut one of them down. This is my damn house and my damn yard, and that tree is staying right where it is until God decides otherwise."

"Lilly, what in the world is wrong with you? You're driving everyone around here crazy with this black mood." He looked at her closely for the first time since he'd entered the room and realized that she'd been crying.

"I'm sorry if I'm driving you and your teenaged wife crazy. Like I said, it's my house, and the sooner you're both out the better."

"Lilly, I am going to ignore that remark," he said quietly, wondering if he and Bridget should find some place to rent until their house became habitable. Buying Lucille Trainer's house after she was moved to a nursing home seemed a brilliant idea at the time he did it. Bridget was thrilled at the prospect of living in the big house next door to Laura. Some days it seemed as if the renovation were going to take years instead of a few months, and he wondered if he had made a mistake. He knew that it was an imposition for Lilly to have them underfoot.

He also knew that their presence alone was not enough to precipitate the kind of reaction his sister had just had.

"I agree that I've overstayed my welcome, but I don't intend to leave this room until you tell me what's wrong. You haven't been yourself since before you left for England."

He rose from the bed and closed the heavy door even though he knew that Desia was busy in the kitchen, Bridget was out taking a walk in the woods, and there was no one else around to overhear their conversation.

"I'm sorry, Kick." She collapsed in a chair with her head in her hands and began to cry again. "I can't talk about it."

"Lilly, I know you better than anyone else in this world does, and I've known for days that you have some major problem. I repeat that I am not leaving this room until you talk about it even if it means growing old standing here."

"Edmund is sick, very sick." She looked up at her brother through her tears.

"Oh, Lilly, I'm so sorry." He crossed the room to sit on the floor at her feet. "Just when the two of you were making noises like you were going to get back together. What awful timing."

"The last couple of weeks with him were wonderful, Kick," she sobbed. "Why did I throw all those years away? I've never loved anybody but him, and now it's too late to do anything about it."

"Well, there's got to be something we can do, Lilly." He looked up at her, hating the misery written on her face. "We'll just find the best doctor there is."

"That's what I suggested," she said bitterly. "He reminded me that there are some problems you can't buy your way out of. It's true, Kick, and it scares me. All our lives we've operated more or less under the assumption that whenever something went wrong we could pay somebody to fix it or to make it go away."

They sat in silence for a few minutes until Kick spoke again. "How is Cait handling all this?"

"She doesn't even know, and I feel so guilty about that," Lilly said miserably. "It just didn't seem right to spoil what should be the happiest time of her life. She and her father are so close, and it's going to be devastating for her when he dies." She drew in her breath sharply. She'd said it out loud, the words hung cold and ugly in the air.

"How long, Lilly?" Kick asked gently.

"How long does anyone have?" she asked. "I thought for a while yesterday that storm was going to blow us away. There's some sort of remission right now, but they've told him that when it comes back it will do so with a vengeance. At that point probably no more than a few weeks."

"Are you going back to Scotland?"

"No, he's very determined that I not do that, and I have to respect his wishes. I left him years ago during what could have been the best of times, and I have no right to ask him now to let me share the worst."

"Lilly, did you ever stop to think that he loves you enough to want to have some say so in your memories?"

"I know you're right, I know he's right, but I look at him, and I look at the mess Laura's making of her life, and sometimes, Kick, it just seems like life's a big bowl of jelly beans, and I keep reaching in for red ones and coming up with those nasty black ones instead."

"I always knew you had a calling." He laughed. "Maybe you should have been a philosopher."

She playfully hit him on the head with a pillow. "You were the one who was going to be a philosopher, remember? You were about thirteen years old when you announced one morning at breakfast that philosophy was your life's ambition. When Grandfather asked you what philosophers did you said they wrote poems that don't rhyme."

"Some poems don't make much sense either, Lilly." He took her face in his big hands and gently wiped away the tears with his thumbs. "Neither does life when you get right down to it. You try to write your own book, and the characters keep doing things you didn't expect them to. Look at what's happened to me. I was so bored, and so restless, and out of the blue along came Bridget."

"I'm still trying to absorb the fact that you've actually pulled the most impetuous stunt of your life," she said as she crossed the room and pulled a thick Aran sweater, a Scottish sweater, from a drawer. "I do like her, Kick, and I truly hope you're going to be happy together."

"As crazy as it all seems, Lilly, I never dreamed a person could be as totally happy as I am. It was like all my life I had this mental image of the person I was meant to be with, and suddenly there she was. It happened very quickly, but believe me I've been looking for her for a very long time. The fact that she's a lot younger than I am has nothing to do with anything. Maybe it was fate, who knows?"

"My brother the philosopher." Lilly laughed. "Let's go see what we can do to help Desia. At the pace she moves these days it might be Christmas before she gets Thanksgiving dinner on the table, and after the kids get here you know it will be bedlam."

"Laura, will you please hurry up in there." Beck rattled the handle of the locked bathroom door. "Marion needs her hair braided."

"Tell her to wear it loose with that plaid bow." Laura lifted her head from its position inches above the toilet bowl and tried to control her nausea.

"Anything you say," he said in what he hoped was a compliant voice. Laura's shrink insisted that he participate in the day-to-day activities of the family, and, for the same reason that he attended the hated sessions, he was trying to comply.

If Jack Connor ever gave up medicine, he could choose a second career in blackmail. Agreeing to the initial appointment to get Jack off his back, Beck never dreamed that his participation in a lot of unnecessary therapy sessions would be a part of the bargain on which Jack continued to follow up. Beck spent as much time in Duncan Eagan's office as Laura did.

He grudgingly admitted that Laura was making surprising changes in her life. Her alarming new assertiveness was something he wasn't sure he was prepared to accept.

Beck wasn't accustomed to having Laura disagree with him, or make even small decisions without first consulting him. He almost fainted when she drove up with a car full of grocery bags and announced her intention to cook pork chops and a squash casserole for dinner.

The addition to the house had been completed in record time thanks to good weather and a generous bonus for the recovering contractor. It amazed Beck when Laura proposed to decorate it herself instead of simply writing checks for the implementation of someone else's ideas. She had done an outstanding job. Lately he found himself wishing he wasn't sleeping a long upstairs hall away from her.

Jack had a serious talk with him about the necessity of avoiding sex until Laura's injuries healed, and he hadn't the nerve to do anything but go along. It didn't take a genius to anticipate the amount of trouble Jack was prepared to cause him.

He looked at the closed bedroom door and resolved to reopen it that night.

While not a changed man, Beck was very much aware that he had been a lucky one in escaping more than minimal repercussions.

Kick and Bridget took off on a quick honeymoon to New York, and Lilly remained in Scotland much longer than originally planned. By the time either one of them saw Laura, the physical evidence was gone.

His mother somehow got wind of the fact that Laura was in the hospital, but fortunately Laura didn't contradict when he told his mother a fabrication about a taxicab accident.

Beck had gotten off fairly lightly. He was minding his manners as far as sex with Laura, or anyone else, was concerned.

The process of interviewing candidates to replace Bridget continued.

Desia reluctantly accepted help with the table setting. Lilly puttered around in the dining room arranging her grandmother's heavy sterling flatware at eight places. Were the children old enough to be included at the grown-ups' table?

If Kick added the leaves the table easily sat twelve. She thought about poor little Marion's uncharacteristic clumsiness in her grandmother's presence and decided to leave things as they were with the children eating in the kitchen with Desia. Lilly wished she could have Thanksgiving dinner in the kitchen with them.

On the sideboard, platters and chased-silver casseroles awaited their steaming contents. For countless Thanksgiving dinners the table had held the same moist cornbread dressing, green beans, sweet potatoes drunk-with-rum nestled under marshmallow blankets, and Desia's specialty, cinnamon-spicy baked apples. From the kitchen came the scents of allspice, cloves, and nutmeg, comforting, home-for-the-holidays smells associated with childhood celebrations.

In the kitchen Kick carved turkey, every other bite going straight into his mouth.

"Don't you forget those eyes in the back of my head," Desia said over her shoulder. "You're going to spoil your lunch and eat up all my turkey besides that. At your age I'd hate to have to pop your hand."

Kick looked at the huge turkey and laughed. On an average day Desia cooked as if she expected a hungry army to materialize at the table, and on holidays she really went overboard.

She dusted flour from her hands, took a hot casserole from the oven, and passed him a spoon.

"What's that for?" he asked innocently.

"For the bite of dressing you're going to sneak when you think I'm not looking," she answered.

"Know me pretty well, don't you?"

They both laughed as he stuffed a big piece of turkey in his mouth.

Beck and Laura, Eleanor, Kick, and the Dudleys were assembled in the library having Bloody Marys before a roaring fire. It created a nice atmosphere but made the room too warm for the day.

Laura sat uncomfortably, wishing that she had called Lilly, begged off lunch with the excuse of an upset stomach, and gone back to bed.

Eleanor, who could be charming when she chose to be, questioned Max about the renovation of Bridget and Kick's new home.

"In what kind of general condition did you find the house?" Eleanor asked. "I can't imagine that anything has been done to that house in years. Of course Kick has never been a very practical man. Just like him to rush into buying something without so much as an inspection." She waited expectantly for his reply that the foundation had serious weaknesses.

"Well, let's just say that Bridget didn't consider saving any of the drapes or wallpaper." Max laughed. "Structurally the house is in excellent shape. You can't duplicate today the craftsmanship available when it was built in the early 1920s. It was first-class construction. My only problem with the house is visualizing my little girl keeping up a place that size."

Lilly stuck her head in the library and interrupted, asking Laura to help her in the kitchen on a pretense of spending some time alone with her sister. Laura reluctantly got to her feet and followed.

"Are you feeling okay?" Lilly frowned at Laura's pallor.

"No, and I probably shouldn't have come," Laura replied in a weak voice. "I've picked up some kind of intestinal flu, and I really feel rotten."

"Laura, I feel like I've hardly talked to you in months." Lilly, without being asked, prepared her sister a cup of weak tea. "Tell me what's going on in your life."

"Oh, not much," Laura hedged. It was a relief to have Lilly out of the country and unaware of the explosion with Beck and their visits to the therapist.

With Lilly away and Kick involved in his book and his new wife, neither had had much recent contact with Laura. They were both in the dark about current events.

Lilly chattered on about Cait's wedding, and Kick, and her efforts to find a Christmas pony for Sam, and Laura felt too wretched to do anything but sit quietly and nod at appropriate times.

Amanda joined Lilly and Laura in the kitchen. The conversation in the library focused on economic matters, a subject that she didn't understand.

"I was just telling Laura how much I love having Bridget in the family." Lilly gave Amanda a warm smile. "I don't think I've ever seen my brother this happy. I do wish that your other children could have joined us for lunch."

"I wouldn't bring that crowd en masse to my worst enemy's house." Amanda rolled her eyes and shook her head. "It's a tradition at our house to share the Thanksgiving meal at night. Hopefully they are at the moment all busy doing their assigned chores."

"It must be nice growing up in a house full of people," Laura said wistfully. "I always made up a lot of imaginary playmates when I was a little girl."

Lilly bit her lip as she looked at her sister's sad, beautiful face and wished she could rewrite the past. Bah humbug on holidays for the sour memories they brought.

The quiet child with the big eyes, dressed up in imported French laces and satin hair ribbons and shown off to relatives at other Thanksgiving dinners, sat today wearing a cream-colored cashmere dress and much the same expression of haunted desperation. How she must hate even coming back to this house.

"Lilly, do you think I could go upstairs and lie down for a few minutes before lunch?" Laura looked as shaky as she felt.

"Of course, Laura," Lilly replied quickly. "We won't eat for at least an hour."

Lilly returned to her guests in the library.

"Where's Laura?" Fidgeting the whole time his wife was closeted with her sister in the kitchen, Beck didn't put it past Lilly to have pulled the whole story, "blow by blow" as it were, out of his wife.

"She's upstairs resting. I don't think she's feeling well," Lilly answered. She accepted a Bloody Mary that she had no intention of drinking from Beck. She knew from past experience how lethal Beck's cocktails could be when the vodka was coming out of someone else's liquor cabinet.

"Every time she goes to that kindergarten she catches something. She's worse than the children," he grumbled, relieved that Lilly wasn't reaching for his throat. "They had some Pilgrim and Indian production the other day, and she insisted on attending because Sam was playing the turkey. I guess she picked this stomach thing up then. Usually it's a raging cold."

"I think she just enjoys poor health," Eleanor added. "I've never known anyone so enamored of running to doctors as Laura seems to be."

"Well, you're certainly looking well, Eleanor. In fact you look younger by the day," Kick said. He couldn't see that the eye tuck had done much good.

"Where are my grandchildren?" Eleanor did not approve of Kick for a lot of reasons, chief among them being the fact that he was impervious to her bullying.

"Outside playing with the dog and getting thoroughly dirty," he answered.

"I've been meaning to bring that up with you, Kick," Beck spoke up. "I understand you offered to buy my children a dog while we were out of town. I don't mind saying I think it was very presumptuous of you. That cat is enough of a nuisance."

"Not the first time I've been accused of being presumptuous is it, Max?" Kick winked at his father-in-law as he declined Beck's proffered crystal pitcher of thick red tomato mixture and instead took the cap off of a bottle of beer.

Involving Bridget's father in planning the architectural alterations to the Trainer house had, as Kick hoped, served to mellow Max's attitude toward his son-in-law. They were now at a stage in their relationship where friendly banter came easily.

"Next time just bring me a puppy," Max said, slapping Kick on the back.

"There you are!" Kick exclaimed as Bridget entered the room dressed in a honey-colored skirt and dark green silk blouse. "You look beautiful."

"A toast to the bride," Beck said loudly, looking Bridget up and down so suggestively that she blushed.

"And to the groom," Max added expansively, not missing the look of total adoration that Kick gave his daughter. It was going to work out after all.

CHAPTER TWENTY ONE

*T*he sky outside the window frowned grey and gloomy. Inside, the dining room table sparkled with the light from the chandelier reflected in cut-crystal wine glasses.

In portraits hung around the room those long absent from this same table smiled benignly down, frozen in time and mood by forgotten artists. Lilly's eyes swept the walls remembering other Thanksgivings when they also took their seats here. She bowed her head as her brother, commanding what to her would always be Grandfather's place at the head of the table, began to say grace.

Unlike his grandfather, Kick was not accomplished at the art of public prayer, and after a few hastily mumbled sentences he concluded. "And bless especially those who are many miles away but very much here in our hearts, bless those who have been here before us, and those who will join this table in the future. Let the child we expect next summer be born safe, and healthy, and strong. Amen." He grinned and blushed as all eyes opened and turned on him.

Max and Amanda exchanged surprised looks, and Beck, who was more than a little drunk, reached for the wine bottle.

Before anyone could voice congratulations to a beaming Bridget, Laura bolted from the room, overturning her chair in the process.

As they all stared after her, Lilly put her napkin down and rose more gracefully from her own place. She bent to give Bridget a quick kiss before following Laura.

"Well! Times certainly change," Eleanor said, casting a disapproving look at her son who downed his wine as if it were water. "You young people are certainly open about private matters. In my day people with taste didn't talk about such things until they became obvious."

The meal proceeded in silence.

Upstairs, Lilly found Laura in the bathroom retching and weeping. "Let me see if we don't have something you can take for that," she said gently, moistening a towel and handing it to her sobbing sister.

"No medicine. I can't take anything." Laura gasped as another wave of nausea shook her.

"Why not? Stomach upsets usually don't last very long, but that's no reason not to get some relief." Lilly rummaged through the cluttered cabinet, pulling out tubes and bottles, finding remedies for everything except nausea.

"This is going to last a lot longer than twenty-four hours," Laura said miserably. "The other three times it lasted nine long awful months."

A bottle of cough syrup slipped from the astonished Lilly's hand. As the red liquid ran all over the bathroom floor, she said dumbly, "I assume you're telling me that Bridget isn't the only one who is pregnant."

"I can't help it, Lilly, I'm so jealous of them sitting down there being so happy about things." Laura cried as Lilly held the cold towel to her forehead.

"What does Beck have to say?"

"He doesn't know. He's going to be so angry, Lilly. I'm afraid to tell him."

"Well, in the first place it's silly to be afraid of your own husband, and in the second place I should hope he knows by now that the process of conception takes two people. I imagine he was not only present at the creation but a more than willing participant in it."

"I was the one who wasn't willing." Laura looked up at Lilly with eyes full of fears and tears. "And it's not silly to be afraid of him. I know only too well what he's capable of doing when he gets mad."

"Laura, I'm not sure what you're trying to say and not sure I want to know, but I think you'd better tell me anyway."

While downstairs the others made a pretense of enjoying the Thanksgiving feast, Laura told Lilly everything.

"So what are you going to do?" Lilly asked. Finally done with both her nausea and her narrative of the past weeks' events, Laura lay on Lilly's big bed staring out the window at the dark clouds rolling in across the grey November sky. The bare trees did a skeleton dance in the wind.

"I don't seem to have a lot of options, do I?"

"Laura, there are always options," Lilly said angrily. Her mind was whirling. She wanted to go downstairs and kill Beck. The only thing keeping her upstairs was the knowledge that Kick might literally do just that when he heard Laura's story.

"Oh, he says he's perfectly happy to get a divorce, but there's no way he'll let me have the children. Kind of ironic, isn't it, for a man who has never paid the slightest amount of attention to them. Suddenly he's super daddy, and I know it's just his way of being conniving. I don't want Eleanor raising my children." She broke into a fresh wave of sobs as Lilly looked on helplessly.

"Does Eleanor know about all of this?"

"She knows some of it, but I don't know how much. Eleanor would like nothing better than to see me locked up in some mental institution, but I'm not going to give her the satisfaction of letting that happen."

"Laura, you know that Kick and I will give you all the emotional support we can, but I think we need to get someone involved who's trained to deal with this sort of thing. I think you both need some professional help."

Lilly thought about her talk with Edmund and cursed herself that now that the opening for a frank discussion about Laura's problems presented itself she couldn't bring herself to squeeze through it. She was afraid.

"That's the only bright spot in all of this," Laura said. "Jack Connor has been wonderful. He told Beck that if he didn't get some counseling he'd go to the police. He found us this wonderful man who's been such a help to me. I think Beck hates the idea of talking to him, but Jack is more or less blackmailing him into going."

"Good for him." Lilly smiled, relieved that Laura was at least doing something concrete to try to dig herself out of the morass of her life. "And what does this wonderful man suggest that you do?"

"So far we've been concentrating on staying calm, doing the things normal people do, without pills, and that's working pretty well. I can actually go in a store without feeling like I'm going to fall out in a dead faint." Laura sat upright, propping herself against the high-backed headboard with pillows. "It's hard to believe that I put myself through all those years of misery. You can't imagine the relief when I found out why I was having all those strange feelings. I'm trying hard now to tell my mind to leave my body alone, and most days it works."

"Honestly, Lilly, my whole life was revolving around how I could avoid certain situations or get another prescription. I was so tired of it, and I didn't know how to stop it."

"Duncan compared it to living in a waking nightmare, and he was certainly right about that. If I hadn't had Duncan I could never have even started crawling out of the big hole I'd dug for myself. Of course once I suspected I was pregnant it got a lot easier. I don't want to do anything to hurt this baby."

"You want this baby, don't you?"

"Of course I do. Despite the circumstances of its conception, it's still my baby." Laura spoke in such a clear even voice that Lilly began to dare to hope that her sister was actually making progress in getting a handle on her life.

"Have you discussed the baby with your psychiatrist?"

"No. No one knows but you and Jack. As smart as he is, sometimes Beck can be so dense that he can't see what's going on right under his nose if it's easier not to."

Lilly bit her lip. Despite the resolution Laura was expressing she wasn't at all sure that her sister needed a baby at this point in her life. She was sure that Beck meant what he said about taking the children in the event of a divorce and that he'd follow through on his threat out of pure spite.

It wouldn't take a lot to convince a court which of the two parents was the more stable, and Lilly doubted a judge would care which was the more loving. Innocent children trapped in the awful sticky spider web spun by adults.

"Do you ever feel funny sleeping in Grandmother's bed?" Laura broke in on Lilly's thoughts. "I loved to sit on this bed and watch Grandmother brush her hair and do her makeup. I loved the smell of her dusting powder and her hand lotion. Remember that powder, Lilly? It was in a little gold monogrammed ivory box."

Lilly smiled at her sister, grateful that at least some of the memories were good ones. "I not only remember it, I still have it." She reached into the dresser drawer.

Laura removed the lid, bent her face to the box, and sniffed the soft scent of the powder. "Oh, Lilly, what did I ever do to deserve ending up like this? You and Kick always seem to succeed at everything you try, and I just mess up everything I touch." Tears welled up in the grey eyes and slid down her cheeks.

"Excuse me while I fall off my pedestal," Lilly said. "Have you forgotten all the schools that sent Kick home in disgrace or the great success I made of my own marriage? Don't forget that you have three fabulous children who adore you and who don't seem to me to be in the least messed up. At least you've stayed there and been a good mother to them which is a lot more than I can say for myself. When the going got tough at my house I just packed my bags and ran." She thought, but didn't add out loud, or look at Mother who stayed at home and ran away.

Laura seemed to read her mind. "Lilly, I'm so afraid I'm just like Mother. I don't know how Kick can sleep in her bed. It would give me nightmares."

Lilly thought of Kick, more than once since coming back home awakening in Marion Lambeth's bed screaming from nightmares in which he heard her downstairs playing the piano.

Lilly closed her eyes. She didn't allow herself to think about her mother very often, and she tried now to shut out the unbidden image of her, a tiny apparition with enormous eyes and a cloud of soft, dark hair.

From the past came an unpleasant memory of herself at Marion's age, trying to sit still while her mother pulled a silver-backed brush through her tangled hair. She hated my hair, Lilly thought, she hated the fact that my hair would not behave.

As a child Lilly wondered if her mother was like she was because of having a daughter with wild unmanageable hair. Was she the cause of her mother's refusal to leave the house?

"No, you're not like Mother," she said firmly. "Or at least you don't have to be. Mother chose to be a victim."

"Don't say that, Lilly. Mother always sang to me before I went to sleep. She had such a beautiful voice."

"Don't hate her, Lilly. She couldn't help it," Laura pleaded. "She loved us, I know she did. I understand how she felt. Poor Mother was terribly afraid of you, and Daddy, and Grandmother."

"Afraid of us?" Lilly laughed bitterly. "You're probably right. She was afraid of her own shadow."

"Think about it, Lilly. Think about how hard it must have been for her living here with Grandmother acting like the Queen of England running the Empire, and you, and Kick, and Daddy, and Grandfather all so loud, and happy, and alive. I think Mother was afraid of everyone in this house except for me and Desia."

Old emotions assaulted Lilly.

She remembered herself as a teenager, looking longingly at other mothers, mothers who seemed always to be cooking, or going to basketball games, or doing half-a-hundred other normal things that mothers were supposed to do. She thought about the times that she wished her mother dead.

Lilly's mother, for all intents and purposes related to the outside world, was dead for many years before she finally, formally reached the cemetery. It surprised no one when Desia took up the breakfast tray one morning and couldn't wake her.

Lilly wondered whether her father didn't care or didn't want to know whether it was death from natural causes or by her own hand. A question to which there would never be an answer.

Kick cried floods of bitter tears and angrily accused Lilly of having no heart when she stood stony-faced and dry-eyed at the funeral.

Their father died less than a year later, much as he had lived, in a violent car crash with the wife of one of his closest friends as his passenger on the road to hell.

Neither Kick nor Lilly evidenced any signs of grief other than concern for their teenaged sister as Paul Lambeth was put into the earth. It was the first time in years that he lay beside his wife.

"Why do you hate them so much?" Laura pulled her older sister from her private thoughts.

Lilly ran her hand through her hair, remembering vividly the day long ago when she had climbed up in the hayloft to look for a lost kitten and had found instead her father and a woman, not her mother, locked in a tight embrace. How could she find the words to explain to this gentle soul the dim memories of her mother desperately trying too hard to please her arrogant, errant husband? No one had even known where to find Paul Lambeth on the day of Laura's birth.

Hate didn't materialize overnight. Its roots were deep and complicated. In answer to Laura's question she simply shook her head and looked away.

"Do you want to stay here tonight?" Lilly asked, worried about involving Kick in all of this. Kick didn't have Lilly's legendary quick and evil temper, but when he did get mad the emotional intensity was frightening.

"No. I have to face things at home," Laura said with a determination that took Lilly by surprise.

"Laura . . . ," Lilly began hesitantly as her sister moved to the dressing table and began to redo her hair and makeup. "It's none of my business, but I have to ask. Do you love Beck?"

"I don't know, Lilly," Laura said evenly as she examined her reflection and frowned at the circles under her eyes. "Maybe what bothers me the most about all of this is not so much that I'm like Mother but that I married Daddy."

Lilly refrained from agreeing.

"Duncan Eagan is helping me, Lilly, I really believe he is." Laura stood up and smoothed the cashmere dress. "And he's cute too." She flashed Lilly a grin and Lilly smiled back, thinking that with all her insecurities Laura had no idea how beautiful she was. Laura's smile could melt your heart.

Late that night Kick and Lilly sat in the library before a fire burned down to little more than embers. Bridget, pleading exhaustion, had already gone up to bed.

Lilly was tired too and glad that she and her brother at last had a chance to talk alone. As much as she wanted Bridget to feel a part of the family, she didn't feel comfortable sharing Laura's problems with anyone other than her brother.

"Want a brandy?" she asked as he kicked off his shoes and leaned back in one of the big, leather chairs flanking the fireplace.

"No, thanks. I ate too much dinner."

The big setter put his head in Lilly's lap for reassurance. He might not understand what they were talking about, but he was enough attuned to Lilly's moods to know that something was very wrong. Lilly sighed as she scratched the dog's ears.

"There's something you need to know," she began. "I'm sure you noticed what kind of state Laura was in this morning."

"Some state other than her normal state-of-confusion?" He yawned again. He didn't take what he called Laura's flights into insanity as seriously as Lilly did.

"Sure you won't take me up on the brandy? It's a long story, and not a particularly happy one," Lilly muttered.

"She needs a baby like a hole in the head," Kick growled after Lilly filled him in on the afternoon's conversation and the events of the preceding weeks. "What she needs is to be rid of the son of a bitch."

"I agree, Kick, but I don't think it's as simple as that," Lilly answered. "Do you want to see Sam in Eleanor's clutches?"

"Unfortunately, you have a point. What's the name of this shrink? I think maybe we should talk to him."

"I don't. For once Laura is trying to deal with her problems on her own terms instead of running to us, and I think we should stay out of it."

Kick tossed another log on the fire. "What do you think the chances are that Beck will be agreeable to her keeping the baby?"

"Pretty remote."

"Speaking of babies, you haven't said one word about my very pleasant news."

"I'm very happy for both of you," she said wearily. "I just hope you're not rushing things. She's awfully young to be tied down with a baby."

"Damn it, Lilly, I'm tired of hearing about how young she is," he grumbled. "Don't forget that you had a baby at her age."

"That's exactly what I meant," she said. He gave her a dirty look, and she felt badly about her remark.

"I apologize, Kick. It's unfair to make comparisons between the two situations. You're nothing like Edmund, and she has a lot more sense than I did at her age."

"Well this is going to work. I know it is. Really, Lilly, men may not have ticking biological clocks or whatever that silly phrase is, but I'm forty-two years old, and if I don't have kids soon I'll be too old to enjoy them."

"How's the house coming?" she asked.

"Some days it goes great guns, and other days it looks like nothing at all has happened. Max says renovation is like that, but it's hard to feel like you're making progress when all they're doing is rerouting heating ducts.

How in the world did Beck get that addition done so quickly?"

"I imagine Mark wanted to get out from under Beck's thumb as fast as he could. You know Laura did all the decorating herself, and even Beck admits that she did a beautiful job. I'm proud of her for trying."

"I am too," he agreed. "Six months ago she would have fallen apart if anyone suggested she select the ashtrays. Maybe Dr. Whatever is actually doing her some good."

"Eagan I think she said. He's new in town. She seems to have a lot of confidence in him, and it sounds like he's helping her. Poor man may go back to wherever he came from when he finds out she's pregnant."

Kick shook his head and stared into the dying fire. "Go back three spaces, Laura, and definitely do not pass go."

CHAPTER TWENTY TWO

*D*uncan Eagan rented a loft apartment in a building which fronted Brierley's town square. On the first Tuesday night in December he returned home from his office to find the usually deserted evening streets thronged with families. He climbed the stairs wondering what all the commotion was about.

Of course. The annual Christmas parade was scheduled to begin at seven o'clock. He'd seen posters in the stores advertising what he presumed was a traditional local event, but holidays, family times, were hard for him, and he tried not to take much notice.

He opened the louvered blinds and looked down at the little knots of people with a lump in his throat. Small boys perched on their fathers' shoulders.

Closing the blinds again, he flipped on the news and tried to shut out the sounds from below and the cries from within.

He was so good at helping other people get a grip on themselves, but all the good advice he dispensed sounded like so much rubbish when applied to his personal situation. He missed his family.

Above the sound of the newscaster's voice he heard a band in the street below. "Jingle Bells." He looked in the refrigerator and wasn't surprised that its contents yielded very little that could be called dinner.

Despite not being very hungry he steeled himself to go downstairs, melt into the crowd, and face Christmas head on. At least he knew no one in Brierley except Jack Connor and the people with clouds on their Christmases who came in and out of his office.

The parade was of modest size. Brierley's answer to Macy's annual extravaganza consisted of a few floats, a Boy Scout flag corps, and the high school band led by a group of frozen looking cheerleaders.

The climax of the parade was the arrival of Santa Claus riding high on a fire engine. Its siren blared as it reached the square, overriding the band's out-of-tune tinkle of "Frosty the Snowman."

As Santa appeared tiny jeweled lights came on in the trees, darkened store fronts were illuminated to reveal their window displays, and the crowd gasped with a collective "aah" as if the scene were more than something they saw repeated every year.

Despite himself he was caught up in it. Christmas did that to you. You could tell yourself it was too commercial, or that you didn't believe in Santa Claus, especially a Santa who was being helped off the truck by firemen instead of elves, but it took a harder heart than Duncan Eagan possessed not to be grabbed by the collective excitement that is Christmas.

Duncan saw in the faces of the children around him the magic of belief, and he wanted desperately to share with them in something inexplicably wonderful.

"Merry Christmas, Duncan."

He turned at the sound of Laura's familiar soft voice and thought again of illusions. Would that this family could be as perfect as they looked.

It was the first time he'd seen Beck and Laura's children, and he tried not to stare as he fixed in his mind the faces of those little frontline hostages caught on the battlefield that was their home.

"Who are you?" Duncan's first reaction was that he was being addressed by a small curly-haired angel. This, he assumed, must be Sam.

"I'm a friend of your mom and dad," he said. "Who are you?"

"Samantha Sutton Kimble." She stuck out a mittened hand. "Where are your children?"

"I don't have any, I'm afraid." He heard his voice break despite himself. "And what is Santa Claus going to bring you for Christmas?"

"Probably ashes and switches." She sighed and stole a glance at her father. "But that's okay because my Aunt Lilly is going to buy me a pony."

"You sound pretty confident of that," a voice spoke from the shadows behind them.

"Aunt Lilly!" Sam cried. Beck's chin hardened and a shadow crossed his face as the trio of Lambeths appeared.

"Merry Christmas, everybody!" Bridget sang out.

Hugs and kisses were exchanged between the Lambeths, and a stiff handshake passed between Kick and Beck. Duncan stood unsure whether to wait to be introduced or to melt away into the crowd.

"I'm sorry." Laura spoke up, aware of his predicament. No one could accuse Laura of lacking manners.

"This is our friend, Duncan Eagan. Duncan, my brother Kick Lambeth, his wife Bridget, and my sister Lilly."

Duncan wished the circumstances of their acquaintance were as casual as they appeared. Beck was glaring at him as if there were somehow something improper in their having a streetside conversation.

"Duncan's new in town," Laura explained.

"So what do you think of Brierley?" Kick asked as he stood with a protective arm around the tiny Bridget.

"Great little town." Duncan watched Lilly rearranging Sam's mane of curls. He noticed that she wore no rings and that Bridget's hand was weighted with the biggest emerald he had ever seen. Nice choice of stone. It complimented her eyes.

"Am I the only one freezing out here?" Beck grumbled, wanting to be done with the annual Christmas spectacle and home in front of the fire with a drink. He spent enough damn time talking to Duncan Eagan as it was.

"Bah humbug on you, Beck," Lilly laughed. "Don't you know it's supposed to be cold at Christmas?"

"My sister's blood froze during the years that she lived in Scotland," Kick teased. "She starts to thaw if she spends too much time in a warm climate."

Duncan couldn't resist the opening. "Didn't someone mention to me that you were married to Edmund McFarland?"

He could have kicked himself when he saw her face constrict. Hadn't Jack said that they still had a friendly relationship?

She recovered her composure so quickly that Kick was the only other person in the group to notice her discomfort. "Yes, as a matter of fact I was," she said graciously. "I'm surprised that you've heard of him."

"I've read all of his books. He's a great hero of mine." He stumbled over his words a little, sorry to have brought the subject up.

She picked up on his discomfort and felt badly knowing that he could have no idea why the mention of Edmund's name could cause her to react with such visible anguish. Lately her dreams of her ex-husband had all included a large, loud, ticking clock in the background.

"He's a hero to me, too, Duncan," she said softly. "He's a very special man."

Now thoroughly confused, Duncan's forehead deepened into the creases it got when he thought rapidly. Lilly smiled at him and decided that her sister's description of "cute" didn't go far enough. This man was absolutely delicious.

"Sorry to break up the fun," Beck broke the silence that suddenly hung over the group. "I've had all the sidewalk small talk I can handle in this weather. Let's see if the bookstore has wine and cheese this year." He took Laura's arm, and, as a family, they moved off down the street.

Duncan started off alone in the opposite direction.

"I need a bathroom more than wine and cheese," Bridget giggled. Kick gave her a look that clearly said "not again." They had already made one stop on the way into town.

"Leave her alone. It goes with the territory," Lilly said as Bridget ducked into the drugstore.

"Why does that guy's name sound familiar?" Kick stuck his gloved hands deeper in the pockets of his overcoat and studied a carousel spinning slowly around in a store window.

"I couldn't place it at first either," Lilly whispered. "That's Laura's friend, the shrink."

"No wonder Beck was so hell-bent on getting away! Bet he can't stand her introducing him as 'our friend' Duncan." He threw his head back and laughed.

"Did you enjoy the parade last night?" Duncan asked as Beck sat down.

Beck responded with a laugh that was more of a snort. "The annual firing up of the commercial crap season? You have to admit that I'm doing things with my children as you suggested, although freezing my rear off to watch Santa Claus come to town on a fire truck is carrying things a bit far. Next year, if they insist on a parade, we'll go to New York."

"Oh, come on, Beck," Duncan said. "Surely you remember how exciting Christmas was when you were their age."

"Let's just say that my mother did not go in for a lot of festivities." Beck's mouth twisted. "Her idea of the perfect gift was always fun-to-play-with things like stock certificates."

"Even when you were a child?" Duncan asked incredulously. Despite the family's meager resources, his mother had always managed to make Christmas the most special day of the year. He remembered fondly the year he got both a skateboard and a complete battlefield set with a hundred toy soldiers.

"Sure. Mother doesn't believe in children any more than she believes in Santa Claus. She considers children to be little adults in training."

"Is that the way she looks at her grandchildren?" Duncan asked. "Lots of people let their hair down more with their grandchildren than they ever did with their own kids."

"Mother feels a special sense of responsibility towards my children. Someone has to instill some discipline in their lives, and obviously it isn't going to be done by Laura." Beck, as was his pattern, alternately criticized and defended his mother.

"What are you giving Laura for Christmas?" Duncan asked.

"I don't know. I just call the jeweler and have him pick something out. There isn't one thing in the world that she needs."

Unfortunately love, and understanding, and appreciation couldn't be ordered over the phone, charged to a credit card, and sent out in a delivery van. The things Laura needed, wanted, deserved couldn't be bought at any price that Beck was willing or able to pay.

"You ever been married, Eagan?" Beck asked suddenly.

"Once," Duncan said, holding fast to his refusal to elaborate on his past.

"Did the sensible thing and canned her, huh? Women can sure be a pain in the butt." Beck ran his hand through his hair. "All this holiday business just brings out the worst in them. I'll be glad when Christmas is over. I've tried for years to get Laura to go out of town and skip the whole thing. At least we're leaving right after the big day."

"Where are you going?" Duncan asked.

"Skiing of course," Beck answered as if everyone went skiing as a follow-up to Christmas. "You ski, Eagan?"

"I have skied once or twice." Today was the first time that Beck had evidenced any interest at all in Duncan's life. "It's an expensive sport. By the time I could afford to get interested I didn't have the time."

"You don't know what expensive is until you've been on a ski trip with Laura," Beck responded. She will buy Marion a different outfit, complete with matching boots, for every day we're there. Of course half of skiing is looking right apres ski, don't you agree?"

"You know, Beck, she's really trying."

To Duncan's surprise, Beck agreed. "Yes, she is. As much as I hate to admit it, I think you're doing her some good. She actually makes decisions occasionally and goes places like the grocery store. Let's not let things get out of hand."

"I don't think I'm following you," Duncan looked at him quizzically.

"I'm glad that she doesn't feel that she has to ask Kick and Lilly's permission to go to the bathroom anymore, but I don't want her getting too independent," Beck answered. "You need to make sure that she remembers who's the boss."

"A good marriage doesn't have a boss, Beck."

"Sure it does. Take my parents for example. As much as my mother likes to run the show she never crossed my father. He was the boss. I'm sure that was the reason Lilly couldn't hold onto her husband. Lilly's much too independent to hold onto any man."

"Your youngest daughter looks a lot like her aunt, doesn't she?"

"Yeah, acts like her too unfortunately. Mother says Sam needs to be shipped off to a good strict boarding school as soon as one will take her. Lilly's a bad influence on her, and it'll be over my dead body that some pony is bought for Christmas. That will only be an excuse for her to spend time out there. It's going to be bad enough having Kick next door. If I had known he was thinking of buying that house I would have bought it myself. Laura's becoming entirely too chummy with Bridget."

"Don't you think it's nice that they're friends?" Duncan asked.

"I think it's funny that Laura is dragging Bridget all over the place buying things for that house. She's spending Kick's money like there's a deadline." He smiled. "The latest thing they've gotten into is some ceramics class. Now can you imagine any place in our house that some piece of homemade ceramic junk would look right? Kindergarten crafts for simple minds."

"I can hardly claim to know Bridget after a five minute encounter on the street," Duncan said. "But she didn't appear to me to be at all simple-minded. I thought she was attractive."

"She probably thought she was smart getting herself pregnant right off the bat, thought that would give her some kind of hold over him. All she'll get is fat as her mother, and when that happens Kick will leave her high and dry. He has laid plenty of women in his day, but until he tries it with a fat pregnant one, he doesn't know the meaning of the word disgusting. All of our kids were small when they were born, and Laura never put on an ounce more than what they weighed, and she was still gross. I'm glad I don't have to go through that nauseating experience ever again."

Duncan had a half hour before Laura followed Beck into his office. He dictated notes into his tape recorder.

"I made something for you." She came in without knocking and gave him a shy smile.

She pulled a little tissue-wrapped item from her coat pocket. Duncan opened it and found a tiny ceramic snowman complete with top hat and minute carrot nose.

"I figured you needed something happy on that desk," she said, pleased at his reaction as he grinned at the snowman. Beck's words about the ceramics class came back to him.

"Thank you. It's wonderful," he said, turning the little snowman in his hands. "Perfect for cheering me up on a cold day."

"The weather man says we could have snow by this weekend," Laura said, tossing her fur coat on the floor as casually as if it were army surplus. "Amazing how cold it's gotten after such a warm fall. Lilly says her horses have put on such thick coats that she has trouble feeling their skin underneath." She shook the ponytail, looking every inch a thoroughbred herself.

"I enjoyed meeting your sister and brother," he said. "There's a lot of family resemblance between your daughter and your sister, isn't there?"

"Poor Sam got that wild hair," Laura said, unconsciously smoothing her own perfect hair.

Laura took a deep breath. She promised Lilly that she'd tell him so she might as well get it over with.

She looked down at her hands again and bit so hard on her lip that she almost drew blood.

"What's the matter, Laura?" he asked gently.

"He isn't going to like it any better the fourth time than he did the first." She looked up at him, the usually expressive eyes enigmatically silent.

"Are you trying to tell me you're pregnant?" He tried to keep his voice level. Duncan felt his stomach knot. Beck and Laura Kimble didn't need, at this juncture in their lives, another child on the way.

She nodded, her expression first miserable and then defiant as she looked him straight in the eye and said, "And I'm going to have this baby whether he likes it or not."

"How far along are you?"

"I know what you're thinking," she said. "How could I want a baby conceived out of violence rather than love? I don't know how I could, but I know that I do."

His worst fears confirmed, he sat quietly for a moment before carefully choosing his words. "I get the feeling that Beck doesn't know about this."

"No, he doesn't." She laughed, a bitter laugh that was in sharp contrast to her normal musical one. "He's so busy eyeing the changes in Bridget's figure that he hasn't even noticed the same signs in his own wife."

"You've got to tell him you know," Duncan said firmly. "Are you afraid of his reaction?"

"I know what his reaction will be," she said. "I don't know how he can stand to look at Sam knowing how hard he tried to convince me to get rid of her. But I can't do that, Duncan, and I won't do it."

"You've got to tell him, Laura," he repeated it all the while hearing Beck's words of earlier that morning echoing in his mind. Duncan looked at Laura and saw, instead of the tears and fears of a month past, a look of pure determination.

CHAPTER TWENTY THREE

*B*eck and Laura lay in bed that night, bodies touching but minds going in two very different directions.

Beck felt satisfied both physically and emotionally. He'd known that if he waited long enough she'd invite him down the hall from his new quarters, and he congratulated himself that it had been worth being celibate for a while to have her do the asking. Tonight had confirmed the fact that she still needed him despite her growing independence.

As he lay in the half-state between sleeping and waking, a drowsy Beck admitted that, despite himself, he felt a measure of gratitude to Duncan Eagan.

"Beck." Fully awake herself, Laura whispered into the back of her sleepy husband's neck.

"Beck, I have to tell you something. It's important." She propped herself up on her elbow, not sure whether she felt more comfortable talking to his back or face-to-face. A dim half-light from the moon came through the crack in the drapes, and the last flickers of the fire she'd laid that afternoon simmered in the fireplace.

Laura had planned the scenario of this seduction very carefully from the fire to the bottle of his favorite wine that now held only dregs.

"Tell me how wonderful I am," he murmured, turning over so that she had no choice but to look at him.

"Beck, I'm pregnant." She blurted it out and involuntarily drew back from him.

"Oh, hell, not again!" He fell back on the pillow. "Laura, I thought you had enough sense not to pull a stunt like this again."

"And just what is that supposed to mean?" she asked.

"You assured me that you could be trusted to use something. I suppose you figured that if you claimed to have forgotten or tried to say that it hadn't worked, I'd go along with you. You tricked me," he said angrily. His head already pounded from the wine.

"Oh, my birth control method works," she said, the anger in her voice equal to his. She was determined to be more offensive than defensive. "Nothing works if someone doesn't warn you in advance that they plan to rape you. You didn't exactly give me a lot of advance notice that afternoon."

"Am I expected to pay for that one afternoon for the rest of my life?" He groaned and slammed his fist into the pillow.

"That's the only time it could have happened," she said coldly. "And if you have to live with the consequences of what you did, then it is, to use your favorite vulgarity, tough shit."

"Oh, no, Laura, there is no way you're going to have another baby." He threw off the covers, stood up, and looked back at her with an expression of pure rage. He went in the bathroom and slammed the door.

Laura got out of bed and pulled on her nightgown. When Beck came out of the bathroom she was sitting in one of the plaid chairs in front of the fireplace with her feet tucked under her.

Beck pulled the sash of his bathrobe tight and sat down in the facing chair. "Laura, I mean it. No more children. Go see your buddy Jack Connor in the morning and find out if he does abortions. It's still early enough to do something about this."

"No." She stared at him.

"What do you mean, no?" He stared back.

"I'm going to have this baby, and there is not one thing you can do about it."

"We'll see about that." He suddenly loomed over her, and she instinctively ducked. "Don't worry. I'm too tired to hit you. I'm going back to bed."

She sat staring moodily into the almost dead fire.

He paused in the doorway. "Go to bed, Laura. You might as well make up your mind to do what you have to do, because I don't intend to discuss it further."

Eleanor marched unchallenged past Mrs. Harris and into her son's office without being announced. She liked to catch him off guard. "I assume you're free for lunch."

"Actually, Mother, I wasn't planning to take time for lunch today." He hedged, knowing only too well that if she intended to have lunch with him he might as well start thinking about what to order.

"You can make time," she said, making no move to remove her coat or to take a seat. "I need to talk to you."

"Sure," he conceded. He got up and reached for his overcoat. "I always have time for lunch with you."

Seated at the best table the country club had to offer, she waited for the cocktail waiter to bring Beck's Scotch and her own dry sherry.

Once served, she wasted no time in getting to the purpose of their meeting. "I received in the mail this morning a solicitation for funds for the Brierley Recycling Center."

Beck squirmed. He liked to stay one step ahead of his mother, and he couldn't for the life of him figure what a recycling center had to do with him.

"I am not pleased that you would allow your wife to permit the group which is promoting such a place to include her name on its board of directors. I would not have believed it if I had not seen it there for myself in black and white." She sipped the sherry.

"Oh, Mother, it can't be that big a deal." He took more than a sip of his drink, trying to figure a way to explain something about which he knew nothing. Damned Lilly was always squawking about the environment. This must be some of her nonsense.

"I think it's good for Laura to get involved in some community efforts just as you have so generously given your time to do over the years. You're such a good role model for her. I do appreciate how much you do for Laura."

"In the first place, Beck, I do not approve of Laura being on the board of anything. How can you contemplate your flighty wife having a role of any importance in anything?"

"Well, Mother, perhaps she's involved in name only, some sort of figurehead role," he said. "She probably has no more responsibility than to show up at the meetings and look nice. She's good at that."

"You don't understand, Beck. The very use of her name is what I object to most. The name of Kimble has always stood for the very highest in civic and social prestige in this community. Certainly it has never been used in connection with a project to collect garbage. Really!"

He tried to make eye contact with the waiter. The second drink was long overdue.

"She seems to resent anything that I try to do to help her," Eleanor sniffed. "Just yesterday I reprimanded that new maid of yours because the doorknobs were tarnished, and Laura seemed to take great offense. She jumped, quite rudely I might add, to the maid's defense. I don't know how she can expect her servants to have an ounce of respect for her when she is disrespectful to me in front of them."

"Please try to forgive her, Mother. I think she's been feeling a little under the weather."

"Again?" Eleanor pursed her lips. "I am still mortified over that episode Thanksgiving Day. It was most inconsiderate of her to expose all of the rest of us to her virus."

The second drink having arrived and been consumed, Beck spoke without thinking. "I don't think you're apt to catch what's ailing Laura, Mother."

"Oh?" She waited for an explanation.

"Seems she's pregnant again," he said, feeling his head spin a little. He'd stormed out of the house early, too angry with Laura to eat any breakfast, and the second Scotch on an empty stomach was having more of an effect than he'd anticipated.

"Really, Beck, how disgusting." Eleanor sighed. "Don't you think four children is a little lower class?"

"I couldn't agree with you more." He felt dangerously close to hiccups. "And I've told her that there is no way she's going to continue this pregnancy."

"Good for you, Beck." She gave him a cold smile. "The sooner this is terminated the better. Thank goodness it's easier today to end a pregnancy than it once was."

"You're right as usual." He smiled crookedly as the waiter brought their food.

Having arranged a few abortions himself, he knew only too well how difficult it once was.

Laura took a deep breath, as she always did before ringing the doorbell of the big red brick house. The air was getting colder, and she could see her breath as she waited, listening for footsteps in the hall.

To her relief, it was the housekeeper, Grace, who answered the door. Maybe Eleanor wasn't at home.

"Good afternoon, Mrs. Kimble." Grace stood framed in the doorway, wearing the formal black uniform her employer required. "Did you come to get your package?"

"Yes, I appreciate your calling about it." Laura smiled at Grace, whom she liked very much. "I can't imagine why it would have been delivered here."

She wanted to get Marion's doll and doll clothes out of the house before Eleanor had a chance to open the package and see the amount of the credit card charge. If she wanted to spend a thousand dollars on doll clothes it was her business, but she knew her mother-in-law wouldn't see it that way.

"Probably because the address label looks like the delivery truck ran over it." Grace grinned. "The only thing you can make out is part of the name. I guess they looked up the wrong address in the phone book. Just a minute and I'll get it for you."

"Thanks, Grace. Laura looked down at the entrance hall rug, a busy neo-classical design of dull golds and red. It was a fine old handwoven Axminster, and Laura thought it was unbearably ugly.

She wrinkled her nose at the musty smell that she associated with Eleanor's house. It was a faintly moldy odor emanating from draperies and upholstery that had hung on the same windows and furniture for years, but it always made Laura feel as if dead mice were hidden somewhere.

The hall was an unpleasantly bilious shade of yellow tinged with green. It was furnished with a serpentine-front Adam console beneath a large por-trait of a sour-faced Kimble ancestor. The painting was flanked by a pair of Georgian sconces which gave off only a little dim light in the fading late afternoon sun of a winter day.

Laura wondered vaguely how long it had been since Eleanor had changed anything in the house, nothing certainly in the years she'd been married to Beck.

Occasionally there was a new addition to Eleanor's valuable collection of celadon, ancient Chinese pottery that varied in color from pale bluish green to olive. Eleanor had people available to act as her representatives in the bidding every time a piece of it went on the auction block in New York or London.

Laura winced as she glanced into the dining room, remembering poor little Marion spilling a glass of orange juice on one of the watered silk chairs. Eleanor had the upholstery cleaned and sent the bill to Laura with a curt note suggesting that she spend more time working on the children's table manners.

Laura looked back at the ancestor, whispered "ugly, old buzzard weren't you?" and was startled when Eleanor spoke back from the dark recesses of the hallway.

"Hello, Laura, I'm glad you're here." Laura spun around. "I need to talk to you, and this will save my having to make a trip over to your house."

"Talk to me about what?" Laura felt as clumsy as Marion did in the woman's presence.

"Shall we go into the living room?" Eleanor proceeded to do just that without waiting for Laura's reply.

Laura followed her into the room which was in deeper shadow than the hall. The walls were off-white, accented by a shade of green that reminded Laura of the color of mold. At least it went well with the dead mice smell.

A dreary oil painting of a cold Glaswegian harbor scene hung over the marble-fronted fireplace. Heavy green silk drapes framed windows covered by partially opened, old-fashioned Venetian blinds.

Eleanor's prized celadon was sprinkled about the room, and Laura felt a pang of sympathy for Grace who had to dust it daily.

Eleanor flipped a wall switch, and the dim bulbs of the chandelier did their feeble best to put a little light in the room. Eleanor took her seat in a deep cushioned wing chair and motioned for Laura to take a stiff French damask chair. Laura shifted around more in an attempt to find a comfortable position on the hard seat than from any nervousness she felt at having been summoned to this audience with her highness her mother-in-law. She was used to Eleanor's commanding the power seat.

"I had lunch with Beck today," Eleanor began. "I was most distressed, as is he of course, to learn of your condition." She spit out the last word as distastefully as if Laura were suffering from something highly contagious and unmentionable in polite society.

"If you're referring to my pregnancy, there is nothing to be distressed about." Laura felt the nausea, which had abated during the past few days, return with a vengeance. She wondered if it were her "condition" or the heavy, sickly sweet gardenia smell of Eleanor's perfume fighting with the mousy odor. Gardenias were the only flower that Laura truly hated. Eleanor's yard was full of gardenia bushes.

"Laura, it is bad enough that your brother has married into that Dudley family with their litter of children. You do not want to lower yourself and my son to that sort of societal level by producing child after child as if you were an animal."

"An animal?" Laura suddenly decided to do as Duncan had suggested and stand up to her, and it felt great. She felt like she had all the power in the world.

"Restraint, Laura. Civilized people use restraint in every aspect of their lives including reproduction. It is unfortunate that this has happened, but I am sure it can easily be remedied, and I want you to assure me that you will do something immediately before anyone suspects."

Laura, accustomed in the past to lowering her eyes and meekly agreeing to whatever Eleanor demanded, surprised them both by returning a stare as cold as Eleanor's as she waited to see if the older woman was finished. She wasn't.

"I insist that you end this pregnancy and avoid any future ones by getting whatever is necessary done to see that this sort of thing doesn't happen again."

"And what if I don't want to?" Laura saw the shock register on Eleanor's face. She smiled, thinking, as Kick had, that the plastic surgeon hadn't done a very good job.

"Laura, Beck and I agree that for the sake of both appearances and your mental health, which we both know, my dear, is tenuous at best, you can't seriously consider going any further with this ridiculous idea."

"My mental health is better than yours, Eleanor," Laura said coolly. "At least I'm doing something positive to improve my mental health. So is Beck. You ought to try it yourself."

"I don't know what you're talking about." Eleanor was becoming coldly furious.

"He's seeing the psychiatrist more often than I am." Laura laughed out loud at Eleanor's obvious discomfort.

Eleanor felt herself go cold with shock and embarrassment. "My son does not need a psychiatrist, young woman. If he had only listened to me, he would have had you locked up several months ago. Your drug habit has caused me considerable anguish and embarrassment, and, as far as I am concerned, it was the blackest day of my son's life when he took the unfortunate step of marrying you. If he is trying valiantly to help you by enumerating your problems to your psychiatrist, then I applaud him." Her voice rose to an uncharacteristic shrillness.

Eleanor shuddered to think that anyone might have seen her son coming or going from a psychiatrist's office. "I repeat, Laura, it is all a matter of restraint, unfortunately a characteristic which has always been in short supply in your family. I realize that you have not had good familial role models in either your parents or your siblings, but I hope for my son's sake that you can rise above your upbringing."

After years and years of baiting, Eleanor finally pushed Laura too far.

"Restraint?" Laura screamed so loudly that Grace, who was listening on the other side of the closed door and silently cheering Laura on, took a step back. "How about a little restraint on Beck's part?"

"I'm afraid I'm not following your ramblings, Laura." Eleanor struggled to keep her voice steady. She was feeling oddly dizzy as her anger mounted.

"I'm not pregnant because of any lack of restraint on my part, Eleanor." Laura did not try to lower her own voice. "I'm pregnant because your precious son, in a total loss of restraint, raped me and then continued to enjoy himself by beating me up. I'm glad you bought that little story about my being in a traffic accident in Barbados because you were the only one who did. You want me to have an abortion before anyone finds out I'm pregnant? Well let me tell you that in this town news travels fast, and half the town is talking about what your son did to me."

Grace, standing wide-eyed and open-mouthed from her vantage point in the entrance hall, waited breathlessly for Eleanor's reply. What she heard instead was a crash followed by Laura's screams for help.

Grace threw open the door and screamed herself. In her fall Eleanor had toppled a small side table. She lay with her mouth and staring eyes wide open in a bed of broken celadon as Laura retched by her side.

CHAPTER TWENTY FOUR

"She's had a severe stroke, Beck." The doctor took a seat next to a stunned Beck and sobbing Laura in the hospital's emergency waiting room.

"She'll get over it, won't she?" Summoned from the office by an hysterical Grace, Beck arrived at the hospital moments after the ambulance. He flinched in horror as they took his mother, the gaping, twisted grin of a mad clown frozen on her face, out on a stretcher.

John Perkins had been the Kimble family doctor for over twenty-five years. He had been summoned when Beck's father keeled over with a fatal heart attack on the golf course and had also seen the family through numerous small complaints. He was not a man to dance around the truth especially with someone he knew as well as he did Beck Kimble.

"She's stable, but that doesn't mean that she won't have another stroke at any minute. Your mother's blood pressure has been a great concern for the last several years, Beck, and I'm sorry to say this doesn't surprise me. Physically she's been a time bomb waiting to explode."

"If she lives, will she be all right?" Beck rubbed his throbbing head.

"She'll probably never again be the person she was earlier in the day if that's what you mean by all right." Perkins hated reading the verdict but knew Beck might as well hear the sentence so that he could begin to deal with whatever prison Eleanor's body might prove to be in the future.

He was prevented from continuing by a fresh wave of loud weeping on Laura's part. He looked over at her, wondering if there was more affection for Eleanor there than he would have expected. At least half the lectures he'd given Eleanor about her blood pressure had come after she'd finished some diatribe about her daughter-in-law. Whatever Laura's feelings for her mother-in-law, the afternoon's experience must have been terribly unsettling. A stroke was an ugly thing to witness.

"We've done a few preliminary tests, enough to know that there's a lot of damage," he went on. "She can't talk, and there's some paralysis. Some of the function may come back, but how much I just don't know. Let's give her a few days and see what happens."

"Will she be able to take care of herself?" Beck looked at the doctor as a small boy seeking reassurance might, and it struck John Perkins that it never got any easier no matter how many times he had similar conversations. No matter how old you were when one of your parents became disabled, it had the effect of throwing you back into childhood, desperately wanting the safety of another time.

"I don't think there's much chance of that," he said slowly. "I expect she'll need nursing care for the rest of her life. I can look into some good facilities if you'd like."

"What about keeping her at home with round-the-clock nurses?" Beck asked.

"That's a possibility of course." Perkins weighed his words. "However, in the long run some type of nursing facility would be my suggestion. It's not something you have to decide tonight, Beck. Why don't you and Laura go home and get some rest? I'll be here all night, and I'll call you if there's any change."

Doubting that Eleanor Kimble would live long enough to require the services of anything other than the local mortician, John Perkins got up to return to his patient.

Beck and Laura sat in silence for a few minutes.

"I'm so sorry, Beck," she whispered. "I'm so sorry."

"Why don't you go home, Laura," he said heavily. "I think I'd like to be by myself."

"If that's what you want me to do." She wanted to reach out for him but didn't. Guilt wrapped around her so thickly that she couldn't fight free of its enfolding shroud.

She got up slowly and took a lonely walk to the parking lot as Beck sat alone, fighting back a small boy's tears.

"Dr. Eagan, this is Lilly Lambeth, and I want to apologize for bothering you at home."

"No problem," he answered as he reached over to turn off the stereo. "What can I do for you?" The gloomy notes of a requiem played by the London Symphony died away.

"You're probably going to think it's totally out of line for me to be calling." Lilly hesitated, but only for a moment. "I'm concerned about my sister."

Duncan drew a sharp intake of breath. "What's wrong with Laura?"

"I just got off the phone with her, and she's hysterical," Lilly rushed on, grateful for the concern she heard in his voice. "Her mother-in-law has had a massive stroke. My brother is in the process of moving into the house next door to Laura, and I called him to go over there."

"Apparently Laura went over to Eleanor's to pick up a package or something, and they had a confrontation that ended with Eleanor having a seizure. Laura is convinced that this is all her fault, and, if Eleanor dies, I'm not sure how well she's going to cope with it."

"I'm not either," he said quietly. "Lilly, are you busy tonight? Could you meet me somewhere so that we can talk about this? I don't feel at all comfortable about Laura."

Relief flooding through her, Lilly didn't hesitate to accept his offer. "Why don't you come out here. I know it's out of the way, but it would be more private. I don't think Lonnie's Tavern is the place to discuss Laura."

"Thank you," Duncan said. "Just give me directions, and I'll be there as soon as I can."

"Come on, kids, I'll fix you a sandwich or something," Bridget said firmly as the Kimble children stared at their weeping mother.

The three were totally unnerved, not so much by the sight of Laura crying, which they'd seen often enough before, as they were by the idea that something could happen to Grandmother.

She took Sam by one hand and gave Brook a little push with the other. Marion followed meekly a few steps behind them as they left the room.

"You've got to calm down, Laura." Kick put his arm around his sister. "Let me help you upstairs." She didn't protest as he pulled her from the sofa and turned her in the direction of the stairs.

He sat beside her on the bed and waited for her to calm down enough to explain the events of the afternoon.

"Oh, Kick, it was awful, and it's all my fault," she wept. "She was saying such nasty things to me, and I just couldn't take it anymore."

"I don't know how you've taken it as long as you have, Laura. Whatever was said, I'm sure what happened was not your fault."

"Beck will think it was." She wiped her eyes, thought about the baby, and tried to make herself breathe normally.

"She wanted me to have an abortion. She and Beck have decided that it's in everybody's best interest to get rid of the baby." She gave Kick a desperate look as the grey eyes filled again.

He could just imagine the conversation.

"Kick, I just can't do that," Laura said miserably, wrapping her arms around herself as if to protect the child.

"Of course you can't," he said in a soothing voice, feeling guilty that it had seemed to him, too, the most obvious course of action when Lilly first told him about Laura's pregnancy.

"She sat there and told me that she and Beck had decided at lunch that we were going kill this baby, and, Kick, I looked at her, and I wished her dead. I mean it. I really did, and now, oh, Kick, it's all my fault."

At a loss for what to say, he simply held his sister's hand.

"Thank you for coming." The porch light glowed over the big double front doors as Lilly appeared before Duncan had a chance to knock.

He followed her into the entrance hall with the massive bulk of the mahogany staircase rising solidly up to the second floor. A draft of cold December air rushed through the hall before she could close the door, and she pulled her beige cardigan sweater more tightly around her as she led him into the library.

"What can I get you to drink?" She held out her hands for his coat.

"Just coffee if it's not too much trouble."

"Exactly what I'm having. I just made a fresh pot. I'll be right back with it."

A fire was burning, and a heavy brass chandelier illuminated worn bindings, a cherry desk with a cracked leather top and green-shaded lamp, and chairs that looked well broken in. Duncan had the impression of a room definitely a man's, a man who surrounded himself with comfortable objects. The room didn't seem to fit the image he had of Kick Lambeth, and he wondered if it bore the stamp of their father.

Lilly reappeared with a tray with a silver coffeepot and two cups. "I guess I always gravitate to this room when I'm bothered about something. Probably sounds silly, but I always came in here as a child when I had a problem. More often than not my grandfather could help me find solutions, and I guess I feel like part of him will always be in this room."

"That doesn't sound silly at all," he said, accepting a cup from her. "I could feel his presence the minute I walked in. It's a comforting room."

Lilly repeated his phrase. "What a nice thing to say. You know you remind me of my grandfather a little bit."

"How's that? You hardly know me." He liked the direct gaze she leveled at him. He was so accustomed to Laura's shy, whispered, indirect mumblings that he didn't know quite how to react to her older sister. Lilly seemed as much in control as Laura was out of control.

"Oh, I don't know. The way you're built maybe, or the vibrations you give off. Just a feeling."

"Well I'll consider it a compliment," he said. "I like your grandfather's taste." He looked in the direction of the painting over the fireplace.

"The Stubbs? That was my grandmother's gift to my grandfather on their fiftieth wedding anniversary. She pretended to look down her nose at his animals, but she loved to whisper about how she had to look all over England until she found an impoverished duke desperate enough to part with that painting." Lilly thought of Anthony's mother and felt a twinge of guilt.

Duncan watched as Lilly walked over and capably tossed another large log on the fire. The thick fall of hair caught the light, and he had a wild impulse to ask if he could lift it to see if it was as heavy as he knew it must be or as light as a sheaf of bundled late summer grass.

"Duncan, may I call you Duncan?" She continued without waiting for confirmation. "You have been an incredible help to Laura in a very short time. You've been like an answer to a prayer, and I'm just sick that this business with Eleanor has happened."

"I can't discuss anything with you that Laura has told me in confidence." He weighed his words carefully, not sure that even being there was proper. "She's making a tremendous effort to get her life together."

"I know she is." Lilly stared into the fire. "Laura has never had to stand on her own two feet and face life, and I'm not sure she has any idea of who she is. It's not her fault."

"Whose fault is it?"

"I'll be the first one to stand up when the blame's handed out. I was fourteen years old when Laura was born. To say that my father and I never got along is putting it mildly. When I came home from boarding school on vacations and saw him treating Laura like some kind of little blonde princess I resented the hell out of the whole situation."

"I guess when my parents died I figured she'd just go right on living here with Desia, and then when she fell into Beck's lap she became his responsibility rather than mine. As much as I hate to admit it, I was relieved when she ran off with Beck."

"Interesting choice of words," Duncan said. "Why should she be anyone's responsibility but her own?"

"I don't know." Lilly was startled by his comment. "Maybe that's just the effect Laura has on people. You want to protect her, or at least feel that somebody is looking after her. I resented that too. Everybody always assumed that I could take care of myself."

"And I expect most of the time that's exactly the way you want it." He laughed, sizing her up.

She gave him the direct open look. "Most of the time it is. But don't you think, Duncan, that occasionally we all want someone to take care of us?"

Before he could answer the back door slammed. "Lilly where are you?" Kick shouted from the kitchen.

He burst into the room before she could answer.

"I'm sorry. I didn't realize you had company." He looked puzzled, wondering what his sister was doing with Duncan Eagan in the library. He hadn't noticed the little car parked in the driveway in front of the house. Very few people ever entered the Lambeths' house by the front door.

"You remember Duncan Eagan?" she said as Duncan rose and extended his hand. "I called him tonight because I was worried about Laura. How's she doing?"

"About like you'd expect given what happened this afternoon." Kick took off his glasses and polished them on his sweater. "What a mess. She's convinced that this is all her fault. Old witch probably did it just to spite her."

"Kick!" Lilly gave him a dark look. "No matter what we think about Eleanor you can't wish what's happened to her on anybody."

"Of course I don't," he said heavily. "I'm just worried to death about Laura. When I left Beck was giving her the third degree about exactly what was said this afternoon."

Duncan and Lilly exchanged looks.

"Don't look at me," Kick said defensively. "He told me to get out of his house, and there wasn't much else I could do at that point. I had already told Laura that she was more than welcome to spend the night at our house or that I'd be glad to bring her out here. I don't know what else I could have done short of dragging her out of there."

Duncan stood. "Thanks for the coffee, Lilly. I think it's time I got home."

"I've got to be going myself," Kick said. "Tonight is our first night in our new house, and I hate to leave Bridget sitting there all by herself."

The two men left the house, one by the back entrance and one by the front, and Lilly, watching the twin tail lights of their cars go down the long driveway, felt very much alone.

"What did you talk about? Was anything said that could have caused this?" Beck asked Laura again and again as she shook her head and cried.

Grace had most likely heard at least some of the exchange. Laura had no idea how much of it she might have repeated to Beck.

Anesthetized by Scotch, Beck finally passed out and slept fitfully on the sofa in the study while Laura tossed and turned the night away upstairs, genuinely wanting to offer him what comfort she could.

Morning finally came, as it always does after even the worst of nights. Laura lay in bed, exhausted. Every time she tried to close her eyes during the night the awful image of Eleanor's twisted face reproduced itself graphically in her mind.

She moved in a daze in the kitchen as the children got ready for school.

"Mom, that coffee isn't going to taste very good." Brook watched her as he poured syrup over a toasted frozen waffle.

"What did you say?" She turned to him, a creature who didn't look much like his mother with her eyes puffy from crying and her hair tangled from her struggle to find a comfortable position in the bed.

"You didn't put any coffee in," he said. "All you're going to get is hot water."

"Oh, I guess I didn't." She stared blankly at the coffeepot.

"Here, let me do it." Marion gave her brother a look that plainly said "can't you see that Mom needs help" and put her arms around her mother.

"I know you're worried, but she's going to be okay." Marion held her mother tightly.

Laura buried her face in the child's long, sweet-smelling hair. "Oh, baby, I hope so. Say a prayer for Grandmother."

"I already have, Mom." Marion disengaged herself and stood on her tiptoes to reach the coffee. Easy, she thought, there were the directions right on the can.

After the third unanswered request for breakfast, Sam started to cry.

"Be quiet, Sam," Marion said. "I'll fix you something. Do you want cereal or waffles?"

"I want potato chips," Sam said petulantly.

"Fine, have potato chips," Laura said absently. All three children stared at her in disbelief. Potato chips for breakfast?

Laura sat down at the table and stared out the kitchen window at the clouds building overhead. She shivered despite the thick velvet robe.

Brook turned on the small television set on the counter, and the morning weatherman smiled the bright little chipmunk smile he always wore whether predicting blue skies and sunshine or possible tornadoes.

"Though winter doesn't officially arrive for a few weeks it looks like fall has fallen!" he chirped. "Hope all you ladies have your furs out of cold storage because tonight could be the coldest ever for this date in December. And kids, think snow, because the possibility does exist. See you at twelve!"

They heard the rumble of the bus at the foot of the driveway, and Marion bent to give her mother a kiss before leaving for school. "Have some coffee, and take a bath, and get dressed, Mom," she said in the perfect role reversal which she had assumed so many times before. "Things will look better after you're cleaned up."

"Thanks, honey. I love you." Laura squeezed her hand, and Brook and Marion disappeared out the door and down the driveway.

Sam watched as Laura continued to stare moodily out the window. She might as well have been invisible despite the crunching of the potato chips.

She stuck out a pudgy hand and speared the last bite of Brook's waffle.

"Your coffee's ready, Mommy."

"What?" Laura looked at her as if she'd just materialized. "Oh, thanks, Sam. It's not my day to drive is it?"

"Nope, you drove yesterday, remember?" Sam wondered if she dared pick up Brook's plate and lick the syrup. Her mommy was goofy this morning, but not goofy in the same way she used to be. Lately she picked up on things that she didn't use to notice. Better leave well enough alone.

Sam's eyes widened as her father came into the room. He looked even worse than her mother. Daddy looked like he'd been crying too, but that was silly because everybody knew Daddys didn't cry. They were both acting goofy.

A horn sounded in the driveway, and Sam, relieved to be freed from a situation she didn't understand, grabbed her jacket and mittens and flew out the door.

"Do you want some coffee, Beck?" Laura asked as the back door slammed behind Sam.

"No, I'll get some at the hospital." He reached in the cabinet for a bottle of aspirin. "I've got a bitch of a headache."

"Beck," she began, unsure of what to say to him.

"Laura, I've got to go. I meant to be there an hour ago." Gulping down the aspirin, he bolted out the door.

Tired, so tired, she propped her elbows on the table and tried to drink the coffee without gagging. He hadn't said a word about the baby.

CHAPTER TWENTY FIVE

Dr. Perkins insisted on taking a haggard Beck to the cafeteria for breakfast. In all the years Perkins had known the younger man he'd never seen Beck unshaven until today.

Beck looked somehow incomplete, and Perkins realized that except on the golf course or tennis courts he'd never seen Beck without a tie either. Beck was the sort of man who looked like he slept in a coat and tie.

This morning, wearing the same wrinkled tattersall shirt that he'd had on the day before, he didn't look as if he'd had any sleep at all.

"She's no better, but she's also no worse," Dr. Perkins said as Beck pushed runny scrambled eggs around on his plate without taking a bite of anything.

"I'd say that if her condition remains stable, and I'll warn you again that I can't guarantee that it will, there will be no reason to keep her here. Have you given any thought to what you're going to do?"

"Do you want to know what I thought about between one and two or between three and four?" Beck asked as he wearily rubbed his bloodshot eyes. "Yes, I've thought about it."

"There's a good place south of town," Perkins said gently. "They have an excellent primary care nursing wing. I don't know how full they are."

"No nursing home," Beck interrupted. "I don't want her in a nursing home full of drooling old people."

"Beck, I think you're laboring under a misconception. Nursing homes aren't what they used to be. The ones I have in mind are first-class establishments. The time will come when there will be no reason to keep her on in the hospital. Not only are we short of beds, it wouldn't be fair to your mother. The sooner she's settled somewhere on a permanent basis the better it

will be for her recovery. I realize that we may be premature in even discussing this, but the more preparation time you have the happier you're
likely to be with the facility you do choose."

"She's going home." Beck looked directly at the older man.

"Beck, that's not a practical solution," John Perkins said slowly. He'd
seen similar situations happen before and knew that Eleanor could drag on
for years in the semi-vegetative state in which she now lay. He couldn't say
for sure how much of her razor sharp mind was left. She was under sedation
to keep her blood pressure down. "She may need round-the-clock nursing
care, not even be able to go to the bathroom on her own."

Beck winced when he thought of his mother unable to perform the sim-
plest bodily functions without the assistance of others. It was the first time in
his life he'd thought of his mother as someone who even had bodily functions.

John Perkins mistook contemplative silence for agreement. "Let me call
Green Hills for you, Beck. You can go out there and have a look around this
afternoon."

"Tell me what equipment we need to buy before taking her home." Beck
ignored the doctor's suggestion. "Who do I contact about providing home
nursing services?"

"All right, if you insist." Perkins sighed. "Grace's not getting any
younger either you know. Have you discussed this with her?"

"I don't need to discuss it with Grace," Beck said firmly. "I'm taking
Mother to my house."

John Perkins spilled coffee in his lap.

"Home with you?" he sputtered as he mopped at his pants. "Beck, you
have a young family. Surely you can't be thinking of bringing your mother,
in the state she's in, into a household with young children. It wouldn't be at
all fair to Laura."

"It's time Laura took some responsibility for something," Beck said coldly. "She's got time on her hands. She can help take care of Mother. Heaven
knows my mother has tried for all these years to take care of Laura. Now it's
Laura's turn."

"Laura's turn to do what?" she asked. Neither of them had noticed as
she hesitantly approached the table.

"We're going to move Mother into the new bedroom at our house," Beck
announced. John Perkins saw Laura go white as a sheet as she grabbed the
back of the chair for support. He automatically pushed back his chair, think-

ing for a moment that she was going to faint.

"Are you all right, Laura?"

"Yes, just a little dizzy." She lowered herself gently into the chair as if she were afraid of falling.

"Beck, we can't take care of your mother," she pleaded.

"Certainly we can," he answered so firmly that John Perkins was left with no doubt that he was going to do exactly what he said. "You've been saying for weeks that what you need is something to do. You can take care of Mother."

Before either Dr. Perkins or Laura could argue further, Beck pushed back his chair and rose from the table. "Now if you'll both excuse me, the nurse said I could go in for five minutes at eight-thirty."

He looked at his watch for confirmation and strode from the room, leaving Laura and the doctor staring in bewilderment at each other across his uneaten breakfast.

"Duncan, I need to see you," Laura watched her breath make little clouds in the cold air as she spoke into the car phone.

"Laura, where are you? I've been worried about you." He leaned forward over his desk and picked up the little snowman with its crooked carrot nose, turning it over and over in his hand.

"I'm in my car in the hospital parking lot. I feel like I've got to run away, and I don't know where to go." Her words tumbled through the cellular phone.

"Come on over. It just happens that my next appointment canceled." He'd had Laura on his mind all morning.

Five minutes later she burst in, her coat this time a three quarter length mink, and Duncan remembered Beck's description of her closets. He wondered if she had one closet reserved just for furs. The animals that had given their lives to keep Laura Kimble warm would have over-populated a small farm.

"Slow down," he said. "Let me get you a soda or something. You look like you're ready to collapse."

"Thanks, that would be great," she said. She fell into one of the chairs without removing the coat. She seemed to shrink inside the fur, and Duncan hurried across the hall to get her a soft drink.

"Take your coat off." He stood over her, holding the can, until she did as she was told.

"You okay?" he asked, leaning over her as she took a sip. She shivered a little, and her eyes looked like grey pools sunk deep in the black shadows surrounding them. Her facial bones were prominent, and he suspected that she was losing rather than gaining the weight that worried Beck so much.

"Have you been eating, Laura?" He frowned at her as he sat down in the chair next to hers.

"I'm trying. I'm so sick most mornings that it doesn't do any good to eat because it just comes right back up. I dread meals."

"You've got to feed that baby you know," Duncan said softly.

"Fatten it up for the kill you mean?" she asked bitterly. She took another small sip from the can.

"Laura, no one can make you abort this baby. But if you're going to keep it you have to take care of it, and yourself."

"I have been taking care of it, Duncan." There was a trace of anger in her voice. "I have not so much as taken an aspirin because I'm trying to protect this baby, but so far I seem to be the only one who's concerned about it."

Duncan didn't answer, knowing he hadn't done a very good job of hiding his shock when she told him her news.

"How's Beck's mother?"

"He's moving her in with us," Laura said in a hopeless voice. She knew Beck well enough to know that when he was determined to do something nothing was going to change his mind.

"He's what?" Duncan couldn't believe his ears.

"The doctor says that at some point she may be able to leave the hospital. Beck wants to bring her to our house. He says taking care of her will give me something to do."

"Laura, that just won't work. He doesn't realize what's involved in caring for someone who has had a stroke."

"I know that, you know that, the doctor knows that, but try to tell him that." She made a face. "This is all my fault, and I suppose it's only fair that I pay for it."

"I'm not going to listen to that," Duncan said angrily. Laura had come too far to take on as penance something that would drive a normal person round-the-bend. He had to talk to Beck before this went any further. "The last place you need is to go on a guilt trip. Guilt trips are all down a dead-end road, and it's hard as hell to get back home once you've booked one."

She turned to go, fastening the fur coat. Outside a light snow began to fall.

The little snowfall of the evening before had accumulated only in the dreams of the children and the childlike. The few patches where it remained in the morning light didn't amount to enough to make a decent snowball.

Lilly looked out the window at the dreary countryside and felt as emotionally stripped as the trees that stood bleakly bereft of their leaves. From downstairs she heard the front door knocker thud a summons.

"Lilly! You've got company!" Desia's voice boomed from the entrance hall below.

Who in the world pays a visit at this hour of the morning she wondered, not wanting to see anyone but the one person it was most impossible to see. She certainly was in no mood to greet anyone who observed the formality of coming to her front door.

"Lilly, did you hear me?" Desia demanded in a voice which clearly implied "mind your manners."

"I'm coming," she called back, dropping her robe on the floor and putting on the same jeans and sweatshirt she'd tossed on the chair the night before.

At the top of the stairs she paused and frowned down at the empty hall. Desia must have taken whoever it was back to the morning room. Lilly was irritated. She had no intention of entertaining anyone this early this morning.

She was taken by surprise when Duncan Eagan rose from one of the wicker chairs.

"This time I'm the one who should do the apologizing for being out of place," he said diffidently, feeling horribly the intruder and suddenly sorry that he had acted on impulse and driven out to the big house. "I don't sleep very well some nights. I was trying to find something to watch on television, and I heard it on the international news from London. I wanted you to know that I'm sorry."

"Oh, Duncan, it was good of you to come," she said heavily. She found herself suddenly very grateful for his presence. Somehow it was easier to share her newborn grief with someone she hardly knew than it would have been with her own family or close friends.

"My daughter called me late last night," she said softly as he poured a cup of the coffee and handed it to her. "I knew it was coming, but I didn't know it would be this soon."

Tears, the biggest, fattest, wettest tears Duncan had ever seen a person cry, rolled down her cheeks, but her voice was even.

"Had he been sick?" he asked gently.

She nodded. "He actually died of a heart attack." She made no move to wipe away the streaming tears, and Duncan picked up a napkin and gently did it for her.

"My daughter had gone into Aberdeen to meet her husband's plane," she continued in a dull voice. "When she got back he was sitting in a chair by the fireplace, and she thought he'd simply fallen asleep there. He did that sometimes. She couldn't wake him up."

"You loved him a lot, didn't you?"

She sat cradling the coffee cup in her hands, her mind a million miles away, and Duncan let her have her silent thoughts.

"You know we had a marriage made in both heaven and hell," she said at last. "I was too young, and he was too old, but from the first day I met him I loved him every day of my life. I just couldn't live with him. Can you understand that Duncan? No one else seems to be able to."

"Of course I can. Opposites attract, and then the very things that make you so different begin to drive you crazy."

"I tried to go back in October," she said. "I wanted to try again as an adult instead of a silly little twenty year old who pouted because he wouldn't take me dancing every night."

"What happened?"

"We had a few wonderful weeks together, and then he made me leave. We made some good memories in those weeks, but I can't help but feel that I once had the chance for a whole lifetime of memories and just threw it away."

"Maybe it was best for both of you that you left when you did, both times."

She put her face in her hands. "I hate this terrible, empty, gut-tearing feeling that death gives you. To know you'll never touch, or talk, or laugh, or even argue again. Maybe the worst of it is that even though I know that pain will ease, I also know it will never entirely go away. To the day that I die there will be something missing that I want back very, very badly."

The quiet tears at last gave way to huge noisy sobs, and Duncan, knowing only too well the truth of her words, moved next to her and held her while she cried.

CHAPTER TWENTY SIX

Lilly flinched as she walked into the library and heard an unmistakable pinging noise. A shower of needles fell from the Christmas tree with every step she took.

She frowned at the tree as if daring it to be totally barren of green by Christmas Day. Kick insisted on cutting his own cedar from the woods behind the house and had tried, as he did every year, to convince her to let him cut one for her as well. She knew that when her expensive, purchased one was dead by Christmas Day he was going to say I told you so. Their tree argument was a Christmas tradition.

She assessed her dilemma and came up with no good solution. Buying another tree was out of the question. The man who operated the only lot in town that sold trees tall enough for a house with twelve foot ceilings had already sold out and closed up shop. Even if this one were no more than a bare-branched stalk of ornaments by Christmas Day, she wasn't going to back down and have one of those nasty, sticky old cedars.

Some Christmases go off like clockwork, and some have a few humbugs despite your best efforts. This year was definitely going to be one of the latter.

Lilly sat down at her grandfather's desk and took a notepad from the drawer. She halfheartedly began making a list, lacking this year the usual enthusiasm for her annual Boxing Day party.

She chewed the end of the pen. Space in the house wasn't a problem nor was the menu. Desia always cooked for fifty as though the number were going to change to a hundred-and-fifty at the last minute. She smiled. Sometimes it did, depending on how many last minute trips to the grocery store she made and who she ran into in the process.

Desia's heavy footsteps in the hall started a fresh hail of dry needles, and Lilly looked again in the direction of the tree. "This Christmas is going to be hard enough as it is," she said sternly. "Behave yourself."

Desia took firm hold of the banister and shook her head before pulling herself upstairs. Talking to Christmas trees was a sure sign of spending too much time alone. Lilly needed to find herself a man.

Laura looked painfully thin as she entered Duncan's office and took her familiar seat.

"Still feeling sick all the time?" he asked. He was concerned about her appearance.

"Not so much as I was. Thank you for asking. I'm just so dead tired, and I have so much to do before Christmas. As usual I have none of my shopping done. All I've bought so far is a doll for Marion." She wasn't sure she could look at Marion's doll without remembering the reason she had gone to Eleanor's that terrible afternoon.

"Having a hard time with Mrs. Kimble?" he asked, knowing the answer before he asked the question.

"I feel sorry for her, Duncan, terribly sorry for her. No one ought to have to live like that, but just when I feel the most sympathy she takes that little pad and makes this huge effort to write me a note saying that she's noticed that the fireplace needs to be cleaned out or something equally dumb, and I get mad despite myself."

"Duncan, as awful as this sounds, when she first got sick I had this terrible feeling of relief that she'd never be back in my house again, never be picking me apart for what I happened to be wearing, or serving for dinner, or because she saw a few cat hairs on the kitchen counter. For just a little while I had the strangest sensation of being free."

"How are things with Beck?"

"The truce is holding," she said with a rueful smile. "He never mentions the baby. He made a bargain with me, keeping the baby in exchange for keeping his mother. He's holding up his end, but some days I think I made a pact with the devil."

Duncan's personal opinion was that Beck was too upset over his mother to expend the energy necessary to bully Laura. Beck was totally undone by Eleanor's incapacitation.

"I got an invitation to Lilly's party." He changed the subject, feeling that she was truly too worn out to examine how she felt about anything.

"The Boxing Day Party?" she asked absently. "You ought to go. That's always fun. I'd never even heard of Boxing Day until Lilly started having her party."

"That makes me feel better," he said. "I'm still not sure what it is."

"Lilly observes more British traditions than the British do," Laura said. "I think originally it was the custom to 'box' up the leftovers that the kitchen help had labored over the day before and distribute it back to them. Lilly told me that it was customary to tip the lamplighter, and since she'd only seen one lamplighter in her life, she just decided to have her friends over instead. Don't ask me to explain anything Lilly does. Lilly's crazy, but she does know how to throw a party. I'm sorry we're going to miss this one, but it's going to be wonderful to get out of town." She closed her eyes.

"That's right. You're going skiing right after Christmas. You need to get away."

She sat with her eyes closed and didn't answer, and he thought for a little while that she might be asleep.

"I've got to get some presents bought if it kills me," she said without opening her eyes. "How about pulling me out of this chair and pushing me out the door."

"Why don't you call your sister or your sister-in-law and get them to help?" he suggested. "I'm sure you could give them a list or something. You need to go crawl in bed and get some sleep."

"Maybe you're right." She rubbed her eyes and yawned. "Are you all through shopping, Duncan?"

"Just about. I don't have much family, so I don't have much to buy."

"Are you going home for Christmas?"

"No, my sister insisted that I come to her house," he said slowly. "But she has more children than space as it is, and I'd be in the way. I guess I've got to call my apartment home now."

Beck looked almost as tired as Laura as he entered Duncan's office. He caustically accused his wife of being addicted to Duncan, but to his surprise he found himself feeling almost the same way.

"Merry Christmas," Duncan said as he took Beck's coat and hung it over his own on the peg on the back of the door.

"I don't know how merry it's going to be," Beck said grumpily. "Sometimes I think it would be a lot easier if everyone just paid some sort of tax that reverted to the merchants as an annual compensation for letting Christmas come and go like any other day."

"There is a reason for Christmas that goes beyond gifts you know," Duncan said.

"Everyone always says that, but the real reason seems to get lost in the shuffle of parties, and gifts, and trying to see who can outspend the neighbors," Beck complained. "On Christmas morning Laura will have thousands of dollars worth of toys under the tree, and by ten o'clock the children will all be complaining that there's nothing to do, or that they wish they'd gotten whatever the kids down the street got."

"Then we will all get dressed up and go out to Lilly's to stuff our faces and try to play the big happy extended family. Same scenario every year. Her tree will be dead as a doorknob, and Kick will be telling her how she should have cut a cedar out in the woods, and Mother will be complaining that Marion has gotten her dress dirty."

He stopped suddenly. "No, I guess Mother won't be complaining this year, will she?"

"Only on paper," Duncan said softly. "Are you going to try to take her to Lilly's?"

"I don't see how we can," Beck said in a miserable tone of voice. "We can get her downstairs in her wheelchair at our house because we have the elevator, but I don't see how we'd manage at Lilly's. Too many steps. I've hired nurses for the time we're going to be skiing, and I suppose I'll just tell them to send someone out a few days early."

"Might be hard to find someone to work Christmas Day," Duncan said.

"If you pay them enough they'll come," Beck said automatically. He hadn't run into anything yet that money wouldn't buy, or at least he wasn't aware that he had.

"It's not easy having your mother in the shape she's in, is it?" Duncan asked sympathetically.

"No, it's not. Amazingly, her mind seems to be fine, and it's got to be terribly frustrating to her that she can't talk or make her body behave. I get impatient with her, but Laura has been amazing. Mother has a bell that she rings when she wants something, and it's like the time Laura put a bell around the cat's neck so that she could find her. Constant ringing. Some nights Laura's up and down all night."

"Don't you ever get up with your mother?" Duncan asked, fully expecting an angry reaction.

To his surprise it didn't come. "I would try to help, Duncan, but I can't. I'm sorry for Laura, but I can't very well help my mother go to the bathroom. It's degrading enough for her as it is."

"Illness is degrading for anyone, Beck." Duncan had watched both of his parents die, and on more than one occasion he had helped his mother into the bathroom. The Eagans didn't have the resources to provide nurses on Christmas or any other day, and he and his sister had tried to share the burden of his mother's last illness with his father.

"I made a mistake," Beck said, his head in his hands. "A terrible mistake. I should have listened when everyone told me not to bring her home."

Duncan almost fell out of his chair.

It had been dark for hours when Beck returned home, tie loosened and smelling strongly of Scotch.

He found his wife sitting alone in the living room which was dark except for the light from one small lamp and the glow of the Christmas tree.

Laura's tree wasn't shedding needles. It was thick, full, artificial, and decorated as it was every year by the local florist who did all of Laura's decorations. She vowed to herself that next year she would have Kick cut her a cedar out of the woods and decorate it herself.

"Is Mother all settled for the night?" Beck asked, flopping down as comfortably as he could on one of the tight cushioned love seats.

"Yes, I fed her dinner, and I think she's asleep," Laura said. "One thing that's undiminished at least is her appetite. I don't know how she can stand that pureed stuff. It reminds me of baby food, and I'm sure she hates the fact that I usually end up getting as much of it on her as I do in her."

"Maybe that's because you always had a nurse around to feed the children when they were babies. I don't recall you spooning in a lot of mashed peaches or whatever it is that babies eat."

"You're right, I didn't." She sat up straighter and looked right into his eyes. "But this time is going to be different. I'm going to do everything with this one that I never did with the other three."

"At least you're not getting grossly obese yet," he said. "I ran into Bridget today, and she already looks like a big fat Irish peasant."

"I think Bridget looks wonderful," Laura objected. "I wish I had more time to spend with her. I think she's lonely when Kick has to go out of town, but he made commitments before he even knew her, and I suppose he can't help being away."

Beck snorted. "Getting a little out of town action, I imagine. I knew he wouldn't be able to stay in the same bed very long."

"Just can't get your mind out of the gutter, can you, Beck?" She stood up. "I'm going to bed."

"Suit yourself," he said. "I'll try not to wake you when I come up."

He stared moodily at the tiny white lights blinking on and off on the tree, at the piles of presents beneath it, and wondered what it was like to want something, anything, for Christmas.

CHAPTER TWENTY SEVEN

On the evening of the day after Christmas Lilly made a final check of the dining room before going upstairs to dress for her party.

She'd served the same menu, cold filet of beef, crabmeat casserole, pasta and vegetable salad, and Desia's hot yeast rolls, for so many years that setting up the buffet table was something she could do blindfolded, but she always made one last inspection trip to be sure everything was in place.

Lilly had given her first Boxing Day party years before, deciding on the spur of the moment one Christmas that she wasn't ready for the holiday to end.

Apparently everyone else felt the same way because the next year she had several calls well in advance of Christmas from people hoping that she was going to repeat the party.

So many Christmases ago she reflected as she put on a trace of makeup and noticed a few wrinkles that she was sure hadn't been there just yesterday. The dusting of grey in her hair had appeared the night Edmund died.

Lilly stared hard at her reflection and wondered where the years had gone and what she'd done with them. She had traveled a lot, from a safari in Africa to a cruise through Alaska. She had read a lot of books, and puttered around outside with her animals, and enjoyed Laura's children. She had had summers shared with Cait.

She had spent years on the go, riding from place to place in beat-up trucks and Bentleys, on the backs of horses, donkeys, and elephants, and high in the air in helicopters, planes, and hot air balloons. Going where? Why couldn't she put her finger on what she'd actually done with her days except to let them go by? It made her sad.

She thought of yesterday's Christmas already now no more than a memory. The humbugs had stayed away through the traditional celebration, but she had had an uneasy feeling all day that they were lurking in the shadows waiting to pounce.

The only ones truly unemotionally unafraid to let go and celebrate had been Kick, Bridget, and Sam.

Lilly had, after much searching, finally found the ideal pony for Sam, a fat, chestnut Welsh gelding with a perfect white star in the center of his face.

Sam had been beside herself with excitement, and Lilly had had to make a trip out to the barn to check on "Punkin Puddin" during the night to make sure he hadn't developed colic from the sheer volume of apples and carrots he'd been fed.

Bridget had been glowing with descriptions of her first Christmas morning in her new house. They had come downstairs to find that Santa had left every imaginable baby toy spread out beneath the tree. Lilly wasn't sure that Bridget didn't really believe that it all had come down the chimney while she slept.

Looking at her watch, Lilly realized that her guests would be arriving momentarily and hurried to dress in brown tweed slacks and the ecru lamb's wool turtleneck sent by Cait as a Christmas gift.

Static electricity from the sweater made her hair look wilder than usual, and on impulse she grabbed a brush and a rubber band, plaited it in a huge fat braid, and pinned it on top of her head just as she heard the first crunch of tires on the gravel drive below.

She hadn't been at all sure that Duncan would even come, but he surprised her by being the first guest. Bearing a gift bottle of wine, he had debated whether "Merry Christmas" or "Happy New Year" was the more appropriate greeting. She flung open the door and wished him, naturally, a "Happy Boxing Day."

"Where did your hair go?" he sputtered as he looked at this very different Lilly.

"In my horse show days I used to be quite adept at braiding thick tails." She laughed and patted the braid. "I decided to try it on my own head though heaven knows I don't think any of my horses ever had this much to work with. Don't you like it?"

Duncan was embarrassed and blushed as she closed the door behind him. She must think him awfully rude to be making personal comments about her hair.

"Well, give me an honest opinion." She continued to laugh.

"I like it. It's just different. It makes you look grown-up or something."

Everything he said came out sounding worse, and Duncan felt as ill-at-ease as a teenager at his first big dance.

Lilly frowned at her reflection in the huge pier mirror that hung in the entrance hall. "I could have sworn that it made me look sophisticated," she complained, turning her head from side to side.

"Maybe that's what bothers me," he said, wanting to bite his tongue. "I like your hair flying all over the place. You always look like you've been out in a windstorm." He blushed. What in the hell was he saying?

"I take that as a compliment." She gave him a warm smile and took his hand. "Come in the library and fix yourself a drink while I run upstairs and free my hair."

Duncan did as he was told and was soon joined by an odd mix of people, the secret of Lilly's success as a hostess. No one ever knew who was going to turn up at her parties, but those who did knew that it would not be a group that anyone else on the Brierley social circuit would dream of assembling in the same place at the same time.

Duncan was enjoying himself socially for the first time since moving to Brierley and was a little embarrassed when he realized that, as midnight approached, he and Kick and Bridget were the last remaining guests.

"Lilly, I hate to leave you to wash the dishes alone, but I've got to get Cinderella here home before she turns into a pumpkin," Kick said as he put his arm around Bridget.

"I well remember how hard it is having to sleep for two." Lilly laughed and gave Bridget a peck on the cheek. "I'm just getting a second wind. I'll have this cleaned up in no time."

Duncan hesitated as Kick and Bridget walked arm-in-arm out the back door. "Lilly, I realize that I have probably committed the ultimate faux pas in being the first to arrive and the last to leave. Can I give you a hand with the clean up?"

"No, but you can come and sit with me while I take off my shoes and have a well-deserved drink. It was always a cardinal rule of my grandmother's that one doesn't drink at one's own parties, and I guess I'll always feel uneasy if I break one of her rules. You won't catch me wearing white shoes before Easter or after Labor Day either."

He joined her before a dying fire. "I usually have a terrible let down feeling after this party which has always been my way of prolonging Christmas one more day," she said, a pensive look on her face. "Somehow this year I'm glad Christmas is over, glad that it's too late for something to spoil it. Is that an awful way to feel?"

"No, I know what you mean," he said, staring into the fire. "Holidays can be very emotional times, Lilly. They're always tied up with people who are no longer here."

"Duncan, am I wrong, or are you as lonely as I am?" she asked quietly.

He looked at her for a long moment, at the reflection of the lights from the bare branches of the dead Christmas tree shining on the long thick hair. She had tears in her eyes.

"I guess it's obvious that I am. The real question is whether we can help each other do something about it."

She wiped her eyes and smiled at him, held out her hand. "If you'll follow me upstairs, I'll show you the rest of the house."

Lilly woke up the next morning to the very pleasant feel of Duncan Eagan's arms around her. She snuggled next to him and began to laugh.

"What's so funny?" he mumbled, nuzzling her neck.

"I can just imagine Desia's expression when she sees that your car's still in the driveway."

"Do you really care what Desia thinks?" he whispered as he rolled her over.

"No. I've never cared what anyone thought." She laughed again. "Duncan Eagan, you are exactly the way I imagined you the first time I met you."

"And how is that?" he asked.

She kissed him before answering. "Delicious, very delicious."

Beck, Laura, and the children arrived in Vail just after lunch.

The condominium was warm and roomy, and Laura was eyeing the sofa in front of the fire and longing for a nap when Beck announced that they had to rent their ski equipment before seven so that they could be on the slopes early the next morning.

"Go ahead with the kids," she said. "I'm going to just curl up here."

"Laura, you know perfectly well that I can't just grab a pair of skis for you. You've got to go with us to be fitted."

"Beck, I have no intention of skiing," she argued. "You know I'm pregnant."

"How could I forget?" he asked, the ice in his voice as thick as that built up on the porch rail outside. "If you think I'm going to spend all the money to bring you out here so that you can sleep and shop, you'd better think again. There's no reason you can't ski. You don't even look pregnant."

She pulled herself up from the sofa and put her coat back on. It was easier to rent the skis than to argue, and since he usually skied more difficult trails than she could handle it made very little difference anyway. He'd never know whether she actually took the tram up the mountain or not.

The blinking red message light on the telephone caught Laura's eye.

Beck held the phone to his ear and closed his eyes tightly. "I understand," he said. "When did it happen?"

Laura felt a cold that had nothing to do with the freezing temperature. She knew the minute she saw the flashing red light on the phone that Eleanor was dead. She could have given him the message right then and there.

She felt the same odd floating sensation she'd experienced after Eleanor first had the stroke, the feeling she'd described to Duncan. This time, though, it really was over.

No matter how guilty she might feel about it, Laura Kimble was from at least one of her demons at last and forever free.

In small southern towns like Brierley, society funerals are much like society weddings. The only difference is that you don't need an invitation to attend a funeral. Everyone who is or wants to be somebody attends the funeral when someone like Eleanor Sutton Kimble is put to rest.

Duncan Eagan stood on the fringes of the crowd listening to the minister memorialize the numerous philanthropic contributions of a woman he'd never met. Despite that fact, he felt he had known her better than had most of the people who stood assembled in the freezing January wind.

Grey clouds so dark they were almost black were rolling in from the west, and the television weatherman had hinted that sleet might cover the new grave by morning.

He looked over the mourners, recognizing a few, people who had attended Lilly's party, people who had shared their private agonies in the confines of his office, and Betsy and Jack Connor with Betsy's mother and father.

Remarkable how the people who populated this little strata of this little society looked so much alike. Eleanor's contemporaries carried their age in varying degrees of preservation. Those ten years younger wore for the most part the hard look that women get with hair that just misses being a natural color and skin already surgically tightened or getting loose around necks rising from fur collars.

Laura's friends were, as a whole, still in the full bloom of their beauty, but they too were beginning to hear the drum beat of time's inevitable march toward age. None of them were truly unattractive. They had the advantages of good clothes, good facials, good hair stylists to make the most of what nature had chosen to bestow.

Under the tent reserved for the family, Laura pulled her fur coat tightly around her and kept her head bent. Beck stared straight ahead, his face a mask. Impossible to know whether Beck grieved or celebrated. Lilly put her arm around the shoulders of a weeping Marion, and Brook elbowed Sam from time to time when she started to fidget. Tiny Bridget stood close to her towering husband in a fur coat full enough to have wrapped them both. Of the women, only Lilly wore a simple khaki raincoat.

"Ashes to ashes, dust to dust," the minister at last concluded as he tossed a symbolic handful of earth into the frozen ground that waited to receive Eleanor Kimble.

The threatening skies seemed to respond as an icy rain began to fall, and the upper crust of Brierley, the people the French call "le gratin," moved as quickly as their feet and their sense of respect would allow back to the warm, dry safety of their big waiting cars.

Southern custom decrees that the funeral is not the end. After the service streams of people pour into the house of some designated family member to drink, and talk, and eat the food that they brought as soon as they learned of the passing of a friend.

It is part of the ritual. It is the reassurance that life goes on, the celebration that while your time is coming this time was someone else's.

As the cars pulled away from the cemetery the maid waited in Laura's kitchen, having made a final inspection of the dining room much as Lilly had done before her party.

There were so many trays of roast beef, and ham, and potato salad that they had filled the Kimbles' two refrigerators and taken the overflow next door to Bridget's house. Lilly had finally called Nelson's and told them to stop delivering.

The flowers were worse than the food. Every surface in the living room held a spray of some kind of appropriate hothouse bloom, and she could only imagine what the arrangements at the cemetery were like.

It was all such a waste. She had heard Mrs. Kimble's sister say that she planned to take the leftover food to the recently opened shelter for the homeless and felt a little better. Tonight would no doubt be the first time most of those poor souls tasted pate de foie gras, but that was obviously what Nelson's was pushing today. Small good the flowers were going to do for anyone who faced spending this bitter night cold and hungry.

She smoothed the skirt of the formal, black uniform and prepared to greet the mourners.

CHAPTER TWENTY EIGHT

"*I* can't believe she's gone," Laura said to Duncan. "I've woken up every night of the past week thinking I hear that bell. I've spent so much of my adult life trying to please Eleanor and coming up short. It's hard to realize that never again will Eleanor tell me what to do."

"Is Beck taking this fairly well?" He remembered the absolutely blank expression her husband wore throughout the funeral.

"I think so." She drew her words out slowly, thinking as she spoke. "He won't talk about it. Maybe he feels like he's been let out of a cage too. He's meeting with the lawyers again this morning. Eleanor's will is complicated beyond belief. I don't understand why she couldn't have just left it all to Beck and the children."

"Nothing for you?"

"Nothing for me." She smiled at him. "But then the last thing on earth I want is Eleanor's money. We've got to go through the house so that we can put it on the market, and I don't want any of her things either, although I expect Beck will."

She shuddered a little thinking of the musty smell.

She had dreamed the night before that she was back in Eleanor's living room opening a drawer and finding it full of the bones of little dead mice.

"That's hard, going through a lifetime of personal possessions," Duncan said.

"You know I don't know what happened to my parents' stuff," she said thoughtfully. "I suppose Lilly did something with most of it, although knowing what a pack-rat my sister is, it may all still be hanging in the closets. I hate to think that someday my children will inherit that old barn and all the junk in the attic. It's like something out of a bad Gothic novel."

"Lilly told me that her house is full of ghosts." Duncan laughed, remembering the serious expression on her face as she said it. He wasn't sure whether or not she meant it.

"Don't laugh. I think she talks to them late at night when she's all alone. It must be spooky living out there all by herself. No wonder she's crazy." Laura made a face.

"I think Lilly enjoys her ghosts. She considers them good company," he said.

"You wouldn't catch me living out there all alone," Laura said, fluffing out her long hair. "The only ghost I'd encounter would be my grandmother saying 'Stand up straight, Laura. A lady must have proper posture.'"

He grinned at her stiff-voiced mimicry. "I gather you don't share Lilly's fond memories of Grandmother."

"Are you kidding?" She laughed with him. "She was another Eleanor. Be careful if you get married in this town, Duncan. There are lots of them out there."

He thought back to the group at the funeral and knew exactly what she meant.

"Do you have to leave again?" Bridget asked as Kick threw clothes into a suitcase.

"I wish I didn't, but someone has to pay for all of this furniture."

"I wish I could take you with me," he continued in a softer voice as he put his arms around her, liking the feel of the little of knot of baby that now came between them. He asked her a dozen times a day when they were going to be able to feel it move.

"I do too." She hugged him back. "All that talk we did about the places we were going to go, and the only place I ever seem to go is to the grocery store. I don't know why that mean old doctor won't let me fly."

He hated the trips out of town, but the book was so close to completion that it required frequent meetings with the publisher. He was working, not to pay for furniture, but because he wanted the book completed in time to dedicate it to Bridget before she had the baby.

"Why don't you take Laura to lunch or something?" he suggested as he closed the suitcase. "See if you can get her to eat something full of calories."

"I certainly don't need anything full of calories." She rolled her eyes. "Maybe I will try to get her to go shopping or something. That always seems to cheer her up."

"My sister, the professional consumer." He laughed. "Just don't try to keep up with her."

"We need something to hang over the dresser and some accessories in the living room," Bridget said. "I cannot believe there is not one decent decorator shop in this town."

"Why don't you open one?" he asked jokingly as he gave her a quick kiss and ran down the stairs, already late for the airport.

Beck appeared to have aged ten years in a week. The suit was beautifully cut wool, the white cotton shirt was starched, the tie was a regimental stripe that went well with the dark jacket, his shoes were polished to a mirror shine.

The face of the man in the custom-tailored clothes looked like that of someone who had spent the morning out breaking rocks.

"You look beat, Beck," Duncan said.

"I am beat." Beck ran his hand through his thick dark hair. "I have spent the morning with lawyers and accountants, and we can't figure out how to handle half the stuff she put in that will. It's a nightmare. Every bequest has so many stipulations that it's like she's trying to control things from the grave."

"I've got to go through that huge house too," Beck sighed. "I'm not sure I'm up to it yet, but I've either got to do it soon or hire some security. There have been too many burglaries right after funerals in this town."

"Sorting through memories isn't easy," Duncan agreed.

"And there's no one to do it but me, is there?" Beck sat quietly, thinking about the opening of drawers, and closets, and the past.

What happened next didn't surprise Duncan. He'd known for several months that it would come at some point, had to come sooner or later.

Beck began to cry. Duncan sat watching silently. It was time for him to crack.

Duncan waited patiently, knowing that the river of tears flowing out of Beck represented the pent-up feelings of a lot of years.

"Duncan, I don't think I know who I am anymore."

"I'm not sure you've ever known," Duncan said gently. "But I think it's time you found out."

"My mother kept telling me to be a man," Beck said miserably. "She always measured me against my father."

"And you never measured up?"

"In some ways I guess I did." Beck had his guard down, and it was scary. "I've made lots of money. I've got all the trappings, the house, and the cars, and the right friends. It just doesn't mean anything."

"No, those things generally don't," Duncan agreed. "The only things we truly have in life outside of ourselves are our relationships with other people, and I don't mind telling you that you haven't been very successful in that department."

"I didn't like my father very much," Beck said. "He had a voice that could cut you down until you felt about two inches tall."

"You know that's exactly the kind of image you've been trying to create with your own children." Duncan stuck in the knife and twisted it hard. Beck had so many false outer layers that cutting through to the real man at the core was going to be a painful process.

"They don't like me any better than I liked my own father," Beck mumbled. "Growing up I thought it would be different if I only had brothers and sisters. I hated being an only child."

"Why don't you like Lilly and Kick?" Duncan asked.

Beck stared out the window, looking inward.

"I guess because they like themselves so much," he said finally. "They seem to feel so damn good about who they are. Don't you find that attitude sort of arrogant?"

"Not at all. Feeling good about who you are is what life is all about. I suspect that you're jealous of them because they're happy."

"What's wrong with wanting to be happy?" Beck asked.

"Nothing, but the way you've gone charging through life is not very conducive to making yourself or anyone else happy. Look at your wife, a woman most men would give anything to have. Look at the way you've treated her, and don't tell me how you've bought her everything money can buy. Have you ever sincerely told her that you loved her?"

Beck automatically started to protest and stopped himself.

"No. I don't suppose I have," he said heavily. "Do you think she loves me?"

"Why else would she have put up with you for all these years, Beck?" Duncan laughed. "Ease up on yourself, man. Go home and enjoy your wife and your kids. You might even find yourself liking the dreaded in-laws if you gave them half a chance to like you. The first thing you need to do though is to tell your mother good-bye."

Bridget and Laura sat in the little flower-filled upstairs sitting room of the Kimbles' house.

"Do you think you could be having twins?" Laura asked, eyeing Bridget's bulging stomach under the maternity smock. "I'm still wearing my regular clothes."

"Stay away from snack foods, Mrs. Lambeth," Bridget mimicked the doctor. "We don't want to end up with an eight pound baby and an eight hundred pound mother." She popped a chocolate chip cookie in her mouth and giggled.

"Give me one of those cookies before you eat the whole plate." Laura laughed with her. She felt closer to Bridget than she'd ever felt to her own sister.

"Laura, Kick gave me an idea this afternoon," Bridget said as she slid the plate toward Laura and out of her own reach. "He was joking when he said it, but I've been thinking about it ever since."

"An idea about what?" Laura reached for a second cookie.

"I was complaining that there is no place to buy art, or decent picture frames, or nice lamp shades in this town," Bridget said. "He suggested that I open a shop. You know what I mean, not a gift shop exactly, sort of a decorator shop, with fabrics and wall coverings too."

"And are you thinking about doing that?"

"Actually, I'm thinking about you and I doing it." Bridget sat back with a pleased expression on her face. "You have such good taste. You know everyone in town. It would be a huge success."

Laura considered the idea and decided that it just might work. "We could offer our expertise too. Both of us have proven ourselves pretty darn good at choosing colors, haven't we?"

"Between your house and mine I don't think there's a color we haven't chosen!" Bridget laughed excitedly. "Kick would love the idea of my telling someone else how to spend their money!"

"Where would we have this shop?" Laura was intrigued by the idea.

"Beats me," Bridget said, dismissing any obstacles as they came along. "You're the one with the husband in real estate. Ask Beck."

Laura's face clouded. "It was a great idea for the few seconds it lasted, Bridget. You know Beck would never let me work."

"Laura, I hate to say this, but isn't it time that you stood up to Beck and told him what you're going to do about something instead of always asking him? You're not Sam's age you know. I can do this on my own, but it would be so much more fun if we did it together. Just think, Laura, it would give you a life of your own, a life outside of Beck."

Laura, sitting in her little flowered hideaway long after Bridget had gone on her way, long after it got dark, and without turning on the lights, did a great deal of thinking.

Beck was also thinking as he nursed his second drink in the dimly lit interior of Lonnie's Tavern. He was disturbed by what had happened in Duncan's office, wondered if he was in some way grieving for the mother he'd told himself he was lucky to be rid of.

A voice from behind startled him. "Didn't anyone ever tell you that it's bad to drink alone?"

Beck looked up into the glittery green eyes of Ginger Borland.

"Hi, Ginger, you and Mark out for the evening?"

"Actually, I'm alone. Mind if I join you?" Ginger slid into the booth without waiting for an answer.

"Beck, I was sorry to hear about your mother. She was really a great lady. I always admired her. She never left any doubt about how she felt about anything."

"I won't argue with that," he said.

"What's wrong, Beck? You look awfully down." Ginger put her hand on his arm, and he noticed that her fingernails were short, and blunt cut, and unpolished. Her perfume was strong, musky, not unpleasant but in sharp contrast to the light floral scent that Laura wore.

"I guess I am sort of down," he said looking directly into the green eyes. "Ginger, are you by chance free for dinner tonight?"

"As a matter of fact I am."

He dropped a twenty on the table, and they left the bar together.

It wasn't unusual for late evening to arrive without Beck having made it home.

It wasn't usual for Laura to try to determine his whereabouts, but she'd made a few decisions, and she was anxious to find him. She called Duncan at home.

"Yes, Laura, he was in my office late this afternoon," Duncan answered. "I can't say for certain where he was going, but I think the first place I'd look is his mother's house. I have a hunch he might go there to sort through a few things. You know losing his mother represents both an end and a beginning for Beck."

"Thanks, Duncan, I've been doing some thinking of my own along the same lines. Beginnings and endings. That sort of thing."

"Laura, are you trying to tell me something?"

She smiled to herself. "You know, Duncan, I've never been inside your apartment. What's the decor like?"

It wasn't the first time that Duncan had absolutely no idea what Laura was talking about. Before he could question her further, she said good-bye and hung up.

He looked at Lilly lying beside him, hair fanned out on the pillow. It was time to write the final chapter in the sad, lonely period of his own life. He was ready to move on, and he sensed that she was too.

Lilly had an unsettling habit of seeming to read his mind. She ran a finger down the thick mat of hair on his chest and said, "You know, Duncan, I couldn't help overhearing that conversation. When does the lease expire on this dump?"

"Next month. Why do you ask?"

"As much fun as the past few weeks of 'your place or mine' has been for us, I think it's going to get real old, real fast. I know a great house out on the Old Post Road that needs a man around it. You wouldn't be interested in the job, would you?"

"Are you trying to hire me on as a handyman?" he asked as he buried his face in her hair.

"I had more in mind hiring you on as a husband."

"Best job offer I've had in years. How soon can I start?"

"Just as soon as you finish the physical part of this interview."

Laura snapped off the television set and faced the children. "I'm going out for a little while. Brook, I'm putting you in charge while I'm gone. If you overstep the authority I'm giving you and mistreat your sisters, you will not be allowed to play in the basketball game this weekend."

The children stared open-mouthed as she took her longest mink coat from the closet, marched down the hall, and out the back door. She certainly didn't sound like the mother they knew.

There were several lights on downstairs when Laura pulled into Eleanor Kimble's driveway. Not Eleanor Kimble's driveway she told herself. Eleanor Kimble is dead. Nothing belongs to Eleanor Kimble now, including me.

It was cold, and she pulled the coat tight as she went up the walk, looking at the house defiantly, telling herself that the heat had been off, the smell would surely have abated.

She twisted the handle. As she'd expected Beck had left the door unlocked. She walked through the downstairs rooms, soft leather boots making little noise.

She'd parked right behind his car so she knew he was somewhere in the house. She thought of him upstairs, going through his mother's most personal possessions and felt a stab of sympathy.

Laura hesitated at the bottom of the stairs. What he was doing couldn't be easy, and she hated to interrupt him with what she had to say. She'd made up her mind though, and it was past time for them to talk about things. She took a deep breath and climbed the stairs.

When she opened the door to Eleanor's bedroom, her first reaction was to scream. Instead she began to laugh.

Ginger Borland and Beck stared as if they were seeing a ghost, and Laura had the feeling that Eleanor might be right behind her, glaring over her shoulder.

Ginger made a clumsy attempt to wrap herself in Eleanor's crewelwork bedspread.

"Be careful, Ginger," Laura said, laughing helplessly. "If you wrinkle Eleanor's bedspread she'll haunt you for the rest of your life."

"What are you doing here, Laura?" Beck asked angrily, too surprised to do anything to cover himself.

"I came to tell you good-bye, Beck, that I'm tired of you, and I'm through with you. It's funny that I've always been so worried about making it on my own. Tonight it suddenly hit me that I couldn't wait to do just that."

She closed the door, reopened it, gave them her sweetest smile. "Sorry I interrupted. Feel free to get back to whatever it was that you were doing."

CHAPTER TWENTY NINE

Squinting in the bright May sunshine, Kick tore open the air-expressed package and tossed the cover letter aside. The completed book was in his hands, accomplished in these four seasons spent back in a small town.

The last picture submitted for the book was the one he had selected for the opening section, and he wanted to make sure that it had reproduced well.

From the first page of *Springtime* the faces of his family smiled back at him. He relaxed. It was perfect.

The editor had questioned his choice of this particular photograph. With the possible exception of the clumsily arranged, ribbon-tied bouquet of daffodils, there were no symbolic, cliched props artificially arranged to speak of the spring.

Looking at the picture, Kick was glad that he had held his ground. Any bride and groom, even a pair obviously middle-aged, epitomized new beginnings.

It was a wonderful picture of Lilly. He admitted to himself that it would have taken no particular skill with a camera to capture such an expression of obvious love as she wore the February morning that she married Duncan in the library of the house on the Old Post Road. Kick knew that, however invisible to the naked eye, among the members of the wedding party hovered at least a few of Lilly's reassuring ghosts.

Studying the photograph, he at last realized what it was that had made her seem somehow different that day. It wasn't, after all, the uncharacteristic creamy lace dress or the high heel shoes borrowed from Laura. It was her hair, for once falling smoothly over her shoulders. Sure of what she was doing, she had made it through the previous night without twisting a single tangle.

From just to the right of Lilly, Bridget's green eyes winked back from the photograph. His earliest impression of his wife still held. She would always be like a videotape of springtime, his to play over and over for the rest of his life.

In the picture she was laughing, arms wrapped around the growing child within her. To Kick, that evolving life was in itself a paean to the springtime.

Let Lilly tease that his epitaph should read "a man who loved women." He was pleased beyond measure when the tests said he could look forward to meeting a newborn daughter.

He closed the book and let his eyes sweep the rose stucco facade of the house, a house that was beginning to feel like home. He felt a real sense of belonging, of joy that he and Bridget could provide for their children and grandchildren a place which would always offer the open arms of peace and comfort, the chance to come back.

He might laugh at Lilly's ghosts, but she was right in her conviction that beneath the roof of a real home the aura of love lingers long and steady and reassuring even after those we love are gone.

Not too many days after telling Duncan that she owed her long life to the fact that she couldn't go on to a well deserved rest until she was sure there was someone to make Lilly behave, Desia died peacefully in her sleep in the kitchen rocking chair. Kick knew that Lilly continued to talk aloud to her, confident that she remained as she always would a strong foundation timber, forever at home among the friendly ghosts.

He walked back into his quiet house. Bridget and Laura were in Atlanta attending market, selecting merchandise for the shop which was scheduled to open in September. Kick was confident that their new business would succeed if on enthusiasm alone.

Springtime, he thought to himself, should also have had a picture of a butterfly emerging from its cocoon. Laura, who a brief year ago found it impossible to decide what to wear in the morning, a few weeks after Lilly's wedding insisted on flying off alone to obtain a quick divorce. She and Bridget continued to grow closer, honing their decorating skills by collaborating on their nurseries.

Kick wondered, decided he really didn't care, how Beck was doing with his new life. Mark Borland divorced his wife immediately after learning that she was carrying a child he could not possibly have fathered. Beck, for once, owned up to responsibility and married Ginger Borland within a few days of the decree.

Bridget had recently come home from the Kut and Kurl full of news about the couple. According to the manicurist, they were living in Beck's mother's house, and Ginger, only a few months into her pregnancy, had already gained more than fifty pounds.